Bloodline

Also by Fiona Mountain

ISABELLA

PALE AS THE DEAD

Bloodline

FIONA MOUNTAIN

ORION

First published in Great Britain in 2004 by Orion,
an imprint of the Orion Publishing Group Ltd.

Copyright © 2004 Fiona Mountain

0 75284 113 0 (trade paperback) 0 75284 112 2 (hardback)

A CIP catalogue record for this book is available
from the British Library.

Typeset by Deltatype Ltd, Birkenhead, Merseyside

Printed in Great Britain by
Clays Ltd, St Ives plc

The Orion Publishing Group Ltd
Orion House
5 Upper Saint Martin's Lane
London, WC2H 9EA

For Tim, Daniel, James and Gabriel
as always

And in memory of my dad, Douglas Swinburn

What might have been and what has been
Point to one end, which is always present.

T.S. Eliot, 'Burnt Norton'

Prologue

FOR MARION LASSITER *the taste of ice cream is a torment that she forces herself to endure.*

She queues in baking sunshine at the ice cream cabin at the top of the beach. The striped awning offers some shade to those at the front, but Marion stopped caring about personal comforts long ago.

The man behind the counter seems surprised to see a smartly-dressed old lady waiting patiently amid the noisy hordes of children. In her practical navy skirt and white blouse and her wide-brimmed sun hat, she's dressed more for a church fête than the seaside. He's even more surprised when she chooses the same ice cream as all the children.

'May I have a Ninety-Nine Sensation, please?' Even his superficial glance catches the unmistakable sadness in the old lady's voice and around her deep-blue eyes.

Almost a reflex action, as the man takes the coins and hands over the ice cream, crusted with coloured vermicelli and bright pink sauce, he looks for a small grandchild hiding in the folds of the old lady's skirt. She cannot possibly be buying a Ninety-Nine Sensation for herself. But she seems to be entirely alone.

Marion Lassiter is not the slightest bit hungry. In fact, as the lurid concoction starts to melt down her bony fingers, she feels rather sick. But she makes herself turn towards the sea and lick.

The ice cream is a punishment in the same way as Marion's choice of career. It took her years of training to qualify as a midwife, to relive the past every day in blood and screams. But after what she had seen, what she did, there could have been no other way for her.

In the white room in the house that stood in the shadow of the trees, the screaming stopped and the silence was far more terrible. It was in the silence that Marion knew she had to run. The dead are beyond help, but there was someone vulnerable she could still save.

She couldn't wait to see what he did with her friend, but she thinks she knows. And that's why the sea disturbs her so, because it sounds just like the wind in the trees, looks so like the woods when they were awash with bluebells. The haze of lilac flowers had seemed to emit a mysterious light along with their insidious fragrance, but at all other times of year it was as if the light had been banished from the place where they grew. Even in January, when the trees were bare, the winter sun had never seemed to penetrate those woods.

The house too reflected the character of the woods that guarded it so well – a house of secrets and shadows and strange echoes, standing entirely alone in the narrow valley, as it had for hundreds of years. Despite its pale painted walls, the high corniced ceilings and the tall windows, there was always a darkness there. And what happened within its aged stone walls will haunt Marion Lassiter for ever.

Standing on the sunny beach now, amid the delighted squeals of the children with their buckets and spades and fishing nets, the darkness of the house and its land still lies deep inside her. Not that she'd be able to enjoy the beach anyway. Coming to such places is also part of her penance. She sometimes considers keeping her Christmas tree up all year, with fairy lights twinkling when the sun goes down. Christmas and summer seashores, the realms of children.

She'd rather be anywhere but here. Drinking a pot of tea in a café, or shut away in her whitewashed cottage with its view of the cobb and the yachts sailing across Lyme Bay. But that would be cheating. Over the past sixty years she's become an expert in self-retribution. Hers is no sentence of self-denial though. She can eat as much ice cream and candy floss and chocolate Easter eggs as she wants. She can buy endless teddy bears and toy cars.

The gleaming paint on the cars and the unblinking eyes of the fluffy toys stare at her from her bed, from every shelf and chair in her cottage. Their pristine newness accuses, just as she intends it to do. The bears should be threadbare and fur-matted, eyes or ears missing from too much love. She keeps buying them for the same reason she goes to the beach when it's packed with families. For the same reason she makes herself eat ice cream. Because it ensures she can never forget what happened, what she did over half a century ago. It reminds her of the life she could have had if she hadn't been so foolish, if she had been a better person.

One

THE ABBREVIATION, *SUS*, next to an entry in the criminal records, was short for the Latin *suspendatur*, meaning 'Let him be hanged'. It never failed to make Natasha Blake break out in goose bumps.

She'd been a genealogist for over a quarter of her twenty-nine-year existence, since she graduated eight years ago, and she'd been coming to the National Archives, what used to be the less grandly titled Public Records Office, in Kew at least once a month since then.

Let him be hanged. Him was a her, in this particular instance.

Alice Hellier was just a parlour maid from Fulbrook, Oxford-shire, until she became a murderess at the age of nineteen, when she shot her 64-year-old employer, Samuel Purrington, on 11 August 1852. A bonafide black sheep to add a splash of colour to the rather humdrum family tree Natasha had spent the past month and a half researching.

What had led her here was a small paragraph she'd stumbled across in the *Oxfordshire Gazette* of August 1853, at the start of Alice's trial. The headline 'MURDEROUS MAID' had been enough to get her going. Now she had come for the official proof. She went over to a computer terminal, keyed in her reader number and searched the online catalogue to order the Burford Gaol Book, which she'd collect downstairs.

This was the type of history she loved best, the reason she did this job. Kings and Queens, famous explorers and military heroes were all very interesting, but what gave her the best buzz were people like Alice. People on whom the spotlight of history shone very faintly and for just a millisecond. Those whose names were recorded in a few dry and dusty old papers that only saw the light of day when someone summoned them from the vaults to touch them with white-gloved hands.

A few minutes later the gaol book was waiting for her at the document collections counter. Impatience kicking in, she found the entry on the way back to her allotted desk.

A whole page was devoted to Alice. In the history of lowly people like her, it was infamy that gave you your fifteen minutes of fame. If you lived a blame-free existence, the odds were that all but your vital statistics – name, dates, address and trade – were lost to future generations. Little of your essence remained. But a brush with the law left a stain that lingered as long as archives were preserved. Natasha often debated committing a crime of passion or staging a heist in an antique arcade, something to create enough intrigue for any family historians who might follow in her footsteps.

Fixed to the centre of the page was a sepia mug shot of Alice. She sat demurely with her hands clasped in her lap, a dark cape around her shoulders, her hair parted in the middle and drawn back from a solemn but pretty, round little face. She looked a lot more like a parlour maid than a murderess.

Natasha added the information to the notes she'd already made on Alice's descendants.

Her baby son, Thomas, was cared for by Alice's aunt after Alice was hanged, and, at the age of thirteen, he would be sentenced to twenty-one days' hard labour for larceny. His previous crimes were listed as arson, setting fire to a stack of wheat, night poaching. By the time he was thirty he had a wife and two children and had served two years in prison for robbery with assault. His son Jack went the same way, sentenced to one month's hard labour for stealing a pair of boots and five years in reformatory school. A bad lot, the Helliers. They came good in the end though. Jack's son became a blacksmith and his son a farmer.

She glanced out of the angled plate glass window. Flaming June, the sun Mediterranean-bright but everything still fresh and green. She hadn't minded the early start this morning, walking across the dewy Cotswold fields with her Red Setter, Boris, at six-thirty so she could catch the seven-fifteen train from Moreton-in-Marsh, with about two seconds to spare thanks to the Sunbeam Alpine. Her beautiful old car relied on its beauty to excuse its refusal to start just when she needed it most.

It was her third trip to London in the last seven days. She'd never worked so hard as she had for the past weeks, or earned as much money in so short a time. Bloody hell, had she earned it. It was no easy task to compile a comprehensive genealogical chart going back about eight generations, to 1750 to be exact, in just thirty-five days.

The precise cut-off point had been imposed by her client, Charles Seagrove, who'd also, mysteriously, demanded confidentiality so complete she wasn't even allowed to tell anyone who she was working for. Why the great secrecy? And why, when Seagrove had gone to some lengths to impress on her that he was a proficient genealogist who'd worked for Debrett's, had he employed her to do this research instead of doing it himself? While she was at it, she'd also like to know why he was so interested in the family of the person at the top of the chart, John Hellier, now aged twenty-one? Why the need for so much detail and all this great hurry to unearth the Hellier roots? Either Charles Seagrove liked to be thorough, or there was something important at stake.

Just what that could possibly be, when it didn't even look as though any of the Helliers were related to her client, she couldn't begin to fathom. She had expected to discover a branch intertwining the Hellier and Seagrove trees, but hadn't found a single one.

Too much work, not enough play and even less sleep – she was breaking all the rules the trusty Internet Doctor offered on how to beat insomnia. No mentally taxing activities late at night, minimize stress, don't take your work to bed with you. She knew what she was supposed to do but doing it was a different matter. Since she and Marcus had split up eighteen months ago, she'd become more a workaholic than ever. She'd had her laptop plugged into the socket by her bedside table, had been up until the early hours trawling online databases after long days at the Family

Records Centre, ploughing through census returns and wills, the trade directories at the Society of Genealogists, coroners' inquests, deeds, old newspapers. She'd practically taken up residence here in the Reading Room and she'd lost count of the numbers of documents she'd requested to view. Military service records, apprenticeship books, correspondence of the Lunacy Commission, calendars of prisoners. She'd spent nearly a whole week, all in all, in the Wellcome Library for the History of Medicine, sifting through clinical and patient records, the first time she'd been asked to do that as part of genealogical research.

Hellier, if not as common as Smith or Jones, was not a rare surname, and, as usual, each line of enquiry had thrown up several possibilities. There were rather more question marks in the Hellier genealogical chart than Natasha's professionalism and perfectionism usually allowed, but that was deadlines for you and time was up. She'd done all she could. But that didn't stop her itching to go back to the contemporary local newspapers, to try to find the original news account of the murder, with the inevitable speculation on the motive, and the trial reports.

On the way to the underground station she rang her friend Toby, a researcher based in London. From a recent conversation she knew his current project was the history of brewing for a television production company.

'You're not by any chance planning a trip to Colindale in the near future?' The newspaper archive was the perfect place to find out more about Alice, but Natasha couldn't justify a special trip there herself now that the job was over.

'Might be,' Toby said, obviously guessing that she was about to ask a favour.

She gave him Alice's details, asked if he would have a scout around, if he had a few minutes to spare.

'I'd be glad to.'

She passed an over-ironed couple heading towards Kew Gardens, discussing the merits of snapdragons, though they didn't call them that.

'What is it with people over fifty?' Natasha said. 'They know the Latin names for every flower, tree and butterfly, whereas I just

7

know the Latin for "let him be hanged". What does that say about me?'

'That you're just a teeny bit twisted perhaps?'

'Bound to be. We make a living out of the dead, don't we? What time is it, by the way?'

'Five to three.'

'Shit. I'm going to be late for my train.' Again.

'The Late Natasha Blake,' Toby said.

She was spending so much time with ghosts she was slowly becoming one.

For once, it was almost as hot in Snowshill as it had been in London. On an idyllic summer's day like today, the village was straight off a shortbread tin, and the way tourists and incomers like Natasha pronounced its name, as spelt, suited it best. But on most days, certainly the winter and autumn months, its quirky and less pretty local pronunciation, 'Snouwsall', was more appropriate.

One of the highest and windiest of the Cotswold hill villages, it didn't tend to appeal to fair weather country-dwellers, but Natasha liked its isolation, the steep drive to get to it and the grey stone cottages huddled round the little green, stumpy church and spooky manor house.

It was the start of the fête season. Every village had one. Natasha must have passed at least half a dozen small roadside signs on the way back from the station, some handwritten and some composed on a computer with clip art and fancy graphics, advertising tombolas, coconut shies and cream teas. She was going to have to borrow her godson, Kieran, the son of her best friend Mary, for an afternoon.

She parked in front of Orchard End and heard Boris set up a frantic barking and wailing. He'd trained himself to recognize the distinctive rumble of the Alpine's engine and gave her about twenty seconds to turn it off, lock up and unlock the front door before he started trying to scratch his way through it.

He welcomed her as if she'd been away for a month and she accepted voracious licks and thrashings with his tail as she said hello and retrieved a trampled white envelope from beneath his hind legs. Boris immediately tried to snatch it. 'Let go, Boris.' He took no notice but she managed to wrest it off him with only a corner missing, gave him a moment to calm, then slid her finger under the seal.

Inside was a single sheet of creamy vellum writing paper, folded in half.

The typeface was courier and it had been composed on a traditional typewriter with a worn printer ribbon that had made some of the letters fainter than others. A single sentence across the centre: *Cinderella is in the Bluebell Woods at Poacher's Dell.*

Like a line from a nursery rhyme, or the clue to a crossword puzzle. Natasha turned the paper over and studied the envelope, looking for a proper clue to tell her who had sent it. Her name and address were in a font that matched the message. The postmark was smudged.

Stuff of nonsense. The paper equivalent of the junk emails with which she was constantly bombarded, jokes and brainteaser chain letters that had been passed on from friend to friend, or sometimes from complete strangers who'd somehow managed to get hold of her address. She chucked the letter onto her desk.

Just someone having a laugh. Trying to tell her, cryptically, that she'd been working too hard and needed a handsome prince to rescue her.

Two

NATASHA WAS LOST.

She knew this road and the surrounding villages as well as the lyrics to a Nick Cave song, but until precisely six weeks ago she'd never even heard of Shadwell Manor Farm, even though she lived less than ten miles away.

It seemed she wasn't the only one. She'd already stopped to ask two locals – an elderly woman with a broad Cotswold accent planting pansies in front of her terraced cottage, and a red-faced man mending a dry stone wall. The man gawped at her blankly before shaking his head and the woman gave her vague and impossibly garbled directions that were no more help than the ones Natasha had taken down over the phone.

The heatwave hadn't broken. She'd fastened her thick, dark-gold hair back in a low ponytail and forsaken her beloved black for a white Victorian chemise and scarlet linen skirt. The hood was down on the Sunbeam Alpine and so far she'd enjoyed the drive through the high sheep pastures and down into the wooded valleys. But now she was getting flustered. Charles Seagrove had told her to meet him at six and at a guess – the best she could do since she didn't wear a watch – she was already quarter of an hour late. The hills and dense trees that ranged on either side of her were guaranteed to impede radio waves and there wasn't a flicker of reception on her mobile.

As she rounded a bend, she nearly ran into a girl who was walking in the middle of the road as if she owned it. She had curly silver-blonde hair, was dressed in white cotton pedal-pushers and vest top, a glossy King Charles Spaniel dancing behind her. She seemed completely unperturbed by her brush with oblivion.

Natasha stopped. 'I'm looking for Shadwell Manor Farm?'

She could have been mistaken, but she'd have sworn the girl eyed her with a mixture of curiosity and surprise, as if she were about to warn her not to venture there after darkness fell. 'The big gates up there on the right.' She pointed.

'Thanks.'

'Cool car by the way.'

Natasha smiled.

A couple of minutes later, half hidden, she came upon two pillars topped with stone globes, ornate iron gates opened just wide enough to drive through. It was as if Shadwell Manor Farm was a place in a fairy tale, its gateway the entrance to another world, only appearing when the sun had started to set or you found a magic key. As she drove on she half expected the gates to swing shut behind her.

The long driveway was trimmed and perfect, not a single stray dandelion poking through the gravel. A neat line of beeches and birches surrounding the house, the rim of a wood, towered overhead. This wasn't one of the ancient Cotswold forests. Instead of vast gnarled oaks, the trunks here were slender, had been growing for decades not centuries. But it didn't take an expert in forestry to see that the trees had been planted a little too close together. They'd had to struggle and compete for the light and air to grow and stay alive, and the fight had made them tall and spindly and some oddly bereft of foliage.

The trees thinned and there was the house, standing in a clearing with a horseshoe courtyard. Manor Farm was an appropriate name, since it was too grand to be a common-or-garden farm but not quite grand enough to be a manor house. With its curved steps leading to an arched front door, its gables and bays, it was beautifully proportioned, like the best Cotswold houses.

She'd mixed with enough of the well-heeled, at Oxford and through her job, not to be intimidated by wealth and status, but as she pulled the old-fashioned doorbell she realized she was nervous, which annoyed her. From her single, brief telephone conversation with Charles Seagrove, to commission her and simultaneously set the date for her to report her findings, she hadn't been looking forward to meeting him.

He answered the door himself and her first impression was of someone very tall and thin. He made up for the fact that he was balding with plenty of facial hair, a grey beard and moustache as neatly trimmed as the drive to his house. He was crisp and smart in a dark suit and white shirt. But his feet were entirely bare, the skin a light coffee colour, dirt under the toenails, suggesting it wasn't unusual for him to forgo his shoes and socks. Was he losing his marbles as well as his footwear? With some effort, she tore her eyes back up to his face.

'I'm sorry I'm late. I had real trouble finding you.'

'That has its advantages,' he said. 'But the directions I gave you should have been sufficient.'

She chose to remain silent. She'd apologized once.

Charles Seagrove must have been at least eighty but he walked with the quick, rigorous stride of a man a quarter of his age, his bare feet flapping on the flagstones as he led her through the hall and held open the door of a study.

It wasn't at all the kind of room you'd imagine in a house like Shadwell. Not the cosy, jumbled, dusty, lived-in sort of place where Natasha would feel quite at home, with rugs and leather chairs and old paintings. Instead, it was light and airy and immaculately tidy, the books lined at right angles on the shelves, not a pile of papers or magazines in sight, the mahogany desk swept clear except for a clean jotter and slim silver ballpoint pen. The wide, open window offered a view of tiered steps that led down to an ornamental pond set in an expansive lawn.

Without asking what she'd like to drink, he poured two cups of pale herb tea from a pot on the window seat and handed her one. 'You're very young.'

What was she supposed to say to that? 'I'm nearly thirty.' She sipped the tea, which tasted like mashed-up grass.

He faced her across the desk, his iron-grey eyes as bright as a raptor's and the bones of his skull showing through the dome of his head, the skin as polished as his desk.

'I must confess,' he said. 'I'm rather surprised not to have heard from you before now. I thought you'd have had some questions.'

She smiled her sweetest smile. 'Your brief was so thorough it pretty much covered everything.' She'd dealt with enough prickly old ladies and pedantic academics in her time to know how to neatly defuse criticism with a compliment.

As she opened her carpet bag – she refused to own anything as conventional and boring as a briefcase – and pulled out the bulging file, she wondered, not for the first time, why she'd agreed to take on this job. The fee, she had to admit, had something to do with it. It would normally take her months to earn as much as she'd earned in the past six weeks.

'As you'll see, the Helliers are an interesting family. I've had fun tracing them. Actually, it would be great to have a little more time, just to—'

'Oh, one could always do with more time. But then nothing would ever be finished, would it? Just give me what you have.'

She leaned forward and spread the family tree out on the desk, spinning it round so it was the right way up for him to read. She felt like a schoolgirl having to explain why she'd not done her homework properly. She sensed that Charles Seagrove was the type who favoured the stick above the carrot and hoped she hadn't slipped up.

Seagrove flicked through the sheaves of papers and photographs, which she'd neatly arranged and indexed in chronological order, certificates and photocopies presented in a good old-fashioned ringbinder, the family tree itself carefully drawn with rulers and ink, as requested.

Charles Seagrove had come to Alice Hellier's page, her photograph and entry from the gaol book. Natasha resisted passing any comment as she watched him deliberate over it, his face unreadable. Ponderously, he turned back a page to Alice's parents, then forward to her son and grandson, then back again to Alice.

Say something. Clearly, he wasn't going to oblige, which meant she didn't feel free to discuss Alice either.

As her client went on studying the documents Natasha studied the room and realized something else that was odd about it. It was a house that cried out for ancestral portraits, the obligatory gallery of gilt-framed oil paintings and formal sepia photographs, faces staring out from every wall, every century. But in the hallway she'd been led through there was nothing and here, in the library, Seagrove's personal study, there were just three unobtrusive photographs. On the desk were a silver-framed graduation portrait, Seagrove's son perhaps, and a colour snap of a little girl standing proudly beside a sheep with a gold rosette pinned to its forehead. Granddaughter? On the small table in the corner by the window was the only old photograph, early nineteen hundreds at a guess: a blonde woman and a little girl.

The lack of ancestral portraits would have been surprising in the house of anyone of Charles Seagrove's standing, but doubly surprising considering his hobby and semi-profession was as a genealogist. Then, who was she to talk? She'd been a professional genealogist for eight years and didn't even know who her real mother and father were. When she was a teenager she'd found out that she was adopted by Steven and Ann, and had kept hoping that, in the course of her work, she'd discover a way back into her own past. But how did you start looking for someone who'd abandoned her baby daughter in hospital a few hours after she was born, a woman who'd left a false name and address?

Charles Seagrove must surely have researched his own family history at some point though. That was how most people got started.

He was looking at her expectantly. What had she missed while she was off with the fairies? 'I'm sorry?'

'For what?'

'I ... um ... Did you say something?'

'Not a word.' He carried on staring at her.

When men were described as undressing a person with their eyes it generally implied something sexual. Charles Seagrove was undressing her now, no doubt about that, but more in the way one might study a prize-winning ewe or ram. Stripping off the layers of her skin to see the cage of her ribs and her heart with its web of veins. The appraising, clinical stare of a horse trader, assessing whether she was healthy and strong, of good stock. It made her feel uncomfortable as well as cross. The sooner this meeting was over and she was out of here the better. Charles Seagrove may have more cash to flash around than most of her clients but he was giving her the creeps like few dead people ever could.

He suddenly broke eye contact, looked down at his desk, tapped the file. 'You're a clever girl.' Had his X-ray vision seen all the way through to her brain tissue?

She took his surprising compliment as justification to get up close and personal herself. She flicked her eyes towards the black-and-white photograph by the window. 'Part of your family tree?'

'No. A German soldier gave that photograph to my father. At Ypres on Christmas Eve nineteen-fourteen.' He looked at her as if she should know exactly what he was talking about.

She racked her brain, wishing she'd read modern instead of medieval history at Oxford, and located an image, not from a textbook but from a Paul McCartney pop video. German and British soldiers fraternizing near the trenches. 'The Pipes of Peace ... I mean ... the Christmas Truce?'

'It wasn't just a fairy story, you know,' he said brusquely.

An amazonian woman popped her head round the door. With her scrubbed face, headscarf, flowery pinafore and broom under her arm, she was a 1940s housewife personified, undoubtedly the person responsible for keeping Shadwell so spick and span. 'Beg pardon for disturbing you, Mr Seagrove, I'll come back later.'

Seagrove rose. 'You carry on, Mavis. Miss Blake and I will continue our conversation outside.' Just then the telephone on his desk started ringing. 'Tell whoever it is that I'm in a meeting.'

Mavis went to pick it up.

'That takes me back to my City days,' Seagrove commented to Natasha, as they made their way towards the hall.

'You worked in the City?'

'In banking. A means to an end. I had to work damned hard for all this.'

A surprise. Natasha had assumed he'd inherited Shadwell, that it was at least partially purchased with old money. He was clearly proud of his achievement.

She was used to running behind Boris on their country rambles, so keeping up with Charles Seagrove as he marched past the orangery and down a shady path that skirted the edge of the trees was a breeze. She wondered at his fitness regime though. Maybe she should stock up on herbal tea.

'So, tell me, what's the appeal of genealogy to someone of your age?'

She could have picked from any number of corny, superficial answers – Because otherwise we just have the present; the rest is history – but after her last flippant remark about the Christmas Truce she didn't want to be glib.

'Sometimes I see my ancestors as puppet masters,' she said eventually. 'It's as if they're there behind the scenes, controlling me, pulling strings I can't see. I'm dancing to their tune, a tune that was written so long ago I can't hear it, unless I know how to listen properly.'

He looked at her. 'That's very eloquently put. I'm relieved to hear you're in the camp that accepts the only difference between a human being and a stone rolling down a hill is that the human thinks he's in charge of his destiny. Not one of those who views the mind as a blank sheet of paper on which experience writes the plot.'

She didn't take kindly to pigeonholing. 'Actually, I'm some-where in the middle.'

She wasn't about to get into an argument right now but she'd devoured enough studies of adopted children to know she could hold her own in any nature versus nurture debate. Could have told him that when a child changes its family environment it leaves surprisingly little mark on his or her personality, for instance, but that an intellectual home makes you more likely to become an intellectual.

'Given a choice I'd rather be shaped ninety-nine per cent by genes and one per cent environment than the other way round. Much better to be determined by forces inside yourself than by outside influences.' Control freak or what?

'Indeed,' Seagrove agreed. He slowed as they reached the woods.

It was chilly, and it was clear the sun never reached this path. The ground was still wet and spongy, tatters of last autumn's decayed foliage still rotting in the undergrowth.

'The Christmas Truce,' he said reflectively, picking up the thread of the conversation again. His pace slowed further. 'My father never talked about his experiences in the war, except to tell me what happened that Christmas after the first battle of Ypres. He didn't need hindsight. He knew at the time that he was part of something momentous, that it would be the most extraordinary experience he would ever have.' They'd come to an opening in a high cypress hedge. 'After you.'

Natasha walked through and found herself in a secret garden. The hedge formed four walls which enclosed a lawn, in the centre of which was a crooked old apple tree with a rope swing. At the far end was a stone statue of a nude young woman, ghostly white and still against the jade backdrop. Life-sized, she sat on a pedestal with her legs tucked under her, hair twisted into a bun, her head tilted to one side and cradling a naked baby who was nestled against her, suckling. The curve of her breast against the child's mouth was both intimate and unsettling as well as peculiarly beautiful.

'My wife, Stella, modelled for it,' Seagrove said.

'The baby is your son?' Natasha said, thinking of the graduation portrait.

'Not Richard, no,' he said eventually. 'The baby is a little girl. There was no model. Stella gave the sculptor a drawing. She calls her Amelia.' He smiled almost apologetically. 'My wife has always been rather fanciful. But Richard used to play here,' he added. 'We could keep an eye on him and know he was safe.'

'It's very peaceful.' Almost unnaturally, eerily quiet, in fact. A place out of time. Natasha looked at the peaceful, cherubic little face of the baby. And Mrs Seagrove, frozen forever as a young woman.

Charles invited her to sit on a stone bench. 'As I was saying, my father was in the London Rifle Brigade near Ploegsteert Wood. There had been torrential rain for weeks but on Christmas Eve the rain stopped. It snowed briefly and then there was frost. The mud hardened, the pools froze over and there was bright moonlight. The huddled shapes of dead men and sheep were white with rime.'

There was something peculiar about the way he was talking, the sentences disjointed. Experience of such conversations told her that he was downloading his father's memory, telling her the story in the exact words it had been told to him, or the words he remembered, the fragments that had stuck in his mind, taking care not to add his own embellishments.

'By the time my father took over the night watch,' Charles continued, 'a row of Christmas trees had been lit with candles along the parapet of the German trenches, stretching as far as the eye could see. My father heard the distant, haunting sound of the German soldiers singing "Silent Night". For the rest of his life he could never hear that carol without being moved to tears. The next morning he heard a voice through the fog. "We are Saxon. You are Anglo-Saxon. Come out and talk to us. We won't fire if you won't." My father and a soldier called Hans Koenig met halfway across No Man's Land. Hans used to be head waiter at the Great Central Hotel so he spoke perfect English and he was the same age as my father, twenty-two. Hans gave my father a bottle of cognac and a photograph of his wife Hilda and daughter Magda, which you saw in my study. My father gave him some tea and the only picture he had of my mother. Hans shook my father's hand and said, "Tomorrow you fight for your country and I fight for mine. Good luck." They arranged to meet after the war, then went back to their own trenches.

'My father said that after that day the war no longer made any sense to him. He'd been chatting to a man who he'd been trying to kill a few hours before. Shaking hands with someone he'd try to pierce with a bullet the next day. "My friend the enemy", my father called him. He was killed less than three months later, in the Battle of Neuve Chapelle. My father said the Christmas Truce taught him the futility of war, and it was because of that night that I learned the importance of family, and family history.'

She didn't understand the connection, but left a respectful silence.

Seagrove pressed his thin hands down on his knees, stretched his back, and stood, with not a trace of stiffness. 'It's my son's birthday on Sunday. We're having a garden party. You must come.'

'I thought you didn't want anybody—'

'It won't matter by then, if people know you've been working for me.'

As usual, curiosity got the better of her. 'Thanks. I'd love to come.'

'We must celebrate the next generation, mustn't we? Remember that we too will become ancestors.'

'Are you descended from the Helliers?' she asked then, finally. 'I kept thinking that I'd find out you were related in some way.'

The stiffness which hadn't been evident in his knees now appeared in his face, a scowl that sent frown lines rippling right up onto the dome of his head.

'Over my dead body,' he said.

Three

NATASHA WAS STILL at her own front door, receiving Boris's enthusiastic welcome, when Mary came out of the Snowshill Arms, baby Kieran balanced on her hip, and shouted hello. She'd shrunk to her pre-pregnancy figure almost instantaneously and was back to wearing the teenage fashion – embroidered bootleg cords and bright, skimpy T-shirts – which fitted and suited her tiny frame better than adult clothes.

'How's my little friend?' Natasha asked.

'Little monkey more like. How did the meeting go?' Mary said, reminding Natasha that one drunken evening, she'd broken her vow of silence and spilled the beans to Mary about her mysterious client's identity. Her excuse was that, before Mary had gone and got herself pregnant, Natasha had been training her as a research assistant.

Natasha wandered across the lane. 'Client satisfied. Job done. My curiosity not quite satisfied but the invoice is almost in the post and the fee's spent already.'

Several times over, in fact, what with the rusting front wing of the Alpine and its balding front tyres, not to mention Orchard End's guttering, which wouldn't cope with another winter. Plus, there was that gorgeous chocolate antique lace dress in the vintage clothing arcade in Cheltenham ...

'Think you'll get any more work out of him?'

'I'm not sure I want it.'

'It's odd, isn't it? When you think that Charles Seagrove has lived not a dozen miles away for over sixty years. And no one round here can tell me a jot about him, not even my father-in-law, who knows everything there is to know about everybody. Apparently Mr Seagrove opens up the gardens and the bluebell woods around Shadwell Manor Farm one day every year, but none of the oldies have ever been, so far as I can tell – I've been asking around. Don't worry, I haven't mentioned you in the conversation.'

'Bluebell woods? Just wait there one moment.' She dashed inside, came back out with the enigmatic letter. Could Charles Seagrove have sent it? Why would he do that? 'What do you make of this?'

Mary frowned as she read. 'I don't know. Not likely to be connected, is it? Never heard of anywhere called Poacher's Dell.'

James, Mary's husband and landlord of the Snowshill Arms, appeared, rolling a beer barrel round from the back.

Mary showed him the letter. 'Someone sent this to Natasha.'

James gave it a glance. 'Cinderella, huh? Probably nothing more than some supposedly clever direct mail teaser campaign for a new brand of dustpan.'

Natasha smiled. 'I'm sure you're right. It's just . . .'

'What?' Mary looked at her and Natasha knew she was thinking the same thing.

'It's like some kind of tip-off about a *body*. Do you think I should go to the police?'

James laughed. 'They'd have you committed.' He handed the letter back.

Mary's father-in-law, Arnold Hyatt, appeared at her shoulder, on his way out. He saluted Natasha and kissed the top of his grandson's fluffy head. Arnold was a farmer and Snowshillian born and bred. He was also, thanks to Mary's influence, a new convert to the local history society. He was a great asset, a one-man walking encyclopaedia of the North Cotswolds. With his snow-white hair and stagy voice, he was perfectly suited to his role as guide at Snowshill Manor, regaling tourists with stories of the house's weird and wonderful contents, and he was old enough to remember Charles Paget Wade, the manor's eccentric owner. You could guess Arnold's plans for the day by his clothes. Braces for tending to his chickens and goats; smart black waistcoat for Snowshill Manor. It was the waistcoat today, so he must be on his way to work.

'Ever heard of a place called Poacher's Dell near Shadwell?' Mary asked.

''Fraid not.'

Mary gave Natasha a shrug.

Natasha went back to the cottage. Another envelope had arrived while she was out and as she retrieved it from behind the door, she half wondered if it was going to be a follow-up. Then she turned it over and saw the handwriting. Unmistakable. And the stamps. Canadian stamps. Her legs went shaky. She slid her finger under the seal. Her hands were shaky too.

It was from Marcus. The man she'd been sure she was going to marry one day. Her friends said they were perfect for each other. Marcus worked with her father – he was a medical artist, someone who recreated the faces of the dead through intricate skull measurements – and was as passionate about history as she was. He loved old houses and dogs, just as she did. He was reasonable and calm, made her feel safe and secure, and he was the only man she'd ever said she loved. But, true to form, she'd not let herself trust him, and it had led to a stupid misunderstanding. Marcus had not rushed to introduce her to his large and close-knit family because he worried she'd feel left out. His kindness backfired. When she heard him talking to a girl on the phone late at night, she jumped to what she thought was the only conclusion. She'd been abandoned once, as a baby, and it was never going to happen to her again. She'd made it her mission always to be the one to leave. She accused Marcus of two-timing her and packed up his things. Too late, she discovered that the girl he'd phoned was his sister, Katie.

He came back after she sent him away, just once. She'd realized her mistake and emailed to say she was sorry, not even daring to hope that he'd even reply. Not long afterwards, she walked into her living room and there he was, sitting by the fire. He spent the night in her bed and left for a sabbatical at the University of Vancouver in the morning, leaving her unsure if he'd forgiven her or had just come to say goodbye. That was ten months ago, and Natasha had had just a couple of emails from him since. Friendly and chatty but no more than that, leaving her wondering if there was anything left between them except thousands of miles.

Why would Marcus send her a letter now instead of an email? Unless he had something important to say, like he'd met someone else. Or unless he was sending her something.

Like a plane ticket.

That's all there was inside the envelope. Just a little folder with an aeroplane in a blue sky and the red maple leaf logo of Air Canada. She opened it, could read her name on the ticket but not the flight itinerary or the date of the seat reservation because her eyes had misted over. Due to the bright sunshine, obviously. Scribbled on the back of the folder she made out a message: *The rainbows over Niagara never fade. Come and see them.*

Now that was the kind of cryptic message she liked. It was so kind and thoughtful and romantic. It was just like him.

It was more than she deserved.

Marcus knew her so well. Knew that if he left it to her to buy her own ticket she'd find a million excuses, because jumping on a plane to go and see him was the action of someone far too needy. She battled down a sting of pride now. Pride, or stubborn independence, depending on how you chose to look at it, had come between them too many times. She stroked the ticket with her finger. She had to stop punishing everyone who tried to get close to her. She finally made out the date on the ticket: 10 July. Exactly one calendar month away.

Go. Don't go. Go. Don't go.

Why was she always at war with herself?

Four

THE SHADWELL MANOR Farm garden party wasn't nearly as big an affair as Natasha had expected. There were about thirty guests, though there seemed to be more because they'd all congregated in the one sunny area that stretched across the terraced steps to the middle of the lawn. Even in the early afternoon the trees which surrounded the house cast long shadows and it was as if everyone had huddled together because they didn't want to stray too close to the woods.

After Mary had mentioned the bluebells here, Natasha had checked her large-scale map of the local area. The woods were simply named Shadwell. Could there be a place within them called Poacher's Dell that Arnold Hyatt didn't know about? There were bluebell woods all over England, she told herself, but wondered who else she could ask.

The note about Cinderella and the bluebell woods of Poacher's Dell aside, there was certainly something about this place, about the way the trees completely enclosed the house. Everywhere you looked they were there. There was no sense of the drive, no sense of a way out. They lined up at the periphery of the lawn, like an angry crowd pushing against an invisible barrier, a still and silent army threatening at any moment to stampede and destroy the formal flowerbeds and the trim lawn, to show how nature restrained was just an illusion that could be shattered in an instant.

Natasha glanced round at the beautiful people sipping Pimm's and champagne, listening to the string quartet that was stationed near the rosebeds, and she couldn't escape the strange sensation that this refined afternoon was transient and fragile, too. The air of falseness and pretension gave her the perverse desire to rip off all her clothes and turn cartwheels across the lawn. Instead she grabbed a glass of Pimm's from a passing tray.

There was a large proportion of young couples, she noticed, the London commuters and weekenders seeking a rural idyll for their children. The usual Cotswold establishment was missing. Where were the retired captains of industry, the barristers, aging academics and county set? Other local farmers, like Arnold Hyatt, were conspicuous by their absence. Maybe Charles Seagrove retained his youthfulness by surrounding himself with the young and avoiding the company of his own generation.

Now sporting a rather jaunty if battered straw hat, he spotted her and put an end to her idle voyeurism. 'Come and meet Richard.'

'You've been fortunate to have sunshine today. The forecast was for rain,' Natasha said politely as they walked across the grass. Hey, she was English. It was her duty to mention the weather at least once in a conversation.

'We've had sunshine on Richard's birthday every year since he was born.' He announced it proudly, as if luck was not involved but divine right.

Unless Charles Seagrove had become a father very late in life, Richard Seagrove must be in his fifties, Natasha calculated. Strange, still to be having your birthday parties at your parents' house. Maybe that was how the other half lived. The ones that still called their parents mummy and daddy when they were mummies and daddies themselves. Perhaps that's what money bought you. The chance to be a child for longer.

'Happy Birthday,' Natasha said, then instantly wondered if she should have chosen a more sophisticated phrase. Congratulations or happy returns would have been more appropriate.

'Thank you.' Richard Seagrove's handshake was so firm it temporarily cut the circulation to her fingers, but at least it was not at all clammy, despite the weather. If she hadn't decided he must be almost the same age as her father, she would definitely have flirted with him. Robert Redford good-looking with sky-blue eyes, he radiated health and well-being. He was not quite as tall as Charles but lean as a lurcher. A golden boy with no gold band on his finger, she couldn't help but notice.

The Seagroves certainly proved that money and privilege were good for your health. Richard's mother, Stella, had skin as soft and gleaming as a teenager's and one of the loveliest faces Natasha had seen. Her wide, blue eyes were just like Richard's, and her blonde hair, still lustrous and shoulder-long, was drawn off her forehead with a tortoiseshell comb but left free to tumble around her shoulders. Around her neck was tossed a luminous extravaganza of organza scarves, a bohemian look carried through in dangling earrings and jangling bracelets.

In a queenly fashion, she offered Natasha her hand. 'I'm glad you could come.'

'I'm sure I saw you yesterday,' Richard Seagrove's tone gave the impression he'd caught her doing something she shouldn't. 'Walking up on Shenberrow Hill. Would you have been exercising a Red Setter?'

'Boris.'

'Beautiful dog.'

'He knows it.'

'Reds are descended from Irish Setters,' Charles Seagrove put in. 'The chosen breed of kings and courtiers through the ages.' So his interest in genealogy stretched to dogs. And why not? Debrett's, where he used to work, talked about a family's pedigree as if they were referring to animals not humans.

Another tray of fluted Pimm's and champagne glasses sailed by. Natasha swiped one and so did Richard. The waitress didn't even offer one to Richard's father, who was drinking what looked like carbonated water with ice and lemon, Natasha noticed.

'My father tells me you're a historian?' Richard said.

'Yes.'

She'd been sworn to secrecy for weeks but it was evidently fine for everyone to know her business now the job was done. Stella Seagrove didn't seem to approve, however, as she had stiffened and turned her head away to listen to the string quartet as soon as Richard mentioned Natasha's profession.

'You'd get on well with my daughter, Rosa,' Richard added. 'She's been fascinated with castles and King Arthur since she was a little girl.'

Stella looked round. 'I wonder where she can have got to?'

'She refuses to come down,' Richard said, turning towards his father pointedly. 'Whatever you two were talking about earlier, you've put her in a foul mood.'

'Charles?' Seagrove was caught in his wife's critical glare. 'What have you done to upset Rosa?'

Her husband's mystification was almost credible. Almost. 'I'm afraid it seems dear Rosa has inherited her mother's hot temper and irrationality.' Charles seemed to remember that Natasha was marooned in the middle of this family summit. 'Take Richard's example as a warning against whirlwind romances. They lead to whirlwind divorces. Still, it also led to Rosa so we can't complain.'

Natasha couldn't quite work out the dynamics of this conversation. There were definite undercurrents, but who was having a dig at whom?

'My father is of the enlightened or irresponsible notion that motherhood and marriage don't necessarily have to go together,' Richard said with barbed amusement. 'He never did like my wife but so long as she gave him a grandchild she was fulfilling her biological duty. What do you make of that?'

Natasha, who at times longed for a baby more than she longed for a husband, could see his point, up to a point. 'Call me old-fashioned. But I think a child needs both a mother and a father if at all possible.'

'If only we lived in a perfect world.' Charles Seagrove touched his son's shoulder and said he must go and mingle. He seemed to have a knack of ending conversations just as they were getting interesting.

'If you've upset Rosa you should go and apologize to her,' Stella Seagrove commanded his retreating back. She glanced at Natasha and inched closer to her son, almost possessively.

Natasha wondered if her long purple sundress, bought especially for the occasion, was perhaps a little too revealing. But it wasn't as if she'd let her hair cascade down her back with the wild abandon it usually did. She'd restrained it demurely into a ballerina's bun, the hairstyle somehow suggested by the black embroidered canvas sandals with strings that tied around her ankles like dancer's shoes. She knew the recent hot spell had given her usually pale cheeks a honey flush, scattered faint freckles across her nose, but her bedroom mirror had also told her that her brown eyes still looked too tired to be wanton. Perennial curse of a chronic insomniac.

'I tried to tempt Rosa outside with a game of tennis this morning but she wouldn't have it,' Richard said.

'That's because you always beat her, darling,' Stella Seagrove simpered, gazing adoringly at her son. 'You should see the trophies lined up in the drawing room,' she said to Natasha. 'Richard won every race and tennis tournament he entered, from his first sports day in infant school. He had an amazing will to win at all costs, right from the start. But he wasn't one of those children who's only gifted on the playing field. He's got academic certificates and awards to match every one of his athletic medals.'

Richard didn't bother faking discomfort at this outpouring. He was clearly used to it and utterly at ease with the world, as if he took it for granted that fortune, like the sun, would always shine on him. It would be easy to despise him but actually, so far, it was impossible not to like him. Too sweet to be wholesome, as Arnold would say.

Silence swept like a tidal wave through the guests. The string quartet had stopped playing and Charles Seagrove was standing in front of the fountain, obviously waiting to make a speech.

'Lunch is served in the orangery. And plenty more champagne. But first I'd like to thank you all for joining us to celebrate Richard's birthday. I know some of you have come a long way to be with us today. Most of you haven't known Richard that long so you won't remember the first parties we had for him. It was jelly and ice cream the first time round, fifty-nine years ago, then clowns and magicians. We moved on to pop music and dancing and lots of pretty girls, and now it's strawberries and cream and a string quartet. All special occasions but none more so than the day

Richard was born. A man can die peacefully when he has a son. Please join me in a toast and raise your glasses. To Richard.'

Natasha had gauged the party wrongly, she decided. It wasn't the usual scenario of the guy in the big house lording it over the local peasants. It wasn't his house or his success or his status that Charles Seagrove was showing off, but his son.

The menu in the orangery was an extension of the herb tea Natasha had first been served at Shadwell. The Seagroves were clearly into health foods of the cranky variety, which was OK with Natasha, who was more than content with a plate of cous cous, sunflower seeds and artichoke hearts.

At the buffet she couldn't help tuning in to hear what Stella Seagrove was saying to her husband, but all she caught was: 'He's been here again.' Stella had leant in close to Charles as she spoke, as if she wanted to be discrete, but a certain urgency in her voice had made her audible, and not just to Natasha.

Richard had overheard too. 'Who are you talking about?'

Stella was instantly dismissive. 'Oh, just someone who wants to talk to your father about old times.'

'Well, invite him in then,' Richard suggested.

'Neither the time nor the place,' his father snapped.

'Has he come up from Kent, then?' Richard pressed.

'Leave it, darling, please,' Stella told her son, firmly.

The heat in the glasshouse was cloying. Natasha could feel sweat trickling down her spine and the combination of warmth, alcohol and severe sleep deficit was threatening finally to drag her under. She went over to the drinks table for a glass of iced mineral water and wandered back across the lawn, sipping the drink, and sat down on a wooden bench under a chestnut tree near the front drive.

There was someone standing in the doorway of the house. A girl with curly blonde hair, a silver slide sweeping a heavy fringe to the side of her face. She'd not dressed for the occasion, was wearing a white sundress and white pumps scuffed with grass stains. It took a second for Natasha to place her as the girl she'd met on the road when she was trying to find Shadwell Manor Farm.

'Rosa, my dear. I was wondering where you'd got to.' Charles

Seagrove strode past Natasha to his granddaughter, his hand outstretched.

The girl folded her arms across her small chest, stepped out onto the lawn. 'Say hello to John, Grandpa.' Defiance rang in her voice. She turned back towards the house where a young man appeared behind her. It wasn't too much of an exaggeration to say that Charles Seagrove stopped dead as if a chasm had opened in the ground in front of him.

Natasha wondered if she should shift out of sight and earshot, at least turn away or try not to listen. But this was people-watching at its best. The three of them were like actors on a stage and there was definitely a scene brewing.

It seemed that Charles Seagrove already knew his granddaughter's companion. No introduction was necessary.

The boy walked towards the older man, his hand outstretched. As he did so, Seagrove slowly put both his hands behind his back, a small, quiet gesture, but one loaded with meaning. Natasha had found him intimidating enough when he wasn't so obviously set against her, so her sympathy at the moment was all with John, whoever he was and whatever he'd done to upset his girlfriend's grandfather. She noticed that he'd made more effort to dress up than Rosa, was wearing a beige linen suit over a white granddad shirt, which looked too big for his boyish frame. He stared down at the ground, awkward beneath a mop of brown curls.

Without one more word, Charles Seagrove turned on his heel and strode away.

Surreptitiously, Natasha watched Rosa. Unshed tears glittered in her eyes, threatening to brim over, but instead of making her look vulnerable or tragic they made her seem somehow stronger and fiercer. She'd tilted her head slightly upwards to stop the tears falling, or to call on the gods for assistance.

'Let's go,' the young man said.

Rosa trained her eyes on her grandfather's retreating back like a laser. 'We're not leaving. No way.' She was mightily sure of herself for someone so young, for someone of any age come to that.

'I know when I'm not wanted,' John said.

'*I* want you.' It was spoken with the force of a command and she'd almost stamped her foot as she'd said it.

It was too private for even Natasha to watch now. She picked up her empty glass and was about to carry it back to the Orangery.

'We met the other day, didn't we?'

Natasha turned to find Rosa homing in on her.

'That's right.'

'My big mistake. Helping you to find us.'

'I'm sorry?'

'Are you?' She struck the same mutinous pose she'd adopted in front of her grandfather. 'Are you really? Or do you just believe in taking the money and running?'

'Hang on a minute,' her boyfriend intervened.

'It's OK,' Natasha said. She was perfectly capable of fighting her own battles, thank you very much. When she'd worked out what the hell she was fighting. 'I'm afraid I don't have a clue what you're talking about.'

The boy put his hand tentatively on Rosa's arm, flashing Natasha a wary look, half apologetic. 'Come on, you can't blame her.'

Rosa shrugged him away, kept her eyes fixed on Natasha. 'Oh but I can. Just ask her. Go on. Ask her if she stopped to think. When my grandfather asked you to do his dirty work for him, did you even wonder, just for one minute, who John Hellier was?'

She had. And now it took only a split second for the penny to drop.

'What gave you the right? I hope he paid you well, for snooping around behind our backs. What's the going rate for spying these days?'

'This whole thing's too weird,' John said. 'You've probably got it all wrong. Old people are peculiar sometimes. I could have offended your grandfather without meaning to. Maybe he knows I use the wrong knife and fork at dinner or something. I think it'd be better if I just left.'

Like many men, his well-meant chivalry shrivelled in the face of adversity. Natasha's father Steven was no different, much as she loved him. But John Hellier was descended from Alice, from a murderess and a string of petty criminals, Natasha thought as she

31

watched him. With his dark curls and eyes and diffident, unassuming stance, he looked, and seemed, the gentle, sensitive sort, as unlike Alice and the arsonist and robbers who'd followed in her wake as he was his more recent ancestors, the blacksmith and the farmer.

Say hello to John, Grandpa.

The Christmas Truce taught my father the futility of war, and it was because of that night that I learned the importance of family, and family history.

Why was Charles Seagrove so interested in *his* family history? What on earth was he playing at? Was what he'd done, what she'd helped him do, even ethical?

'You're my guest and I want you to stay,' Rosa said to John. 'If you leave now he's won.'

John didn't deny it. 'Look. I'll call you.'

Natasha had heard that one before.

This was probably the first time Rosa Seagrove hadn't had things go exactly her own way, but she looked so crestfallen that Natasha's big-sister instincts were kicking in. She wanted to put her arm round Rosa, offer her a tissue to blow her nose.

'Look, Rosa. What your grandfather wanted me to find out for him isn't the sort of information that usually does anyone any lasting harm.' But it could. It did. She thought of paternity suits and lost inheritances and all the cupboard doors that could be opened to let skeletons come rattling out.

'Then how do you explain this?' Rosa dug her hands deep into her pockets, less angry now, more concerned with hiding her disappointment. 'John's studying agriculture at Cirencester, like me, so when I introduced him to Grandpa they clicked right away. About a month ago we told Grandpa that we were going to get married and he even suggested that the ceremony be held in the college chapel, which John said was perfect. Grandpa was so happy for us, he really liked John. Until he had that meeting with you.' She broke off, fighting tears still. The stiff upper lip hadn't gone out of fashion in some circles evidently. Natasha rummaged in her pocket and found a tissue. Rosa took it and rammed it against her eyes, then scrunched it in her hand.

So John was at agricultural college with Rosa. Not the hale and hearty variety of farmer that populated the Snowshill Arms, Natasha decided, but a more poetic type. A nature lover perhaps. From her short encounter with him, she could easily picture him as a little boy, collecting tadpoles and dry leaves, putting food out for birds and nursing hedgehogs and baby owls with broken wings.

'Dad said he knew my grandfather would want to know about John's family history,' she said. 'He's obsessive about that kind of thing, can't help himself. But you've told him something, I'm sure you have. And I have a right to know what it is.'

It won't matter by then, if people know you've been working for me. Presumably Charles hadn't wanted John or Rosa, perhaps even his wife or son, to find out what he was doing until he'd reached some kind of verdict.

'Rosa, I honestly haven't a clue.' This couldn't have anything to do with Alice Hellier surely? She cast her mind back to assess what she could remember of John Hellier's more recent past. His parents and grandparents were all upstanding people, so far as she'd been able to ascertain. Paternal grandfather decorated in the Second World War, father an arable farmer, mother a veterinary nurse who died a couple of years ago in a riding accident. 'I'm sure he'll come round.'

Rosa shook her head vehemently. Natasha worried for her. Real life wasn't star-crossed lovers overcoming all obstacles and opposition to be together. Relationships crashed on far less rocky ground than family disapproval.

'Where there's a will there's a way,' Natasha said, and Rosa had a will stronger than most, she suspected. 'I'm a great believer in that. If you want something badly enough you'll work out a way to get it.'

'Sure. In fairy stories.'

Natasha hid a smile. If you couldn't be bitter and cynical as an adolescent when could you be?

She hated the feeling that she'd let herself be used. If Charles Seagrove had told her he wanted to investigate his granddaughter's lover she'd have said no. Wouldn't she? She knew Rosa's remarks about dirty work and spying were over the top, but there was enough truth in them to give her more reasons to stay awake. How could she put this right?

'Look. You're welcome to see a copy of John's family tree, and the summary that I wrote for your grandfather.'

'It's John who should see all that crap, not me.'

'Yes, he should.'

No prizes for guessing how Charles Seagrove would feel about the work he'd commissioned being taken behind enemy lines. Was it too late for him to stop the cheque? Probably is, but not too late for him to demand his money back. However John Hellier, *did* have a right to see his own family tree.

He's not welcome in this house.

If there *was* something more explosive than Alice, she hadn't seen it. What had she missed?

Five

TWO DAYS LATER, the Air Canada ticket was still goading Natasha from its position of prominence by her computer screen. She picked it up, opened her desk drawer and was about to put it away, then wavered, set it back carefully in its place. She'd not even rung him or emailed to say she'd received it. *Go. Don't go.* Her internal battle was no closer to being resolved.

If she ripped the ticket in half would it stop her doing the same thing to herself? Would it stop her losing more sleep over it?

She checked her emails. One from Toby: 'Got what you wanted about Alice Hellier. Shall we have lunch so I can share it? I fancy a day in the country. Shall I come up to you?' His emails always read like an old-fashioned telegram. You could imagine each sentence interspersed with 'stop'.

Natasha responded: 'Lunch would be great. Stop. Suggest The Crown on Thursday. Stop. I'll pick you up. Stop. Love Natasha. Stop. Over and out.'

She opened her appointments programme. Client meeting in Winchcombe at three this afternoon. Tomorrow another visit to the Family Records Centre. The day after to Eastleach to interview another client's aged aunt. At some point she had to squeeze in a trip to Sevenhampton to photograph a church for an American woman whose great-grandmother had been baptized, married and buried there. She'd promised her friend Heidi a game of tennis on Thursday, to cook supper for her ex-colleagues Will and Emily at the weekend and to go to the Cotswold Wildlife Park with Mary and Kieran if the sun kept its hat on. Her diary for the next few weeks continued in the same vein. She hadn't been to see John Hellier in Cirencester, didn't have time. She didn't have time go to Canada either.

Not having time was always a poor excuse, and she knew it. But she had a niggling suspicion that before she saw John, she should tell Charles Seagrove, her client after all, and give him a chance to explain. She unfolded a map of the Cotswolds. Shadwell was halfway to Winchcombe, Sevenhampton a few miles further south. She could kill three birds with one stone today.

Mavis told her she'd find Charles Seagrove weeding in the kitchen garden, round the back.

The sun was hot on her face as she walked down the terrace and emerged from the long shade cast by the house, but as soon as she came to the rose garden she left the sun behind once again. This time the shadows were cast by the high redbrick wall, adorned with honeysuckle and Virginia Creeper.

The way in to the kitchen garden wasn't immediately evident so she followed the wall, passing two carefully tended greenhouses and what looked like a potting shed. She found it hard to imagine someone like Charles Seagrove on his hands and knees, digging his own garden, but if that was what he was doing right now, behind the wall, he was being very quiet about it. There was no clang and scrape of a trowel or a rake, or of trundling barrow wheels. In fact, there were no sounds at all except the occasional drone of a bee alighting on the honeysuckle.

She came to an open door in the wall, walked through. Froze.

She could see the wheelbarrow now, next to a tray of lettuces.

The trowel was lying on the ground beside the tray.

And lying on the ground beside the trowel, face down in dark, newly-turned earth, his arms and legs spread across the brick path, one arm bent under him and the other flung out in front, was Charles Seagrove.

No sign of movement, of breath. No sign of life at all.

'Mr Seagrove . . .' Somehow, Natasha knew immediately that he was dead. But that didn't stop her calling out to him as if he might somehow still hear her.

She dashed forward, an assumption leaping into her mind. Heart attack. Old man dies gardening; it was often the way. Frantically trying to decide if she'd be better to run for help, dial 999 or try to revive him, she dropped to her knees and reached out her hand to touch his shoulder. And as she did she took in the rest of the scene.

On the ground a few metres from the wheelbarrow was a shotgun. And, adjacent to Charles Seagrove's chest, the faded red of the old brick path was stained with the darker, glossier red of newly-spilt blood.

His head was turned to the side. His eyes were open and so was his mouth, as if he'd died gasping for air or shouting for help.

She snatched her hand away. The blood was warm and sticky on her fingers. She wasn't sure if she screamed out loud or if that only happened inside her own head.

Nobody came.

She made herself reach out again and touch his hand. The skin was still warm. She lifted his wrist, felt for a pulse, knowing, from his face and from the amount of blood, that she couldn't possibly find one.

When she stood, her legs felt as though she'd just stepped off a fairground ride, as if it was she who'd been shot, her own blood that was seeping out to dry in the warmth of the June sun.

She stared at Charles Seagrove's feet. The dirty toenails were peeking out from worn leather sandals.

She turned and ran.

Stella Seagrove was seated in her husband's chair behind the desk in the study. Natasha was in the chair she had used when first she'd met Charles Seagrove. Rosa was perched on the window seat, plaiting one of the curtain tassels.

Outside, the police had arrived and were doing whatever it was they had to do when someone had been murdered. Photograph the body and then remove it? Begin the search for evidence? Richard was on his way back from London and the police had asked Natasha to wait with the Seagroves until someone came to talk to her.

Her eyes were drawn back to Stella Seagrove. It was she Natasha had found when she'd charged into the house. She couldn't remember now exactly what she'd said but Stella had hurried back with her to the vegetable plot. She hadn't screamed, hadn't fainted. She'd just stared at the gun and whispered, 'That's Charles's shotgun.'

Natasha was wishing now that she'd handled it differently, that she'd somehow prevented Stella from having to see her husband with his own gun on the ground beside him, his blood slowly creeping towards it.

Gone now was Stella's elegant posture. She was hunched down in the chair as if she wanted it to swallow her up, and she was almost as still as her dead husband, except for the fingers of her left hand which gently caressed the worn arm of the chair. She'd got blood on her fingers too and a faint stain of it had rubbed off onto the green leather. It would never come out.

Natasha looked down at her own hands. She'd washed them half a dozen times since she'd come back from the garden but she still imagined she could see red under her nails, just as there had been soil beneath Charles Seagrove's toenails. She went to the bathroom and immersed her hands in soapy water again, scrubbed at her skin with a paper towel.

Mavis had poured them all a cup of tea. Natasha drank hers quickly, wouldn't have minded another, or something stronger, but Stella's sat untouched on the desk. Beside it, and open, Natasha noticed for the first time, was the Hellier file she'd given to Charles Seagrove just over a week ago. She could just see the photocopied picture of Alice Hellier.

Presently, there was a knock at the door. It was the policeman who'd introduced himself earlier as Sergeant Archie Fletcher. He conformed to policeman stereotype in that he was young, tall and clean-shaven, but his hazel eyes were unstereotypically exuberant and his light-brown hair was cut in a surprisingly trendy style, short at the back and floppy on top. Quite sexy, Natasha decided, then was instantly appalled that there was room in her brain for such thoughts right now.

Sergeant Fletcher asked Rosa to take her grandmother into the drawing room while he interviewed Natasha. 'Then I'll need to talk to both of you, and your son, Mrs Seagrove, as soon as he arrives, I'm afraid.' He did sound truly afraid, and uncomfortable, as if taking statements from the recently bereaved was alien to him. Natasha felt sorry for him, wondered how many murder inquiries he'd handled before.

He sat opposite her in Charles Seagrove's chair, cleared his throat and took out a notepad and pencil. He asked her to go over again exactly how she'd come to find Seagrove's body.

She tried to describe it without seeing it all again in her mind, but images flashed up at her like slides on a projector screen: staring eyes, the pool of blood, his bare and dirty toes.

Sergeant Fletcher had asked one of his junior officers to go off in search of more tea and she now appeared with a tray, set it on the desk. As Natasha talked, the sergeant poured milk, added the tea and then a generous helping of sugar. He hadn't asked her if she wanted any, just following the great tradition of soothing the traumatized. Warm and sweetly did it.

'What exactly was the nature of your relationship with Mr Seagrove?'

She sipped the tea, surprised to see the surface of it ripple. Which must be because her hand was shaking. 'He was my client. He asked me to do some genealogical research for him.'

'Family history?'

'Not the Seagroves'. Rosa's boyfriend, fiancé, John. The Helliers.'

She glanced at the file still open on the desk. The police would surely want to talk to John Hellier. There was someone, she realized with a sickening jolt, who might be relieved, pleased even, that Charles Seagrove was dead.

'How well would you say you knew Mr Seagrove?'

'I only met him twice. The first time was in this room, when I presented my findings, and then we went for a walk and he talked to me about his father who was in the First World War.' Despite the bright sun beyond the window, the room felt icy, as if mere mention of the snowy night in Flanders was somehow affecting the air quality. She wrapped her hands around the mug and glanced at the black-and-white photograph by the window. She wondered what had happened to Hilda and Magda Koenig.

'And the second time?'

'The garden party.'

He made a note. 'The garden party. Ah, yes. You were seen arguing with Charles Seagrove's granddaughter. What was that about?'

'She was, understandably, upset that her grandfather had asked me to dig around in her boyfriend's family history. You should talk to Rosa about it.'

'Oh, don't worry, we'll do exactly that.'

Archie Fletcher drew the Helliers' file towards him, with one finger on the corner of the page. 'This was the cause of the disagreement Rosa had with her grandfather, the cause of your disagreement with her?'

'That's right.'

'Were you angry with Mr Seagrove, too? Is that why you came back to talk to him today?'

Something in his tone made her feel even colder than before. She put her cup down, met the policeman's eyes. 'You're not seriously suggesting that I might have—'

'It's not my place to suggest, just to ask questions.'

'I wanted to give Mr Seagrove a chance to tell me his side of the story.' She stopped herself fiddling with her hair, twisting it round her finger like she used to do in exams when she was trying to think fast. 'There is something else that might be important. At the garden party. I heard Stella Seagrove mention a man who'd wanted to talk to Mr Seagrove. I got the impression Charles wasn't that keen to see him, and not just because it was an inconvenient time. Mrs Seagrove made some comment like, "He's here again", as if whoever it was had made a few attempts to see Mr Seagrove. Richard asked his mother who it was and she brushed him off, as if she didn't want to go into it.'

The sergeant made a note, then closed his notebook. 'Well, I think that's all for now, Miss Blake, thank you. Here's my card. If you remember anything else give me a call. And if I need anything else I know where to contact you.'

'If your investigation takes longer than a few weeks you'll have to call me in Canada.' Since when had that decision been made? Right now she wanted to be as far away from Shadwell as possible.

'It'd be better if you postponed.'

The knot in her throat was so big it felt as though her air supply was being cut off. 'I'm sorry?'

'I can't *stop* you going but it would be useful if you were around until all this is sewn up. It might only take a couple of weeks but these things can drag on for months. You were the one who found Mr Seagrove. And it seems there is a chance that his death has something to do with the work you were doing for him.'

The same thought had already occurred to her.

Six

BEFORE SHE'D LEFT Shadwell, Sergeant Fletcher had asked her if she was all right. She'd said yes, but in truth she wasn't sure how she was.

Charles Seagrove was dead and she knew the sight of his prostrate body would live with her for ever, would not fade over time.

The person she wanted right now was her dad, Steven. He'd offer just the right dose of compassion and level-headedness. But he was away at a conference in Germany. She tried calling him but his mobile was off. She'd be able to reach her mother at home in Derbyshire but Ann would ask more questions than the police, and her sister, Abby, was always one to make a drama out of the tiniest crisis.

She ran a hot, almost scalding bath, held her breath and submerged, feeling the heat and the caress of the water relaxing her tense head and neck muscles. When she sat up, letting the water cascade down her body, she examined her hands carefully. They looked entirely clean, but all the same she took a metal nail file and dug at her nails until there was blood on them again, her own blood.

Afterwards came an overwhelming urge to see a friendly face and at the Snowhill Arms everything was reassuringly familiar. On the way she managed to say hello to Violet, the Twig Lady, who even now, in the summer, was on her perpetual hunt around the village for kindling. A couple of the other village 'characters' were ensconced in the low-beamed inn: Gerald, who never uttered a word until turning out time when he had a habit of singing 'Silence is Golden' at the top of his voice, and Jock Hunter, an eccentric for the fact that he was a pig farmer whose entire family had turned vegetarian.

Besides Gerald and Jock, Arnold Hyatt was already at the bar, plus the regular domino duo on a table at the back. Along with James, Vanessa Deacon was serving. A teenager from Stanway, she wore a red jewel stud in her nose, coloured braids and hair extensions, and was generally about as wild as it got around here. Natasha would miss her when she went up to Durham University after the summer.

When Natasha first moved to Snowshill she'd considered it imperative to check out the local, knowing full well that as a single girl she'd need somewhere welcoming and friendly, and the first time she'd walked into the Snowshill Arms, nobody had halted their conversation or turned to stare at her. They did now though.

She looked at Arnold, faked a smile. 'Did I just grow another head?' She couldn't believe bad news could have spread so fast.

Mary came round from behind the bar and gave Natasha a vodka and a sympathetic hug. 'Vanessa's mum's friend cleans up at Shadwell,' she explained quietly. 'She told us half an hour ago.'

So by now the whole village would know not only that Charles Seagrove had been shot but that Natasha had been the one to find his body.

'It must have been so awful for you,' Mary added quietly.

For a while everyone left her alone and she sat at the bar and drank her vodka in quiet companionship, though she was aware of Mary and James casting solicitous glances in her direction. She wished they'd take off their kid gloves and treat her normally.

Arnold wasn't quite so cautious, or perhaps curiosity was a more powerful driving force, as she guessed it would be with her had their roles been reversed. 'Have the police any idea who did it yet?' he asked.

Natasha knocked back the vodka, grateful to him for not tiptoeing round her. 'They don't appear to have.'

After a moment. 'How long had he been dead when you found him?'

'I don't know.' She saw the pool of blood, still wet on the path, and she felt that if she swallowed another mouthful of vodka it would come right back up. She didn't know how long Charles had been dead but it couldn't have been long. In which case, how far away was his murderer when she walked into the kitchen garden? In her shock and panic it hadn't even occurred to look up. For all she knew the person who had fired the fatal shot could have still been there, inside the wall, watching her.

Someone else was talking. She made an effort to concentrate on that instead.

'I remember when he bought that house up at Shadwell.' It was one of the domino players, a grey-haired woman with red thread-veins criss-crossing her cheeks like the cracked glaze on an Old Master. 'We lived over that way at the time. I was only a youngster but I remember they both attracted a lot of attention.'

'How do you mean?' Arnold asked.

'His wife was the worst. Sweet as pie to you one day and yelling her head off the next.' Natasha found that hard to believe. Stella Seagrove? 'People thought he was strange too, and with good reason.' The domino queen broke off to select another piece and add it to the snaking formation on the table, then took a tissue out of the pocket of her quilted jacket and wiped her nose. 'People said he slept outside, in the garden in the summer, aye, and winter too, and that he swam naked in the river. He was an extraordinary sight. He used to wander round the village with no shoes. I can still see his toes poking out beneath his grass-stained trousers, dirty and calloused they were.'

Natasha could still see them too. 'What's wrong with swimming naked in the river?' she said. She'd done the odd bit of skinny-dipping herself. There was nothing like it for a sense of freedom and abandon.

The domino player sniffed and went back to concentrating on her next move.

'You knew him well though, didn't you?' Vanessa said to Natasha. 'You were working for him?'

When Toby came to stay at Orchard End he sometimes asked how she put up with everyone knowing her business. She quite liked it in a way, found it reassuring. If she fell and broke her leg out walking Boris, it wouldn't take long for the alarm to be raised and a search sent out. If she wound up in hospital she was guaranteed a steady stream of visitors, even though she'd no family nearby. But it had its downside. So little happened here that it was no wonder Shadwell was the prime topic of conversation. A drama worthy of *Crime Watch* unfolding not far from their doorstep and Natasha had a starring role. Unfortunately. She suddenly wanted to go home.

Mary hurried after her, caught her up at the front door of her cottage. 'Are you going to be all right?'

'Yes,' she said, just as she'd assured Sergeant Fletcher.

But she knew she was in for a long night, dreaded closing her eyes because she knew what she would be seeing in the darkness.

She turned on the television. The story made the national late night round-up of TV news: 'An eighty-three-year-old man was found shot dead early this afternoon at Shadwell, near Winchcombe. A murder incident unit has been set up at Chipping Campden police station.'

The young reporter, filmed standing outside the gates to Shadwell, was playing up the enormity of the news, commenting on how deeply shocked locals were and how the tranquil villages that surrounded Shadwell were places where people still left their doors unlocked and felt entirely safe walking their dogs out late at night. There was an interview with a woman from Stanton who was visibly traumatized: 'Nothing like this has ever happened round here before. It's horrific. I'm almost afraid to venture into my own garden.' A spokesperson from the police station was interviewed, telling locals not be to be alarmed, inferring that there wasn't an armed madman on the loose and that whoever had killed Charles Seagrove had been specifically out to get him.

The story was followed by another about people enjoying the heatwave. Natasha stared at images of children splashing on a beach.

In bed she tried to read a novel but her mind seemed incapable of conjuring the story's landscape, too preoccupied with other, more realistic images. Blood and bricks and dark, crumbling earth.

Charles Seagrove's eyes. The last things they'd seen must have been the person who held the shotgun, unless the shot had come from nowhere, out of the blue.

At two in the morning she couldn't stand it any longer. She went to sit in the garden, then wandered barefoot on the dewy grass, like Charles Seagrove used to do.

At 9 a.m. she didn't feel too bad. But she knew the after-effects of a sleepless night would kick in about mid-afternoon. She couldn't face going to London as she'd planned, or the interview in Eastleach. She remembered then that she'd been due to go to meet a client in Winchcombe after she'd left Shadwell and she'd never made it. Her client, an elderly lady, would be furious. But she couldn't even bring herself to pick up the phone to apologize and explain why she'd let her down. She'd do it later.

She distracted herself with replies to some emails, then managed to get absorbed drafting an article she'd been commissioned to write for RootsWeb on tracing convict ancestors. It didn't need to be finished until the middle of July but she'd started it a couple of days ago, to get it out of the way, just in case she wasn't going to be around next month.

She closed the file. No need to hurry now. She flicked her eyes towards the ticket with its bold red maple leaf. Unusually, her desk was tidy and the ticket was the only item not in a neat pile.

Excluding the odd long weekend in the Dales or the Lakes, when Marcus had been based at Manchester University, she hadn't had a proper holiday for nearly three years. One of the penalties of being self-employed. This time she didn't try to stop her brain clicking into calculator mode and start totting up lost days in terms of lost income. It helped, just a tiny bit, as the decision had been made for her. Would she have gone if she could? It seemed important to know the answer to that. A couple of days ago she'd spent hours tidying and filing and generally putting things in order, for all the world as if she were intending to go to Canada. She'd realized it would be surprisingly easy. She'd already checked her passport, mentally arranged for Mary and James to look after Boris, made the all-important decisions about what clothes she would take and had even started to put some into her suitcase, which now teased her in the hallway as much as the ticket did, sitting there on her desk. She'd have sent a message to her work contacts telling them she'd be away for a couple of weeks, and diverted her landline through to her mobile. Where would a girl be without technology? Not on her way to Canada, that was for sure.

Someone was hammering on the door. Richard Seagrove.

It was shocking how quickly someone could change. His sun had disappeared behind a cloud for the first time. Even his blue eyes didn't seem to be shining so brightly, the blueness of them faded, like the over-washed denim jeans he was wearing with a cotton pullover.

He didn't give her a chance to invite him in.

'I want to know what you're planning to do to help repair the damage you've done to my family.' He made his request sound perfectly reasonable and rational, and yet Natasha could tell immediately that Richard Seagrove was neither of those things right now, which of course was perfectly understandable consider-ing the shock and grief he must be suffering. If Steven had been . . . she couldn't bear to think of it.

'I can only imagine how you must be feeling.'

'Oh, can you? I doubt that very much.' He was surrounded by a force-field of naked aggression that repelled any attempts at sympathy. 'I won't let you just walk away from this.'

'Look, I'd be glad to do whatever I can to help,' she said, 'but I honestly don't know what you want from me.'

He reached out and grabbed her arms. 'I want some answers, that's what.'

It was broad daylight in the middle of a village, but she felt a hot stab of shock and fear at the sudden contact, which threatened to swamp her sympathy for him. She glanced down the lane; there was nobody about.

'I should think the police are more likely to provide you with the answers you need,' she managed.

He released her. 'They don't have your particular expertise.'

She really didn't want to get any more involved in this than she already was. 'I don't mean to sound insensitive, but my skills are generally more useful for solving mysterious deaths that happened at least a hundred years ago.'

'This is what you're going to do,' he said, ignoring her. 'You're going to carry on where you left off with the research you were doing for my father. I know it has something to do with why he died. And this time you report back to me, understand?'

She felt she should do it. She'd wanted to follow up her initial research and now she needed to, for her own peace of mind as well as Richard Seagrove's. He was right – there was more to the story than met the eye. But what could she possibly find that would relate to Charles Seagrove's death?

'I won't do it this time unless I have John Hellier's permission.'

'Leave that to me. I'll talk to him. One final thing: this arrangement is strictly between you and me. Is that perfectly clear?'

Like father like son. 'I can't promise I'll discover anything that will help you.'

He stared hard at her. 'You have to.'

Seven

NATASHA NEARLY TRIPPED over her suitcase as she bolted upstairs. She gave it a frustrated kick and made for her bedroom, where she pulled her hair back into a ponytail, and pushed her swimming costume, goggles, shampoo and towel into her bag. Almost running back down to the hall, she couldn't wait to get into the cool silence of the pool, her regular solace.

There were two people sitting at her kitchen table. Mr Samuels and Miss Dodsworth. Mr Samuels held out a grocery bag filled with home-grown tomatoes.

With a carefully concealed sigh, Natasha slid her swimming bag off her shoulder, went to put the kettle on again and find the biscuits.

Before she bought Orchard End, six years ago, it had been the home of May Rainbow, who'd lived there for one hundred years, from the day she was born to the day she died, at least, almost. All her life, she'd never known a single day of ill health, or so the legend now went. She'd never even visited a doctor until a week prior to her death when she developed an infection in her toe. She was taken to the Cheltenham General, contracted pneumonia and passed away two days later.

Some potential buyers might have been put off by the benign but lingering spectre of Miss Rainbow, but for Natasha the house's history was what sold it to her. She liked the feeling she was taking on the care of a place that had been so well-loved and she liked the sense of permanence, of living somewhere that had watched its previous occupant pass from the cradle to the grave within its own four walls.

On the day she moved in, Natasha found May Rainbow's simple grave in the churchyard at St Barnabus and laid a bouquet of wild flowers on it. It seemed inconceivable to her that she would never come back to Orchard End, and she'd wanted to make sure they were friends, that Miss Rainbow wouldn't resent the person who'd moved into her home. But it wasn't only May Rainbow who returned to haunt her old house, it was all her elderly living friends.

In her first week at Orchard End Natasha had received separate visits from two old women from the other end of the village, Mrs Osborne and Miss Dodsworth, as well as old Mr Samuels, who'd come by bus from Stanton. All wandered in to Natasha's house without knocking, Mrs Osborne and Miss Dodsworth bringing jars of homemade lemon curd and apple pies, and Mr Samuels his home-grown tomatoes.

Natasha had made them all cups of tea and they had stayed and chatted to her, sitting at her kitchen table as if they'd known her all their lives, as they had Miss Rainbow. It was as if they'd transferred all of their affections for their old friend, lock, stock and barrel, onto her successor.

Mrs Osborne had joined Miss Rainbow in the graveyard now but Miss Dodsworth still popped in when she was passing, armed with more pies and jam and chutney and curd, and Mr Samuels continued the habit of a lifetime, catching the bus to Snowshill about once a fortnight, with a grocery bag full of his home-grown groceries.

As Natasha poured yet another cup of tea now, Mr Samuels told her about his recent trip to see his daughter in Wales and Miss Dodsworth filled her in on the goings-on at the bring-and-buy sale in the village hall and the antics of Mr Huggins, ex-milkman and self-appointed Mayor of Snowshill.

Natasha's job had bestowed upon her a gift, which came from hours spent drinking pots of tea in the company of other people's aged uncles and great-grandmothers, looking through boxes of their old photographs and hearing the ordinary, extraordinary stories the pictures told. She could see through the liver-spotted skin and white hair to bright eyes and strong limbs and a heart that was not worn out, to a time when their hopes and dreams outnumbered memories. Arnold told her that was her special talent, why she was 'so good with the grannies', why they all took to her immediately and why she managed to get them to tell her things they'd never told another living soul, to recall things they'd thought they'd forgotten.

Mr Samuels was remembering a hot summer from his childhood when there was a plague of ladybirds.

Natasha refilled his mug, spooning in two heaps of sugar, the way she knew he liked it. She'd also opened a fresh packet of shortbread. 'You heard about Charles Seagrove?' she ventured finally.

'Well, you reap what you sow. Charles Seagrove called himself a farmer. He of all people should have known that.' Mr Samuels dunked his biscuit, not about to elaborate.

'How do you mean?'

'What comes around goes around.'

It was clear from his closed expression that idioms were all she was going to get for now and she was running late for Toby's arrival at Moreton station. She'd tackle Mr Samuels again. But the implication was clear: Charles Seagrove had got his just reward.

Toby's floppy brown fringe was hanging over his eyes as he rummaged in his battered leather satchel and took out a foolscap pad and chewed lead pencil. Two years younger than Natasha, he was addicted to computer games and text messaging but was a dogged traditionalist when it came to his work, and to clothes and food. In a blazer, cream checked shirt, light canvas trousers and brogues, he still looked a lot like the schoolboy he was when Natasha and his big brother were flatmates in Oxford.

'You'd never think a paper trail could be so exciting,' Toby said, shrugging off his blazer and pushing a photocopied article from the *Oxfordshire Gazette* at her across the table. 'The first news piece doesn't tell us much more than we already know about Alice Hellier, but I found this, written on the day after the trial.'

They'd driven to The Crown, ten minutes down the road on Blockley High Street. It had the atmosphere of an old coaching inn, served French cuisine in the brasserie and daily specials in the bar. They'd both ordered mussels with crusty baguette, though Natasha didn't feel much like eating any of it. Whatever Toby had found out for her would have to make up her first report to Richard Seagrove. She regretted agreeing to his demands now. For demands they had certainly been. And it was odd how she'd felt almost powerless to refuse him, a combination of guilt and fear. Yet she couldn't have said precisely why she felt guilty or what she was afraid of.

'Alice Hellier's not the only murderer I've got to think about now,' she said, trying to stop her voice wavering. 'Someone shot my client.'

'No way!' He sounded as incredulous and eager as an eight-year-old for whom pistols were merely playthings you filled with water.

Death was like the ripples on a pond, she thought, its impact diminishing the further removed you became. The victim's family grief-stricken for months, family friends for just a few weeks, acquaintances for a few days or just hours. Those who knew the deceased only by name, like Toby, were more interested than shocked. Not fair to blame him for that.

'I found him.' She stared down at her fingers.

'You mean you . . .' He reached out and touched her arm. 'No. Shit. That's awful. You poor thing.' But she sensed he was morbidly fascinated.

It was stiflingly hot in the inn and she wished she'd suggested somewhere where they could eat outside. But it was even hotter out there. She was wearing a crocheted black shawl over a long peacock-blue strappy silk dress. Cut on the bias, the fabric was water-cool as it swished about her bare ankles, but already she could feel the heat soaking through. She slipped the shawl off her shoulders and sucked some mineral water up the straw.

More for herself than for Toby's benefit, she made herself fill him in on the details of Charles Seagrove's death, as far as she knew them. She found it harder, if anything, to talk to Toby about it than it had been to talk to Sergeant Fletcher. The healing process in reverse? Or maybe it was simply more difficult because Toby was such a close friend.

'Did he seem the type someone would want to kill?' Toby said.

She hadn't really thought about that. 'No, and yes.' She could easily imagine Seagrove causing offence, snubbing someone, but enough to make them resort to such violence?

'Did you have to give a statement to the police?'

'I think I'm on their list of suspects.'

'You're joking.'

'I wish.' Richard Seagrove was right. She couldn't even begin to imagine what he was going through and Toby couldn't come close to really understanding her. She suddenly felt very lonely.

'I suppose they have to consider everyone a suspect until they find the person who did it,' Toby said.

'I suppose so.' He was doing his best. She picked up the newscutting from the *Oxfordshire Gazette*.

Toby watched her, sipping his pint of Hook Norton beer. 'Oh, I get it. I know you're a great believer in history repeating and the past haunting the present and all that, but you don't seriously, for one second, think Alice Hellier could possibly have anything to do with this chap's murder?'

'I'm doing my best not to think very much right now.'

'You must try not to let this get to you too much, you know, Tasha.' He made a characteristic endearing swing from schoolboy to caring old uncle. 'I know it wasn't a nice way to go but he was an old man. People die all the time.'

She attempted a smile. 'You don't say?'

She read the article.

'Poor Alice.'

'Poor Alice?' Toby was incredulous. 'How can you say that, you of all people? After what you just told me. What about the poor old bugger she killed? He was no different to Charles Seagrove.'

'Probably, but I can't help siding with her. Call me sexist.' The attempt at their usual banter didn't come easy. Yet she felt under some strange pressure to go through the motions, to carry on as usual.

'You naturally assume Mr Purrington tried to have his wicked way with his parlour maid?'

'I'd bet anything.'

'Maybe Alice just took teenage angst too far. Dread to think what you were like at eighteen.'

'Oh, I could quite cheerfully have murdered everyone then. My teachers for starters, for telling me I couldn't paint my nails black. My parents when they didn't let me sleep in a tent with my friends at Glastonbury. My little sister when she borrowed my bangles without asking. And my first boyfriend, Josh, when he refused to stop being the only decent guy in the sixth form and fulfil my depraved fantasy of losing my virginity at a Halloween party. What I could murder right now though is a glass of chilled white wine.' At least the last sentence was spoken from the heart.

Toby offered to go to the bar and order.

Where did the paper trail lead now? she wondered as she looked at the photocopied article again. Alice's story posed more questions than it answered.

Alice had applied for the position of parlour maid at Elm House in Burford. She had good references and the housekeeper praised her hard work. Her employer, Samuel Purrington, was a banker. On 11 August 1852 he invited two dozen of his acquaintances and colleagues to drink champagne in his garden. At three-thirty Alice, a sweet-faced and until then sweet-natured girl, approached him with a pistol concealed in her skirts, a pistol she stole while dusting her employer's own study. She fired a single shot at point blank range. The bullet entered Samuel Purrington's chest and he fell backwards to the ground. His blood splattered the stone steps and the pale summer dresses of three of his guests to whom he'd been suggesting a game of croquet. For a few minutes he struggled for breath with a hissing, gurgling sound. Alice lowered the gun and announced that Mr Purrington was a bad man who deserved to die. Alice repeated her statement in court. It was her only defence.

Alice's aunt, a washerwoman, came forward to provide an

explanation. Alice's mother, Molly, had also once been a maid in Samuel Purrington's household. Alice was born illegitimate when her mother was fifteen. Molly had arranged for her to be cared for by a woman who ran a boarding house while Molly worked to support herself and her child. But when Purrington discovered she had a bastard he sacked her, turning both her and the baby Alice out on the streets. They ended up in the workhouse where Molly died of cholera two months later. Alice blamed Purrington for her mother's death and threatened to have her revenge. 'She showed no fear for her fate and no remorse for the cold-blooded killing. God have mercy on her soul,' the newspaper report concluded.

A sad story. But Natasha had read countless such stories over the years. You only had to log on to Old Bailey Online to access thousands of tales of desperate girls throwing their illegitimate babies into the river or selling their bodies for a loaf of bread.

Then, suddenly, words leapt out from the sheet of photocopied paper as if someone had taken a luminous pen and highlighted them in citrus yellow or lime green: *champagne in his garden ... Sweet-faced girl ... Banker ... Pistol she stole from her employer's own study ... Shot him at point blank range ...*

Mr Purrington had not been in his vegetable patch, he had died during a garden party not three days after it, and his own pistol was used not his own shotgun.

But the similarities were still too close for comfort.

Eight

NATASHA'S FRIENDS WATCHED as she twirled the sycamore stick between her palms, pressing down lightly into the hearth wood. When her hands had travelled down the drill she moved them back to the top and started again, gradually increasing pressure and speed. Her face broke out into a grin as smoke began to rise from the notch she'd carved in the bottom piece of wood. She felt like a sorceress as she held the tinder up to her face, blowing on it gently until the smoke was thick and white, then dimmed to a greenish colour just before it burst into flames.

'That's amazing,' Mary said, clapping her hands in delight. 'Where did you learn to do that?'

'Steven, my dad, taught me.'

Natasha had thought Steven was a magician the first time she'd seen him rub two sticks together to create fire, telling her how her ancestors had done it just the same way thousands of years ago. She was about eight and as usual she was spending her summer holidays with him on an archaeological dig. They were excavating the remains of a medieval monastery in Suffolk and they'd found some flints and Stone Age tools among the Dark Age coins and jewellery.

Some of her best times had been spent beside a campfire, talking and telling stories, singing old folk songs with a guitar. The flames entranced her, the glow they cast like an ancient spell that made time spool backwards. At eight years old she'd felt a deep connection to those who'd sat round firesides just as she was doing, as if she carried their experiences within her. When Steven taught her to summon fire in the traditional way, she liked to imagine that primal bond strengthening. She got a real kick out of discarding the trappings of the modern world.

She reached for her glass of Shiraz and with the other hand carefully turned the tuna steaks and vegetable kebabs on the barbecue. Natasha, Mary, and Heidi, a black-haired potter with a raucous laugh who'd recently moved into The Old Forge, got together once a month for a girls' night in or out. Or on one mad occasion, Mary's birthday, shaking it all about in Cheltenham. Natasha had never considered herself a creature of habit but there was something nice about this routine, which had been going strong for about a year. It had started just after Mary had given birth and complained that mums needed a social life which didn't feature balloons and jelly. Monday was an odd night to choose but it worked because the bar at the Snowshill Arms tended to be fairly quiet. If Arnold offered to babysit, the girls went out on the town in Campden or Broadway. If Kieran had to come along, like tonight because he was teething and needed his mum, the venue was one of their kitchens, or gardens. This time he was happily making soil castles under the honeysuckle in Natasha's little garden, which, like everything in Snowshill, was on the slant, rising steeply from the back of the cottage.

Heidi topped up the glasses. 'I wish someone would send me a plane ticket.' She'd spotted it when she'd gone inside to use the bathroom and brought it out, demanding a full explanation. 'It's so romantic.'

'Non transferable and non-refundable,' Mary read out from the back of the ticket. 'Nobody else can use it but the named holder, Natasha Blake. He can't get his money back either. If you don't go he'll have wasted five hundred dollars.'

'I've already read the small print,' Natasha said. 'Trouble is, there's small print attached to everything. If I go to Canada the subtext is: I miss you, I love you, forgive me, let's start again. And if I don't go ...'

'You'd be a complete idiot,' Mary finished.

Natasha forced a smile. 'So what's new?'

'What's wrong with saying I miss you?' Heidi asked.

'Oh, stop ganging up on me, you two.' She'd been determined not to let Charles Seagrove enter into the conversation tonight, had asked Mary to help her out and have a quiet word with Heidi beforehand. Surely there was nothing wrong in at least pretending to have a nice evening, even if she did feel guilty for enjoying herself? It wasn't working anyway.

'I can't go, OK, even if I wanted to.' Tears pricked her eyes. 'The police have told me to stay in the country.'

When the girls had gone she knew she couldn't put it off any longer. She swivelled her chair sideways so the ticket with its maple leaf logo, back on her desk, was no longer in her line of sight. It was more a torment than a tease now, but she couldn't bring herself to put it away. You always want what you can't have.

She picked up the phone, dialled the number she'd committed to memory even though she'd never used it before now.

Before Marcus moved semi-permanently into Orchard End and when he was working away, they used to call each other at least once a day. The habit had started immediately after their first date. There'd been no playing hard to get, no taking it slowly, yet there was nothing rushed about their relationship either. They'd met when she'd gone up to see Steven at a conference in Manchester and then Marcus had come to Snowshill to see her. Through Steven, they knew plenty about each other already and their being together had seemed the most natural, easy thing in the world.

After twelve rings she should have hung up but having got this far she was determined to follow through.

'Hello.' His voice was muffled but the sound of it made her realize for the first time how much she'd been looking forward to seeing him. It took an effort to hold her own voice steady.

'Marcus, it's me.'

'That's OK then. If anyone else called at six in the morning I'd tell them where to go.'

She'd entirely forgotten the eight-hour time difference between the UK and Vancouver. Telephones are cruel, she thought, with their illusion of closeness. You can hear but you can't touch or see.

More intimate sometimes than a face-to-face conversation. So near and yet so far.

'How are you?' he asked.

'Fine.' She couldn't even tell *him* the truth. But she'd decided that she wasn't going to spoil their conversation by talking about Charles Seagrove unless she absolutely had to.

'So describe it all to me,' Marcus said. 'What are you wearing? Do you have make-up on? Is your hair down or up or wet from the shower?'

She laughed. 'You're crazy.'

'Not crazy at all. I just want to see you.'

'Well, if you insist. My hair's in a ponytail. I'm wearing a long russet-coloured skirt and a cream basque-type top that was some Edwardian lady's underwear. I have gold eye-shadow above my eyes and dark shadows under them, darker than usual because I've been working too hard. I'm drinking a cup of coffee which is rapidly going cold. Does that satisfy you?'

'Where are you?'

'In the living room.'

'Have you got your head cocked on one side, like Boris, with the phone tucked under your chin?'

'I have actually.'

'Are you sitting cross-legged on a cushion or curled up on the sofa?'

'This is almost phone sex.'

'Now you're talking.'

She giggled. Why had she worried? Nothing had changed between them at all.

'Phone sex is the best offer I've had for the past few months.'

His considerate way of letting her know, because he understood how insecure she could be, that even half a world a way, there was no one else.

'Actually, I'm not sitting I'm standing. By the window.'

He was silent for a moment. 'You only stand by the window when you're about to start pacing about the room, when you're in the middle of a phonecall you're nervy about making.'

She tried to laugh. 'That's not true.' They both knew different.

It was kind of scary, and also nice, for someone to know you so well. But it left you nowhere to hide.

'Well, so long as you're not nervy because you're calling to tell me you're not coming.'

'Actually, something's come up—'

'I'm not hearing this.' He'd used those exact words when she'd wrongly accused him of having an affair and thrown all his belongings into the boot of his Renault, erasing him from the cottage and from her life. The memory momentarily threw her, robbed her of the ability to form a coherent sentence. 'Something always comes up with you, doesn't it?' he went on. 'An ivory tower. A bloody brick wall. Ten feet high with razor wire on top.'

She was so cross that he'd jumped to conclusions, refused to let her get a word in edgeways. 'Will you just let me explain?'

She didn't get a chance. There was no stopping him. 'I don't need you to explain. I don't need this at the crack of dawn, OK? I don't need this full stop. This is the last time, Natasha. I'm not going to bother trying to get through to you again. It's too much like hard work.'

'Marcus, please . . .'

He'd hung up. It served her right. She'd been the one to set the pattern. That last morning, it was she who'd not given him a chance to explain. So they were quits now. They'd cancelled each other out.

Or maybe she'd just picked a bad time. Let's face it, the crack of dawn wasn't exactly a good time for many people and Marcus was the deepest sleeper she'd ever known. Sign of an untroubled conscience, she used to tell him. It maddened her and at the same time filled her with contentment, to watch him sleeping beside her when she couldn't sleep. He was like a diver who got the bends if he was made to surface too quickly. Leave him to wake in his own sweet time and he was the sweetest-natured person you could hope to meet. For a moment, she'd almost had him back. Almost.

So near and yet so far.

She glowered at her 1940s vintage phone and wished she wasn't so respectful of old things and could hurl it across the room. Damn and blast Charles Seagrove. He had come between them, albeit inadvertently. Not so blameless where his granddaughter and her lover were concerned though.

It was a relief to tune on to Rosa and John. So much easier to think about other people's problems than her own, even when, in a way, their problems had become hers.

Rosa had told the police she rowed with her grandfather about what he'd hired Natasha to do, because of something she'd found out about John Hellier. Archie Fletcher hadn't ruled out the possibility that her research might in some way be connected with what happened at Shadwell. If the scenario was right, then she'd been the catalyst that led to Charles Seagrove's death. Richard Seagrove certainly believed that. She hadn't aimed the shotgun but she had released the trigger. She may have washed it away but, in the metaphorical sense, there was still blood on her hands.

She went across to her desk, averting her eyes from the ticket, and opened up the Hellier folder on her iMac.

It wasn't her usual practice to go into such detail. But for reasons best known to himself, and now probably never to be known by anyone else, Charles Seagrove hadn't been satisfied with birth, marriage and death certificates illuminated with the usual gems to be found in trade directories and census returns. It was he who'd specifically asked her to provide the names of the schools and universities John's ancestors attended, apprenticeships, qualifications and full CVs. He'd been adamant about her checking medical records and wills, as well as verifying if each and every member of John's clan, maternal and paternal side, cropped up in the numerous criminal registers.

Which of course they did – quite spectacularly – in the form of Alice.

Again she hit the buffers. Alice was no reason, surely, for him to reject John as a possible grandson-in-law. But could she be? Could she be connected to his death?

Richard Seagrove had already left a curt message, demanding an update. She was about to call him back then she wondered: Did John Hellier know about his great-grandmother?

She closed the file. It felt wrong, other people knowing so much more about his family than he probably knew himself.

Nine

REBELLIOUSLY, SHE ROLLED back the hood of the Alpine. She was young, free and, it seemed, single. She may as well act the part and enjoy the perks.

She cut across the hills on minor roads, through the wide open fields that surrounded Temple Guiting and the water meadows of the River Windrush, on to the Slaughters where she joined the straight Roman road of the Fosse Way down to the market town of Northleach.

To the casual observer, the Cotswold Hills could look monotonous and bleak from this road, even lit by soft morning sunshine, just acres of stone-walled fields populated only by sheep. It was only when you turned off the high roads and descended into the wooded valleys that you discovered the little settlements tucked away in hollows, old stone cottages clustered round a village green, a quaint pub and an ancient church. She was crossing the River Coln at Fossebridge when her mobile rang. She pulled over and answered it.

Toby, calling from a London bus. 'Where are you?'

The drone of heavy traffic at the other end of the line made her feel she was on a different planet. 'On my way to the Royal Agricultural College in Cirencester.'

'Don't tell me you've actually bought that field you've been banging on about for ages?'

It was one of her more attainable fantasies, to buy a small patch of land one day and have a few sheep and chickens, maybe even a goat. 'While I'm there I just might enrol on a crash course in egg laying and milking. I quite fancy the simple life right now.'

'Personally, I'd rather have my eggs served up nicely poached with bacon on the side.' He seemed to be talking slightly loud and fast in the way of people in cities. She felt herself doing the same when she was in London. Busy in the Cotswolds was two gear-shifts below, sleepy in a way she seldom was at night. 'Have the police caught that chap's murderer yet?'

'Not that I'm aware of.'

'How are you bearing up?'

'I'm fine.' Maybe if she said it often enough she'd convince herself it was true.

'You know where I am if you need a shoulder.'

'Thanks, Toby.' She was sure she knew precisely where he was at this very moment. He'd be sure to be riding on the top deck, in the front seat if it had been free. 'I'm on my way to see John Hellier.'

'To tell him his dead ancestress has risen from the grave to kill again?'

'Oh, shut up.' She wished he wouldn't try to jolly her along.

'Have fun, won't you?'

'It's bound to be a barrel of laughs.'

She hadn't even called in advance to tell John Hellier she was coming. It seemed a better plan just to wing it.

The Royal Agricultural College was just over a mile south-west of the town.

She turned off the Tetbury Road and drove up the long, wide avenue of limes. Even under the circumstances, she couldn't help admiring the main college building that stood at the end. The central battlemented tower, flanked with five gabled bays, was an imposing Tudor Gothic blend of Oxford College and traditional Cotswold architecture. Fitting surroundings for the sons of the landed gentry who'd been coming here for over a century to learn how to care for their birthright.

The mobile rang again.

Richard Seagrove. 'How are you getting on?'

She asked how he was, then told a half-lie, that she was going to interview John about his take on his family history.

He seemed satisfied with that, for now, but she sensed his satisfaction would be very short-lived. She wondered at his insistence, a mechanism for displacing grief perhaps, but jarring nonetheless. Putting him from her mind, she followed the signs for the main car park then walked back to the reception past the traceried chapel of St George the Martyr in which Rosa and John had planned to get married.

The receptionist looked up John's name on the computer. 'He should be attending the agricultural marketing lecture in the Garner Theatre. Otherwise you'll probably find him in the Union Club.' She handed Natasha a map of the grounds.

As she crossed the quadrangle, enclosed by beautiful gothic buildings and a clock tower on the central turreted gable, she felt as though she were back at Oxford. Sometimes she thought she'd altered beyond all recognition since her student days but in these surroundings she didn't feel different. She could quite happily head to the common room and hang out with a beer, or pack a rucksack with books and find a quiet spot in the arboretum or by the cricket pavilion to read and make notes. Better still, have a catnap in the sunshine. Maybe people didn't change that much underneath, even over centuries. On the surface, she thought, you'd not think you'd have much in common with a parlour maid who wore a starched pinafore and ended up in the workhouse because her mother hadn't been married. But if you transplanted her to the twenty-first century, fixed her up with an office job, a car and a pair of jeans, she'd be just like you.

The Garner Lecture Theatre was a modern building with a stacked, longitudinal slate roof, adjoined to the library. Natasha crept in and peered through an open door into the darkened auditorium. It was newly furnished, pine tongue-and-groove walls, with rainbow formations of blue upholstered chairs. A plasma screen above a stage was showing pictures of cows. There were perhaps two dozen students conscientiously taking notes or slouching on the back rows.

Natasha loitered outside with a couple of students drinking cans of Coke. With her mane of wavy hair, her faded flared jeans and red gypsy top, she merged in very well.

A gangly lad with ginger hair and a freckly face slipped out of the theatre.

'Excuse me. Do you know John Hellier?'

'Sure. He's in my tutorial group.'

'Is he in there?' She nodded towards the theatre door.

'Sure thing.'

'Is it due to finish soon?'

''Nother hour to go yet.'

It was on the tip of her tongue to ask if he was sure about that but she said thanks instead and headed back to the quad and the common room.

As common rooms went you couldn't expect a nicer place to chill out. Located in the old Tithe Barn, according to the map, it still had its original vaulted, beamed roof, whitewashed stone walls and a grand stone fireplace.

Rosa was sitting on her own, staring at a closed text book and polystyrene coffee cup on the small, round table in front of her.

Natasha slid in opposite. She knew better than to ask Rosa how she was, so all she said was, 'Hi.'

Rosa barely glanced up.

Sometimes words were utterly inadequate and Rosa seemed to have given up trying to find them. Suffering set you apart, gave you a different set of rules to other people. You didn't need to bother with social niceties, as if Rosa had put them top of her list of priorities before. She snapped a chunk of rim off her cup. It broke with a crack, flakes crumbling onto the table. You could feel waves of pent-up misery rolling off her.

'I didn't expect you to be here.'

'Why not?' She snapped the rim at the other side. 'There's nothing I can do at home. Dad's looking after Grandma.' She was like a hedgehog, tightly rolled into herself, all needles and prickly defences. 'I'd go mad if I stayed there.'

'I'm sure you're doing the right thing.'

She shrugged, as if to say that wrong and right had no meaning for her any more. Different set of rules again.

'I came to see John really. I wanted to give him his family tree, as you suggested. How is he?'

'How should I know?'

Natasha pushed the CD-Rom across the table. She'd burned all the Hellier documents onto it. She'd also scanned the Alice Hellier articles. 'Perhaps you could give it to him for me.'

Rosa looked but didn't touch. 'That'd be difficult. I'm public enemy number one so far as his parents are concerned. No doubt they've told him to stay well away and John's not the rebellious type. I expect they're even less keen on me right now than my grandfather was on John, if that's possible. You can't really blame them, can you? Totally screwed up family. Divorced parents. Nutty old man. John told them about your . . . about Grandpa's research, and the next thing they know he's been shot and the police want to know where John was at the time. They blame me for getting him mixed up in everything.'

'It's not your fault.'

'You mean you don't think I killed my granddad?' She spat the words, violet eyes hard and cold and bright as Arctic light. 'So I could marry John and protect my inheritance?'

Rosa's speech set off a rapid fire game of word association in Natasha's brain: Inheritance. Last Will and Testament. A saying bandied about in the Family Records Centre: Where there's a will there's a law suit. Her advice to Rosa: *Where there's a will there's a way*.

And something else that Charles Seagrove had said when she'd asked him if John Hellier fitted into his family tree: *Over my dead body*.

Right now it wasn't impossible to imagine that Rosa Seagrove was capable of murder. Or was that just the corrupting power of suspicion? Rosa was the type to play up to any accusation, like a child who's told she's bad so often that in the end she decides she might as well fulfil everyone's expectations.

Natasha picked up the CD-Rom. 'Take it. It'll give you an excuse to talk to him at least.'

After a long moment Rosa pocketed the disk. 'Why is it up to me?'

How many times had love withered while two people waited by silent phones, refusing to pick them up until they rang?

'He's probably thinking the same thing.'

They left the common room and walked back across the quad. 'Your grandfather was right about the chapel. It's lovely.'

Rosa nodded towards a slightly more humble old stone building attached to the main façade. 'John wanted to have our wedding reception by candlelight in the Bathurst wing. It's part of the sixteenth-century farmhouse that was here before they built the college.' There was contempt in her voice for the innocent plans and future that had occupied her mind before her grandfather's death.

'It sounds like the wedding arrangements were pretty advanced.'

'Oh, John was the one who had it all worked out. He said he'd imagined what his wedding day would be like since he was a little boy. I told him if that was the case he should have been a little girl.'

Most girls' wedding plans were pretty advanced by the age of four, Natasha agreed. She'd known exactly what dress she'd wear a full decade before her first kiss: old gold lace with a crimson velvet cloak and black-red roses in her bouquet. How would she feel if her vision never became reality? She wasn't exactly on the shelf, but with her track record there was a distinct possibility she might end up there.

'Have you got a lecture to go to?'

'Introduction to mechanization.'

'Sounds interesting.' That raised a smile at least.

'I prefer the livestock side of things.' Her tone was slightly less hostile. 'I'm interested in animal behaviour and breeding management. I asked Grandpa once what his favourite subject was at school. Considering his job, as a financier, and his interest in genealogy, you'd think he'd have said maths or history. But he told me it was biology. Life was what interested him, he said.'

Natasha had a sudden vision of the wheelbarrow in the kitchen garden, and beside it the tray of tiny lettuces, fresh green shoots of life which Charles Seagrove had never got around to planting before his own life was extinguished.

She cleared her throat. 'Did your granddad encourage you to study here?'

'Even at his age, he'd never got stuck in his ways.' She was using the past tense already. It was supposed to be therapeutic, healthy, to talk about the dead. But still it was surprising that Rosa could do it so easily so soon. 'He wanted a breakdown on what I'd been learning,' she went on. 'He said it was important to always keep your mind open to new ideas. They're really hot here on the environment, ethical issues and animal welfare, but Grandpa always cared for our animals well, even when there weren't all these public pressures. He had ideas about breeding programmes that were way ahead of his time.' Still no sign of a crack in her voice. She was a tough cookie, all right.

'It was an unusual career path. For him to go from the City to farming.'

'Not really. He only became a banker to make money to buy land.'

'That takes some determination.'

'You said it. Where there's a will there's a way.' Rosa's tone was hard. 'He'd have agreed with you there.'

Natasha tried to read Rosa's eyes but they were inscrutable.

'A weaker person than him would have given up two years ago,' Rosa went on. 'We lost a couple of Short Horns to BSE but Foot and Mouth was even worse. I was in my first year here and I had to stay away from the farm until the holidays. When I did get to go back, Grandpa met me at the top of the drive and everything had to be sprayed.'

'The precautions worked?'

'For a while. But our whole flock had to be slaughtered in the end, five hundred of them, everything he had worked for. He'd built them up from two original sheep. They were all healthy, not a sign of the disease, but the animals in the farm next to ours were infected so we had no choice but to have ours culled.'

'It must have been hard for him.'

'He got very depressed afterwards, then this spring he seemed back to his usual self again. We just started again. That's why I'm determined to do well here. To learn how to make sure Shadwell is never one of the farms that goes under and gets sold to greedy developers. I promised Grandpa I'd never let people convert our barns into houses and park their Range Rovers in our stables.'

The large building ahead of them was signed Mechanization Building and Rural Skills Centre. Beyond the large open doors at the far end were all manner of tractors and combines, ploughs and seed drills.

'Your father's not interested in taking over the farm?'

Rosa looked directly at Natasha. 'Dad made it clear right from the start he'd never give up teaching and Grandpa doesn't believe in absentee landlords. He always told me that it'd be all mine when he'd gone. He wanted to see what he's built up over the years continue for another generation, and that's what I want too. I feel as if I'm inheriting a responsibility and a privilege. Grandpa said a farm is like your own little world. What better way is there to spend your life?' No wonder Rosa had been closer to her grandfather than to Richard. 'As soon as he knew John was studying for a diploma in agriculture and farm management he said Shadwell would be in good hands if I married him.' She paused before adding, meaningfully, 'Then he changed his mind.'

'Are you certain it was my meeting with him that made him do it?'

'I told you, he liked John. Right from the start he wanted to know all about him, his opinions and what he planned to do with his life. When he knew we were going to get married he asked loads more questions. Where did John grow up? What does his dad do for a living? Are his grandparents still alive? I thought it was nice that he was so interested. I came over for the day just before the party, when you nearly ran over me in the road, and everything was still fine. I left at sixish, without saying bye to Grandpa because I didn't want to disturb his meeting with you. He'd said I must invite John to this stupid party and we were supposed to come back over to Shadwell the night before, but I had an essay to finish. When I arrived in the morning, everything went pear-shaped. Grandpa said he didn't ever want to see John again or hear me mention his name.'

'What did your father have to say about it?'

'The only thing he ever gets worked up about is winning silly sports races and matches. He swore he didn't know anything about any of it. He was cross with Grandpa for not telling me what he was up to, but he never fell out with him, unless of course Grandpa was foolish enough to beat Dad at tennis.'

'He's a bad loser?'

She snorted. 'That's an understatement. Swearing, disputing points and throwing his racket around.'

Natasha had seen it already, wondered now if the hostility Richard had displayed when he'd come round to the cottage just after his father's death was a reflection of his behaviour on the tennis court.

'Dad doesn't like to see me upset but when it comes down to it he'd always side with his father, belongs to the generation that believes you should respect your elders.'

'Dads never think anyone is good enough for their little girls.'

'He'd never risk upsetting Gran either and she made it totally clear she wanted nothing to do with any of it.'

'What about your mum. Where's she?'

Rosa shrugged. 'Sweden. Austria? Who knows? Who gives a fuck? My parents divorced when I was four and my mother ran off with her ski instructor.'

'I'm sorry.'

'S'OK.'

'Is that why you're so close to your grandparents?'

'Grandpa even chose my name. He was proud of that. They looked after me a lot, when Dad had to go to weekend away matches or trips with his school, which was all the time. I didn't mind though. I loved going to Shadwell, staying in the house. Grandpa let me keep rabbits and guinea pigs. I liked lambing time best though. And the pheasants. Grandma hates hunting and blood sports but Grandpa taught me to use a shotgun when I was twelve. We put two hundred birds down every year. I did the rearing from day-old chicks to fully grown birds.'

And then you went out and shot them, Natasha added silently. Rosa was certainly an interesting girl, but that was country folk, no squeamish sentimentality.

Rosa did look squeamish now though. She'd turned completely white. 'I just realized. The gun Grandpa taught me to shoot with is the same one that was used to kill him.'

Ten

IN A PARALLEL universe, where Charles Seagrove hadn't been shot, Natasha would have indulged in the excitement of going shopping for a new outfit to take to Canada. Probably. Maybe. Perhaps. The world she inhabited now was in limbo.

She headed into Cirencester town centre anyway, found a cash machine to fund lunch, checked her bank balance while she was at it. Charles Seagrove had had the decency not to get killed before his cheque had been cleared, and so absolve her of any conscience about Rosa's inheritance being used to pay for a project which had so upset her. But the unusual health of her business account still gave Natasha a pang of guilt. The only thing to do was reduce both simultaneously. Canada or no Canada, she could still go shopping. She parked near the Cricklade Street end of the Market Place, wandered round the craft shops in Brewery Court and bought a ludicrously expensive bulbous pitcher for Mary's birthday next month.

Renaissance, a boutique on Dyer Street, was her favourite shop, which she had to pass on her way back to the car. Always impulsive, it took her all of ten minutes to purchase a long clingy moss-green jersey dress and a sheer blouse in amber.

She found a little bakery and bought a slice of chocolate-coated flapjack. A sugar boost sometimes compensated for lack of sleep. Sometimes. Next door was a newsagent's. Charles Seagrove's death was splashed across the front page of the *Cotswold Journal* and the *Gloucestershire Echo*. The *Journal* had gone for alliteration

– 'SHOOTING AT SHADWELL' – while the *Echo* had stuck to the brutal facts: 'LOCAL FARMER MURDERED.'

She stashed her purchases in the boot, wanting them out of sight. It might be a touch melodramatic, but she suddenly felt they'd been purchased with blood money. Although tracing bloodlines was her business. Maybe every penny she earned was blood money in a sense. She felt once more the warm stickiness of Charles Seagrove's blood on her fingers.

She slammed the boot, ran round to the front of the car and doused her hands with bottled mineral water, rubbed them almost raw with the windscreen cloth. Then stared at them. Was she going mad? She must have had a dozen showers, had been swimming twice since the murder. There was no blood left on her skin now.

There had been so much of it on the bricks . . .

Until she'd seen Charles Seagrove's dead body the most real blood she'd ever seen was when she cut her finger on a dig. Steven had bandaged it and praised her for being brave. She didn't feel brave now.

She made herself go back and buy copies of both newspapers, then drove back up past the medieval High Cross and the seventeenth-century houses of Coxwell Street. Her eyelids were drooping and she was having enough trouble just concentrating on the road. She pressed her fingers against her eyeballs. It was worse than being drunk, each small decision requiring huge effort, each movement needing to be deliberate and slow. She wasn't really fit to drive. Had Charles Seagrove had trouble sleeping at night? She remembered Mr Samuel's words: *You reap what you sow.*

Back at Orchard End she took a breath and picked up the *Journal.* The portrait they had used was of a younger Charles Seagrove, dignified and gallant, with his chin lifted, face turned to the side. Underneath was the undignified caption. 'Shot in cabbage patch.'

It was difficult to believe a person could murder an old man in his garden. According to the article, that's what the Shadwell cleaner and the gardener had thought when they heard a gun shot. Just someone out shooting rabbits or clay pigeons on the estate.

No exact time was given for that shot, of course, it only really mattered to the police and to Natasha, who still wanted to know if the killer had been anywhere near when she'd discovered what he, or she, had done.

After the skimpiest report on the scant details the police had released on the shooting itself, the rest of the article in the *Journal* read like a straight obituary. The journalist hadn't used the opportunity to demonstrate his investigative powers, however, and had obviously found Charles Seagrove as elusive as everyone else. 'A banker and landowner who'd worked for Debrett's in his retirement' was about the sum of it, a list of occupations. Which told you not very much about a person usually.

It was the first question you were asked at parties: 'What do you do?' Meaning, for a living. People were pigeonholed by their jobs, and before you were old enough to have one, by the jobs of your parents. Professional father equalled well-balanced, well-mannered, middle-class child. An unreliable shorthand. Charles Seagrove had said his stint as a banker was a means to an end, so it shouldn't be used to define him. If you hated your job your entire identity was wrongly skewed. An accountant who liked climbing mountains. A bus driver who lived to see Tottenham play at the weekends. 'What do you do?' should mean what do you do for fun, not money.

But Charles Seagrove had been passionate about two of his occupations: farming and genealogy, an odd combination.

She turned to the *Echo*.

Charles Seagrove, born in Rochester, Kent in 1921, was made a CBE for his services to agriculture, an active member of the National Union of Farmers, the Galton Institute and the Soil Association. A firm campaigner in support of hunting, he joined the Countryside Alliance's recent march in London, despite being in his eighties.

But why had the Hellier file been open on his desk on the day he died? He'd looked at it and then he had told her about his father, the Christmas Truce and the German soldier, Hans Koenig. Had he implied a connection? She tried to remember. She opened her copy of the Hellier file and checked. But there were no Koenigs in John's family tree. A long shot, excuse the pun.

The Christmas Truce taught my father the futility of war, and it was because of that night that I learned the importance of family, and family history.

Who or what had taught him that?

The little living room at Orchard End, with its crooked, black-beamed ceiling and enormous inglenook, its cosy rugs and tapestry cushions, had always seemed like a cosy cocoon, a burrow to curl up in. But for the first time she felt trapped and suffocated by it. Her garden was little better, tangled and slightly wild the way she liked it, the Cotswold Ridge bearing down.

She dragged on her boots, took Boris and walked round the side of the Snowshill Arms to Mary and James's cottage. Mary was hanging terry nappies on the washing line, Kieran playing beside her. She'd read a whole book on how disposables were clogging up landfill sites. That was progress for you.

From the kitchen came the whistling of the kettle on the hob. Natasha swooped Kieran into her arms and buried her face against the soft creases of his neck.

It was easy to understand why innocent people took the risk of making themselves look extremely guilty by running away. Or why middle-aged men, finding themselves burdened with huge mortgages and school fees or crippling debts, just upped sticks and disappeared. Unburdened with any commitments or debts, at least not of the crippling kind, Natasha had had the urge to escape once or twice herself. The pull was usually strongest in train stations. On the way to a job interview or, in more recent years, a client meeting, she'd sometimes looked up at the destinations board and been tempted to climb aboard the Orient Express or the train bound for Brighton. A sense of responsibility had always prevailed, boringly.

Now, when she came back from the pub and was confronted with her still partially packed suitcase, she seriously considered driving to Heathrow, taking the first available flight to Canada, or anywhere, leaving all this mess behind. But of course you took your mess with you wherever you went. The phone was ringing.

'Are you busy for the next few days?' Steven Blake always launched right in with what he wanted to say. It was one of the many things she loved about her father. Another was the almost telepathic way he seemed to know when she needed to talk to him, what she needed before she knew it herself.

'Actually, my diary's just been wiped.'

'How about a trip up here? I'm home for a few days. It'd be great to catch up.'

She was about to tell him about the murder but decided it'd be easier if she did it face-to-face. Derbyshire wasn't quite Vancouver, or the Orient Express, but it would do. 'If I leave now I can be with you for tea.' Despite not having lived in Derbyshire since she was eighteen, Natasha hadn't entirely shaken off her northern roots. It still felt pretentious to refer to an evening meal as supper or dinner. She'd never quite got to grips with which of the two terms was correct anyway.

She looked up the number for Chipping Campden police station, asked for Sergeant Fletcher. 'I take it I'm allowed to visit my parents in Castleton?'

'Of course.'

'How's it going, the investigation, I mean?'

'It's going. I'm afraid I'm not allowed to give details.'

A knock at the door made her leave it at that.

Richard Seagrove was standing outside again, an unwieldy cardboard box cradled in the crook of his arm. It looked heavy, but it wasn't only that which made him look weighed down. He appeared more exhausted than the last time he'd paid her a visit.

'I'm sorry to arrive unannounced like this. I'm not disturbing you, am I?' He was all charm and unassuming politeness, a complete contrast to how he'd been before. Such radical shifts in personality were unnerving, she thought, but she was prepared to blame his previous outburst and dubious telephone manner on stress and sorrow.

He glanced past her to the suitcase. 'Off somewhere nice?'

'I'm just about to leave for Derbyshire.' The suitcase was hardly weekend-sized and she wouldn't be taking it to Castleton but she didn't need to go into that. 'I need to take Boris for a good walk before the journey. You're welcome to join me.' She eyed the box. His car, a green Peugeot, was parked down the road. So the box must be for her. Beware of strangers bearing strange gifts, she almost said out loud.

He set the box on the floor. 'It's just some of my father's papers. I want you to take a look at them.'

I want, not *I wondered if you'd mind*. She sighed.

She clipped Boris onto his leash as they left the Stanway Road and climbed a broken-down wooden stile into a field of sheep. Once through the kissing gate in the next dry stone wall she let Boris free to bound on ahead, agile as a gazelle, red coat streaming in the last rays of the sun. Ridiculously, she felt freer to talk when he was safely out of earshot. Substitute child or what?

'Unusual job, genealogy,' Richard said. 'I'm a great believer in making a career out of what most folk do for fun.'

He was, she thought, a little too chatty for someone whose father had just been murdered. Perhaps he was running on nervous energy, trying to be normal, as she herself had tried to do. Although Charles Seagrove wasn't her father.

'Is that what you've done, made a career out of your hobby?'

'Absolutely. I'm a PE teacher. Get to spend every day playing cricket, tennis and football. Except for the twelve weeks holiday and then I carry on playing cricket, tennis and football. Pay could be better but what's the point in making pots of money if you can't enjoy it?'

So spoke a person who had never been short of a few pennies, Natasha thought. And she'd make a bet the touchlines and terraces at his matches had more than their fair share of mums cheering him on. But she agreed with him, nonetheless. Genealogy wasn't exactly a passport to untold riches.

'My boys won the county cup last Saturday,' Richard said. He couldn't have sounded more proud if it had been the World Cup.

Natasha found herself smiling. 'Which school do you work at?'

'Plaistow Road. East End.'

You could have knocked her over with a feather. The guy was

definitely too good to be true. She'd been sure he was going to say Harrow or Eton, an exclusive private school with tiptop facilities.

She remembered his parents' pride in him at the garden party. But by conventional standards, Richard could have been something of a disappointment. An only child, the son, or sun, around which his parents world revolved. A member of the elite class, born to rule. Top-flight private education, every advantage money could buy and the brains and charm to make the most of those advantages. You'd have thought his parents would only be content if he'd gone on to be a doctor or a lawyer. But PE teacher in an East End school seemed fine so far as they were concerned. Well, good for them. They'd not made the fundamental error of the overly-attentive parent who wanted their child to have everything and failed to consider that he or she might not want it. Good for Richard too. He could so easily have gone down the road of many a trust-fund kid, those reared on fatted calves and parental eulogies. He could have become a drifter, a drop-out, happy to coast through life, pleasing no one but himself.

Charles and Stella had every right to be proud, though the fierceness of their pride had still been extraordinary.

She was striding at her usual brisk pace, then noted that Richard Seagrove was taking in the views, the sun turning orange and slowly sinking over the fields, a change to the East End. She slowed down so he could enjoy it some more.

'People are too ready to dismiss sport,' he said. 'But there's no underestimating the benefits of physical exercise, and the confidence boost it can give to kids who don't have much.' He spoke with conviction, not as if he was repeating some pat justification for his chosen profession. 'They get a real sense of achievement from taking part, and from winning of course. Sport teaches you competitiveness and team spirit. Without those there'd be no successful businesses, no economy full stop.'

'You don't take your father's view that sporting prowess is fixed at birth, determined by genes alone?'

'It's a circle. People like doing what they are good at and they are good at what they like doing. Having sporty genes makes you want to practise at sport, so you get better at it.' A certain smugness had crept into his smile.

Natasha smiled back, all innocence. 'I suppose teachers are bound to credit the skills of their students to external influences but claim that the talents of their own children are inherited.'

The aggravated look on Richard's face revealed him as someone who had to have the last word, didn't take kindly to points being scored against him, in even the most light-hearted debate. She sensed he wanted to fire back at her but was resisting. Because he wanted her on his side?

'You're in good shape. What's your sport?' he said instead.

'Swimming mostly.'

'Lonely.'

'I like my own company.'

He gave her a smile. 'That's selfish of you.' He made it sound like a compliment. She wondered then why he hadn't re-married. He was a good-looking man after all. What was it that put women off? 'My father was a good swimmer,' he added. There was a choke in his voice.

She left a few respectful moments of silence. 'Did you ever want to play sport professionally?'

'I beg your pardon.' He pretended to be indignant. 'I thought that's what I was doing.'

Once more, she was having real difficulty believing the person she was talking to now was the same person who'd come knocking on her door the previous week, demanding she carried on with her research. The change in him was dramatic. She thought about the box of his father's papers sitting in the hall and felt wary.

'But it must be a wonderful feeling to play for your country, come home a hero and all that,' Richard continued. 'I'd have loved to be a professional cricketer but I suppose the trouble is that winning matters to me too much. I'd rather shine against amateurs than appear run of the mill amongst a crowd of sportsmen more talented than me. I sometimes think, if only I could just have played one match, so I got a chance to meet all my heroes.'

His enthusiasm reminded her of Steven, and Toby in a way.

Like Steven, he was also, clearly, an outdoor person, someone for whom a shirt and tie were as constraining as a prison cell.

'The police searched my father's office, of course. I don't think they found much. But I don't think they were looking in the right places. And they left something behind.'

'Not the something that's currently in the box in my hallway by any chance?'

They descended over a gated footbridge into woodland and emerged along the track that led eventually to the picturesque village of Buckland and the Cotswold Way. The stark profile of Broadway Tower dominated the crimson skyline, with Middle Hill House lower down to the right.

'There's an old bread oven in the fireplace. It has a cast-iron door which has rusted quite badly. If the police did try to open it they probably gave up, thought it was just ornamental. I knew that wasn't the case because I remembered hoarding sweets there as a child. And I remembered seeing a small ebonized casket inside. It was still there when I looked yesterday. It was locked but I prised it open. There's just—'

'Hold it right there.' She stopped and jammed her hands over her ears. 'You can't just go taking things from a police search area.'

'It's only old papers, family history stuff,' he said, his tone cajoling. She unclamped her ears slightly. 'Nothing to do with the Seagroves, but I vaguely recognized the name. Local family, I think.' She flicked a look at him out of the corner of her eye but kept quiet. 'The police wouldn't have looked at it twice. They would have dismissed it as irrelevant.'

'Of course they would,' she said, loading on the sarcasm, 'except that anything hidden immediately becomes intriguing in a murder inquiry. Have the police made any progress?'

'They play their cards very close to their chest but I get the impression they don't have many leads. They've scrutinized every inch of the house for fingerprints, had a search team combing the woods, eyes to the ground, no doubt hunting for anything that had been dropped, or footprints that might have been left by someone on their way to the garden or running from it. I know for a fact that there was no sign of anyone breaking into the house, and the staff didn't let anyone in. Apart from you, afterwards.' He stared straight ahead.

'How did someone manage to get hold of your father's gun?' She didn't want to talk about her part in the events of that day.

'The gun is the real mystery,' Richard conceded. 'It's usually locked away in a cupboard under the stairs. The door wasn't forced, so maybe my father intended to go into the woods and hunt rabbits, already had it outside with him, I really don't know. A woman from the CID did tell my mother that there were no prints on it. There were loads of genealogical papers in the office,' Richard said, getting back to his point. 'The police took it all. Including—'

'The stuff I did. Yeah, I know.' She combed her hair off her face with her fingers. 'I meant what I said about doing anything I can to help, Richard, but there are limits. I mean, how's it going to look? It could land us both in serious shit.'

'Some of us are already in it.'

She was mortified, vowed to go home and write out two hundred times: I must not be flippant. I must not be flippant.

'In the casket is a chart, tree, whatever you call them,' Richard said. 'For someone called Marion Lassiter. The last birth or death date I can find on it is about sixty years ago.'

'I thought your father's interest in genealogy was a recent thing, a retirement hobby?'

'So did I. I can't imagine, when he was working up in London or building up the farm, that he had much time to take on commissions.'

She shook her head. 'I'm sorry. I can't do this.' She started walking again but when she realized he hadn't moved she turned back to him.

'Nothing is so hard to ignore as the wishes of a dead person,' he said, his voice low and quiet. 'The police are only interested in finding who killed my father but I need more than that, for my daughter's sake.' His voice was fierce again, but softened slightly, perhaps by compassion and fatherly concern. 'John Hellier keeps ringing the house to ask me to get her to talk to him. He says she's avoiding him at college. At first she pretended it was him who didn't want anything to do with her. Some nonsense about his parents thinking she was a bad influence. But I knew that wasn't true and I got it out of her eventually. She's vowed to herself that it's over between them. Her queer way of honouring my father. If he were still alive she'd have argued with him until the cows come home. She was very close to him and she wouldn't have wanted to hurt him, but she'd have done her utmost to change his mind, nag him into submission. By dying he's won, he's got his way, without a fight. She's got it into her head that she'd be betraying him if she carried on with John, their marriage would be cursed. But she loves him, I know that. The whole thing is tearing her in two. I'm well aware that there's not many who'd put up with her. She's not the easiest person.'

A fine speech, which proved the power of fatherly love. Mary said she found the ferocity of her maternal instincts almost shocking. But at least, in Richard's case, it wasn't blind. *She's not the easiest person.* You could say that again.

'She can be a lovely kid,' Richard went on. 'You've only seen her worst side.' He allowed a weak smile. 'She was a different person before my father tried to make her choose between him and John. She was so happy, softer, more relaxed.' Natasha remembered now that in fact she had had one glimpse of the other Rosa, when she'd stopped to ask her for directions to Shadwell. There'd been no trace of sullenness or hostility then. *Cool car,* Rosa had said.

'John adores her and he's good for her,' Richard concluded. 'So the only solution is to find out exactly why my father was so set against him. And, as I said to you before, it might help to find out why my father died.' He paused. 'I'll pay the going rate, of course.'

'The police haven't come up with any ideas?' She remembered the tip she'd given Sergeant Fletcher about the man who'd tried to gatecrash the party and wondered if he'd interviewed Stella about it.

'The only people they've spoken to so far are my family,' Richard said. 'I know neither my daughter nor my mother did it. I know damn well I didn't. I don't have a clue who would harm him and I don't think the police have much of one either. He kept himself to himself. Didn't have any enemies that I know of. But he must have had, mustn't he? I get the impression Sergeant Fletcher has pretty much ruled out any wrong place at the wrong time random scenario. Someone wanted my father dead and I won't be able to rest until I know why. Those papers were hidden. That has to mean something.'

'How did you get into the study?' she asked reluctantly. 'Surely the police locked it?'

Matter-of-factly: 'I have a spare key.'

She threw her head back in exasperation. Then she levelled her eyes at him, her mind made up. 'So you want me to do what precisely?'

'Whatever you think best.'

She stretched her back, took a deep breath. 'We could start by trying to track down the person at the top of the tree, Marion Lassiter, asking if she hired your father to do the research. There's generally no reason why you'd be interested in another family's history, one not related to yours, unless a member of that family paid you to be interested.' She thought of John Hellier as she spoke. Were the hidden papers connected to John? There was a chance they might be, she supposed, given that Seagrove had been equally secretive about the Hellier family tree.

'That's settled then?'

'I guess so.'

'I want you to be committed to this. Half measures won't do.' The warmth had gone from his voice quite suddenly. She could imagine him using the same tone in the cloakrooms, turning on the pressure to fire his team up and spur them on to ever greater effort. No room for excuses, no negotiation.

She stuck her fingers in her mouth and whistled to Boris, who came tearing back across the meadow, tongue lolling, as full of energy as when they set out. A fine companion for a three-hour car journey.

It seemed a slim chance that some ghost from Seagrove's past had come to take his revenge now. But you could never be too sure. Politicians relied on people having short memories but

Natasha knew, and Alice Hellier had proved, that people were capable of bearing grudges for the longest time.

Eleven

MARION LASSITER'S PRETTY whitewashed cottage is modern and everything is fitted: carpets, kitchen, cupboards and wardrobe in the bedroom. Formica table in the kitchen, blue plastic bath and overhead shower, UPVC double-glazed windows. She can't fathom this trend for nostalgia, why young, often unmarried couples these days are intent on kitting out their starter homes with claw-footed baths and pine dressers, Victorian fireplaces and brass bedsteads. Out with the old, in with the new. There was nothing good about the past. She certainly doesn't want it to come knocking at her door.

She hardly ever receives visitors, so she presumes it must be the electricity man come to read the meter or perhaps the Jehovah's Witnesses come to save her soul – several years too late.

She opens the door and drops her tea cup. The thick carpet stops it shattering but the hot tea splashes her hand and her stockinged ankles. She hardly feels it.

A man is standing there, a man who looks exactly how she imagines her son must now look. All babies are born with blue eyes but her baby's eyes would have remained blue, she is sure of that. This man has blue eyes, and greying fair hair. He is wearing a smart navy suit and white shirt.

'I'm Peter,' he says. And then he smiles and his smile is not the bold, almost impudent smile of his mother, but the same supreme inner confidence emanates from it and Marion is instantly transported back in time to a Cotswold orchard. She is up a ladder propped against an apple tree, dropping rosy ripe fruit into a basket as German bombs drop over English cities.

'You know who I am, don't you?'

Oh yes, she knows who he is.

'What are you doing here, Peter?' She can hear her own blood, turbulent and seething. How much does he know? 'If you want me to help you understand, I can't do that. If you want my apology then you have it. I'm sorry, you'll never know how much.'

'You haven't heard, have you?' He steps into her house and glances round the room. 'Do you watch much television?'

'I prefer books.'

'He's dead. Charles Seagrove is dead.'

She isn't at all sure how this information makes her feel. It makes no difference to her life now. The world is a better place without him but it's hardly justice.

'They say he was murdered.'

Her immediate thought: Which one of us?

'He had plenty of enemies, didn't he?' Peter says softly. 'I tried to see him. A few days before he died.'

He did it, Marion thinks. She recollects his mother's hot temper and pushy confidence, his father's cold fanaticism.

'Don't tell me you never wanted him dead,' Peter says. 'Seagrove knew everything there was to know about us, about our families, but the one thing we knew about him could have ruined him for ever. Richard could have done it, if he found out.'

Marion's hand is pulsing where it was doused with scalding tea. She brings the wound to her mouth, sucks the angry red blotch.

'How could Richard know anything? Seagrove would never have told him.'

'Stella?'

But Marion shakes her head firmly. Stella Seagrove has too much to lose.

Twelve

NATASHA LAY ON her stomach on the narrow pine sleigh bed in her childhood bedroom, the pretty white duvet embroidered with blue stars and crescent moons. She'd set off on her first sleep-walking expeditions from that bed, had learned to combat silence and darkness with a book and torchlight under the covers, or headphones and a walkman and the Sisters of Mercy. But last night she hadn't needed any of those things.

She'd stayed up late, talking to Steven about what had happened, and he'd managed to lessen some of the horror of what she'd seen, using the same methods he'd used to dispel her childhood nightmares – a few select words and a hug.

Afterwards, she'd closed her eyes in bed and for the first time since it had happened, she didn't see Charles Seagrove's sightless eyes and his open mouth. She'd managed a straight seven and a half hours of sleep, a personal best, and had woken recharged and relaxed.

Fortunately, sleep debt didn't work the same way as the usual kind. You didn't have to pay back exactly the same as you owed. A token gesture was all that was required. You could have lost several hours over several days but one good night and the slate was wiped clean. She was back in the black. Her best colour.

Even curiosity had deserted her for once. She had no burning desire to open Charles Seagrove's box, was more than happy to leave it where it was, underneath a pile of clothes at the bottom of her carpet bag.

As she'd packed the box she'd noted that it was a beautiful

object, Victorian ebonized oak, carved with heraldic emblems, chevrons and shields and lions rampant, and shaped like a treasure chest. It reminded her of the coffer at the foot of her bed in Orchard End, in which she kept the white knitted shawl and the note with her name on it, all that her real mother had left with her at the hospital twenty-nine years ago. You kept precious and private things in pretty carved boxes.

Richard Seagrove had already left one message on her mobile, his impatience at not being able to reach her evident. She had the niggling concern that he was going to be like a blackmailer who kept coming back for more and more. Give an inch and he'd take a mile. Except that Richard Seagrove wasn't blackmailing her, she reminded herself. She was doing this out of choice, wasn't she? Because she felt an obligation to the family she had so disrupted?

She knew she'd have to look through Charles Seagrove's papers eventually, even if just to satisfy her own nosiness. For now though, she idly thumbed through a dog-eared copy of Noel Streatfeild's *Ballet Shoes* instead. She'd lost count of the number of times she'd read it growing up, lying in this same little bedroom under the eaves, with the view of the Hope Valley enclosed at the western end by Mam Tor, the shivering mountain. The novel was her security blanket, her gateway back to childhood innocence. From the age of seven she'd modelled herself on Posy, Petrova and Pauline Fossil, wearing a leotard and little tutu round the house and dancing the dying swan. Then, when she was seventeen and saw her birth certificate, she found out that her life emulated the adopted Fossil girls more than she could have possibly imagined. Though in a way, it was as if she'd always known, had always felt different.

She was whiling away half an hour while Steven made a few phone calls, the constant chase for funding for his next dig, before they went to walk off the scrambled egg, bacon and mushrooms Ann had just served for breakfast. When Natasha lived at home her mother's constant jibe was that she 'treated the place as an hotel'. But now she'd left, Ann seemed keen for Natasha's childhood home to resemble a guesthouse when she came back for a visit. There were clean fluffy towels neatly folded on the bed, fresh flowers from the garden on the dressing table, and the full English breakfast was complemented with homemade bread, orange marmalade and Earl Grey tea, which made Natasha feel wonderfully pampered. For a while she even allowed herself to indulge in the illusion that her parents still had the power to protect her from the world, to sort out all her problems. Even though Ann was far more concerned in sorting out her 'real' daughter, Abby. Abby's love life, Abby's promotion, her annual leave, her new sofa. Natasha couldn't help feeling a little left out by the detail Ann knew about her sister's day-to-day life. She resented Ann asking her probing questions and she resented it when she didn't. No wonder she drove people mad.

She closed *Ballet Shoes*, rolled over on to her side, sat up and plugged in her iBook. It was almost a relief to look at a computer screen without having to contend with the red maple leaf floating in the corner of her vision. She vowed to get rid of the ticket as soon as she got home.

She downloaded four emails, watched as John Hellier's name popped up in the inbox. When she'd read his message she thought: Here is incontrovertible proof that the art of letter writing is not dead, that it just lives on in an altered state, in cyberspace. She wanted to print off John Hellier's message and tie it up with ribbon, to be saved for the family historians of the future.

Hello Natasha

It was thoughtful of you to leave the disk at college for me. Rosa gave it to someone on my course and asked him to pass it on. She's avoiding me – almost as if she blames me for her grandfather's death. So please feel free to dig around in my family's sordid past to your heart's content! Rosa's father says you are continuing your research and I told him you have my total blessing. I hope something comes of it.

I have this terrible feeling that if I lose Rosa I lose everything and my life will be ruined. Can a life be ruined at twenty-two? I think that it probably can.

From our brief meeting at that ill-fated garden party I can't imagine what you must think of me, no doubt you see me as someone who gives up too easily. But there are other ways of fighting for what you care about, for winning the woman you love, than riding with pistols at dawn. (I wish I could convince the police how much I hate guns!) I wish I could convince Rosa that we're meant for each other.

When my mother died two years ago my dad said he could never marry or love anyone else. He is fifty-five and he still believes that each of us is destined for only one person, that we have only one true love. He believed that Rosa was mine and I was hers. I still believe it, with all my heart.

It would be wonderful if you could help us to understand why Charles Seagrove didn't agree.

With very best wishes
John Hellier

'You ready then?' Steven's voice was a call to arms.

'I'm ready.'

She hit reply.

Dear John
Thank you for your message. I will do my best.
Natasha

She was a sucker for a sob story. When faced with a torrent of tears what else was there to do but go with the flow?

Castleton was a bustling little market town dominated by the surrounding gritstone hills and moors and the impenetrable square keep of Peveril Castle. It was as much a honeypot for tourists as Chipping Campden, with more than its fair share of gift and souvenir shops. Most sold only one thing though: 'Blue John'. Earrings, necklaces, keyrings, goblets – all were adorned with the peacock blue Fluorspar that came from the local caves, the colour of childhood and of home for Natasha.

The air here was fresher and thinner than in Gloucestershire, the sunlight somehow not as rich and deep. But it was pleasantly warm as the three of them, Natasha, Steven and Boris, walked down the steep incline of the main road, past the rows of traditional pubs and shops displaying their wares on pavement stalls.

You never knew or understood a place properly, certainly couldn't really love it, until you knew its history, what made it the way it was. She knew Castleton's past far better than she knew her own. Steven had taught her to read its landscape, get under its skin. She knew that the whole of this area was once part of the Royal Forest of the Peak. He'd shown her the remains of Longbarrows at Longstone Moor, the chambered tombs at Tideslow, the hill forts on Karl Wark and on the windswept summit of Mam Tor, built by the Celtic Brigantes tribe.

They walked down to the square which contained the garrison church and the Celtic memorial to the eight residents of the town killed in the First World War. Despite its fine houses, the square was in the shadow of the castle as much as the rest of the town. It was a narrow, zigzagged and steep climb through rough grassland to its curtain walls. 'It'll be worth it when you get to the top,' Steven had encouraged her when she was six years old. A good motto, she'd always thought, with its promise that effort paid off, that it was worth striving for something. Boris was lagging, not believing a word of it.

There was a definite wind chill factor up here, prickling her bare arms. The desolate moors and outcrops of Derbyshire had prepared her well for living with the changeable weather in the Cotswold hills, where the landscape was wild and open but never bleak like this. She wasn't truly sure where she felt most at home any more. Always that nagging feeling deep inside that she hadn't yet found the place to which she belonged. The map was written in her blood, locked inside her DNA, but she didn't have the key to crack the code.

Steven was entirely different. He was as much a part of Derbyshire as the prehistoric limestone foundations and flints he'd unearthed as a teenager on the first archaeological digs that had set the course of his life. He roamed the world for skeletons and tombs and ruins but he carried his home inside him. How she envied that.

He was wearing battered hiking boots and thick socks, khaki canvas shorts and a navy T-shirt. He walked with his arms behind his back, making his already honed body even more streamlined, his limbs sinewy and sun-darkened as his face. Indoors he seemed clumsy but here, ascending a mountain to an ancient castle, he was graceful and at ease, in his element.

As they ascended, the view opened out across the Hope valley but it had changed dramatically since Natasha had come here as a child. Your eyes were drawn to the Mam Tor landslip, a huge gash in the side of the hill that looked as if it had been hacked away by a giant shovel to reveal a dark gritstone scar, the road that once linked Sheffield to Manchester now ripped and twisted like a scene of devastation following an earthquake.

She glanced at her father. Since she'd arrived, there had been something different about him, but she couldn't put her finger on quite what it was. He seemed preoccupied, but not in an anxious way. There was a strange complacency about him, and now, somewhat annoyingly, he kept whistling little snatches of a melody as they walked. If she didn't know him better she'd almost believe . . .

She stopped dead in her tracks, feeling as if the giant who'd wreaked havoc on Mam Tor was back, ripping the ground from under her feet 'You haven't fallen in love with someone, have you?'

He flicked his eyes towards her, drew to a halt.

'Oh my God.'

'Is it really so obvious?' He was almost squirming.

They'd exchanged positions. She the angered parent, he the contrite child. He stared off towards the Great Ridge, the features of which Natasha knew by name, like old friends – Grinslow Knoll, Hollins Cross, Back Tor and Lose Hill – but her eyes were drawn back to the gaping wound of Mam Tor. She should have seen this coming.

Her father's flings were infamous. She'd been blissfully unaware of them as a small child because he'd never allowed them to encroach on his family life, but when, as a teenager, she'd started to accompany Steven on his trips abroad he'd not been able to keep them from her. The first girl she found out about was a young anthropologist from Milan, named Flavia. Archetypal Italian, she was frighteningly fashionable and sexy, even in dusty jeans and a T-shirt. Natasha was fascinated by her, wanted to be her, studied her every move. So it didn't take long to notice the way she looked at Steven, talked to him, touched him, the way Steven responded. Natasha spied on Flavia one evening, after the communal campfire meal, saw her disappearing into Steven's tent with a bottle of wine and two glasses.

In her upfront way she'd stormed right in there and challenged them both. Steven calmly asked Flavia to leave him and his daughter alone, immediately owned up, then just as calmly proceeded to answer all Natasha's questions on this, and previous affairs. He told her he wanted to show her the respect she deserved, treat her like an adult. She was fourteen years old and she wanted to be treated like a child. But she'd known then that her childhood was over.

Since that summer, she'd never kidded herself that her parents' marriage was anywhere close to being ideal. But because Steven had confined his extra-curricular activities to foreign digs, she suspected her mother simply turned a blind eye, knowing none of the flings were serious, ever threatened her. In her own way, Natasha too did her best to ignore anything that might dent her perfect image of her father. Her parents' marriage seemed to work. It had seemed permanent. But nothing lasts for ever, not even Mam Tor.

'Who is she?'

'No one you know.' He took a deep breath, let it out in a sigh. 'Her name's Rowena. She's a student...' He held up his hand, noting the horrified expression on her face. 'Mature student. She's doing an MA in medieval archaeology.'

'How mature exactly?'

'Twenty-six.'

'Shit, Steven.' For once she wished she'd not stopped calling him Dad when she discovered she was adopted. Right now she wanted to claim him as her own, use a name to which she, and Abby, had exclusive rights. 'She's younger than me.'

'You'd like her.'

'Like fuck I would.'

'There's no need to swear,' Steven said.

She snorted. 'I don't think you're in any position to claim the moral high ground right now. How could you? How *could you* be so selfish and stupid? I don't get it, I really don't. What about us? You have a wife and two daughters, remember?'

'You're not children any more, you—'

She spun away from him, couldn't bear to see his face. Most of all she didn't want him to see the tears in her eyes. 'That's it? We can stand on our own two feet now, so it's OK for you to betray your family?'

'I'll always be there if you need me, you know that.' He reached out to touch her arm but she jerked back from him. 'Look, I should have realized this would be especially hard for you.'

'What's that supposed to mean?' She glared at him as understanding dawned. 'Don't you dare. Don't you dare try to pretend I'm overreacting just because I'm some poor little abandoned kid. I'm right to think that nobody can be trusted, aren't I? Girls grow up assuming their dad is a typical man, you know. Maybe you're to blame more than my real mother for the fact that I don't trust anyone.'

It was no doubt true. His affairs probably had taken their toll on her personal life, seeped into her subconscious, even though she'd done her best to ignore them.

She was lashing out because she felt betrayed by Steven but also because of what was going on between her and Marcus. Nothing he'd ever done suggested that he was remotely like her father, even though she'd accused him of being just the same. Falsely accused him, she reminded herself. Yet she knew that what had happened today would keep those seeds of doubt well watered.

Marcus had been Steven's colleague and friend long before he became hers and, somehow, the discovery of Steven's latest affair made her feel less optimistic than ever about the chances of things working out between her and Marcus. *Nobody can be trusted.* Her father had just proved her right and reconfirmed her worst fears.

She could read Steven's body language well enough to know he was reining himself in, struggling not to show how upset he was. What did he expect? Understanding? Did he really think they were so alike? She may have done some stupid and rash things in her time but she could honestly say she'd never two-timed anyone.

'Does Ann know?'

He looked suitably pained, shook his head.

'You're fooling yourself. She must suspect something. You're not usually so bloody cheerful.'

Maybe Ann was oblivious. She'd never been on the same wavelength as Steven in the way Natasha had. Growing up, Natasha had always sided with her dad in family disagreements. Steven and Natasha against Abby and Ann, against the world. Now she felt the wrench of divided loyalties. For once she didn't relish her role as his confidante.

'How long has it been going on?'

'Six months.'

'It's serious then?'

'I think so, yes.' He looked confused.

She felt a flare of anger. He was old enough to know better. 'Does Rowena,' she could barely say the name, 'feel the same?'

'She says she does.'

Natasha groaned.

Steven was fifty-six years old, but it was easy enough to understand how someone in their twenties would find him attractive. Always Natasha's hero, there was something heroic about him that was there for anyone to see. An adventurous, cavalier charisma. As if all those years spent in the ruins of castles and abbeys had filtered through to shape his very being. Tall and toned, he still had a swashbuckling physique and the peppering of grey in his black hair, the crows' feet around his dark eyes only enhanced his piratical demeanour, made his strong, rugged face all the more interesting.

'You're not going to run off with her or anything, are you?' She could hear the panic in her own voice.

'I don't know what I'm going to do.'

She stared out across the curved, enclosed fields to the distant Derwent Moors. Her throat felt as if she'd swallowed a knife.

Ann once told Natasha that being a mother completely fulfilled her. She'd had five years as a museum curator, five as an interior designer, and motherhood was her next career move. She approached its schedule of baking and ballet lessons, shopping and swimming, with complete professionalism. Now that job was finished, and possibly her marriage with it. Would she be like Stella Seagrove, living out the rest of her life through her children?

Maybe that was the way it often went. Maybe it was about time Natasha accepted that she was too idealistic, that her dreams of romantic love were just dreams, formed by too many nineteenth-century novels and not by the real world.

If I lose Rosa I lose everything . . . each of us is destined for only one person . . . we have only one true love.

John Hellier resisted the real world, too. Irrespective of Richard Seagrove, there and then she vowed to redouble her efforts to help him.

The front of the casket was chipped and scarred around the brass lock where Richard Seagrove had levered it open. Natasha sat cross-legged on the sleigh bed, opened the lid and lifted out the contents. She'd swung the window wide to let some air into the little room and the breeze carried a scent of the moors; peat, gorse and bracken, indefinably northern.

There was a bundle of paper, tied with string. She carefully unwrapped it. A genealogical chart, with a black-and-white photograph of a young girl clipped to the top right-hand corner next to the name at the head of the chart: Marion Lassiter.

The writing sheet used for the chart was good quality vellum, weakened along the folds from years of confinement. She spread it out on the bed. Charles Seagrove's monogram was at the bottom, a large bold C interlocking the S. At the very top of the chart, above Marion Lassiter's name and unconnected by any of the standard genealogical lines or annotated with the usual dates, was a single underscored name: Karl Briegel.

Almost unconsciously she realized she'd been looking for the name Cinderella, Hans Koenig or someone she recognized from John Hellier's family tree. Nothing though.

Natasha had been on courses to learn how to date photographs and Marion's hairstyle, curls scraped up at the sides, firmly placed her in the 1940s. She was dressed in a V-neck jumper, shirt and tie, the unmistakable uniform of the women's land army. She had a strong and striking rather than pretty face. Under her name was a single date, preceded by the letter 'b', signifying that it was that of her birth: 1927.

If Marion had ever married she'd seemingly not done so by the time the chart was researched and drawn up. Scanning the other members of the clan, the most recent date was 1943, a marriage. There was another wedding in 1938 and a death in 1940. Which would all indicate that the research was done some time in the mid-1940s.

Natasha laid the chart aside and studied the rest of the supporting material.

As with any proper study, the history was illustrated with other photographs, sepia studio shots of girls in ball gowns, cricketers and soldiers, a posed Edwardian wedding group. Unusually, however, none of the pictures were originals, just taken from newspapers and society pages. The file also contained corresponding certificates and paperwork. Natasha had more of an insight now as to why Seagrove's brief to her had been so thorough. This research project of his contained the same information he'd wanted her to give him on the Helliers.

But Marion had nothing obvious in common with John Hellier. Her family tree glowed so bright you needed sunglasses just to read it. Her family had gentrified origins: eighteenth-century landowners and squires, Members of Parliament, army generals and local magistrates. Department store owners and tea merchants were about as lowly as it went.

There was not a single Assize report or debtors jail entry, no asylum or borstal records. Instead there was a neatly handwritten sheet with a cross against each item in an exhaustive list of all the criminal records Seagrove had obviously checked. Not even a single petty thief or bankrupt amongst them. Of university and glittering military records there was an abundance. Natasha gave them a cursory skim. Not sure what she was looking for, it was hard to make out what she was looking *at*.

Plenty of hospital admission forms and clinical records and something else, protected in a buff envelope. It was the first time she'd seen a chest X-ray included in a family tree dossier. She held it up to the light, pale ribs like ghostly branches. As she knew very well, from her weeks at the Wellcome Medical Library, patient records were closed for years, could only be obtained with the consent of the patient or next of kin. Marion's clinical records certainly wouldn't have been open for public inspection in the 1940s. How and why had Charles Seagrove got hold of them?

Had Marion wanted Charles Seagrove to research her history? Or had he undertaken the study behind her back as he had with John Hellier? The photographs in her dossier took on a new significance. If you were researching an official family history, elderly relatives were all too willing to hunt through their attics for old negatives and prints. But if you were researching someone's history without their consent, it would be a different matter. All you'd be left with were pictures from newspapers and magazines. In which case, Seagrove would have had to find another way to obtain medical files. But if that was what he had done, the question was still, why? What motive could he have had? Not the same one that made him do the background check on John Hellier. If he had been vetting possible brides, she thought, who was the groom?

There was another possible explanation which she pushed to the back of her mind. But she had a feeling that, like a troubled spirit, it wouldn't go away quietly.

Thirteen

LIKE NATASHA, ARNOLD Hyatt didn't wear a watch. He operated on the earliest method of timekeeping known to man, his routine dictated by the rising and the setting of the sun. On long summer days, 9 a.m. was practically midday for him.

But when Natasha knocked on the turquoise tongue-and-groove front door some time after ten the next morning there was no reply. She lifted the latch on the wooden gate at the side of the cottage and led Boris up the brick path that led to the back garden. Arnold was at the top, beyond the vegetable patch and an encampment of cane wigwams of runner beans, scattering grain for the hens. Dressed in black Wellington boots crusted with dried mud, with a length of rope instead of a belt to hold his trousers over his rounded belly, he looked like old Mr McGregor, minus the angry glint in his eye that made small rabbits run for their lives. He raised his hand in greeting now and came towards her, Pied Piper to two chickens and a bantam-pheasant cross he called 'Phantom'.

She had been relieved to leave Castleton. Her father's news had shattered the illusion that she had escaped to a temporary refuge. The cruel world caught up with you wherever you fled, had stealthily ripped apart a marriage that had lasted for over thirty-five years.

She had found it excruciating even being in the same room as Ann, eating the delicious roast dinner she'd lovingly prepared. She was terrified that if Ann looked into her eyes she'd see what she'd failed to see in the eyes of her husband. When Natasha watched

Steven return Ann's kiss as she stood at the cooker making custard for the apple crumble, she felt herself in serious danger of despising him.

The birds threw Boris into a frenzy. It took all Natasha's strength to rein him in. Both hands on his leash, she rocked back on her heels as he strained, springing up on his back legs. 'Leave the poor things alone,' she scolded. She shouldn't have brought him but he'd refused to be left behind when he'd sussed, from her boots and jeans, that she was going for a walk. 'Pick on someone your own size.'

Arnold ruffled the russet fur on Boris's head and instantly, magically, he calmed down, plonked himself obediently at Arnold's feet for all the world as if he were in the company of Doctor Dolittle. 'Good boy,' Arnold cooed softly, then to Natasha, 'Follow me. I've got something to show you.'

He led her to the ramshackle wooden garage, swung open the doors. From Mr McGregor to Doctor Dolittle to Willy Wonka. The garage resembled a crazy laboratory, a maze of bubbling tubes and cylinders and gauges.

'What on earth are you up to?'

He gave her a gleeful grin. 'You mean you don't recognize cider brandy distilling equipment when you see it?'

'I'm guessing you don't have a licence.'

'Who's to know?'

'Me now, for one. But what's a little moonshine?' She spied the barrel loads of apples in the corner of the shed. 'Where d'you get all those?'

Arnold tapped his finger against his nose. 'Let's just say I've had a few windfalls lately.'

'But you only have one apple tree.'

'Aye, but there's dozens of 'em round the village.'

'And everyone's agreed to give their apples to you?'

Arnold looked sheepish.

Natasha widened her eyes. 'You don't just help yourself?'

'Few folk are into baking apple pies and making chutney any more. They just leave them rotting on the ground, never even notice if some disappear overnight. Sin to see 'em going to waste.'

'Very enterprising, I'm sure.'

'Now I think of it, there's a fine little orchard at Shadwell, isn't there? With all that's going on up there lately I bet nobody's had time to tend to—'

'Don't even think about it.'

He chuckled, nudged her arm. 'Want to sample some?'

'Oh, go on then.'

He dipped a small ladle in to an oak barrel, poured the clear liquid into a sherry glass.

It made her cry.

'Better than the stuff you get from Calvados, wouldn't you say?'

She wiped her eyes.

He edged her back outside. 'Anyway, to what do I owe this pleasure?'

'Not sure I can remember now.' She inspected the empty glass. 'You're just about old enough to remember the war, aren't you, Mr Hyatt?'

'Old enough to think young folk these days are a might too cheeky. But yes, you could say I was historically advantaged.'

Natasha laughed. 'I like that. A historical advantage is exactly what I need right now.'

The brick patio area by the kitchen door was a real suntrap so, with Boris spread out under the bench, more kitten than lion now, they drank mugs of tea. Arnold insisted Natasha took the striped deck chair, which threw her back into a semi-supine position so that she couldn't see his face, or much else apart from the wide open sky. Arnold sat ramrod straight on a small three-legged stool similar to the one he perpetually occupied at the Snowshill Arms.

'I remember the war all right but I don't know what I can tell you that'd be of any use,' he said. 'I only got to see it from a distance. I couldn't wait to go and fight but first off I was too young and then my father insisted he needed help on the farm.'

Natasha twisted sideways so she could look at him properly, pulled up her knees to get comfy. 'I'd have thought nothing would drag you away from here.'

'Ah, but you see it's a love of the land that makes you want to fight to protect it.'

'Well, it's not battles and air raids that I'm interested in. It's war in the Cotswolds that I need to know about.' The war as Charles Seagrove and Marion Lassiter experienced it. 'Did you have land girls at Oat Hill?'

'Aye,' Arnold smiled wistfully. 'Sally. From Birmingham-way. Lovely wavy black hair. Didn't know a ram from a bullock or a carrot from field of corn but she was a hard worker and she had a smile as sweet as honey, set the day off to a fine start for sure. I can still see her, lugging a pail of milk in the frost, cheeks all glowing and pink, like a little ripe Bramley. Her bottom as firm and ripe as—'

'My Hyatt!'

'Oh, dear, getting a bit carried away there, wasn't I?'

'It's certainly brought some colour to *your* cheeks.'

He composed himself. 'You were saying?'

'Did most of the farms round here have land girls?'

'Off and on. Someone had to do the ploughing and harvesting and tend to the flocks. Farmers scoffed at the notion of women doing a man's job but they saved the day those girls.'

'How did it work? I mean, how did they get trained and recruited and allocated?'

Arnold dunked a shortbread biscuit in his tea, bit it, slurping slightly. 'You mean to tell me you've not been able to find all this out on the internet?' He was impishly victorious, full of I-told-you-so. When Natasha occasionally went with him to the local history group he always made a point of demonstrating to her how it was quicker to go back to the original source than to surf.

In this instance, she couldn't argue with that. 'I've learnt plenty about how to get hold of reproduction land army socks and where I can buy a copy of an old recruitment poster, praising the paradise of rural life, but not a lot more, I admit.'

'The county War Agricultural Committees handled everything. If I remember correctly, the little museum in Winchcombe has some wonderful Second World War memorabilia. The history group donated some photographs to add to their collection of pictures of the airbases and POW camps. We had prisoners of war as well as land girls helping us on the farm at lambing and shearing time. Italians were lazy and cheerful and the Germans were a surly and hard-working lot, I do remember that much. I used to cycle to Moreton to see them all coming off the trains and being marched up to the camps. The Italians formed a brass band that used to play on Sundays.'

Natasha suddenly felt ignorant. She was well versed in the centuries-old history of the Cotswolds, the site of Roman villas and roads, but except for the obvious signs like the disused hangers and airstrips at Rissington, she didn't know nearly as much about her local area during wartime. Yet this was living history, experienced by people who were still around to talk about it, for a little while longer at least. Though all too quickly, those doors to the past were closing.

Karl Briegel, she wondered, remembering the stray name at the top of Marion's genealogical tree. A Germanic name. A German prisoner who had worked here during the war?

'Where were the camps?'

'Oh, all over. Springhill, Studely Castle, Bourton-on-the-Hill, Northwick Park. If you do go to Winchcombe, let me know and I might tag along. I rather fancy a trip down memory lane, especially if I can travel down it in that snazzy little car of yours.'

'How about right now?'

'Well, why not?'

Arnold locked up and climbed into the passenger seat of the Alpine, clearly chuffed with the prospect of an impromptu outing. 'Have the top down, shall we?'

Natasha obliged and they set off, dropping Boris back at the cottage.

'I kept in touch with a little evacuee lad we had to stay at the farm.' Arnold chatted as they turned onto the minor road that arched over the open sheep pastures. 'Stanley his name was. He died about ten years back. There were twelve children in my class at school and then suddenly there were over forty. All snivelling and homesick.'

'It must have been a terrible wrench for their parents too.'

'I dare say. I can't imagine Mary and James packing little Kieran off to live with strangers.'

'I can't imagine Kieran's granddad letting him go that easily either.'

He smiled thoughtfully. 'It must have been the toughest decision. If you kept them with you and they were wounded or killed in an air raid, how would you ever live with that?'

There it was, finally, a situation where it was in the child's best interests to be parted from its mother. If there was one example, maybe there were others. Natasha clutched that thought for a moment.

'Mary told me you went for a bit of a holiday up north?'

'Some holiday. My father's gone and fallen in love with a student.'

'Oh dear, it's always a bit awkward when you realize your folks are as capable of messing things up as you are.' He looked at her. 'You've just got to let 'em get on with it. Same as we have to let you young 'uns make your own mistakes. That's the biggest shock when you become a parent, realizing kiddies aren't there for you to mould and coach. Taking care of them's about all you can do.'

Natasha forced herself back to the matter in hand. 'So what do you know about Charles Seagrove?'

'Not much but as much as anyone round here, save our local domino champion. I grant that he lived not much over ten miles distant but it might as well be a hundred. Us old folk still calculate distance in terms of how long it'd take to walk through snowdrifts. I will say this though. People seemed to keep their distance from Seagrove. Whether that was more of his making or theirs I can't say. I don't like to speak ill of the dead but I get the impression he wasn't everyone's cup of tea, gripes left over from the war but I've never known the root of them. Can't have been that people thought he was yellow though. Farmers were exempt from being called up. Needed for food production.'

The town of Winchcombe wasn't nearly so well manicured as Chipping Campden. Rare in the Cotswolds now, there was chipped paint still to be found on doors and windows of some of the beautiful medieval and Georgian houses. The Victorian school was empty – old rolled carpets and an obsolete cash register visible through the grimy windows. But there were warning signs of hungry developers beginning to swarm, drawn to the scent of potential killings to be made.

She and Arnold walked back up past the entrance to Winchcombe Abbey to the Folk Museum, which was housed on the second floor of the redbrick town hall.

A wonderful resource for family historians, the little museum was a single, high-ceilinged room with cornices and faded red velvet drapes, permanently kept shut to protect the exhibits which made up a vivid picture of Winchcombe through the ages.

There were display cases of Roman coins and canon balls, a brass fireman's bell and shepherd's smock displayed on a tailor's dummy. A roped-off area displayed a Victorian kitchen scene, with a statue sitting by the fireside, bellows and paraffin lamps and a sewing machine, beside which were old farm and industrial implements, horseshoes and glove-makers' dollies and farriers' nails.

Arnold directed her to the Second World War cabinet in the centre of the room. Ration books and gas masks and a group photograph of the Home Guard as well as a delicate bone knife made by a German prisoner of war. On a bench running the length of the museum were presentation albums, like scrap books with excerpts from parish magazines, news cuttings and diaries.

At the reception desk, an elderly volunteer summoned the curator for them. In her forties, small and trim except for her out of control curly grey hair, she introduced herself as Janet.

'I'm after any information you might have on the land army as well as prisoner of war camps,' Natasha said.

Janet directed Natasha to an album of photographs, including an assortment of land girls in their breeches and boots, with pitchforks and carts and milk churns. She looked carefully but could see no one resembling Marion.

'Do you know if there's a record, anywhere, of the names of land girls who worked on the local farms?' she said then.

Janet shook her head regretfully.

'Or of the prisoners of war held at the local camps?' Arnold added.

Another shake. 'After the war people just wanted to forget it.

We've done our best to collect as many memories as we can though.' She picked up another thick presentation file, its plastic leaves filled with transcripts of interviews, painstakingly typed up on a manual typewriter, mistakes touched up with white correction fluid. 'You might find something of use in here.'

Natasha often said a silent thank you to the army of unpaid amateur historians whose labours of love preserved so much of the minor, vital details of heritage and history, people who spent hours collecting, collating and cataloguing information that otherwise would be lost for ever.

Helpfully, there was a detailed index of all the people and places mentioned in the interviews. Marion Lassiter's name leapt off the page. She was part of the short dictated memoir of someone called Muriel Mulholland, who worked for her father Fred on his market garden: *Marion Lassiter from Cutsdean complained of backache from potato picking but not about the calluses on her pretty hands.*

'Marion Lassiter was assigned to Fred Mulholland's market garden, not to Shadwell Manor Farm,' Natasha muttered. That was one theory blasted out of the water. So how had Charles and Marion met?

Arnold reckoned he'd be able to track down Muriel. His well-established network of farmers, small-holders and market gardeners spidered across three counties. On the outskirts of Weston-Sub-Edge, in the no man's land between the Cotswolds and the Vale of Evesham, Mulholland's market garden was long ago submerged under a small development of stone houses and disproportionately enormous garages, but Arnold was sure they wouldn't have covered up the scent. Then, just as they turned to leave, Natasha spotted an antique map of Winchcombe and its surrounding area. Idly she found Snowshill, and Shadwell. And in italics, just to the west of Shadwell, in the middle of the woods, was a small grove marked Poacher's Dell.

Fourteen

AS SOON AS Natasha came home from Derbyshire she'd reverted to her nocturnal habits. So it was a good job that she often did her best thinking lying in bed, that reading over papers in the soft glow of a bedside lamp was sometimes beneficial because it gave her an entirely different perspective.

That was what she was looking for when she took Marion Lassiter's chart upstairs with her, putting Poacher's Dell to the back of her mind. According to the tree Charles had drawn up, Marion had a brother, Victor, seven years her junior. His birth certificate, like Marion's, gave an address in Cutsdean.

What had been snagging in her brain ever since she'd opened Charles Seagrove's box was the German connection. On Marion's chart there was a German name, Karl Briegel, and Charles Seagrove had spoken of the German soldier his father had met at the Christmas Truce, Hans Koenig, *my friend the enemy*. Was there a chance Karl Briegel, and therefore Marion in some way, was connected to Hans Koenig.

Dragging on a T-shirt, she went back down and logged on to the online telephone directory which covered the whole of the UK. The first time she'd used it it had freaked her out a little, to discover how easy it would be for anyone to find out where you lived, the very thing that made it one of the most indispensable tools of her trade. Three Mr V. Lassiters were listed in Gloucester-shire, none in Cutsdean.

She went back to bed and dozed until what she considered an acceptable hour to call strangers on a weekday morning. She tried all three numbers, going through the whole spiel about being a genealogist researching the family name and trying to track down relatives so long lost no one had realized they even existed until now. No go. One V. Lassiter turned out to be a typing error, not Mr at all but Mrs Lucy, while another spoke with a broad Dublin accent. The third, the most promising, in Toddington, was picked up by Mrs Lassiter who said her husband was on his way to the bowling club but no, he didn't have a sister named Marion. She left her number anyway.

Sometimes the living could be as elusive and difficult to trace as those who'd died over a hundred and fifty years ago. Before 1851 there were no such things as census returns, and after 1901 the data protection act kept their contents secret. She could carry on stabbing around in the dark for months, eventually find Marion or at least one of her living relatives. Perhaps. But hand on heart, she'd already done as much as Richard Seagrove could reasonably have expected her to do. She could at least try calling him and telling him she could see no obvious reason his father had kept those papers hidden, no reason he had kept them at all.

She took a deep breath and dialled the number for Shadwell Manor Farm. The phone was snatched up on the first ring. Rosa Seagrove's anxious 'hello' was that of someone waiting by the phone for news and dreading what that news might be.

'Hi, it's Natasha Blake. Is your dad there?'

'You of all people should know damn well where he is.' Rosa hung up.

It wasn't her morning. 'What have I done to upset her now?' Natasha asked the purring of the open line.

Archie Fletcher answered her question, later that afternoon, when he came knocking on her door.

'May I come in?'

Why did she feel nervous when she'd done nothing wrong? 'Do I have a choice?'

He smiled. 'I didn't bring a search warrant but I do need to talk to you.'

Boris was nosing the policeman's trousers in a very intimate fashion. Sergeant Fletcher fished out a bone-shaped biscuit and Boris gobbled it up, then went back to sniffing.

'You've been doing background checks on me and you've discovered I have a dog who can be bribed?'

'I've got one too. A golden Labrador.' His lively eyes twinkled. 'She's called Custard – because she's a tart.'

Natasha managed a laugh. Sergeant Fletcher was clearly good company, in practically any other circumstance.

The sergeant gently pushed Boris off. 'We arrested Richard Seagrove yesterday evening.' He scrutinized her face. 'For the murder of his father.'

She could feel what precious energy she had draining away, leaving her arms and legs heavy as lead. Tiredness, combined with the sun streaming in the window, felt like heatstroke, making her shivery. Limp as a rag doll, she dragged out a kitchen chair, slumped in it, elbows on the table. She jammed her fingers into her hair to support the heaviness of her head. Richard Seagrove had killed his father? She didn't know what to think.

'It was definitely him? You have proof?'

'He's not been charged yet but we're working on it.' He paused. 'He had means and motive, and what's more he had the key to his father's shotgun cupboard in his jacket pocket.'

'But he took the keys so he could unlock . . .' She resisted the reflex to clamp her hand over her mouth. Too late.

'To unlock his father's study?'

So the police knew about that already.

'Did you think I was going to say we'd arrested him for tampering with evidence from a murder investigation?'

'I didn't think anything.'

Archie Fletcher sat himself down opposite her. 'I don't believe that at all. I had you down as someone who thinks too much for her own good.'

'And your job depends on you being a good judge of character, I suppose?'

'As a matter of fact that's my big failing, according to my appraisals. I always see the best in people. Not the ideal qualification for a copper.' He lowered his voice as if someone might be listening, though there were only the two of them in the house, excluding Boris. 'My gut feeling is you're a good person and pretty clued up. But, like I say, I could easily be wrong. I can't work out how a clued-up person could do something so dumb. I could arrest you as well, you know? For theft and perverting the course of justice. Maybe even aiding and abetting a murderer. You knew very well where those papers came from and you knew it was wrong to take them. I need them back, of course.'

Sniffing the scent of danger in the air, Boris had remained loyally at Natasha's side. Now, his doleful black eyes flicked back and forth between the two of them in the fashion of a spectator at a tennis match.

She could always say she didn't know the papers were stolen. But lies had a habit of coming back to bite you. She was wary of them, ever since she'd discovered that she was adopted, that she'd lived the first seventeen years of her life under a fundamental falsehood.

'What did you think you were doing?' The way Archie Fletcher pursed his lips and tutted was over-emphasized, like a mime artist. He'd be a good person to have on hand if you were feeling glum. She could picture him, clowning around, pulling sillier and sillier faces, not giving up until he elicited a laugh.

'I felt bad, about upsetting Rosa. I was just trying to help.'

Archie Fletcher smiled. 'That's more than Miss Seagrove is doing for sure. She's not taking kindly to our involvement at all.'

Natasha could well imagine how the girl's manner would get the police's backs up. She remembered the icy laser of Rosa's eyes. *I hope he paid you well, for snooping around behind our backs. What's the going rate for spying these days?*

She was suddenly angry. 'She *has* just lost her grandfather in the most horrible way and now you've arrested her father for it. How would you feel?' She pulled herself straight. 'I bet you're all secretly enjoying this, aren't you? I mean, you join the police because you want action, to play Starsky and Hutch, and opportunities are a bit thin on the ground in the Cotswolds. The last local crime of note was probably when Mr Johnson's pedigree boxer puppy went missing.'

Sergeant Fletcher closed his notebook thoughtfully. 'There does seem more point in coming to work than usual, if I'm honest.'

His frankness, and the fact that his answer seemed to worry him, made her soften towards him even more than she had when she'd found out he carried dog biscuits in the pockets of his work clothes.

'I wanted to be Luke Skywalker actually,' he said. '"May the force be with you." I can't go along with us becoming the police service. "May the service be with you" isn't the same at all.' He patted Boris's head. 'You were wrong about the last local crime though. It's actually a Peeping Tom with a fancy for pensioners. Three old ladies have reported someone snooping round their garden late at night.'

'If I see anything I'll be sure to let you know.'

There was a knock at the door. Arnold.

'Just popped by to say I've spoken to . . .' He froze mid-sentence.

Natasha looked over her shoulder. Archie Fletcher had wandered into the hall.

'Mr Hyatt, this is Sergeant Fletcher. Sergeant Fletcher, this is Mr Hyatt.'

Arnold practically ran for it.

'I have that effect, sometimes,' Archie said. 'Usually only on criminals though. What's old Mr Hyatt got to hide?'

It struck her. She'd make a bet that Arnold was the Peeping Tom with the preference for pensioners, or rather pensioners with apples in their garden.

To hide her smile, she went through to the living room, came back with Charles Seagrove's wooden box and set it carefully on the table in front of him, like an expensive gift.

He looked at it circumspectly. 'No doubt your fingerprints are all over it but I won't make matters worse by adding my own. So perhaps you could tell me what's inside.'

'A sixty-year-old family tree. Nothing very exciting.'

'But you find it exciting?'

'Yeah, well, I'm strange like that.'

'It's the family tree of a girl named Marion Lassiter, correct?'

She went cold, wondering for a split second if she'd been watched all this time. 'How do you know that?'

'I have my sources, as they say.'

Networks and grapevines were one and the same. Arnold had promised to ask around, tap into his network, and the police picked it up on the grapevine, the kind that always flourishes in small, rural communities. Or maybe Richard Seagrove had told them.

'What happens now?'

Using a tea towel, Archie Fletcher slid the box into a clear plastic bag, zipped it. 'If this turns out to be insignificant I doubt it'll be taken further.'

'And Richard Seagrove?'

'There's a memorial service for his father at the local church in three days time. Whatever happens, he'll be allowed to attend that, even if only under supervision.'

The phone was ringing.

'Saved by the bell. I can see myself out, don't worry.'

Did that mean don't worry about Richard Seagrove, or about perverting the course of justice or just that he knew the way to her front door?

She didn't get it. If Richard had murdered his father, why make her carry on with her research? Were his reasons simply, as he said, to heal the rift between Rosa and John or was she being drawn into something she wasn't even close to comprehending? Had he been toying with her, playing her for a fool? She couldn't think straight. From her desk the red maple leaf swam into focus. Did Richard's arrest mean it would all be over soon? That, so far as the police were concerned at least, she'd be free to go to Canada?

She went through to her desk and picked up the receiver.

'Has he gone yet?' It was Arnold, sounding very furtive.

She waited until she heard the front door close. 'Just.' She realized, too late, that she'd not told Sergeant Fletcher about Poacher's Dell, and the note.

'You didn't say anything, did you?'

'About what?'

'You know.' Arnold's consternation came over loud and clear.

'Do you mean the newly-opened Snowshill distillery or our friendly local apple thief? Don't worry, Mr Hyatt. Your secret's safe with me.'

Arnold had popped round to say that he'd spoken to Muriel Mulholland. He'd ascertained that she hadn't kept in touch with Marion Lassiter but had arranged to visit her in Mickleton anyway.

The phone rang again just as she put it down.

'It's Victor Lassiter. You spoke to my wife an hour ago.'

'That's right.'

'You were asking about Marion. My wife told you that I don't have a sister but that's not actually true. Hilary, my wife, has never met Marion, you see. I haven't set eyes on her in sixty years.'

Fifteen

VICTOR LASSITER AND his wife lived in the tiniest cottage Natasha had ever seen, nestled down by the old railway line on the outskirts of Toddington. It had a long, narrow cottage garden packed with sweet peas, azaleas and peonies, and a greenhouse bursting with tomato plants. Inside the house itself there was just one main downstairs room, dominated by an inglenook fireplace.

The Lassiters reminded Natasha of the figures in a weather vane; she with a grey bun and half-moon granny glasses and him dressed in slippers and a woollen cardigan with leather patches at the elbows.

At first, as Mr Lassiter commiserated with his wife over some inconsequential slight she believed she'd suffered at the hand of the parish council, Natasha wondered if their minds had shrunk to fit their house and their bodies. Then, as she watched Mrs Lassiter go through a ritual of making tea, first warming the pot with water that had almost boiled, stirring the tea leaves, then pouring milk into a tiny jug and laying the tray with tea strainer and sugar lumps in a pottery bowl with silver teaspoons, she realized she was being unfair. They were the kind of people who placed great emphasis on matters others would think inconsequential, gentle relics from a time when everyone had more time. There was a certain charm in that, but it made Natasha more worried about what she might be stirring up.

On the way over she'd tried to imagine what terrible thing had happened to make Victor Lassiter sever ties with Marion to such an extent that his wife didn't even know she existed. How was Mrs

Lassiter going to feel about discovering her husband had a long-lost sister, that he had kept such an important part of his life from her all this time?

But she seemed to have accepted it with remarkable serenity. The atmosphere between them suggested that she fully expected surprise siblings to crawl out of the woodwork every day. Old age had its consolations, foundations so well set that no extent of seismic activity could even shake them. Natasha felt a pang at the realization that she'd never see Ann and Steven in a similar state. Her father had already left for Tuscany but he'd tried her mobile several times since she'd come back from Derbyshire. She wasn't returning his calls.

Mrs Lassiter poured tea and her husband offered round a plate of homemade fruitcake.

'You grew up in Cutsdean?' Natasha said.

'Lovely old house. Be worth a small fortune now but we sold it right after my mother died, before property prices round here went through the roof. We did have a bigger place ourselves, and a whacking great mortgage to match, but I decided to come down in the world so I could retire at fifty.'

'Lots of people would love to come down to a pretty place like this,' Natasha said, eyeing the crowds of china figurines and the large oak sideboard and dining table that hadn't adapted to the downsizing half so well as their owners.

'Don't get me wrong, I'm not complaining,' Victor Lassiter said. 'The steam trains pass right by the bottom of the garden, every hour on summer weekends. Couldn't think of a better place to see out my days. It's a treat to see all the children waving at us from the carriage windows. At Christmas the train takes them off to see Santa Claus. Greenland's just a few miles up the line, very near Winchcombe in fact,' he added with a twinkle. 'Bet you didn't know that.'

'I'll call in on the way home,' Natasha smiled.

'Let him know you've been a good girl?'

'That's debatable.' She tucked into the cake that was laced with sherry, happy to let Mr Lassiter take his own time to bring up the reason for her visit.

'Anyway, it's Marion you're here to talk about, isn't it?' He set his small cup on a nest of tables. 'Who did you say you're working for?'

'Someone whose father might have known your sister when she was in the land army. You know how it is. You reach a certain stage in life and people you met years ago suddenly seem more important.'

'Not one of our distant relations then?'

'Depends how far back you go. Everyone turns out to be related to everyone else eventually.'

Thankfully, he seemed satisfied enough with the flimsy explanation. 'It was the fellow Marion got mixed up with that caused all the bother.'

With the number of bases around the area it was no doubt a hot bed for wartime romances. 'Was he a soldier?'

'Not in the way you're thinking. A dreadful scandal it was.' He shook his head slowly, as if he still couldn't accept what had happened. 'Marion was a headstrong girl. She should have been born twenty years later. She'd have been the first to burn her bra and practise free love.'

'Love's never free,' Mrs Lassiter said.

But priceless, Natasha added, silently.

'My mother blamed it all on her getting in with the wrong crowd,' Victor Lassiter explained. 'She had one bosom pal at school, you know the type, always up to no good. My mother said she gave Marion ideas, although my sister had plenty of her own. But she was always champing at the bit, our Marion. She wasn't your typical land army girl, straight from the city terraces and the cotton mills of Lancashire. But several girls I knew from round here joined up and worked locally. It was right up Marion's street. She was training to be a shorthand typist but when she saw the posters of healthy lasses cuddling lambs and leading cart horses she was well and truly smitten.' Victor Lassiter's voice was growing gradually quieter and slower, as if he were feeling his way back with great care. The act of remembering for him was a journey down an unfamiliar dark passage in which he wasn't sure of the way or what he might find. 'In those days women didn't leave home until they got married and Marion saw it as a way to gain some independence and a chance to prove she could do a man's work. She wasn't a feminist as such, she had no hostility towards the opposite sex, but she certainly considered herself their equal. Soon as she was seventeen, spring of forty-four, that was it, she was off.'

Natasha knew she could sit back and listen now. Experienced interviewer that she was, she could pinpoint the precise point when she'd done enough coaxing and digging. Like a miner, she'd gently led Mr Lassiter down far enough to tap into the rich vein of memory which would just fall away now without any further probing.

'My father was furious, spitting pips.' Victor Lassiter chuckled. 'He said the land army was beneath her, she was wasting her education, should join the WRNS. Marion turned round to him and said, cool as a cucumber, how she'd rather grow things than destroy them. She could always hold her own in an argument, a real clever clogs she was all right.'

Natasha glanced at Mrs Lassiter who was listening avidly, a sad expression on her face, sympathy for her husband's loss and for her own loss of this spirited sister-in-law she'd never known but who might have been her friend had things been different.

'Marion took to farming like she was born to it,' her brother said. 'The outdoor life suited her. She was terrifically sporty, always off playing hockey and tennis. And she'd never been a bit squeamish. I could never make her squeal like the other girls when I came at her with worms or put frogs in her bed. So the muck didn't phase her. She could wade through manure and help deliver lambs without batting an eyelid. Wasn't scared of walking down pitch-dark lanes to fetch milk or harness towering shire-horses either, and she thought driving around in tractors was the bees knees. She fitted in well with the other land girls from the city, too well, I suppose, with their four-inch heels and eye veils and film star hairstyles. I was too young to take much notice at the time but, looking back, my parents must have been worried sick. The land girls had a bit of a reputation, not entirely justified, for being free and easy. Back to the land was the slogan used by the Ministry of Agriculture to tempt enlistment. Well, it soon became *backs* to the land. The villagers didn't like their sons mixing with the girls, by jingo they didn't, but that didn't stop them holding dances on Friday nights at the village hall. Marion was a beauty, always turned heads. Lovely blonde hair and blue eyes. Little Bo Peep I used to call her, what with her being a shepherdess. That first summer there was a lot of droving to be done. She once told me she'd taken over a hundred ewes and lambs eleven miles and then drove another ninety sheep back again. She was that proud of herself. No doubt she could have had her pick of lads but, sadly, the one she picked was on the wrong side.'

Mr Lassiter paused and reached for a piece of the cake, chewed on it slowly as if his false teeth were troubling him. He was approaching the hardest part of his expedition.

'There was a big prisoner of war camp up at Springhill. Near Chipping Campden, on the crossroads there. You can still see it. Full of Germans and Italians it was. Some of them were sent out to help on the land. Well, didn't Marion go and fall for a German.'

'What was his name?' Natasha knew what he was going to say seconds before he said it, and she was on the edge of her seat.

'Karl . . . Karl . . . Briegel. Yes, I'm pretty sure that was it. Only seventeen years old himself. Then the woman who came to bring our eggs said she'd seen Karl and Marion holding hands in the orchard. Well, that did it. I thought it was just in cartoons and comics that people went purple with rage but that's what my father did. Just sat at the table with a plate of peas and potatoes in front of him and went the colour of the plums in the pudding we were expecting to eat for afters but never did. In this day and age you might think he was overreacting, being too harsh. But he fought in the Great War and it was like a slap in the face, an insult, to think of his own daughter gallivanting with the Hun.' He broke off, shook his head sadly. 'He forbade Marion from seeing Karl again if she still wanted to call herself his daughter. Well, it was *her* we never saw again. I think she wrote to my mother a few times but that was it. Gone. Almost as if she'd died, except no one was allowed to mourn.'

'It's just like *West Side Story*,' Mrs Lassiter sighed.

Her husband shook his head. 'That has always been the mystery of it for me. Family was important to her. I never accepted that she'd turn her back on us all for someone she'd only known a few weeks. She was too level-headed. And more to the point, I heard a while afterwards that Karl was still around after Marion had flown the nest, and apparently was entangled with another pretty English girl.'

Natasha put the cake back on the plate, pushed it away from her. She had to ask. 'Do you know if Marion was ... all right?'

'All right?' Victor Lassiter looked at her and she saw understanding in his eyes. 'Oh, I see what you mean. She wrote to my mother a few times, never said where she was or what she was doing, just that she couldn't face coming home and wanted us to know she was well.'

Natasha gave a sigh of relief.

'Maybe the poor child couldn't handle the shame of it all,' Mrs Lassiter said sadly.

'Maybe. But it would have all blown over, eventually. There's that German prisoner of war who married a local girl, lives over Hailes way. Nobody holds any grudges against them now. On the contrary. They're quite a curiosity, local celebrities almost, symbols of buried hatchets. Marion could get in touch now, if the thing with Karl was all that was keeping her away. I'm sure there was a lot more to it. I was too young to take it all in really, no doubt a lot of it went over my head. I wish I'd asked my folks more about the whole episode while I still could. But it was like an unspoken family rule that her name should never be uttered. I suppose over the years I've tried to put her out of my mind. Easier that way, isn't it?'

So much for blood being thicker than water. It was a sad story but not unique. It was amazing how many families drifted apart.

'My poor mother never got over it,' Victor said.

'Didn't she go to see this Karl Briegel?' Mrs Lassiter was indignant.

Again Victor Lassiter shook his head. 'I've a feeling it had something to do with the man who owned the farm where they'd been working. My mother didn't want anything to do with him.

Maybe she blamed him for taking Marion's side, letting her fall for a German under his very nose, something like that. You know how gossip feeds off itself. I do remember her saying he was a bad man.'

'This was Fred Mulholland?' She must pass this on to Arnold before he went to see Muriel Mulholland.

'I wish she'd stayed at Mulholland's. She was trained there,' Victor said. 'She lived at the hostel at Mickleton then, before she went over to Shadwell.'

Natasha was on the edge of her seat again. So Marion *had* been at Shadwell. 'Not the man who got shot?' Mrs Lassiter said, her hand flown to her throat.

'What man?'

'Oh, Victor, you know? What was his name?'

'Charles Seagrove,' Natasha offered.

'That's right.' Mrs Lassiter turned to her. 'Victor's got no time for the news, says it's too depressing. Says he needs good news at his age.'

Karl Briegel and Marion were both at Shadwell. 'So you have no idea where your sister is now?'

'No. But like I say, I know for a fact she's not with Briegel. I dare say she's probably tied the knot with some other fellow, changed her name.'

'Couldn't you look her up in the marriage registers?' Mrs Lassiter said.

'If only it was that easy,' Natasha said. If it was, she'd have done it herself. 'Trouble is, unless Marion married locally, which seems unlikely, you'd not know which one was her. There'll be literally hundreds of Marion Lassiters listed since nineteen forty.'

'The peculiar thing was, Marion's friend went AWOL at about the same time,' Victor added. 'Got herself in the family way and ran off with the fellow, or so the tittle-tattles had us all believe.'

'Do you remember her name?' Natasha asked.

'Ella. Ella Pateman. Her mother was a music hall dancer. I remember because Ella was short for Cinderella, believe it or not.'

Sixteen

FROM BEHIND THE glass partition Natasha could just hear the shorn-headed young sergeant and another uniformed officer discussing the policing of a village fête in Stanway. She'd been waiting in the lobby of the police station to see Archie Fletcher for twenty minutes.

According to the sergeant, there was to be an animal carnival at Stanton, the children from the primary school parading through the village in costume. Traffic round the cricket ground would have to be diverted. Life went on. But not for Charles Seagrove. And not for Cinderella Pateman, Natasha had become more and more convinced as she'd driven to the station.

'Can I get you a coffee?' the sergeant eventually broke off to ask her.

'No thanks.' She was jumpy enough as it was, her heart still racing as fast as if she'd downed a dozen cups of espresso in half an hour.

The letter, in its envelope at the bottom of her bag, was ominous as a ticking bomb. She wished Archie Fletcher would hurry up and finish his telephone call.

'I'm sorry to keep you. Come through.' As he led her through a large room with a snooker table, she glanced towards a door which looked as if it led to the cells, where Richard Seagrove was being held. She wanted desperately to know what was happening. Had he been charged?

They came to a smaller office Sergeant Fletcher shared with three others, sickly green gloss walls and a line-up of sickly looking plants on the high window sills. His in-tray was reassuringly overflowing and there was a framed picture of his Labrador, Custard, pinned to a cork noticeboard on the wall behind his desk. A chewed ball lay at her feet and she appeared to be smiling for the camera, black lips pulled back in a grimace. For some silly reason, it made Natasha relax a little.

Archie pinched an extra swivel chair from the next desk.

She sat down opposite him and took the envelope out of the bag, handed it over. 'It came last week.'

He held it by diagonal corners with his fingertips, looked at it, then at her, kept his eyes on her face as he pulled out the letter, then lowered them to read it. Which was more than Natasha could do with his expression.

'I thought nothing of it until someone happened to mention a girl called Cinderella Pateman who went missing near here sixty years ago.'

'Someone happened to mention?'

'Someone I was interviewing. And there are bluebell woods at Shadwell.'

'Very true.'

'And on an old map, there's a place called Poacher's Dell, right in the middle of them.'

'Interesting.'

Dust motes danced in the ray of sunlight that slanted in through the small, high window. Down the hall a man was shouting. There was the smell of coffee and onion from someone's sandwiches. She noticed that Archie's desk calendar was behind by two months. Still April. Before she'd even heard of Charles Seagrove.

She couldn't stand the suspense. 'For someone who's used to catching stray pets you're being pretty cool about this, I must say.'

Fortunately Sergeant Fletcher chose not to be insulted. He reached into his drawer, slipped the letter into a plastic bag that looked like a freezer bag. He studied it again through the plastic, then pulled over a notepad. 'Have you any idea who might have sent it?'

'No.'

'This Cinderella who went missing, what do you know about her?'

'Cinderella Pateman, also called Ella. She was Marion Lassiter's schoolfriend.'

He stopped writing and leant back in his chair. 'How was Derbyshire?'

The change of subject threw her. It seemed an age since she was in Castleton. 'Eventful.'

'Stunning scenery. Have you ever been paragliding off Stanage?'

'Can't say I have. Stanage is one of the best places in the country to do it.'

'You're into dangerous sports, I take it?' The small talk was making her feel better, more normal, safe. She'd be quite happy to sit here all day. What better place than a police station was there to be if someone was sending you scary letters?

'Extreme pursuits. Like you said, I joined the police for a bit of action, and mostly I get to chase lost pets and Peeping Toms. Have to get my kicks elsewhere. You should give it a go.'

'I don't think I'm brave enough to throw myself off anything higher than the side of a swimming pool.'

He smiled at her with his lively brown eyes. 'Oh, I'm sure that's not true.' He studied her for a moment, then turned his attention back to the letter. 'Cinderella Pateman was just Marion Lassiter's friend you say, not a relative?' His puzzlement was exaggerated. She knew what he was getting at. Cinderella's name wasn't in Charles Seagrove's box, so how did she know who she was? When it came to interview skills she'd met her match in Archie Fletcher.

'I went to see Marion's brother. It was he who told me that Cinderella and his sister were friends.' She looked up at him through her eyelashes. 'No harm in that, is there, Officer?'

'Perhaps you'd be so kind as to share the rest of your discoveries.'

'Marion Lassiter had an affair with a German prisoner of war. It caused a scandal. Her father disowned her and her brother's not seen her for sixty years.'

She could almost see his brain computing. 'I can't see there's any solid connection to Charles Seagrove's murder. Have you mentioned this letter to anyone else? Richard Seagrove? His daughter?'

'No.' Her voice sounded weedy. It had never occurred to her that either of them might have sent it. But they seemed unlikely candidates to her. Rosa was way too young to have known Cinderella and Marion. Richard was – almost. 'I really believed Richard only wanted to find who murdered his father and put things right between his daughter and her boyfriend.'

'You'd get "too trusting" stamped on your appraisal, just like me.'

'I'd have thought you're exactly the type the police force, sorry *service*, needs.'

'Thanks.'

'You need to find Marion Lassiter and search Poacher's Dell.'

'Oh, do I now?' He leant forward on his desk, arms folded, an amused expression in his eyes.

In another life, Natasha might have liked to go into the police. It suited the way her brain worked, piecing together clues, following leads. She'd not even mind the mundane detail and paperwork. There was enough of that in genealogy. But genealogy was a safer way to be a detective, on the whole.

'I wasn't trying to tell you how to do your job.'

'That's exactly what you were doing, but I'm not a proud chap, I'll take friendly advice whenever it comes my way. As it happens, I'm inclined to agree about Poacher's Dell, *if*, and it's a big if, Cinderella Pateman turns out to be recorded as missing. A mysterious note naming a place and someone who disappeared? Logic would dictate that we might be led to a body. It's certainly worth following up, with or without it having any relevance to the Seagrove murder. Which I have to admit I'm more than a little sceptical about. That said, we are currently detaining someone who grew up with the Shadwell woods as his playground. But tell me, why is Marion Lassiter so important?'

'I'm not really sure, just—'

'A hunch? Female intuition? As it happens I'm a great believer in both those things. Let's try to find Cinderella first, shall we? I can't believe anyone would land their kid with a name like that.'

'I've heard worse,' Natasha said. Her job meant she had a constant source of unfortunate names to contribute. 'Jenny Taylor?'

'You're not serious?' Archie fell about laughing, until one of his colleagues put a stop to his fun by winking at him and then at Natasha.

'We'll be sure to run some checks on Cinderella,' Archie said.

'And if you find she's listed as missing?'

He took a deep breath. 'Then it doesn't look very good, I'm afraid. Does it?'

Once again she was left wondering precisely what he was getting at. Did he mean it wouldn't look good for Cinderella Pateman, for Richard Seagrove, or for herself?

Seventeen

USUALLY, WHEN SHE went for a swim to unwind at the pool in the Lygon Arms Hotel in Broadway, she completed a whole length holding her breath in the cool, blue, underwater silence, then came up for air and swam a few more lengths at an easy pace, alternating between slow crawl and breast stroke, flipping over on her back and letting the water cushion her head, gazing up at the sky through the glass roof.

This time she cut up and down the lanes like a shark going in for the kill. It was late, so she had the pool to herself, fortunately, and there was no one to get in her way, which made a nice change to the real world. Despite the chill of the water her face felt hot and sweat prickled her hair. Head down, arms slicing the water, legs like pistons, she reached the end, kicked and spun, filling and emptying her lungs, pushing through until the cramping pain in her muscles subsided, back and forth, back and forth, using the water almost as a punch bag.

After which, she was in a far better state to do something unethical.

There was a chance she might find Marion Lassiter through her school friends. Thank the Lord for FriendsReunited.com. And to the thoroughness of Charles Seagrove's research, which meant she knew the secondary school Marion Lassiter and Cinderella Pateman had attended.

It was the only option left. It was obvious that the police weren't going to attempt to find Marion, although she had hopes that Archie Fletcher would indeed search the missing person records for Cinderella. She was convinced that everything led back to Marion, just as surely as the lines on the family trees that Charles Seagrove had drawn up half a century ago.

Notebook to hand, she entered the name of Marion's school, Chipping Campden Grammar. Marion's name was not on the list, of course. That would have been too good to be true. But there were ten others from Marion's year group. She clicked on each one. Some had just registered their names, others had posted messages: 'Married with two kids. Living and working in Leeds. Get in touch if you remember me, please.' Natasha made notes of any that might be worth following up in the phone directories and then sent the same email through to every one: 'Is anyone still in contact with Marion Lassiter or Cinderella Pateman?'

The site now had sections for ex-neighbours and ex-work colleagues, plus a new genealogy section. In such ways the world wide web lived up to its name. Forging links, joining one group to another and to another, millions of gigantic invisible webs cast across the globe. The internet, symbol of the modern world, was proving a powerful tool in hooking people up to their pasts. Marion and Cinderella's friends would be elderly, but silver surfers were taking over the virtual world.

There was another site that was worth a try, War Friends. *My friend the enemy.* The internet gave you total anonymity, and Natasha had fewer qualms than some about using an alias. After all, her whole life had been lived under a false identity. Today she became a land girl who'd been based at the hostel in Mickleton, Gloucestershire and was looking for a girl she'd once known, called Marion. She asked about Cinderella there again too. Unlike Marion, her name hadn't been included in land army recollections at Winchcombe Museum, but if Marion and she were such close friends, they may have joined together.

School friends, war friends, work friends. There was probably a site somewhere devoted to reuniting you with your ex-boyfriends. Now there was an idea. Wasn't everyone curious about their exs? Wouldn't Marion Lassiter be interested to know what happened to Karl Briegel?

Job done, she sat back in her chair. She turned towards the

airline ticket, reached for it and picked it up, slowly turned it over and read the inscription, not as if she needed to read it to remember: *The rainbows over Niagra never fade.* She held the ticket for a moment then carefully set it back in its place. She just couldn't bring herself to put it away, let alone throw it away. It had become a familiar fixture on her desk, almost as much a part of her living room decoration as the framed engravings and oil paintings that hung on the walls. Tickets were always emotive objects, symbols of promise and hope. Just having it sitting in front of her made her feel closer to Canada, to Marcus. Right now, it seemed the only promise of escape she had.

What had entirely escaped her mind was that, in a rash moment, she'd agreed to be on hand at the History Open Day at Snowshill Manor the next morning, to talk to visitors about genealogy. When Arnold had asked her to do it, ages ago, she'd agreed, and probably jotted the date down somewhere, because it was far enough away not to have to worry about. It was surprising how quickly the future arrived.

She grabbed her mascara and business cards now, and opened the door.

Richard Seagrove was standing on the step.

She couldn't stop her sharp intake of breath, 'They told me you'd been—'

'They had to let me go after forty-eight hours. Not one shred of evidence.' He was holding a bouquet of purple irises tied with lilac ribbon and his skin was as waxy as the petals. He looked awful, his eyes bloodshot, hair unwashed, face unshaven. His lean physique, which before had made him look as if he'd come straight from the tennis court or a Wild West ranch, now made him appear haggard and drawn. He could barely stand, as if he'd not slept for the two days he'd been in the cells.

He handed her the flowers, brandished them almost, she thought, charm his chief weapon. 'I'm sorry for getting you into trouble. I had to come clean about the keys and the box.'

She waved her hand. 'I'm a big girl. I knew what I was doing.'

'I don't think I did. Aren't you going to invite me in?'

She hesitated. No evidence didn't mean the police no longer believed he'd murdered his father. What did she believe? She didn't know.

He walked into her hallway anyway, nearly tripping over the suitcase. 'Off somewhere again?'

Reluctantly, she led him through to the kitchen, fetched a clear glass vase shaped like a daffodil trumpet and filled it with water from the tap.

'I wasn't thinking straight,' he said. 'I thought it could help and instead it made things worse.'

'Well, it's water under the bridge.' Natasha made her voice bright. She trimmed the end of each stalk, cutting across it diagonally the way Ann had shown her, to help the flower to take up water, her actions soothing her. She arranged the irises in the vase. 'I've found nothing significant in the papers in any case.'

'I suppose they told you they'd found the keys to my father's gun cupboard in my jacket.'

She didn't turn round.

'I explained that I didn't know what that particular key was. It was attached to a bunch and all I was interested in was the study key.'

She didn't know whether to believe him or not. 'You told me before that the gun cupboard wasn't forced open. The police must have asked about keys to it right away?'

'They did. My mother told them there was a spare set but she couldn't find them.'

Natasha felt her heart hammering. 'You'd taken them so soon?'

'They were in Rosa's room.'

Natasha put the last flower into the water, turned slowly to face him.

'It looks bad for her, I know. But she'd only taken them because she wanted to get a look at the Hellier files you'd given to my father.'

'She didn't need to do that,' Natasha whispered, her voice hoarse. 'I offered her a copy at the party.'

Richard shrugged. 'She wouldn't want to let you think you were doing her a favour.' He paused. 'I'm not in the clear yet,' he said.

'Sergeant Fletcher made that very plain. They need to solve this soon and I don't think they are getting very far. They'll not let go of their suspicions, and who knows what they'll be able to pin on me? I need your support more than ever.'

Knowing the police suspected Richard of murder should have made her refuse, right there and then, to have anything more to do with him.

'The memorial service tomorrow is the vicar's idea,' Richard was saying. 'He thought it might be good for my mother. Give her some sort of closure, as our Atlantic cousins would say. A proper funeral would be much better of course, but they might not be able to release his body for weeks yet.'

One mention of Charles Seagrove's corpse and the horror returned. She knew now what it was to see red. Often all she could see was red blood on red bricks.

'Surely there's only so much examination they can do?'

'They may keep him until they catch whoever did it. Apparently when someone is accused of murder they have a right to demand that the victim is re-examined.' He looked bewildered then, as though he'd woken up and found himself in someone else's life, speaking lines that were not his own.

Natasha set the vase in the centre of the table, concentrating on the bright colour of the petals. 'Purple's my favourite colour.'

'I thought it might be,' he said kindly. 'You were wearing a purple dress at the party.'

She remembered her own reaction to Archie Fletcher's news. It hadn't actually come as a great surprise that Richard had been arrested, she thought now. What did that say? More proof that she never trusted anyone? Or that she had learnt enough about the human condition to know that people were capable of anything. That given the right motives, even the kindest most charming people could be driven to kill. Or that killers could appear just as charming as anyone else. She cleared her throat. 'What time's the service?'

'Eleven.'

'I'll be there.'

'I'd appreciate that.' Then, as though worried he'd sounded too personal, 'Rosa and my mother too.'

That, she doubted very much.

Once he'd gone she realized he had made no mention of a police search of Shadwell woods. On the one hand she was hugely relieved and on the other she was fuming. Didn't the police take her seriously?

'I amaze myself,' Arnold said as they sat side by side behind a little table in a room near the top of the house, which was filled with old penny-farthing bicycles and spinning wheels. 'I thought my memory was going. By suppertime these days, I usually haven't the faintest idea what I ate for breakfast. Mind you, I have no problem remembering all the words to "She Moves Through the Fair". It was Eve's favourite song. She used to sing it to James when he was a baby, to get him to go to sleep.'

Arnold's wife died of breast cancer when she was forty-three. He hardly ever spoke of her. Except once, just after Kieran was born, when he'd said he was glad James had had a son, because what happened to Eve couldn't happen to either of them. Breast cancer could be genetic. Was that the reason Charles Seagrove had asked for medical records? Was John Hellier's family afflicted with a hereditary medical condition? It would be hard to blame him for wanting to protect his family from future pain. Yet such interventionist measures were alarming. It was like playing God. Natasha couldn't work out where she stood at all. Besides, to her untrained eye, the death certificates and medical reports in the Hellier family tree, and in Marion Lassiter's, seemed to give the families a clean bill of health. Old age had killed the majority of them.

Arnold slapped a small notebook on the table. 'Anyway. That's why I wrote it all down.'

'What?' Natasha looked at him, thinking for a moment that he was handing her song lyrics.

'I got the bus and took myself off to see Mulholland's daughter. It's all there. Everything she told me. You're in for a few surprises, I shouldn't wonder.'

She grimaced. 'I'm not sure how many more surprises I can take.'

There'd been a steady trickle of interest at their desk and now a woman with spectacles hanging on a chain around her neck came to tell Arnold that her father remembered Vita Sackville-West visiting Snowshill in the days of Charles Paget Wade.

Once she'd gone, Arnold turned back to Natasha. 'It turns out Marion Lassiter only worked at Mulholland's market garden for about a month. She never lived there either. She stayed up at the land army hostel in Mickleton and Mr Mulholland called for her each morning in his cart, brought her back each night after she'd helped dig up potatoes or plant lettuces.' So much she knew already, but she let him carry on. 'According to Muriel Mulholland, Charles Seagrove got the hots for Marion.' He paused to let that sink in. 'He drove up to the Mickleton hostel to collect a couple of girls to help with lambing and what not. When he first laid eyes on Marion no one else would do, so Muriel says. He insisted on having her instead of the girl he'd been allocated. Mulholland arrived to pick Marion up, so he was party to all the goings on. He was an easy-going sort of chap, told Charles if he was that particular it was no great shakes to him. He'd have the girl who was allocated to Shadwell. Not half so pretty but greener fingers apparently, so everyone was happy.'

'Wait a minute—'

'Going too fast for you, am I?' Arnold chuckled. 'The quick and the dead, eh? Well, there's plenty more. Marion didn't come back to the hostel after that. Seagrove said he needed help with the lambing at all hours so she'd have to live up at Shadwell Manor Farm. See, I didn't need records this time, let alone any of your fancy technology. Just a packet of bourbon creams and a few hours to chat.'

Eighteen

IT WASN'T THE day for a memorial service. Cloudless skies, bright sunshine, trees in thick leaf, all too vibrant and cheerful, too full of colour and of life. Funeral scenes in movies never looked like this. No pathetic fallacy here. Nature wasn't mirroring sentiment, more mocking it.

In the absence of a grave, the wreaths and bouquets had been laid by the church door. In their cellophane wrappings, the flowers were already starting to wither and wilt.

Natasha had lived in Snowshill long enough to have witnessed the funerals of a few village elders. They were mini state occasions, talked about in the pub before and after, obituaries posted in the parish newsletter, the roads outside the church lined with cars, the whole place coming to a standstill while the service took place.

But there were only three cars parked outside Shadwell's Church of St Peter, a small Norman chapel with a square tower around which the swifts were wheeling in great arcs. As at the garden party, it was impossible not to notice how few old faces were waiting to file into the church for Charles Seagrove's memorial. How few faces full stop. No more than a dozen. Only a tiny fraction of those who had happily drunk his Champagne now came to fill the box pews to pay their respects and say goodbye. Only Basil Wilkinson, a sheep farmer from Stanton, was there to represent the old brigade. There was a wizened man in a wheelchair, pushed by someone who could have either been a nurse or his daughter. Natasha didn't recognize either of them.

Maybe it was the nature of Charles Seagrove's death that kept people away. As if violence and tragedy were contagious diseases, and getting yourself shot was a disgrace.

Natasha's black linen skirt soaked up the heat, and the faces of the other mourners were equally flushed above their stiff white collars and black ties.

Reverend Clarkson was in attendance at the church door, a rotund man who looked more like an opera singer than a vicar in his flowing robes. His greeting to Natasha was inappropriately cheerful. She'd met him a few times, professionally, in his capacity as keeper of the parish registers for this part of Gloucestershire. Funerals were just another part of his daily job. 'In sure and certain hope of the resurrection,' would pass his lips nearly as often as a waiter might say, 'May I take your order, please?'

Natasha slid into a pew next to Archie. She was longing to ask him how things were progressing with Cinderella, if a search of the Shadwell woods was imminent, how he felt about releasing Richard Seagrove, but this wasn't exactly the right time to do it.

As she sat down, Archie leant towards her and whispered, 'I hate these things.'

'You're not supposed to enjoy them.'

They stopped talking. Rosa, Richard and his mother had begun to make a slow procession up the aisle to the front. Rosa was wearing a plain white dress with a long flowing skirt, like a bride walking towards the altar on the arm of her father. Her outfit was raising a few scornful eyebrows but Natasha wanted to shout at them all to leave her alone. This was her grandfather's funeral. She'd loved him more than any of them, so let her wear what she liked.

Stella Seagrove was gripping Richard's right arm as if she couldn't support herself. It had never occurred to Natasha that emotional anguish could show in a person's face the same way as physical pain. Even Stella's black hat with its wide brim and small veil couldn't hide the bloodless pallor of her cheeks and lines of pain which had etched themselves around her eyes. It was cooler in the church though still close and airless, but Stella Seagrove didn't look even warm. As she took her place beside Richard and Rosa, she hugged her arms around herself.

From their brief interaction at the garden party and the evident friction between them, Natasha was surprised at the depth of Stella's despair. But then, elderly couples were often like that, bickering like children, constantly criticizing, but deeply devoted and dependent, sometimes if only through habit.

The organ was playing a stirring classical piece Natasha recognized but couldn't put a name to. It was peculiar, this funeral with no coffin, no grave, no dead body. Almost as if Charles Seagrove wasn't really dead at all.

Everyone rose to sing 'The Lord's My Shepherd' and then Reverend Clarkson spoke a few words of tribute to Charles Seagrove, another shepherd. It was obvious the Reverend didn't know him at all, that he'd been primed by Richard. But he mentioned a deep love for his family and his farm, the two things it was obvious he had cared about most. The man in the wheelchair was introduced as Dr Jarratt, who'd known Seagrove from his Kent days. He was taken up to the front to read from chapter fifteen of I Corinthians: 'The last enemy that shall be destroyed is death.' She wondered then what kind of doctor Dr Jarratt was. Might he have provided Charles Seagrove with access to medical files?

Then Rosa went up to the lectern. Her voice clear and strong as a bell, she read a verse from Wordsworth's 'The Prelude': 'There is /one great society alone on earth, / The noble Living, and the noble Dead.' Unusual to hear, at a Christian burial, the words of a pantheist, who believed in the presence of spirits in stones and trees and mountains.

Richard's was the final reading, another irregular choice, a passage from *Chronicle of Ancient Sunlight* by Henry Williamson, a writer, he informed them, who'd been altered for ever by his experience of the Christmas Truce. Richard had washed and shaved since last she'd seen him but his voice sounded more exhausted, the reading a strain, as if, underneath, he'd still not even begun to recover from the murder of his father or his stay in the police cell.

When the organ started playing 'Silent Night' she felt tears prick her eyes. It was surreal, singing a Christmas carol with the bright summer sunshine streaming in through the stained glass, but it was appropriate, considering what that carol had meant to Charles Seagrove and his father.

Of course he hadn't been able to predict or choose in which season he was going to die but he'd seen to everything else with the greatest precision. He was not one to leave it to those left behind to see he got a decent send-off. Like a member of the royal family, he had, so Richard told Natasha afterwards, left detailed instructions about exactly who was to be invited, the readings and the music he wanted to be played.

Richard had carried out his father's last wishes as best he could but he was clearly disappointed at the poor turnout. He thanked Natasha for coming, said he was grateful to her for her support. For making up the numbers, he implied. Eighty-five years on this earth and only a dozen people care when you finally leave it.

'My father drafted the list of all the people he wanted to be invited years ago,' Richard explained. 'Colleagues from his City days, other farmers he'd met through the Union. But he was a bit of a recluse in his old age, and he'd not been in touch with most of them for thirty years or more. A few have sent cards or flowers but you can't blame them for not coming all this way. Some of them have moved on and no doubt there's a whole bunch who aren't even with us any more.'

'That can be the downside of living a long time,' Natasha said gently. 'How's your mother bearing up?'

Not at all well by the look of her. Stella was standing by a tabletop tomb, talking to the doctor in the wheelchair, her arms still crossed in front of her. She seemed to sense they were talking about her and looked over. Natasha smiled but Stella looked right through her, as if she wasn't there.

'She's a strong person,' Richard said. 'But she'd been married to my father for over sixty years. I wonder if I've done the right thing, going ahead with today, if I haven't made it harder for her. We're going to have to do this all over again when the police eventually let us have his body.' He cast his eyes over the graves. 'My father spent a fortune on a good plot, south-facing, beneath one of the yew trees.' He indicated the spot, just rough grass and wild flowers for now. 'I hope he can be left in peace there soon.'

It was likely that in a Kent churchyard, where, according to the newspaper obituary, Charles Seagrove had been born, there'd be a plot in which generations of his ancestors were interred. With an eye to assisting future historians, a good many genealogists she knew had left instructions to be taken back home and buried with their forebears. Instead of which Charles Seagrove had chosen, and paid dearly, for a prominent plot in this churchyard. He must have booked his space long ago, while he was still a young man, for the graveyard, as with so many village burial grounds, had been full for several years. The distinguishing mark between a true born-and-bred local or an incomer was whether or not you had a plot in the churchyard, or had to find a last resting place in the cemetery, or else be burned and scattered on the winds.

Charles Seagrove had taken care to ensure he had his traditional place amongst the great and the good of Shadwell. No doubt he had planned a fine oak coffin, an elaborate headstone and fittingly grand inscription. But instead of his coffin laying atop his relations, he would be buried as he had lived for the later years of his life, alone.

The Seagroves' BMW had drawn up outside the lychgate.

Richard took his mother's right arm. Rosa moved to the other side of her grandmother. In her white dress and her pale hair, she was like an apparition amidst the black-clad mourners. As they started to walk she made to slip her arm through Stella's.

Stella flinched, as if her emotions were so raw she could feel them in her skin and bone, as if Rosa's touch burned her.

Rosa looked distraught. She stood, riveted to the spot, streaks of black mascara running down her face, while Richard led his mother away.

Nineteen

THE TELEPHONE WOKE Natasha from fitful sleep two mornings later.

'It's me.' Her sister, Abby, sounded tearful. 'I've been trying to get you for days.'

'Did you leave a message?'

'No.'

Natasha rubbed her eyes. 'Well then, how was I supposed to know—'

'What's going on with Mum and Dad?'

'How do you mean?'

'They're not talking. Do you know what's happened?'

'Not really.' The lie was heavy as lead on Natasha's heart. 'Look, why don't you come up sometime next week after work? You could stay over and get the train back to London next morning.'

'How about Wednesday?'

'Fine.' She wanted to see Abby but dreaded the conversation.

At the Snowshill Arms that lunchtime, Heidi was keeping company with the regulars, the Dynamic Domino Duo and Silent Gerald. In front of her on the table by the fireplace was one bowl of salad and another of chips.

'Saint and sinner all in one, that's me,' she said when she spied Natasha.

Natasha sat down and Heidi shoved the chips in her direction. She dipped one in some ketchup and bit it, forced it down her tight throat. She realized she'd hardly eaten all day. It was a worrying fact that you could live longer without food than you could without sleep.

'What have you been up to anyway?'

Natasha waved her hand, shooing everything away. 'Talk about something nice.'

'Hmmm. Let me see now. Crème brûlé to follow the chips?'

Heidi persuaded her to forsake vodka and join her with the Jack Daniels. Which took her right back to her rock and roll days and her first swig of whisky from Steven's hip flask. She was about twelve years old and they were on a dig in France. 'Don't tell your mother,' he'd warned as he'd slipped her the flask. She'd loved the fire in her throat, loved even more the shared conspiracy with her father. She no longer loved that conspiracy. Too wrapped up in the Helliers and the Seagroves, she hadn't given her own family a moment's thought for days.

Arnold arrived as Natasha was fiddling with the spoon, cracking the burnt, sugary crust of the brûlé. He was in his waistcoat, fresh from his morning shift at Snowshill Manor. 'We had a horde of school kiddies,' he grinned. 'Couldn't get enough of the stories about whether or not Charles Paget Wade was a bonafide vampire.'

'I thought you were supposed to stick to the truth, not recycle old rumours.'

'What is it they say? Repeat a rumour long enough and it becomes the truth.'

He delved in his pocket and pulled out a photocopied newspaper article, not unlike the one Toby had given to her about Alice Hellier. 'I was going to push this through your letterbox on my way back. Been putting my historical advantage to good use again.'

Arnold's enthusiasm was heartening and amusing. 'For someone who, until about a year ago, thought genealogy was the study of little spirits that come popping up when you rub bottles, you're a bit keen, aren't you?' Natasha read the headline out of the corner of her eye: 'WINDOWS SMASHED AT SHADWELL'.

It was enough to guarantee she read the rest with both eyes fully focused.

Police were called out last night when bricks were thrown through the windows at Shadwell Manor Farm. No one was injured. It is likely the incident relates to the considerable bad feeling surrounding the house's owner, Charles Seagrove.

The article was dated January 1945.

There was a photo of the front of the house, windows still intact. The woods were not so tall back then, not so well-established.

'What bad feeling?'

Heidi peered at the date. 'I suppose back in the forties everything was more gentlemanly, even the media.' She arched her beautifully plucked eyebrow at Arnold. 'The *Gloucester Journal* wouldn't want to print pure speculation and rumour.'

'No smoke without fire though,' Arnold said. 'Do you want me to find out what this particular blaze might have been?'

'Why not?' Natasha said.

Arnold rubbed his hands with glee. 'Marvellous. I'm getting a proper taste for this.'

When she checked her emails later, an unfamiliar name popped into her inbox, an Edith Connolly.

I was at school with Cinderella Pateman. I haven't kept in touch with her, I'm afraid, but a few years ago my mother, who was still living near Cutsdean at the time, did bump into a chap who said he was related to Cinderella. Noah Hearn his name was. He might still be living locally.
Edith

She focused on the maple leaf while waiting for the connection to the online directory. She wasn't quick enough to stop her brain adding up the days. It was 24 June. Only fifteen days to go, the ticket seemed to whisper. Fifteen days and you could be thousands of miles away from all this. Except for two small problems. One: Cinderella Pateman entangled her with Shadwell even further. The police would be even less keen on her leaving the country if a body was found at Poacher's Dell. Two: She'd told Marcus she wasn't coming. He'd told her it was the last time, he wasn't going to bother with her any more. She'd blown it. She wanted to see him. She didn't want to see him.

Back in the real world, she found that there weren't too many Hearns living in the Cutsdean area, just one with the initial 'N'. She dialled, listened to the universal message, 'the person you are calling knows you are waiting'. She always thought it sounded vaguely threatening, like an anonymous note. I'm watching. I know who you are. Cinderella is in the Bluebell Woods at Poacher's Dell. She listened to the refrain begin its second repetition. It was cut off in mid-sentence.

'Hello.' The voice was male and promisingly middle-aged, with a pronounced Gloucestershire accent.

'Noah Hearn?'

'Who wants to know?'

She ran through her introductory patter, this time finished off with, 'I wondered if you are related to a girl called Cinderella Pateman.'

Again, a hesitancy before answering, as if it was an international call. 'Cinderella, you say? Is this some kind of joke?'

She'd had a similar reaction when she'd first read the note, but the hesitation before Mr Hearn had spoken made her wonder if he knew more than he was letting on.

'Does the name Marion Lassiter mean anything to you?'

The time lag of silence was even longer, as if Hearn was drifting even further away.

'How about Charles Seagrove?'

That seemed to hook him. 'Are you from the police?'

She didn't blame him for being cagey. Many people were when a stranger called them out of the blue to ask questions about their family. But Hearn was cagier than most.

'I'm a genealogist, Mr Hearn.'

'I don't have time to talk to you.'

'But you'd have time to talk to the police?' As if they'd be remotely interested in this hare-brained line of inquiry.

Silence. 'Please, Mr Hearn, I—'

Like a family with no male heirs, the line was dead.

Twenty

SERGEANT FLETCHER KNOCKED on his inspector's door at half past ten the following morning, found his boss examining a model of an aircraft carrier he kept on permanent display on his filing cabinet. Resisting any quips about naval-gazing, since his boss's beer-belly was the butt of too many jokes already, Archie walked straight in and came straight out with it, reading from the file he'd called up from the archives.

'Sir, Cinderella Pateman's father reported her missing in October nineteen forty-five. Despite extensive searches, over several months at first and then years, she's never been found. The file went cold and was officially closed five decades ago, case never solved. Cinderella ceases to exist after nineteen forty-five. No bank account, no employment records, no emigration papers, no nothing.'

'Double negative, Sergeant. No nothing means there is something. Are you absolutely sure there is? I'd hate you to be wasting your and everyone else's time. We've got enough on our hands trying to find who murdered Charles Seagrove and I'm not at all convinced this is going to help one jot.'

'Neither am I, sir. Having said that, the fact that Charles Seagrove was murdered a few days after someone who was working for him was sent the letter about Cinderella *does* seem to point to some connection. But, with all due respect, enough questions have been raised in my mind to make me think we should be looking for Cinderella in any case. A girl was reported missing and now we have a note which apparently tells us where to look for her. And she certainly isn't going to be in those woods having a picnic. She may be lying there dead, sir, and I don't need to remind you that there's no statute of limitations on murder. If she is where I suspect she might be, we have two killers at large and, technically at least, just because one killing is more recent than the other it doesn't make it any less important, especially given that we have nothing to suggest Charles Seagrove's murderer is a risk to anyone else's safety. Of course, there is the issue of acting quickly before a trail goes cold, so I agree that to some degree the Seagrove case must take precedence. But the murder team have pretty much taken over. I can follow this up without it encroaching on the work I'm doing on that investigation.'

Butterworth gave a slow nod of acquiescence. 'So you reckon poor Cinders never got to go to the ball.'

Archie tried not to groan. Butterworth's hatred of incorrect grammar was equalled by his love of tabloid word play. The newspapers were going to have a field day, if, or when, they announced they'd found this girl's body.

'Here's the really interesting thing,' he pressed on. 'Guess who was originally questioned about her disappearance?'

'The fairy godmother, the handsome prince? No, of course, it'd have to be the ugly sisters.' Butterworth roared with laughter. He wasn't taking this seriously. The only thing the inspector was taking seriously at the moment was his forthcoming reincarnation as a fifty-something beach bum. He'd handed in his notice and was emigrating to Australia at the end of the month. He'd been demob happy for weeks. He probably already had his wetsuit on beneath his navy polyester one. For Butterworth, Charles Seagrove's murder couldn't have come at a worse time, disrupting his plans to cruise through his last weeks before he could pretend to surf on Bondi.

'Charles Seagrove was one of the first who was asked to give a statement when Cinderella's father reported her missing,' Archie said, wondering why he was bothering. 'According to him, Cinderella came to see her friend Marion Lassiter and then left Shadwell. He knew not where. But our predecessors seemed to think it was worth asking again. He was questioned twice.'

'Marion, you say? The girl whose family history was in the box that rather foxy young genealogist waltzed off with.'

Butterworth hadn't totally zoned out then. 'That's right, sir.'

'Then if you are determined to follow this through I suggest you get to it.'

'I'll do my best, but I'm not a historian.'

'Ah, but you know a girl who is, now don't you, son?'

When Archie called Natasha ten minutes later, all he had to say was, 'I thought you should know, we're following the instructions in the letter.'

He didn't have to elaborate. 'I understand.'

Finally, they were looking for Cinderella Pateman in the bluebell woods that surrounded Shadwell Manor Farm.

'We could use your help actually.'

'You *are* joking?'

'Of course we don't want you to assist us with the actual search. We'd just like you to carry on with your own kind of digging, investigating that family tree you found in Charles Seagrove's study. There may be a link.'

'Oh, *found* is it now? Not stealing evidence from a crime scene any more?'

'Just let me know if there's anything relevant, will you?'

She put down the phone and stared into space. She should have told Archie that Richard was already paying her to continue her research. The cheques had been arriving like clockwork, and at the same generous rate that Charles Seagrove had offered. Conflict of interest wasn't usually a problem she encountered in her profession. But working for the police and a suspect in a murder investigation at the same time . . . letting Richard Seagrove pay her to find information she might also hand over to the murder inquiry team . . . not so much a conflict as an all-out war. Question was, if push came to shove, whose side would she be on?

She reminded herself that the police were on Richard's side too, weren't they?

If you lost enough sleep you reached a state where flashes of dreams broke through into your waking consciousness, like hallucinations, the lucid dreams of opium smokers. Maybe that was what was happening to her, explained the image that lurked like a shadow at the back of her mind, a nightmare of a forest haunted by skeletons.

She wandered about the house in a kind of paralysis, picking things up and then putting them down, making a cheese sandwich and only taking one bite. When she was about to pour milk into the washing machine ball instead of a coffee mug she knew she had to get out before she did some serious damage.

The weather had changed overnight, the sky almost without colour, a dense, dull opacity that made the sunshine seem like another kind of dream. But it was still humid, the unbroken clouds a blanket that trapped the heat.

Driving made her feel even worse. Each time she blinked it was harder to open her eyes. There was a vice clamping her head, an ache in her joints as if her body was fighting off a virus. She turned on the radio but she couldn't pick up a signal, just the hiss of white noise. She found herself taking the turning for Shadwell Manor Farm, steering the Alpine up the drive through the woods. Woods and forests, enchanted places, land of fairy-tales. But the Cinderella who might be buried beneath the trees came straight out of a horror story.

There was blue tape strung between the tree trunks like party ribbons. White figures flitting about in the shadow, like the gauzy white maidens of *Giselle*, dancing the Dance of Death. But this was no company of ghosts. Natasha didn't need anyone to explain the procedure. When a skeleton was unearthed on archaeological digs, similar cross-contamination suits were worn, a barrier between this world and the next, to make sure the dead didn't infect the living or the living pollute the dead. Two marked police cars were parked up by the edge of the grass, their tyre marks still fresh, cutting across the immaculate lawn where the string quartet had once played. Shadwell looked utterly different to how it had then, but with its forest and shady drive, narrow gables and mullions, it wore its sinister mantle well, as if it was born to it. The perfect place to hide a body.

She hadn't expected Rosa Seagrove to have come back from Cirencester for the unveiling but there was a blue Golf parked next to Richard's green Peugeot in the drive. And there she was, watching the proceedings, standing sentinel-still outside the front door of the house. It gave Natasha the creepiest sense of déjà vu. She put it down to the fact that she'd seen Rosa standing in exactly the same position at the garden party, just before she'd argued with her grandfather.

Rosa's recent traumas hadn't made her abandon interest in her appearance, in fact she seemed to have paid her make-up and outfit more attention that she had at the party. She was wearing a pale-blue knitted cardigan and well-pressed white jeans, her silver hair glossily combed around her face and her lips painted a deep matt red. Unusually for someone suffering stress, she seemed to have put on a little weight, but it suited her, softened her.

That the softness was only skin deep was soon clear. She turned imperiously to Natasha as she climbed out of the car, pretending she'd only just noticed her. 'Why can't you leave us alone?'

'I wish I could.' She looked over at Richard who was walking towards his daughter, as if to present a united front. 'I'm—'

'Sorry?' he finished for her. 'For sending them here? It's too late for that.' He was dressed in navy tracksuit bottoms and faded blue sweatshirt as last time she'd seen him, and he was slightly breathless as if he'd only just stopped running. 'You didn't need to come, too.'

'Why have you?' Rosa spoke in the same chilly monotone.

Natasha glanced at Richard as she worked out how to answer. 'None of this seems real. But normal life doesn't seem real either? If you know what I mean?' She sounded strange, even to her own ears, spaced out, trippy, as if she was drunk or on drugs.

'I know exactly what you mean.' His smile was suddenly sincere and almost relieved, as if in her space-cadet speak she'd stumbled upon words that eased the tension, expressed how he too was feeling. 'I can't bear to watch but I can't bear not to watch,' he added.

She felt truly sorry for him then. Maybe the belligerence he sometimes displayed did merely come from extreme anxiety.

'How long have they been here?'

'About an hour.' He took a deep breath. 'In the normal scheme of things, so Inspector Butterworth told me,' he lifted his fingers and drew ironical quotation marks in the air, 'they wouldn't necessarily be giving this such high priority, directing so much of their effort and resources towards a person who'd been missing for sixty years. It's the timing that's tipped it. The fact that my father was murdered a few days after you got that letter. It could be significant, he says. Why do police people all talk in such a stilted way? Why can't they talk like the rest of us? I wish you'd told me about the letter first' he added, but didn't wait for her response. 'They haven't found anything yet, and these things can take time, the inspector says.' Then he announced that he was making a pot of tea if anyone was interested.

He led the way through the hall, into a narrow, rough-plastered back corridor and then to the cavernous kitchen, complete with aged cream Aga, beside which Stella Seagrove was standing, stirring something on the hob, as glamorous as always, her black dress set off with more of the theatrically colourful scarves and dangling earrings she'd worn at the garden party.

She looked through Natasha just as she had at the memorial, carried on with what she was doing, concentrating on moving the wooden spoon in slow, even circles around the iron saucepan. She looked fragile, was holding her body stiffly as if she might crumble to dust if she let herself relax for an instant. Her shoulders were slightly stooped in a way that Natasha hadn't noticed at the garden party or even at the church.

Even under the current clouds, real and metaphorical, the ambience in the kitchen was entirely different from Charles Seagrove's study, as comfortable, bright and homely as his domain had been austere, with pretty flowered china and dried herbs and flowers. An enormous Welsh dresser took up one wall and a long farmhouse table stood in the middle of the room. There were the remains of breakfast things, honey and jam, a big bowl of fruit.

A glossy King Charles Spaniel was curled up on a settle,

gnawing a bone. She had lifted her head expectantly at the sound of feet, and then let it fall back onto her paws, her black eyes turned mournfully up to Richard.

'She's pining for my father,' he explained. 'Keeps hoping he'll walk through the door. I keep thinking he will too.'

'He had such a strong personality,' Natasha said, half to herself and sounding more spacey than ever. 'Maybe she can sense him still.'

Stella Seagrove stopped stirring. Natasha couldn't see her face but in her experience such notions were almost always a consolation for the bereaved.

'Do you honestly believe that?' Richard Seagrove asked.

'One way or another.' She said it carefully, forcing herself to connect, to think before she spoke. 'An essence, maybe.'

Stella picked up a jug and poured in some milk, put the jug down and stirred again, stopped, sprinkled in grated cheese. Her actions seemed awkward, as if she were finding everything an effort.

Natasha bent down to stroke the dog who rolled over to have her tummy tickled.

'She's expecting in six weeks,' Richard said. 'Her first little brood. It took my father ages to find her a lover.'

He met Natasha's eyes when she looked up, the last word still echoing almost suggestively. Stella stopped stirring again.

Animals didn't have lovers. They had mates. Perhaps Richard wasn't being saucy in front of his mother. He was just thinking aloud. Of how his father had selected a partner for his dog, no doubt verifying its pedigree, in the same way he had been checking out his granddaughter's future husband, her lover, before he died. Richard wasn't stupid. If Natasha had worked that much out, then there was a strong chance he had too. Did it make Richard wonder if Charles had done the same thing with his ex-wife? Had he? How would all that make Richard feel about his father? In his eyes she saw only a deep dismay.

'Could I use the bathroom?' Not a particularly original exit strategy but the best she could think of.

'Up the stairs and along the corridor on the right,' Stella said faintly.

At a better moment, she would have admired the carved elm staircase which must have been an original feature of the seventeenth-century house. The hallway led off in both directions, beautiful elm floorboards as dark and shiny as conkers and as wide as a motorway. On one side of the corridor were closed doors and on the other, low window seats looking out onto the gardens and the wood. The Seagroves were clearly fresh air fiends. All the windows were open and the cooler air funnelling through them prickled Natasha's skin. There was a wind getting up now, the clouds scudding across the sky like a cheap backdrop scene from an old movie, where the train carriage and its passengers are still and the world moves past outside.

She opened one door onto the most beautiful carved four-poster bed. Hung with blue and red tapestry, it was made for Sleeping Beauty, for Cinderella and her handsome prince. The other furnishings in the room, a carved trunk and washstand, were equally lovely and obviously valuable.

She tried the next door, making an excuse to herself. It was OK. She was looking for a bathroom, not just being nosy. An ornately carved Louis XIV bed in this room, which was clearly occupied. The linen sheets were rumpled, a Paisley toilet bag standing on a chest of drawers, a comb and shower gel standing next to it. Men's things. Richard's room.

Waves of drowsiness made her feel as if she were sleepwalking. When she used to do it as a child, it was in houses just like this that she often dreamed she was wandering. Houses with rooms in which you might find a big, old wardrobe that led to Narnia, and outside a Secret Garden . . . There *was* a secret garden here, with a statue of a mother and a baby. Stella and Amelia. She must be so exhausted that snatches of dreams were breaking through again. She shut her eyes tight, opened them again, pinched herself. But still she could hear it. Faint and far away but unmistakable. *The sound of a baby crying.*

She tried to work out where it was coming from, if not just from inside her own head. She knew only too well that old houses played tricks with noises, as they did with drafts and heat. Thick walls insulated but gaps in floorboards and around warped doors and weathered window frames could make voices upstairs sound as if they were coming from the next room, or from just outside the door.

She walked back to the stairs and still she could hear it, slightly closer now, if anything, high-pitched and insistent, distressed. She waited for a moment to see if it stopped, if someone picked the baby up, if the dream was going to end. But it carried on. She told herself that even if it was a real baby it was no concern of hers. The Seagroves hadn't told her they had houseguests but why should they? Something about the cries of a baby though, more impossible to ignore than a ringing phone. The sound seemed to trigger some primeval maternal instinct. Or maybe it was some other more recent memory it rekindled. What it felt like to be abandoned. To be left behind, at three days old, in a hospital ward with strangers. Dream or no dream, she wanted only to make the crying stop, to comfort and console. She couldn't walk away.

She crossed the landing to the other side of the stairs, walked slowly along the corridor. She was sure now, the sound was coming from somewhere above her. There was a narrow, winding staircase at this end of the corridor. She put her foot on the first creaking stair. The crying instantly ceased.

She hesitated, turned back, put her foot on the next step, carried on climbing. At the top of the stairs was a low and narrow door. She knocked. No reply. She turned the brass knob.

'Hello?' No answer. She pushed the door, let it swing open on creaking hinges.

A long attic room with sloping eaves and rafters. Completely empty. Except for three, white-painted wooden cots lined up along the back wall. Next to them were three old-fashioned carriage prams. Natasha stared at them, gripped in a force field of panic that sizzled over her skin like static. The windows were all shut up here, dust and cobwebs sealing the panes, the corpses of bluebottles littering the floor beneath them, as if the flies had died trying to escape. No way out except for the way she'd just come.

She backed away, banging the door shut. She stared at it for a moment, then turned; adrenaline kicked in and she took the steps two at a time.

She would have knocked Stella Seagrove flying if the old woman had not been clutching the banister as if she needed to drag herself up.

'Are you all right?' Stella inquired, her blue eyes suddenly searching and sharp.

Natasha nodded, her lips too tight to speak.

'My mother was feeling faint,' Richard said, leaning against the range. Rosa had taken over stirring the cheese sauce. 'I've sent her upstairs to lie down.' He closed his eyes and pinched the bridge of his nose. 'I don't know how much more of this we can all take.'

Rosa put her hand over his. Her cheeks were flushed from the heat of the hot plate and the steam had kinked the soft strands of hair around her face. Her shell-blue cashmere twinset – turtle-necked top and cardigan – was so old-fashioned it was now the height of fashion again, as was the Aga where she stirred the sauce in steady circles. Maybe that's what did it. Other ways that history goes in circles, Natasha was thinking. But when Rosa turned, there was something suddenly familiar about her. Natasha stared at her, reaching for the connection. Then it came.

Twenty-One

NATASHA STUCK A coin in the balding front tyre, then decided she couldn't risk getting more entangled with the police. She drove only as far as the station and caught the train to Oxford.

She hit throngs of Monday-morning shoppers as she walked towards the WestGate Centre which housed Oxfordshire's local studies archive, made her way through the turnstile and up the two flights of stairs. The archive was relatively quiet, a couple of researchers leafing through old photographs of local scenes, another couple in the aural history section. She headed straight to the carousels of microfiches of the GRO indexes, copies of the originals that were housed in the Family Records Centre.

Her job kept her brain in training, agile enough to make great leaps and twists and turns, to tie complex knots. As she'd watched Rosa Seagrove standing by the Aga, another image had lined up beside it: Marion Lassiter's photo attached to her chart. Their bone structure was the same, and a similar, ready-for-anything glint in their eyes. Then came a date Victor Lassiter had mentioned and she united both with something Charles Seagrove had said.

Victor said Marion had joined the land army in the spring of 1944 and at the garden party Charles Seagrove said that there had been jellies and ice cream fifty-nine years ago, on Richard's first birthday. Which meant that Richard was born sometime in the summer of 1945.

The glimmering idea now sparked and took light as she'd feared it might. She hadn't wanted it to be true, for Richard's sake.

She walked her fingers through the columns of microfiches,

selected the index covering the second and third quarter of 1945, inserted the film and scanned down to July. The hypocrisy of what she was doing wasn't lost on her. She'd accused Archie Fletcher of revelling in Charles Seagrove's murder because it had made his job more exciting, and now here she was, about to shatter Richard Seagrove's world, his whole identity, if she found what she thought she might find. It was disturbing, the sensation of freewheeling, of not being able to stop herself even if she wanted to, the way the pure thrill of the chase, the heady excitement of being sure she was on to something, outweighed the implications of what that discovery might mean.

But there were no Richard Seagroves recorded in the Gloucestershire registration district. No Richard Lassiters either. She jotted the details on her pad, writing as speed typists do, scribbling blindly, without taking her eyes off what she was copying. She slipped one acetate file out and slid in another: the Adoption Children Register for 1945–6. The indexes were arranged chronologically and alphabetically by the name of the adopted child, who could be called by birth name or adopted name. But again there were no Richard Seagroves. No Richard Lassiters.

Her conviction was only slightly shaken. She needed fuel if she was in for the long haul, went back outside to the pavement booth selling refreshments, bought an iced coffee and drank it where she was standing.

For the next two hours she worked systematically through the registers of the years preceding and following Richard Seagrove's birth. She looked under Lassiter and Seagrove and found a couple of possibilities, ordered certificates. But she knew none was him.

Then she worked her way through the marriage registers for 1944 to 1946, looking for Marion Lassiter, on the off-chance she had married locally after her brother had lost contact with her, after Charles Seagrove had drafted her family tree. If her baby, therefore, just might have been registered under a married name. Could she have married Karl Briegel after all? She kept a look out for that name too. Nothing.

She closed her eyes and thought it all through step-by-step, reining in her brain. She didn't need great leaps of faith, just logical, well-reasoned and indisputable conclusions. Legislation and a registry were introduced in 1926 for the control of adoption but private arrangements were still widespread. Childless couples had been bringing up unwanted children since time began, and the informal fostering of illegitimate babies within families had always been commonplace.

Some adoptions were never documented. Births often slipped through the net too, some babies never being registered, especially among the poor. On the other hand, registration dodging was rare after 1940, especially during the war, when evidence of registration was needed for the issue of ration books. A new baby was given precious rations. Why would Charles Seagrove sacrifice that for the sake of signing a piece of paper to say he was Richard's father? But then rations would be not nearly so vital in the country as they were in the cities. You could grow your own vegetables, had access to unlimited amounts of fresh eggs and milk.

Sometimes wills gave an indication of adoption. She wouldn't be allowed to read Charles Seagrove's will although she knew one thing about it already. Richard Seagrove was not named in it, but Rosa was. She thought about this, then decided it told her nothing.

She had no proof that Richard was adopted by the Seagroves, no proof that he was Marion Lassiter's baby. But she did know that if Richard was Charles and Stella Seagrove's baby, for some reason, they had never registered his birth.

Ann always said her favourite game as a little girl had been mummies and daddies. It must have been devastating for her when she found that she couldn't have a baby of her own, to have to accept that her only way to be a mummy would be to bring up someone else's baby. Had it been the same for Charles and Stella Seagrove?

Not being able to have a child of his blood must have been equally shattering for Charles. They'd have tried to have their own baby first surely. And when they couldn't ... They'd somehow persuaded Marion to give them hers?

But if she *was* right, how did someone as passionate about ancestry as Charles Seagrove cope with knowing that his own line had come to an end? He had an heir, but for Charles, blood was everything. Yet Richard was seemingly no less precious to Charles. In fact, he almost seemed *more* special.

Then she thought of an alternative hypothesis. Muriel Mulholland had said that Charles had 'had the hots' for Marion. If Stella Seagrove couldn't have his children, had he made Marion the mother of his baby?

So now what? While she was here there was someone else she had to look up. She was half surprised to find the entry for Cinderella Pateman's birth. Such an unusual name, she'd almost expected her to have been registered under another, more conventional one. She went to a terminal, logged onto the GRO site and ordered a copy of the certificate, priority service, which meant it should be dispatched the next working day. She should have it on Wednesday.

She managed to catch the ten to three train, collected the Alpine at Moreton Station and drove directly to Shadwell church. One more try and then she was done.

The rector's telephone number was displayed in gilt lettering on the oak notice board above the churchyard wall. She punched it into her mobile.

'It's Natasha Blake. I was wondering if I could have a quick look at the parish registers.'

'This afternoon?'

'I'm right outside the church now, if you're free.'

She leant back against the dry stone wall, her head filled with the screaming of the swifts as they swooped around the tower. They reminded her of the dream she'd had the previous night, a dream filled with the baby's cries she'd heard, or believed she'd heard, at Shadwell. Just the products of exhaustion, stress, an overwrought imagination. That was the only explanation, the only rational explanation at least. Sleep the elusive cure.

She'd dreamed last night of the statue in the garden at Shadwell. In her dream the sculpture of the mother breastfeeding her child had come alive, pale as the face in a black-and-white photograph, pale as a ghost. The face wasn't Stella Seagrove's but Marion Lassiter's, and the baby was not a girl called Amelia but a baby boy called Richard. Marion kissed him and stroked him and laid him down in an old-fashioned carriage pram which she wheeled out of the bright sun, towards the shade of the bluebell woods. As she slowly walked away she was followed by the sound of his high-pitched cries. They echoed around the trees and carried all the way to the empty rooms of the house, until Stella Seagrove came. She picked the baby up and tried to soothe him, cradling his head against her shoulder and crooning softly just as his mother had done. But nothing she could do would make him quieten. Babies know, from just a few days old, to whom they truly belong.

She'd not had one single dream, or nightmare, about Charles Seagrove's murder, or not one that she could remember at least. But then dreams often tapped into the subconscious, into half-buried fears and memories. And the memory of Charles Seagrove's murder was still very much in her consciousness. It was there, lurking in her waking thoughts, throughout every moment of the day. That morning, she'd stood in front of the mirror putting on her lipstick and the red stickiness of it had repulsed her. She'd had to wipe it off, flushing the red-smeared tissue down the toilet so she wouldn't see it in the rubbish bin. She'd stopped polishing her nails because she couldn't bear to look at them for long, could still see red trapped beneath them.

In the far corner of the churchyard, a couple of metres from Charles Seagrove's waiting plot, a mound of fresh earth marked a newly-occupied grave. Flowers but no headstone yet.

Reverend Clarkson jingled and clanked up the path like a knight in chain mail, thanks to his impressive bunch of keys.

'I hope you realize you've deprived me of an hour listening to Mrs Bourne bemoaning her bunions.'

From the dealings she'd had with Reverend Clarkson, Natasha had decided it was a blessing he'd been called to the Anglican ministry rather than the Roman Catholic. As a compulsive gossip he would have made the most terrible priest.

He selected the kind of ornate, heavy key that should have been used to open the door to a castle, led Natasha through to the small, whitewashed vestry furnished with a neat chair and small desk with an inkwell. The three dusty parish registers, for birth, marriage and death, were kept in a locked metal safe concealed inside a slim cupboard.

'Looking for anyone I know?' Like anyone given to indiscretion, Reverend Clarkson expected no less in return.

'I doubt it.' Lying in church, and to a member of the clergy at that. She braced herself for the lightning bolt.

'It was good of you to come to Charles Seagrove's memorial the other day. Do you know the family well?' How much did Reverend Clarkson know of her involvement? If God was all seeing, all knowing, had he seen fit to share his omniscience with his mortal portal?

'Not really. I did some work for Charles recently, that's all. How about you?'

'Hardly at all.'

'He wasn't a regular church-goer then?'

'Never set foot in here once to my knowledge, neither did Mrs Seagrove, except for their son's wedding.'

'Richard was married here?'

'Yes. His wife, ex-wife, was, is, Swedish, Norwegian.' He waved his hand. 'Scandinavian at any rate. They met in Oslo, if I remember correctly. Anyway, she didn't have a home parish to go back to as English brides do.'

Rosa did have a Nordic look about her, with her white-blonde hair and violet eyes. But by the same token Richard could also have been Scandinavian. So could Stella. But she was here because she'd decided that Stella didn't share the same genes as Richard and Rosa. Did she? Had she imagined the resemblance between Rosa and a sixty-year-old photograph?

'I'll leave you to it then,' Reverend Clarkson said, grudgingly.

She pulled up the rickety spindle chair and took the three registers out one by one. Shadwell was a small parish, no more than two dozen baptisms a year, so the register begun in 1935 wasn't yet full. The entries for 1942 to 1946 were all written in the same careful bold hand.

She flicked her eyes down the page, searching for Richard Seagrove's name. There was a time when even babies whose births weren't registered were more than likely to have been baptised, when infant mortality was high and mothers were anxious to secure them a place in heaven. Baptisms were less universal in the twentieth century, but the threat of German bombs ensured a greater proportion of tiny souls were given into God's care. Besides, the Seagroves were so proud of Richard she'd have thought they'd use any excuse to celebrate him. Unless, of course, he was already baptised when he came to them, if the ceremony had taken place when he was still with his birth mother.

Richard James Simpson, Richard Alexander Gowan and Richard Francis Bennett were all christened between the summers of 1945 and 1946. It was easier to find people in individual parish registers than in national indexes. The likelihood of two individuals having the same name in one community was small. Once again, there was no Richard Seagrove or Lassiter. Not a single Seagrove or Lassiter at all.

She slid that register back in the safe and took out the one for weddings. There were fewer marriages than baptisms, but this register was started in 1967 and was only a third full. Given Rosa's age, about twenty years ago was a good place to start. She turned the pages until she came to the early eighties. Richard Seagrove's wedding took place on 1 May 1981. His bride was called Kristen Johanssen.

Natasha put the register away and went out to find the Reverend who was at the altar on his knees, not praying but emptying a vase and arranging fresh flowers in it.

'Save our cleaner the bother,' he said, grunting as his legs struggled to straighten under the weight of his stout torso. 'Did you get what you came for?'

'Not exactly.'

They walked together down the aisle, the vicar clutching a bouquet of desiccated roses.

'Crossed off some possibilities at least?'

'Just added some more questions to an ever-lengthening list.'

'A bit of a waste of time for you then?'

'No,' she said. 'Not at all. Sometimes questions are as important as answers, aren't they?'

'Well, indeed they are.' She'd known those words of wisdom

would go down well. 'Perhaps you'd like to give the sermon this Sunday.' He closed the heavy church door with a Gothic thud. 'Now, you'll appreciate my current dilemma, what with your interest in tombstones and such.' He nodded towards the new grave. 'We buried Ronald Davies last week and I'm having a spot of bother with his son about the inscription to go on the tombstone. Young Mr Davies is adamant that he wants something along the lines of: "The best dad in the world. He had a good innings." Ronald was a keen cricketer, you understand. But I'm not at all keen, not even on the dad bit. Father it should be, or else we're dumbing-down the dead.'

'You could argue that gravestones should reflect current culture, in the way Victorian ones reflected Victorian sentimentality.'

'Ah, but Victorian sentimentality is a lot more picturesque than pop culture. Before you know it we'll have "Dearly beloved Cuddles" and "To My Darling Squidgy" and the whole place will resemble a pet's cemetery.'

Natasha laughed. 'Well, I'm sure you can rely on the Seagroves to not lower the tone.'

The Reverend looked pensive. 'Maybe. But I'm not sure Charles Seagrove is going to prove the ideal addition to our peaceful God's acre.' The cheery smile had vanished from Reverend Clarkson's face, replaced by a look of uncertainty. 'There's been some mightily peculiar goings-on since his memorial.'

'What sort of goings-on?' Natasha felt her scalp tingle.

'It started the night after the service.' He'd lowered his voice. 'The next morning we found all the bouquets that had been left by the mourners ripped to shreds, strewn around the grass, the heads and leaves torn off and scattered. Our poor warden was the first to see them and was most upset.'

'You told the police?'

'Naturally. But what can they do? It's not even desecrating a grave, since there is no grave yet. Vandalism, they assume, hard to find the culprits. At least they kept it out of the papers. So distressing for poor Mrs Seagrove.' He pursed his lips. 'But then it was she who did the next odd thing. I was preparing for Mr Davies's funeral and I saw her walk along the path with a fresh bouquet of those giant daisies. Understandably, I suppose, she didn't put it where all the other flowers had been left, on her husband's plot, but over in the far corner there, under the lilac tree. I checked it hadn't been touched the next morning and I happened to catch what was written on the card. I fully expected it to say "from Stella" or "to Charles", but there was just a single word, a name: Amelia. The card was decorated like a children's birthday card, with stars and a little fairy. I find it most puzzling and for some reason I can't quite put my finger on, it bothers me. But at least the daisies were left alone until they perished, thankfully.'

'That's good.' Natasha's mouth was dry.

Amelia. A little girl immortalized in a stone statue. *My wife is rather fanciful.* Natasha wondered if she should have looked for her in the birth registers for the years before the Seagroves' marriage. And again in the adoption registers, or the registers of death? But what surname? No, it was a pointless exercise. Too many unknowns even to begin.

'So you'll understand why I hesitated when the young foreign lady came to the Vicarage this morning, asking where Charles Seagrove's plot was,' Reverend Clarkson was saying. 'I wasn't sure if I should tell her. She seemed a good sort of person, said she just wanted to leave a wreath, but I must admit that, what with everything, I couldn't help but wonder if her request was entirely above suspicion.' He nodded over towards the yew tree. 'Seemingly, I needn't have worried.'

To Natasha it was like a splash of blood. A fresh crown of dark-red roses resting on the grass precisely where Charles Seagrove's grave would one day be dug.

'Foreign, you say?'

'She had a strong accent. German, perhaps. Hard to tell.'

Natasha walked over, bent down to the blooms. The roses were interspersed with tiny white chrysanthemums. All the flowers were perfect, all fully opened – red mouths open for air – but despite the heat of the morning sun, not one of them showed any sign of wilting. They must have been left only a matter of minutes before. She'd not have missed them on her earlier wander round

161

the graveyard. She looked up and around. The lane and surrounding fields were empty except for Reverend Clarkson's battered
Vauxhall. The foreign woman hadn't been tempted to stand and
contemplate Charles Seagrove's last resting place. If the souls of
the murdered were ever allowed to rest. From what the vicar had
said, it seemed Charles Seagrove's resting time hadn't yet come.

She carefully lifted the waxy jade petals, taking care of the broad
thorns, and found, nestled among the woven stalks, a glossy white
card, the writing bold and black. All that was written on it were
the letters, a kind of pierced V and then XM. Her first thought was
that it was a Roman numeral.

X marks the spot, X for love. The X must be a kiss. XM
translated to 'love from M'. M for Marion? V for what? Victory?

'What did she look like?'

'Late fifties, I'd say. Well dressed. Short dark hair.'

Not Marion Lassiter then. But she could have sent someone to
leave a wreath on her behalf.

Natasha wondered if it would still be intact in the morning, or
ruined like the other bouquets, by whatever dark avenging angel
had come before. It was almost easier to believe in something
paranormal than in random vandalism. Easier certainly to accept
that the grave of a murdered person had been violated for specific,
personal reasons. Who? Why? Questions may be as important as
answers, she thought, but right now some answers would be good.

After she'd said goodbye and thank you to the vicar, she turned
the Alpine's ignition key and keyed the number for Chipping
Campden police station into her mobile. She was put through to
Archie Fletcher as she released the brake.

'Can I ask you something?'

'So long as you pull over and turn off the engine. I can't be
encouraging driving while talking on a mobile phone.'

So much for staying on the right side of the law. She did as she
was told.

'Amongst Charles Seagrove's papers, was there by any chance a
genealogical chart for a woman named Kristen Johanssen? Richard
Seagrove's ex-wife.'

'I'm afraid I can't disclose those kinds of details.'

'Can't or won't?'

Silence. Then: 'What has Kristen Johanssen's chart have to do with Marion Lassiter?'

'So Kristen does have a chart then?'

She took the next silence as a confirmation.

'Why are you interested?'

'I'm not sure yet.'

'Will you tell me when you are?'

She paused. 'Maybe. If you give me a proper yes or no to one other question.'

'Bribery is it now?'

'Call it a trade. I thought the police did that all the time. Or is that just on TV?'

'Go on.'

'Did you find Charles Seagrove's own genealogical tree?'

'Should we have?'

Yes. Most definitely. But they obviously hadn't. 'How about Stella Seagrove's?'

'I thought you just had the one question.'

'They're all linked. Call this question one, part c.'

'There was a chart for Mrs Seagrove, or Stella Randall as she was then. Are you going to tell me what all this is about?'

If she could draw conclusions from silence, so could he.

One silence she couldn't work out was the one coming from Richard Seagrove. There'd been no contact from him since she'd seen him at Shadwell. She'd expected him to be much angrier about her sending the police up there with spades.

She couldn't even begin to work out what she would tell him if he did call. She couldn't tell him she'd switched her attention to his own parentage. Perhaps he'd finally given up on her or had just decided he couldn't trust her. Maybe events at Shadwell had overtaken him.

She stared out towards Shadwell Manor Farm, where black clouds were gathering in the sky, for anyone who believed in signs and portents to make of that what they would. She imagined she could see the edge of the woods where the police were searching right now for Cinderella Pateman. Had those trees given up their secret yet? Richard Seagrove's family tree certainly hadn't. But did his parentage, or his marriage really matter?

Somehow. Somehow. Like Alice Hellier's story, she had the feeling it all mattered very much.

Twenty-Two

IT FELT AS though she were turning the ignition beneath a sea of treacle. Her limbs felt leaded, her eyelids even more so. Sleep eluded her when she craved it and threatened to swamp her when she needed to keep awake. Probably with good cause. Expert on her condition that she'd become, she knew that sleep was often the mind's safety valve, its fuse when faced with overload.

She gulped down oxygen as she drew away from Shadwell church. The hum of the engine like a lullaby, the rocking motion a cradle. Each time she closed her eyes it was harder to open them.

Whatever else the black clouds over Shadwell might prophesy, the rain came on hard and sudden. She didn't rush to put the hood up, enjoyed the feel of the drops like hot needles on her skin, smell the scents released from the earth. She was driving towards blue sky to the west where the sun was still shining, a faint rainbow arching over the fields ahead. Her last clear thought before it happened was of the rainbows that never fade over Niagara Falls.

A blue Golf like the one Rosa Seagrove drove was coming at her very fast down the narrow, tree-lined lane.

In an instant, she and the car were almost upon one another, and it was still hurtling straight towards her, showing no sign of pulling to one side.

Both hands on the steering wheel, she put the whole weight of her body behind a yank to the left. The Alpine skidded on the rain-slicked road on its bald front tyres, then tilted and jolted violently as it veered up into the trees. The ground scraped the car's low-slung underbelly; it sounded as if the bottom was being ripped out of it. The branches of the birches tore at her face and her hair. She felt herself thrown back, then forwards, saw the steering wheel coming up at her. Then nothing.

She came to a few seconds later. Her head was throbbing.

She touched her forehead and felt a ghastly familiar sticky wetness, red on her fingers. She stared at it, paralysed by a precarious unreality. She couldn't totally convince herself that it wasn't Charles Seagrove's blood on her skin again, that somehow time hadn't spun backwards.

She flung open the door and was violently sick.

Where had the blood come from?

Her bag had been thrown to the floor, the contents spilled. She found her cosmetics case, the mirror, checked the damage. Just a graze, nothing serious, except that the face staring back at her was out of focus and trembling.

What had happened?

She'd glimpsed Rosa's face through the dappled windscreen as she'd sped past, both hands gripping the wheel, her face grey and set as the stone statue in the garden.

On shaking legs she climbed out of the car. The front bumper was buckled, the bonnet dented, but the thick grass had acted as a brake and the birch tree had taken the brunt of the impact, its bark ripped away to reveal a yellow-green gash of exposed wood.

She could barely hold her foot steady on the clutch or turn the ignition to restart the engine. She stalled it. Turned the key again. She probably shouldn't be driving but she knew she'd get no signal on her mobile here and she wasn't in the mood to sit and wait on the off chance that someone helpful might pass by. She wasn't sure if she was shaking with shock or rage. Rosa hadn't even seemed to notice there was another car on the road. She had been driving as though she wanted to get herself killed and didn't care who else she took with her.

Natasha lived her life surrounded by death, she'd recently witnessed it in all its gory brutality, but rarely had she felt it brush so close, try to claim her. Beneath the shock and anger was a strange hum of elation. The world looked achingly beautiful, raindrops dazzling on the leaves, tumbling to the ground like a spray of tiny jewels. Was this what it would feel like to be reborn?

She reversed, pulled away, the tyres spinning and grinding into the soil before gaining a foothold. The exhaust pipe clanked on a rock as it bounced back onto the road.

The flowery-aproned cleaner answered the door of Shadwell Manor Farm, dustpan and brush in hand. Natasha said she wanted to speak to Richard, aware that her voice sounded much surer and stronger than she felt. She was led through to the drawing room. 'Your daughter almost . . .'

Archie Fletcher was standing with Richard by the mullion windows. She'd called him at the station about a quarter of an hour before the crash and now here he was. She must have been out cold for longer than a few seconds.

Archie's hands were lightly clasped behind his back but Richard had his jammed into the pockets of his tracksuit. Natasha's feeling of detached elation evaporated along with any residual anger as she saw the grave expression mirrored on both their faces. 'You've found her.'

'Half an hour ago,' Archie confirmed. 'What happened to you?'

She touched her head, ran to the bathroom and threw up again.

She drank some water and then carefully wiped the blood out of her hair, off her forehead. She was disgusted at herself. She wasn't usually such a wimp.

Richard Seagrove knocked gently on the door, asked her if she was all right.

She opened it and looked at him. 'I'm fine, but Rosa . . .' Archie appeared in the drawing-room doorway and instinctively, Natasha switched tack, not wanting to add reckless driving to the girl's list of troubles. 'I passed her on the way here. She didn't look in a proper state to be driving.' Even as she said it she wondered why she was covering for someone who could have killed her. The look Archie gave her told her she hadn't fooled him anyway, but her head felt too muddy to worry about any of it.

'I should go after her.' Richard patted his pockets, searching for his car keys.

Archie put his hand on Richard's shoulder. 'How about I put a call through to the station, ask the patrol car to check she's sticking to the speed limit? Where would she have been going?'

'Cirencester, I suppose.'

He took out his radio and went outside to place the call.

'Rosa's taken this pretty badly,' Richard said quietly. 'It's too much for her, my father's death and now this.' His words seemed to lodge in his throat. 'He could do no wrong in her eyes.'

His words were like a strange echo inside her head. Ann used to say exactly the same thing: *Your father can do no wrong in your eyes.* But all that was changing now. Natasha suddenly felt a deep empathy with Rosa. Maybe that was why she'd automatically protected her. By all accounts Rosa had adored her grandfather just as Natasha adored Steven. So her own family problems gave her an insight into what Rosa was going through, how hard it would be for her to come to the realization that she had never really known her grandfather, that he had a dark side, that there were people out there who wanted to kill him, that he knew perhaps how Cinderella Pateman came to be buried in the grounds of his house.

More precisely, as Archie explained when he returned to the house, how she came to be buried face down beneath the birches, in the bluebell woods, at Poacher's Dell, just where the letter had said she would be found.

Her body, or what was left of it, would be taken away to be examined, Archie explained, when Natasha was sitting down with a large glass of brandy: evidently, the medicinal powers of sweet tea were no longer deemed a strong enough antidote to these current traumas.

Thanks to Marcus, she knew more about the degenerative rate of corpses than she would sometimes have liked. If Cinderella had died around the time she'd disappeared, in the 1940s, it meant she'd been in the woods for sixty years. The Gloucestershire soil didn't have the preservative qualities of peat or permafrost. After such a long time there wouldn't be much left. Human bodies were eminently biodegradable, the ultimate in eco-friendliness. Cinderella's hair, her eyes, her nails, even the clothes she'd been wearing when she died, would all have rotted away. Earth to earth. All that would be left were bones.

If she'd been found by chance one day by the gardener, digging to plant spring bulbs or a new conifer, if the police didn't have any starting point, any idea who she might be, they'd probably have called in a medical artist like Marcus. Someone who'd take careful notes of the dimensions of the different features of her skull, the distance between her eyes and the bridge of her nose. A medical artist would use those measurements to reconstruct a face, to bring Cinderella Pateman slowly back from the dead in the hopes that someone might recognize her, claim her. Put a name to a face.

Genealogy was all about hunting and finding the dead, unearthing them. But it had never happened quite so literally before. Or with such profound implications.

Two girls had gone missing around the same time, two friends: Marion Lassiter and Cinderella Pateman. The body of one of them had been buried in the woods. Was Marion out there too?

Cinderella was lost and now she was found. But what else were the police going to uncover? It didn't take a genius to work out that whoever had buried Cinderella also, in all probability, had a hand in her death. Archie said that the note Natasha had been sent would be re-examined, was now central to the investigation. It was also central to the questions tearing around her sore head. She wanted very much to know who had written it. How did that person know where Cinderella was? Why had they kept quiet about it for so long? And why, of all the people in all the world, had they chosen to share their knowledge with her?

Twenty-Three

THIS WAS PRECISELY what one of Archie's colleagues wanted to know when she came round to Natasha's cottage the next morning. PC Harman, or Hard Woman, as Natasha instantly rechristened her, was a tall, broad-shouldered girl with wiry hair and a sharp tongue. She looked as if she were so used to holding her own in a male environment that she didn't know how to let go when she was out of it.

'I was thinking,' Natasha said. 'It was written on an old-fashioned typewriter. So perhaps it was sent by someone who wasn't computer literate.' Like Charles Seagrove.

PC Hard Woman smiled sympathetically, as you would to a willing but slow child. 'Or maybe whoever sent it wants us to look for someone who's not computer literate.'

'Of course.' She wasn't normally so gullible. But she was still feeling sick, and dizzy.

'How'd you get that nasty bump on your head?' PC Hard Woman made it sound like an accusation.

'I walked into a door.'

Fortunately, James had already gone over to the garage in Toddington to get the Alpine ironed out, so at least it wasn't sitting outside inviting more questions than she'd be able to answer. She'd decided not to add to complications by involving her insurance company. The quote for the work was about seven hundred pounds. Which would wipe out a good chunk of what she'd earned from her work for Charles Seagrove. Poetic justice perhaps.

'You should look where you're going,' PC Hard Woman volunteered.

'I'll try to remember that.'

'It would be useful if you could also try to remember anything that might help us to understand why that letter was sent to you.'

Notebook in hand, stern exterior firmly fixed in place, she took down details of everyone Natasha had spoken to on the trail of Marion Lassiter. Victor Lassiter and his wife, John Hellier, even the curator at the Winchcombe Museum and, ridiculously, Arnold Hyatt. She'd have to ring Arnold and warn him that the police would be coming round or he'd have a heart attack, thinking they were interested in the contents of his shed.

Hard Woman had finished scribbling. 'I thought you were employed by Mr Seagrove Senior. Why have you carried on working the case after he died?'

She could keep the arrangement private no longer. 'Richard Seagrove asked me to.'

'And John Hellier?' More a statement than a question. 'He's told us you'd offered to help patch things up between him and Miss Seagrove.'

'That's right.'

'I bet playing cupid never looked so complicated.' The girl could give lessons in how to patronize. She couldn't help wishing Archie Fletcher had come instead. He knew the difference between asking questions and interrogating. Or maybe it was just that she generally got on better with men, had always claimed that she'd rather work for an uncomplicated man than a scheming woman. Not that she was saying she was any different from the rest of her sex. She could scheme with the best of them. When her brain was firing on all its cylinders. Right now she'd have a problem scheming the way to her own front door.

'Did you find Rosa Seagrove? Is she OK?'

That seemed to bring PC Hard Woman up short, as if Natasha was privy to information she shouldn't have had.

'Know where she is, do you?'

'No.' Now Natasha was utterly confused.

She called Richard as soon as the PC had left.

'Rosa's disappeared.' He sounded wrung out. 'The patrol car spotted her on the way back to her hall of residence. She went back to her room and packed her holdall with clothes and now no one knows where she is. The police are trying to find her.'

'I'm sure they will.' Natasha had meant to offer comfort but that wasn't how it sounded to her. The police would make it their mission to find Rosa Seagrove. Because running away made it look as if she had something to hide.

Richard said Rosa had withdrawn all the funds, five hundred pounds, from her bank account. The police had not been able to find her passport anywhere in her room. John Hellier told them he had no idea where Rosa might have gone. The authorities were checking ports and airports.

Even if she was innocent of everything but leaving without saying where she was going, she was guilty of causing her father more anxiety that he needed.

Natasha was beginning to doubt that Rosa deserved her help. That, after all, was part of what all this had been about. Ostensibly, Richard had asked her to carry on with her research for Rosa's benefit, to mend the rift between his daughter and John. John had given her permission to carry on delving into his past because he wanted Rosa back. Well, maybe he would be better off without her.

After PC Hard Woman had gone, Natasha's simple wish was to have a normal day. Normal being a leisurely shower followed by toast followed by a tramp across the fields with Boris, and a couple of hours at her desk. An attractive bruise was forming on her forehead.

She accomplished the first part of her plan, got as far as making a cup of coffee and answering an email from a production company that was making a television programme about how to trace your family history. The Society of Genealogists had given them her contact details, suggesting her as an on-screen adviser. So long as she didn't have to talk about her own background. She and Charles Seagrove must be the only genealogists who'd not got addicted to the subject through compiling their own family trees.

Why *hadn't* Charles Seagrove researched his own genealogy, when he was so preoccupied with other peoples?

She spent another hour composing a client's chart. Not with ink and rulers as she'd had to do for Charles Seagrove, but using slick software which sketched all the lines for you. This was just as well, because her eyes still didn't seem to be working well enough to draw a straight line freehand. The characters on the computer screen seemed fuzzy and distorted. She was all thumbs, seemed to have lost the ability to type. She wondered if she should see a doctor, but she hated being fussed over, the thought that she'd be sent to hospital for poking and prodding.

She gave up with the charts and went for a swim, her own form of meditation and healing. She made herself concentrate on regular strokes, the in and out of her breath. Despite the fact that the hire car she'd been loaned by the garage, a Fiat Uno, was a comedown after her beloved Alpine, she drove home feeling only pleasantly floaty, as if she were still borne up by the water.

She landed with a bang when she saw John Hellier pacing up and down the lane outside her cottage. Dressed in muddy boots, a navy sweater and green gilet, he was every inch the gentleman farmer. Albeit an unshaven, agitated one.

'How are you doing?' He'd pounced before she'd even climbed out of the car.

'I'll survive.'

'I meant in finding out what Charles Seagrove had against me.'

'Ah.' She shut the car door, pushed her hands into her jeans pockets. 'Not so good, I'm afraid, John.'

'Then you have to try harder.'

'I beg your pardon?'

There was nothing remotely threatening about him but he was not so much on edge as on *the* edge, strung out, his dark eyes darting back and forth.

'You've got one week,' he said. 'One week, starting from today, to find out what this has all been about, or something awful is going to happen.'

'What do you mean, John?'

He shook his head, in denial.

'Plenty of pretty awful things have been happening lately,' she added softly. 'What are you talking about?'

He slumped against the car, let his back slide down it as his legs buckled. 'Someone else is going die.'

He'd said it so quietly that she wasn't sure she'd heard him right.

'What did you just say?'

He looked up at her with black, soulful eyes that reminded her of Boris. 'If I can't convince Rosa that we should be together, somebody else will die. Someone totally innocent, who doesn't deserve ...' He bit his lip, screwed up his eyes.

'Who, John? What do you mean?' She tried to keep the alarm out of her voice.

He didn't seem to have heard a word, was staring at the thistles in the grass by his feet.

'Who's going to die? How do you know this?'

'I can't tell you.'

Was this a threat or a warning?

Frustration took over. 'I'm sorry but that just won't do.' She made herself calm down, squatted so she was at his level. 'Why are you telling me this? Why haven't you gone to the police?'

'They're no use. You're the only one who can help.' But he sounded beyond help, without hope.

'Is it Rosa. Is that it? Is she in some kind of danger? Do you know where she is? Why did she run, John? Tell me?' She was firing questions at him without giving him time to answer, challenging him to say something just to shut her up, but it wasn't working. *If I lose Rosa I lose everything and my life will be ruined.* 'It's not yourself you're talking about? You're not thinking of doing anything crazy?'

The look he gave her did little to convince her of his sanity, but she felt certain about one thing: One of his great-grandmothers might have been a murderess but he wasn't capable of hurting a blade of grass.

'She had to get away from the house,' he said, quietly. 'She said she was hearing things.'

'What things?'

He ignored her. 'I told her it was just her conscience but she was adamant that it was some kind of sign. She couldn't stand it. She was determined to do it anyway.'

'Rosa? That's who you're talking about, right? When did you see her? Where is she? What is she going to do? What do you mean when you say you told her it was just her conscience. What has she done?'

He wasn't going to answer. She wanted to take hold of his shoulders and shake him. 'Look, John, I won't . . . I can't help you, unless you tell me exactly what's going on.'

He stared her out and for a moment she thought he'd give in, but he scrambled to his feet, pushing her roughly away, and started to run back through the village.

She considered chasing after him but, suddenly, she had no reserves left, she just didn't have the energy to make her legs move.

Arnold handed her a generous measure of his illicit cider brandy.

She downed it in one.

'Sounds to me like the poor lad's gone a bit doolally. Start talking about people hearing things and seeing signs and it's guaranteed that people are going to stop taking you seriously.'

From Natasha's personal experiences at Shadwell, the opposite was true. She'd be the last to dismiss anyone as crazy for hearing strange things in that house.

'Haven't found anything more about the Shadwell window-smashing scandal by the way, but I'm still working on it.'

'Thanks.'

'One week, you say,' Arnold mused. 'That'd make it what? Tuesday, July the fourth. Anything significant about that date so far as you know?'

'American Independence Day?'

'Hardly counts for much round here.'

That made her smile. 'Ever the good world citizen, aren't you, Mr Hyatt?'

'Go beyond Winchcombe and you fall into the sea.'

'Marion Lassiter's brother told me I'd find Father Christmas.' She held out her glass for some more brandy. You couldn't be charged for walking under the influence, drunk while in charge of a pair of legs, and perhaps it would banish her persistent headache. 'So what should I do now?'

'What do you think? You're much smarter than me, the most turned-on girl I've ever met.'

She laughed.

'Now what have I said?'

'Switched on, you mean. Turned on means something quite different.'

'Does it really?' He was all innocence, except for his naughty grin. 'Well anyway. You go and have a chat to your young friend, Archie.'

'Who'll haul John Hellier straight down to the station.'

'What choice do you have?'

What indeed.

Except, when she called the station she was told that Archie Fletcher had gone whitewater rafting in Wales for three days. Two murder inquiries weren't providing him with enough thrills evidently. 'Can it wait?'

'I don't know. I can't believe he's gone away now.'

'Booked ages ago apparently. The boss said they could spare him and he's been working solidly for the past two weeks, needed to recuperate. Do you want to speak to PC Harman?'

'It's OK, thanks. I'll call Sergeant Fletcher when he gets back.'

Friday. Which still gave four days until Independence Day.

Maybe the time had come to ask Richard Seagrove directly about his birth. But she knew she'd never be able to do it. Her own situation made her ultra-sensitive to others who might face the same discovery. She knew what it could mean. It would be brutally unfair to raise questions in Richard's mind before she could answer at least some of them for him. Deep down she was sure he'd never questioned the fact that Stella and Charles were his real parents.

Perhaps there was another way around it.

She couldn't reach Toby at home so she tried his mobile. It rang, connected, then went dead. She hit redial and this time went straight through to a voice message saying the phone was switched off. She asked him to turn on ASAP. She didn't expect this to be a matter of seconds.

'Sorry, I lost you,' Toby said. 'I'm on a train and I was in one of those designated quiet carriages. Some old girl gave me such a filthy look when the phone rang I didn't dare pick up. Don't know why she had to get so steamed up.'

'Is your ring tone still *Mission Impossible* by any chance?'

'So?'

'So that explains a lot. Speaking of missions, can you find out anything there is to find out about Charles Seagrove?'

'Don't be too specific, will you?'

'I thought you liked to be given your head.'

Toby's blush was so hot she almost had to let go of the phone. Bless him.

'I'm on my way back from a party in Brighton but I can be at the Record Centre in an hour,' he said, prim as a vicar's wife.

She wanted to hug him. 'Are you sure about that?'

'Have I ever broken a promise?'

She couldn't even think of a single instant when he'd not called her precisely when he'd said he would. She, on the other hand, was a habitual breaker of such promises, and he never held it against her.

Next day, a knock at the door sent Boris into his usual frenzied barking.

Who this time? John Hellier? Richard Seagrove again? The police? Natasha had come to dread opening her own front door. Sure to be trouble, whoever it was.

The one person she hadn't expected to see was Stella Seagrove. But she had been right about the trouble. Stella was like moulded steel after it had cooled from a furnace, her slight frame belying its strength, slightly stooped now, but no longer weak and malleable, set rigid in its altered shape. This time her black dress wasn't enlivened with the scarves and she could have been a ghostly widow who'd somehow become stranded in the wrong age, left behind from a bygone era when, for grieving relatives, life didn't go on after death.

Her demands were all too real though. 'Please stay away from my family.' There was no civility in her tone. 'Don't try to pretend you don't know what I'm talking about. I can see it all over your face when you look at him, when you look at my granddaughter.' Her blue eyes were strikingly similar to Rosa's, which would have made Natasha doubt her theories about Richard's adoption if what Stella was saying didn't seem to confirm them.

'You'd better come in.' She needed to buy time to work out what to say. But Stella shook her head, so it seemed there was no option but to have the conversation in the lane, in full view of the lunchtime crowd coming from and going to the Snowshill Arms.

'I'm asking for Richard's sake.'

'Does he know you're here?'

'Of course not.' Stella held her right arm across her chest, almost as if it were suspended in an invisible sling. She crossed her other arm over it, holding her elbow, in a position that was oddly like the way little girls pretended to cradle and rock a baby. A position a real mother could never use without dropping the little bundle.

'Please, come inside and sit down,' Natasha tried again.

'You don't have children, do you?'

'No.'

'Then this might be hard for you to understand. Richard is sixty years old but he's still my little boy. I used to stop him climbing trees so he didn't fall and break his arm. Told him not to play too near the lake in case he drowned. I didn't discuss it with him, I just told him it wasn't safe. And that's what I'm doing now. I'm protecting him, stopping him from hurting himself. I'm asking you to help me.'

'I'm not sure I can do that, Mrs Seagrove.'

The current thinking was that adopted children should never be under any illusion, should be brought up with the knowledge. Which would, no doubt, make it easier for them but painful for the adoptive parents, who usually wanted so desperately to make believe that their little family was just like everyone else's.

She couldn't help wondering if Stella was protecting Richard or herself.

'It will destroy him,' Stella said.

It was not unusual for Natasha to begin a research project and end up finding something a client would rather not know. People usually entered into studying their family trees lightly, for fun, because they were interested in history, wanted a unique present to give to an elderly relative or an heirloom to pass on to subsequent generations. They usually didn't expect any great surprises; family scandals, yes, but far enough removed by time not to matter any more. What they sometimes forgot was that to get back to the past you had to start with the present. Regular feuds and fallings-out were at one end of the spectrum and at the other was illegitimacy, along with all manner of convoluted relationships and misdemeanours. The person you'd grown up calling uncle was really your father. Your grandmother was conceived after her own father raped her. In her time, Natasha had unearthed both those stories and worse. Most people dealt with them remarkably well.

The big difference was that Richard Seagrove had asked her to research Marion Lassiter and John Hellier's family trees, not his own personal history. She was a trespasser in his past. There was a reason why adoption searches, until now, had been a one-way street. Why it was always left to the adopted child to instigate the search. But if she hadn't known it before, she knew she was on to something now. Her investigations may not have to do with Charles Seagrove's death but they certainly had something to do with the death of Cinderella Pateman and with the life of Marion Lassiter. People had been murdered. You couldn't just leave that alone.

Stella Seagrove was staring at her, waiting for a response. 'I shall only ask you one more time.' A hint of desperation had crept into her voice. 'What business is this of yours? I ask you that. Just who do you think you are?'

Whoever she was she wasn't feeling her usual self, and Stella Seagrove's comment caught a raw nerve. The words were out before she could stop them. 'As a matter of fact, I don't know who I am, Mrs Seagrove. I was a teenager when I found out I was adopted. It was tough, but it didn't destroy me. And for what it's worth, knowing the truth hasn't made me love my parents, my adoptive parents, any less.' She focused on Stella's eyes but the hard light in them didn't soften. She hadn't intended a cheap shot at a sympathy vote, but had wanted to gauge Stella's reaction to the mention of adoption.

Sure enough, she'd pulled down the shutters. 'You think you've got it all worked out, don't you?' There was contempt in Stella Seagrove's voice now. 'But you don't know the half of it. You don't know what you're getting involved in. You mark my words. You'll live to regret this.'

She turned and walked slowly back up the lane to where the gardener from Shadwell was acting as chauffeur, waiting in the blue BMW to drive her home.

Natasha closed the door firmly, scowled at it. She was tempted to ram the bolt across. She'd had enough. Richard Seagrove and John Hellier driving her on and on to delve deeper and deeper, Richard's mother warning her to back off. Next time someone came knocking they could take a hike. Maybe that's what she should do. Rather than barricade herself inside she should go somewhere where nobody could find her. She'd cleared her inbox but there was still a teetering pile of unopened snail mail by her desk, a dozen phone calls she had to make before her sister came that evening. Escape was too tempting to resist.

After the short burst of rain the other day, the hot weather had returned with a vengeance and it was the kind of long summer afternoon that you only usually saw in childhood memories, the countryside suffused with a kind of clotted sunlight, rich and thick and sweet.

As she busied about the kitchen she tried not to be tripped up by Boris who was skipping about in front of her, knowing plans were afoot. 'All your birthdays have come at once, boy.'

She filled a flask with tea, made up some peanut butter sandwiches, packed them in a rucksack with fruit and a map, plus a bottle of water and bowl for Boris.

She walked west until she picked up the Cotswold Way, was starting to feel hot and a little dizzy again, stripped off her fleece, tied it round her waist. The steady pace of walking helped her to think.

Always the first to give herself a hard time, she didn't try to deceive herself. She knew what she was doing was wish fulfilment by proxy. There was a chance she could tell Richard the truth about his birth in a way that no one had ever been able to tell her.

It will destroy him. Natasha was certain Richard was made of sterner stuff. When she had found out about her own adoption her world had not so much been turned upside down as spun out of its orbit, entered a different alien galaxy without water or oxygen. But she had learnt to survive there. She was not destroyed. It was not a simple adoption that Stella Seagrove did not want her to uncover, but something darker and far more sinister.

She let Boris carry on with his game of scratch and sniff under a chestnut tree, slid her rucksack off her shoulders and slung it on the ground. She found a comfy rock to sit on, got out a notepad and biro, and doodled:

Charles Seagrove compiled genealogies for:

- Kristen Johanssen – his son's future wife
- Stella Seagrove née Randall – his future wife
- John Hellier – his granddaughter's prospective husband
- Marion Lassiter – a landgirl

There are no genealogical charts for:

- Charles Seagrove himself
- Karl Briegel – the German prisoner of war who'd worked at Shadwell and Marion Lassiter's lover

She turned onto a clean page, and wrote:

Richard Seagrove born in 1945, son of Charles and Stella Seagrove or son of Marion Lassiter and Karl Briegel?

She shoved the notebook back in the rucksack. What was she

playing at? And what did all these people have to do with the body of Cinderella Pateman, buried in the Bluebell Woods at Poacher's Dell?

Twenty-Four

NATASHA'S SISTER, ABIGAIL, arrived bang on time in her brand-new turquoise Mini.

'Glad to see you've changed that old banger you used to have parked outside.' She kissed Natasha's cheek.

'It's at the garage. I'd never.'

Abby was still in her work clothes, the kind Natasha had never possessed in her life. Pinstriped navy tailored trousers, a white shirt, sling-back navy sandals. She insisted on changing before they went over to the pub so Natasha poured them both a glass of chilled white wine and put some music on, knowing how long it took her sister to get ready. She had to smile when Abby appeared half an hour later in pale-pink cords and a pink-and-blue striped T-shirt, colour-coordinated and accessorized down to a pink leather clutch bag and matching pink-and-blue beaded necklace, earrings and bangle.

They had risotto at the Snowshill Arms, chatted about cars and men and clothes and Abby's new flat, which boasted a living room twice the size of Natasha's entire cottage. Abby's half of their grandmother's small legacy had just about covered the deposit. Natasha's half had bought Orchard End almost outright, but Abby said she wanted to push herself. Her life was all about ladders now, property ladder, career ladder, both of which she was rapidly ascending.

When they were little Natasha had been the climber. Trees, walls, the wrong way up slides, while Abby had been happy to play on the grass with her Sindy doll.

'Have you had your place valued?' she said as she sipped her wine. 'I bet you'd make a fortune if you sold it now.'

Natasha could sense May Rainbow wincing. 'I've got to live somewhere. And I can hardly down-size, unless it's to a caravan.'

'You could buy a palace in Scotland for the price of a two-up two-down round here.'

'Except I don't want to live in Scotland, or in a palace for that matter. This is my home, not a business investment.'

Abby shrugged in a way that said suit yourself.

Natasha had never seen her little sister as being particularly ambitious. Taking after Ann, she was the archetypal little girl, obsessed with dressing up as a princess and twirling round in her little bathing costume with its white frilly skirt. Her bedroom had been full of butterflies. Butterfly fridge magnets and hair slides and trinket boxes and cushions. In a way she was still like a little butterfly – bright, beautiful and effervescent as the Verve Cliquot champagne she liked to drink. She wasn't so much climbing ladders as letting her bubbliness and pretty wings carry her upwards.

She showed Natasha the furniture she'd chosen from an Ikea catalogue, proving she was going to be as colour coordinated when it came to soft furnishings as she was with fashion.

Natasha wondered if Ann was a hermaphrodite, if she'd managed to conceive her baby solely from her own egg, her own genes. There seemed to be nothing of Steven in Abby. Natasha was far more like him. How did that work?

'Mum's been acting very strangely lately,' Abby said eventually, picking at the strap of her bag. 'When Dad called from Italy the other night she said she didn't want to talk to him, and their wedding photograph's gone from her bedside table. I don't like it at all. What's he up to?'

'You know what they say, the two people involved in a relationship are the only ones who really understand it.'

'Except there's always been at least three people involved in their marriage, hasn't there? Mum and Dad and whoever Dad was shagging at the time. He's having an affair, isn't he?'

'Yes.'

Abby slammed her glass onto the table, nearly snapping the stem. 'And how long have you known about it?'

'Not long. Look, Abby, let's not argue. Please. If our family's falling apart at the top, let's not cause another split.'

'You do think it's falling apart then?'

'If it is, there's nothing we can do about it except be there for them, both of them.'

'They're just going through a rough patch, surely? Dad's not going to ask for a divorce or anything, is he?'

'It might not be him who wants to call it a day. Oh, I don't know, Abby. I'm a historian not a prophet. I can't see into the future any more than you can.'

'What would Mum do though? I mean, Dad has his precious work but Mum . . .'

'Has you,' Natasha finished kindly.

'And you.'

'She is used to Dad not being around.'

Abby nodded, sipped her wine. 'How's Marcus?'

'He's sent me a plane ticket to Canada.' If Steven found out she'd told this to Abby before him he'd feel more than snubbed. Another rift. The Blakes were in serious danger of disintegration. They'd been a tight enough little unit before, quirky, but a unit that worked well enough for Natasha to have been able to view other families she was researching with some degree of complacency. It wasn't so hard to see how the likes of the Lassiters had been scattered to the four winds.

'That's so sweet of him,' Abby said. 'So when are you going?'

'I'm not.'

'You're mad.'

'Very probably.'

'Well, if you don't want that ticket I'll have it. And if you don't want Marcus I'll have him too.' She must have seen Natasha's face. 'Only joking. But he is gorgeous, those smiling Cornish eyes and mop of curls. How can you resist?'

Natasha knew Marcus wasn't Abby's type. She was even more certain that Abby wasn't Marcus's. So why was that familiar squirm of jealousy and possessiveness there in her stomach again, like the bitter worm at the bottom of a tequila bottle? She could feel it turning her sour, into a person she didn't like, didn't know, couldn't control.

Her mobile rang. The long-anticipated call from Richard Seagrove.

'Our driver let slip that he brought my mother over to see you. What was that about?'

There was nothing for it but to be honest. 'She wanted me to call a stop to my research.'

'Why?'

'I honestly don't know.' Silence. 'Do you want me to do as she asks?'

'No.' He said it so loudly and emphatically that Abby heard and pulled a face.

'Is there any news of Rosa?'

'No.' It was clear he didn't want to talk about her. 'I've not heard from you for a while.'

'I'm investigating a German prisoner of war who might have been Marion's lover.' She was becoming a purveyor of half-truths.

'Cinderella Pateman went missing during the war years.'

'That's right.'

'You think there's a connection?'

'That's what I'm trying to find out.'

He paused. 'And my mother knows something?'

She took that as a rhetorical question.

'Anything you find out you tell me and me alone, is that clear?'

'As a bell.'

Abby was frowning at her as she put the phone down. 'Client from hell?'

'Maybe.' She took their plates and glasses back to the bar.

Mary signalled for her to lean across the bar, then whispered in her ear. 'Don't look now, but we have a B&B guest who might interest you, a German lady. She's sitting over there, under the photograph of the maypole dancing. Her name is Inge Oster-meier.'

Natasha drew back, sneaked a peek. The woman was probably in her fifties, was dressed in cherry corduroy jeans and a black silk shirt, her chestnut hair cut into a bobbed fringe, no make-up on a lightly tanned face. A plate of tagliatelle, a glass of red wine and a copy of *Cotswold Life* were on the table in front of her.

'She says her mother knew someone who lived nearby,' Mary said, with great emphasis. 'And she's only booked for one more night. So if you want to talk to her you'd best be quick.'

Definitely. Tomorrow was Thursday, 29 June. Only five days to go.

'I can't abandon Abby. But maybe if I came over for breakfast tomorrow you could see to it that we're sitting together? I'll talk to her then.'

Twenty-Five

MARY LET NATASHA in through the cottage kitchen at the side of the pub the next morning. At the pine table, Kieran was enthroned in his highchair, sticky bib for a cloak, spooning a bowl of Coco Pops into his mouth and onto the flagstones in equal measure. Toast was toasting, not for the B&B guests but to make into Marmite soldiers. Mary buttered a slice, cut off the crusts and ate them. 'Mummies live on leftovers.'

Unless they were paying guests. James was in the 'professional kitchen', frying up bacon and eggs and sausages, the smell of which wafted through and made Natasha's mouth water.

After Mary quickly removed all choking hazards from Kieran's highchair table, replacing them with a wooden spoon for him to use as a drumstick, she led the way through to the restaurant off the back of the pub where the guests were served. She showed Natasha to an empty table in the bay, neatly set for one. The knives and forks and plate were cleverly positioned, towards the window, diagonally opposite Inge Ostermeier who sat at the next table facing into the room. She was leafing through a Cotswold guidebook as she sipped a cup of coffee.

At the far side, by the fireplace, a family of four were planning the first day of their holiday. The only other people were a middle-aged couple in sweatshirts who were sitting together, but alone, behind a double-skinned wall of broadsheet newspapers.

'What can I get you?' Mary asked, mischievously.

'Might as well go for the full English breakfast, please,' Natasha said. 'And a pot of tea.'

'Certainly, madam. It'll just be a couple of minutes.'

A table at the back of the room was laid out with a variety of miniature boxes of cereals, pots of yoghurt, bowls of fruit and pottery pitchers of orange and pineapple juice. Natasha helped herself to a glass of orange, thinking she should do this more often.

As two single women breakfasting alone, it was easy enough to strike up a conversation. Natasha caught Inge Ostermeier's wide topaz eyes and smiled. Inge smiled back.

'Are you here on holiday?'

'In a way.' Her enunciation was careful and precise, her strong German accent at once glamorous and somehow startling. 'And you?'

'Oh, I live just over the road,' Natasha said. 'I can't be bothered to cook for myself this morning.' Which was the truth.

'What a good idea,' Inge said.

Natasha wondered if the German accent truly sounded severe or if she'd just been conditioned to hear it that way from watching too many war movies. Inge's manner was anything but severe though. She seemed friendly but shy, as if she wasn't used to travelling alone in a foreign country, was happy to have someone to talk to.

'Whereabouts are you from?'

'Wassenberg, on the Austrian border.'

Natasha had been skiing in the foothills of the Alps. 'The Cotswold hills must seem a bit tame.'

'Equally as beautiful. I imagine it can get very cold too.'

'It can,' Natasha said, with feeling. 'Have you visited before?'

'No, I'm sorry to say I haven't. My mother always wanted to come. I'm here on her behalf really. She knew a man who lived in Shadwell.'

'Oh yes?'

'Charles Seagrove.'

Natasha couldn't bring herself to fake surprise.

'You knew him, yes?'

'Yes.'

'My mother was invited to his memorial service but she's not well enough to travel. She's in her nineties. Very frail, you know?'

'The service was a few days ago.'

'She thought it would be better if I came after it was over.'

Stella Seagrove must have known her husband had a female acquaintance in Germany. Otherwise Richard wouldn't have invited her to the memorial service. So why hadn't Inge's mother wanted her to be there on the actual day? Was she connected to Karl Briegel? she wondered then.

'Have you spoken to Richard Seagrove, Charles's son? I'm sure he'd love to meet you.'

'I don't want to intrude on his family's grief. The vicar kindly showed me where the grave would be. I promised I'd leave a wreath there, that was all she wanted me to do. It meant so much to her.'

When Natasha watched someone or started talking to them, she immediately started filling in the blanks. It was all there, in those few sentences Inge Ostermeier had spoken. Well educated but not well travelled, she'd come on an errand she didn't fully understand. She'd left her home, her husband, children, a job maybe, to make this journey alone, to fly hundreds of miles to a village church in a country she did not know, because she realized she had a debt to pay to the generations who'd gone before her. She was only in her fifties, but old enough to able to empathize with the old. To realize that one day she would be one of them. One day, much sooner, her mother would be gone. She was doing this one small, big thing, for her, but also for herself.

'Your mother's name is?'

'Magda. Magda Koenig.'

Someone walked over Natasha's grave. And laid a wreath of red roses. M for Magda, not Marion. The only black-and-white photograph in Charles Seagrove's study – a woman and her child, Hilda and Magda, the family of Hans Koenig, the German soldier Charles Seagrove's father had met in no man's land on Christmas Eve of 1914.

James came though with two laden plates. He set one before Inge and the other before Natasha.

When he'd gone, she said, 'Charles told me the story. The last time I saw him, a few days before he died. He told me how his father, and your, it must be your grandfather, Hans, exchanged photographs of their families. He called your grandfather, "my friend the enemy".'

Inge was sprinkling pepper over her egg. She stopped, looked up. 'My mother told me the very same story.'

'Charles said his father wrote to your grandmother after the war.'

Inge nodded. 'I've read his letter. My mother has it still. It's one of our family's treasures. It was so open and honest. He said meeting my grandfather changed the whole way he thought about war. And about life. How it was the most special thing that had ever happened to him.'

'He told his son that too,' Natasha said. 'They kept in touch, Robert and your grandmother?'

'Yes. He wrote many more times.'

'Do you have the letters?' She smiled. 'Excuse me for sounding so inquisitive. But I have a professional interest in old letters, and in the Seagrove family,' she ventured. 'I'm a family historian. I was working for Charles Seagrove.'

'I'm afraid Robert Seagrove's letters are back home in Germany, otherwise you'd be most welcome to see them.'

'Have you read them?'

'Oh, yes, several times. They are very sad. You can see it clearly. How he was fading. He was a broken man. He wasn't too proud to admit that he drank too much, like so many who came back from the Somme, he felt marked off from other men. Also, he was, how do you say it, shell-shocked and he suffered still from the gas poisoning. He found it difficult to settle back into civilian life I think, to . . .' she searched for the right word again, 'hold down his work, after all he'd seen, all he'd suffered. He lost the family business somehow. Couldn't manage his money, fell into debt. My grandmother invited him several times to visit her but he never did. I expect it was too expensive, if he wasn't working and then he was ill. I think it was the alcohol that finally killed him. It was Charles who came finally, to see my mother, after Robert died. It would have been about nineteen thirty-six, the first time. He didn't want to talk about his father but I believe the drinking was a severe problem. Made him violent and even more depressed. Charles stayed for a couple of weeks. I don't think he wanted to go back home. He and my mother got on well, they were close in age.'

Was Karl Briegel related to the Koenigs in some way? Even as Natasha asked the silent question she was sure he wasn't. But there was a connection. Just as the First World War could be blamed for causing the Second. Charles Seagrove's association with Karl Briegel had everything to do with his friendship with Magda Koenig, The 'hots' he had for Marion Lassiter, Cinderella Pateman's disappearance and with what happened to his father, in no man's land in the Great War.

'What did the V stand for, on the card you left with the wreath?'

Inge abruptly looked down, concentrated hard on buttering a slice of toast. She knew but she wasn't telling.

Twenty-Six

NATASHA'S MOBILE BEEPED, a text message from Toby asking her to call him. When she rang him back, from home, he was in an amusement arcade, by the sound of the simulated laser guns. Just his own living room probably.

He called a ceasefire and said, 'Here's the sitch with Charles Seagrove.'

Natasha tucked the receiver under her chin and opened up a fresh document on the screen. As Arnold was often keen to point out, she was losing the ability to use good old pen and paper, felt almost handicapped if she had to compose a letter in longhand, could certainly type faster than she could write.

'Charles was an only child,' Toby said. 'His parents, Robert and Susan, were at the lower end of the upper class, owned a small distillery in Rochester, Kent.'

'At least you can claim this as part of your brewery research, then.' A distillery wasn't the ideal environment for an alcoholic. It must have been very hard on Charles. He himself didn't drink, she remembered.

'The business had been established and built up by Charles's paternal grandfather, who died in his fifties. The story about Robert Seagrove at the Western Front checks out. After he came back from the war Robert went back to running the business but he must have lost it or sold it because when he died in nineteen twenty-seven, it was no longer his to bequeath, no mention of it in the will. Wasn't mention of much in fact. He left his poor son and widow almost destitute by today's standards. But Susan was a survivor. She ran a small guest house, then became licensee of a less than salubrious pub near the Chatham docks, the Red Lion. Charles's maternal grandfather was in the merchant navy and died aged eighty-two. Obviously I need to confirm all this with the certificates when they arrive. That's as far back as I managed to get but, moving swiftly forward, I checked the National Farm Survey.'

'Well done. I meant to ask you to do that.'

'Fortunately, I can read your mind.'

'I hope not.'

She could read his too, could feel him smiling down the phone. 'No wonder they called it the second Domesday survey,' Toby said. 'It may have been set up to decide post-war agricultural planning but it's a genealogist's dream. I bet the inspectors who conducted it were less than popular though, giving farmers marks from A to C depending on how well they were managing their land. Some cutting remarks about personal failings: "Dilatory, generally untidy, doesn't like parting with money." I'm surprised they got out alive. No wonder we weren't allowed to look at any of this until ten years ago. Charles Seagrove scored straight As though. Conditions of farmhouse, roads, fences, ditches, farm cottages, arable and pasture land all marked as good. No infestation of rabbits, moles, rats or mice. Running water, electricity and a tractor. According to the forms, the livestock was chiefly sheep with a couple of acres for small fruit. Seagrove had owned three hundred acres for the past three years, employed five farm workers, all male, no names given, but I reckon one of them probably was a tenant of one of the farm cottages, Samuel Green.'

'I know his wife, widow, Rebecca Green. She lives in Snowshill. If it's the same Greens. Thanks, Toby.'

'You're welcome.'

'You get back to your work,' she said. 'I'm sure you've got some aliens to blast. Me, I'm in the middle of a real life shoot 'em up situation. So if you've got any tips?'

'If you see them coming at you, run like hell.'

Had the Greens still been tenants at Shadwell when Marion came?

One thing was for sure, Rebecca Green hadn't seen fit to attend her former landlord's memorial, hadn't even acknowledged that she knew Charles Seagrove at all. Samuel Green had departed Snowshill for the afterlife about six years ago, just after Natasha arrived, but his legacy was still a prominent feature of the village.

Over the years he'd accumulated an impressive heap of bits from old tractors and cars he intended to rebuild but never did, which had turned the Greens' land into a metal garden. Rusting exhaust pipes, wheel hubs and cylinders spilled out of the broken-down garage and vied for space with broken body parts of old Massey Fergusons and Morris Minors.

Either Mrs Green was too attached to her husband's collection to get rid of it or she couldn't be bothered. Judging by the old washing machine and shopping trolley that were now parked in the tractor graveyard, the second option was the most likely.

The Greens' cottage was tucked down the back lane by the woods, its aging thatched roof covered in thick green moss, except for the patch that had worn away so badly it let the rain in and had, ever since Natasha had been walking Boris past it, been covered in a sheet of bright blue tarpaulin.

Before he died, Natasha had donned her invisible anorak to listen to Mr Green reminisce about the Sunbeam Alpine's glory racing days but she'd never exchanged more than a smile with his wife.

Rebecca Green opened the door no more than a foot and peered round it at Natasha. Even in the hot weather she wore several layers of baggy woollen cardigans and jumpers, which had all merged into a homogenous brown colour.

'Hi, I'm sorry to bother you, Mrs Green. I was wondering if you could tell me about Charles Seagrove.'

'Humph. Not another one.'

'Pardon?'

'Ne'er mind.'

'You and your husband lived up at Shadwell in the forties, didn't you?'

'We might have.'

Not a promising start. 'Do you mind me asking when you left?'

'Forty-five.'

'Can I ask you why you moved away?'

'You can ask.'

Over Mrs Green's shoulder Natasha could see into the murk of the front room. At the risk of sounding like her mother, it didn't look as though it had been cleaned for decades. Piles of papers and magazines and newspapers, old tins and overflowing shoeboxes, clothes, mugs and plates covered every surface.

'Am I right in thinking you weren't too fond of Mr Seagrove?'

'He was pleasant enough, to start with. It was his ideas and his friends I wasn't too fond of. My husband was a strong man, he could have managed, but Mr Seagrove insisted on bringing in help.' The door opened a fraction wider. Mrs Green was enjoying the chance to give her grievances an airing along with her front room. 'It was an insult, to expect my Samuel to work alongside a German prisoner.'

'That's the reason you left Shadwell?'

'Oh, no. It took more than that to shift us. We had a nice place to live, and Mr Seagrove paid well. But I didn't like to see what was going on. Most of the prisoners could speak good enough English, knew the words for ladder and rake. No reason for Mr Seagrove to start having conversations in a foreign language. It was quite a shock, I can tell you, finding out a country gent like Mr Seagrove spoke German fluent as a native. I wasn't the only one heard him. And it didn't go down too well, as you can imagine. As for that wife of his, seemed peculiar in the head sometimes. Too friendly with the German too, if you know what I mean? All in all, I thought we were best out of it,' Mrs Green finished. 'That satisfy you?'

'That's very helpful. Thank—'

The click of the latch.

Too late, Natasha remembered Mrs Green's opening comment. *Not another one.*

She rapped hard on the door. When it didn't open she shouted as loud as she could, 'Has someone else been here talking to you, Mrs Green?'

The sound of the chain going across.

'Mrs Green?'

The door opened a fraction. 'Your friend Mr Hyatt. Here about an hour ago he was.'

Natasha had to smile. Arnold's circuitous research route had got him there ahead of her again. She was never going to live this down.

Back at Orchard End she read through the notes she'd taken down from Toby about Charles Seagrove. Humbler beginnings than he might have wished, judging by the antiques and grand house that must have been chosen to look like they'd been bequeathed by great-aunts, but on the surface at least, apart from his father's alcoholism, there was nothing he needed to hide or be ashamed of. But if there was one thing she had learnt, it was that you always had to look beneath the surface.

To Karl Briegel. She'd only really been interested in how he related to Marion. But now she had an image of he and Charles Seagrove talking together in German. Of locals smashing the windows at Shadwell because Charles was friends with the enemy. And Stella who'd been more than friends with Karl.

She minimized the notes, logged onto the National Archives website, clicked through to the leaflets section and scrolled down until she found 'Prisoners of War in British Hands: 1698–1949'. She whizzed past the Napoleonic Wars, the Crimean War and Boer War until she came to section 7, the Second World War.

It held very few lists of enemy PoWs and informed her that it was difficult to trace individual prisoners held by the British. Surviving records had been transferred to the appropriate countries. It suggested contacting various organizations such as the International Committee of the Red Cross in Geneva, but said that most would probably require proof of kinship, a service number or ship and regiment. None of which Natasha had. One thing she did have though, following her years at Generations, was the contact details for Konrad Wolff, a genealogist based in Berlin. She fired off an email.

Then she tackled the pile of snail mail and quickly found what she was looking for.

Archie and his gang would no doubt have a copy of Cinderella's birth certificate in the police files, but they might not understand its significance.

At first glance it was unrevealing, but she studied it.

The address of Cinderella's parents was given as 'a horse cart, Maugersbury, Stow-on-the-Wold'. Her father's occupation was 'tree surgeon and fruit-picker'. Horse cart? Of course. A gypsy wagon.

She found the telephone number for the Romany and Traveller Family History Society, a private number, so the fact she was calling outside office hours didn't matter. Yes, the secretary informed her, Cinderella was a popular female given name amongst gypsies. Pateman was a very common gypsy surname.

Cinderella was a gypsy. And a German prisoner of war had been working on Charles Seagrove's land at the time she disappeared. All she could think of now was the Nazi persecution of Jews and gypsies. It was hard to ignore the obvious, much as you might want to.

The PC who picked up the phone said Inspector Butterworth was busy, but when Natasha gave her name and said she had information about the body found at Shadwell, he was busy no longer. 'Wouldn't you rather speak to Sergeant Fletcher?'

'I thought he was off until tomorrow.'

'Summoned back early.'

Dental records had proved that the body in the bluebell woods was that of Cinderella Pateman. No relatives had been traced, so details were about to be released to the press. Natasha wondered if she should mention Noah Hearn, the man Cinderella's schoolmate had mentioned in the email. But the only Noah Hearn she'd located had denied all knowledge of Cinderella.

'Another reason for cutting the trip short,' Archie added when he came on the line. 'My mate went and dislocated his shoulder doing some impromptu rock-climbing. Sometimes all you have to do is lift your arm and it pops back in but Phil had no such luck and we were twenty miles downstream from the nearest hospital.'

'What did you do?' She was impatient with the chit-chat.

'Put my foot in his armpit, gave his arm a pull. Which did the trick. The muscles went into spasm though, and he was getting stabbing pains every time he tried to move his arm. Won't be better for weeks. So we had to call it a day.'

This time Natasha's questions were ones Archie was prepared to answer.

No. There was no news of Rosa but they were still looking. 'You might try to persuade her father to put out an appeal for her to contact him. He flatly refuses. Says she's old enough to look after herself.'

'You can't really argue with that.'

'Oh, but we can. She must have known how it would look.'

Maybe she didn't care. Maybe it looked the way it was.

'Before you ask, I'm afraid we've made no progress with your anonymous letter. It's been checked for fingerprints and it's clean.'

And yes, they did know Cinderella was a gypsy. Her family was originally from one of the gypsy settlements at Epping Forest but came up to the Stow Fair every year and spent the summer hop- and fruit-picking in the Vale of Evesham. Eventually, her father had been given the tenancy of a farm cottage at Didbrook.

'According to Mrs Green, who lives in Snowshill and worked on the Shadwell Estate during the war, there was a German prisoner, Karl Briegel, working at Shadwell around the time Cinderella would have been there. Charles Seagrove seems to have been very friendly with him.'

'I'll make a note of that.'

'Is that all?'

'What else do you want me to do? Unless you can give me this prisoner's address so I can bring him in for questioning.'

Which she couldn't, unless Konrad Wolff came up trumps. 'I think there's someone else you should question again.'

She felt like a traitor as she repeated what John Hellier had told her, but she convinced herself it was for John's own good. She'd wondered if she should edit out the bit about Rosa hearing things, so John would be taken more seriously, but in a way she didn't want him to be taken too seriously, just wanted the police to keep an eye on him. So she gave Archie Fletcher the lot. 'John seemed pretty stressed out.'

'We'll talk to him.'

Thursday was nearly over. Another day gone and it didn't feel as though she'd made any progress.

She could sense Archie was keen to get rid of her, so he could get to it, but she wasn't quite done yet.

No, there was no evidence of Cinderella's precise cause of death. No blow to the head or sign of a bullet wound. But a bullet could have been fatal passing only through organs and flesh, not chipping bone. 'That just about brings you up to date, I think.'

'Can you tell if she ever had a baby?'

'Why do you ask that?' She wasn't even sure herself. She didn't suspect that Richard was Cinderella's son. But something Victor Lassiter had mentioned sprang to mind: *Got herself in the family way and ran off with the fellow.* She could hear Archie rustling papers. 'Says here Cinderella was definitely pregnant and gave birth at some point in her life.'

'Is it possible to tell if she carried to full term?' She didn't need to see Archie's face to know she was the first to ask that question. Which was astonishing. 'You have women police officers there, don't you?' Perhaps not. PC Hard Woman didn't look as if she even possessed a womb. 'Is there any way of telling if she had a miscarriage, or an abortion, or if she gave birth to a full-term baby. In which case, where is that baby now?'

'Who knows?' Archie said, off-hand. 'And to be honest, I can't see what you're getting at. Cinderella's baby wouldn't have been old enough to bury its mother in the woods.'

Impatience made him sound callous. She hoped the investigation wasn't hardening him up, making him lose that fault which she saw as a distinct ability, to see the best in people.

'Aren't you forgetting something?' she said crossly. 'Cinderella's child, if he or she survived, is certainly old enough to have killed Charles Seagrove.'

Twenty-Seven

ONLY THOSE MOST familiar with Natasha's sleeping habits, or sleep*less* habits, would risk calling at half past eleven at night. As it was, Natasha was wide awake. There wasn't much she could do between the hours of 10 p.m and 8 a.m, except think and read and worry, but even that felt better than sleeping, resting, doing nothing.

'I wondered if I could come down to see you.' Ann sounded as if she was preparing herself for Natasha to say that she had other things planned, that she was too busy. Which would have been no exaggeration.

She swallowed hard. 'That'd be lovely.' She was keen to ask Ann why she wanted to come but there was no way to do it without it coming out all wrong. A mother didn't need a reason to visit her eldest daughter, even if it was something she'd never been known to do before. 'How about next week, Tuesday evening?' The date John Hellier had set her. By the evening it would be over, for better or for worse.

They made arrangements.

Counting sheep may induce sleep but counting days certainly didn't. After her conversation with Ann, dates and numbers spun in her head. Friday, the last day of June, would start in a few minutes. Four full days left until 4 July. In eleven days she should have been driving to Heathrow airport.

When she woke the next morning, the foggy-headedness seemed to have lifted a little, fortunately, but she didn't feel entirely back on form. And Konrad Wolff's speed and efficiency made her feel incompetent.

He rang to tell her that, from the Military Archive of the Federal Records Office in Freiburg and the Personnel Archives in Aachen, he'd discovered Karl Briegel had joined the Waffen-SS 12th Panzer Division, Hitlerjugend in 1944, at the age of seventeen.

'This was the first Waffen SS formation to go into action against the Allies in Normandy in the summer of 1944,' Konrad explained. 'Its teenaged soldiers came from the ranks of the Hitler Youth. Instead of the usual cigarette and schnapps ration they were issued with milk and sweets. But as soon as they had a chance to demonstrate their courage, loyalty and disregard for human life, it soon put an end to the jokes.' His spoken English was precise and formal, sentences peppered with words you'd only usually see written down, as you'd expect from someone whose career, as a historian and researcher, meant he'd be more used to reading English than speaking it.

He went on to explain how the Hitlerjugend fought ruthlessly in infantry combat and in close-quarter action against tanks and gained themselves a fearsome reputation amongst the Allied soldiers. The division was implicated in several atrocities against the Canadian and British forces during the Normandy battles, including the murder of prisoners from the Nova Scotia Highlanders. The Hitlerjugend held Caen for thirty-three days and suffered appalling casualties. It was here that many were captured.

Konrad hadn't managed to locate details of what exactly had happened to the Hitlerjugend members but he hazarded a guess. After the Allied invasion of western Europe, those captured were often transported on large barges over the English Channel to major ports where they were put aboard trains to take them to holding camps set up at racecourses and football grounds. They were interrogated on military matters and their loyalty to the Nazi regime before being sent to one of the six hundred camps around Britain. Towards the end of 1944 the screening process became somewhat hurried due to large volumes of prisoners arriving in the country, which resulted in Nazis being mixed in camps with the moderates.

Neither the German War Veterans Organization, HIAG, the Waffen-SS veterans organization or its magazine *Der Freiwillige*, had any contact with Karl Briegel. He didn't show up in any of the general records after the war.

His pre-war history was easier to trace. His family were originally from Düsseldorf, his father was a carpenter. His mother's maiden name was Becker, 'No relation to Boris.' No relation to Hans Koenig either.

In his comprehensive report, which Konrad emailed over, he suggested avenues Natasha could explore next, going on to say that it was possible Karl had changed his identity, gone into hiding, like many former members of the SS. He concluded:

> *The International Military Tribunal at Nuremberg declared many organizations of the National Socialist period in Germany to be criminal. These included the SS. Under the provisions of Military Government Ordinance No 69 of 31 December 1946, former members of such organizations were liable to trial before German tribunals and various other courts set up by the occupying powers. This major operation was code-named 'Old Lace'.*
>
> *As you probably know* [she didn't], *the most comprehensive accumulation of papers on 'Old Lace' is to be found among the records of the Control Commission for Germany's Legal Division in the National Archives in London. I would suggest that it would be worth looking for Karl Briegel there.*

This was one job she felt she couldn't delegate to Toby, had to do herself.

She re-read, extracting what she needed. For now what seemed most relevant was this: Karl Briegel had gone underground. He had belonged to a military unit that was courageous, ruthless, fearsome and disregarded human life.

But all that was a long time ago. How often did you come across a gun-totting octogenarian? On the other hand leopards were proverbially loyal to their spots.

Natasha went across to the Snowshill Arms for lunch.

Heidi had done the same.

'I should really be grabbing ten minutes to do some housework before my mother arrives,' Natasha said. 'It's about the only opportunity I'm going to get.'

She, Heidi and Mary had often discussed the puzzling need to enter into a scrubbing and polishing frenzy in honour of your mother's visit, as common amongst her generation as it was for Ann's to inspect their offspring's corners for crumbs. 'We may be allowed into universities and boardrooms now but when it comes to it we're still judged by our skills with a mop,' Heidi grinned.

'Standards of cleanliness are slipping along with morals and the ability to ride side-saddle,' Natasha decided. 'Our kiddies will probably revert to Medieval manners, eat their dinner with their fingers and then burp very loudly.'

'My kiddie already does,' Mary shouted over from the bar.

For now though, the vacuum would have to go and whistle, Natasha said. She'd feel guilty spending precious time cleaning.

Mary and James were busy behind the bar so she went over to pay for the lasagne. Mary insisted that everyone who stayed for B&B signed the guest book left open beside the till, and as Natasha waited for the credit card machine to do its thing, she glanced at the latest page. The second to last entry was Inge Ostermeier. The address she'd written down wasn't Wassenberg, where she told Natasha she'd come from, but Steinhoring, *near* Wassenberg.

Tenacious as a dandelion, Natasha fired off a quick speculative email to Konrad Wolff to ask if Steinhoring struck any relevant bells.

She went upstairs to have a shower to try to wake herself up. She stepped out, grabbed two towels, turbaned one round her head. As soon as she'd dried off she felt hot again. She pulled a violet tiered skirt from her wardrobe, was reaching behind her back to hook up her bra strap when she heard something downstairs. The rustling of paper, a scraping sound, like a chair being moved.

Boris was guarding the threshold of her bedroom door. He'd heard it too, his ears pricked forward, twitching like radars alert to any further sound.

She dragged on a vest top. It was broad daylight, nothing to be scared of.

She crept out onto the landing, peered down to the hall below. The front door was ajar. She was sure she'd not left it like that.

She fished her mobile out of her bag, hit 999 so all she'd have to do was punch 'send' if need be. She could almost see her own heart pulsating in her chest. Boris slunk downstairs behind her legs. Some guard dog. She just hoped that if he knew she was in real trouble he'd leap to her defence.

From her kitchen came a slight, wheezy breath.

A voice she recognized.

'You two gave me a real fright.'

'Sorry, my dear.' Mr Samuels and Miss Dodsworth were ensconced at the table, their offerings before them, a pie and enough tomatoes and lettuces to feed the entire village. Miss Dodsworth had got out her knitting, a lemon mohair sleeve.

They'd never once bothered to ask if they were interrupting or if she had other plans.

Kettle. Biscuits.

This time she made a conscious effort to steer Mr Samuels back to his previous comments about Charles Seagrove. Not difficult, given that Shadwell was still a prime topic of conversation in the village. 'I was thinking about what you said about him reaping what he sowed. Did you mean that you think he got his just desserts?'

'I meant only that he upset a lot of people and that's bound to have repercussions.'

'How did he upset them?'

'There were mothers here whose sons went to war and didn't come back, girls who lost their sweethearts and husbands, and sometimes it was hard to tell whose side Charles Seagrove was on.'

'Are you saying he was a sympathizer?'

'I believe he called himself a pacifist. Was heard saying that war was pointless. That doesn't go down too well when you want to think your son or husband died a hero, for a good cause.'

Natasha couldn't get much more out of them than that but she kept their memories focused on the Second World War. Mr

Samuels obliged with morsels about the garage on the High Street in Chipping Campden, which had once been a factory for the manufacture of Spitfire parts, a bee colony at the Springhill camp which produced the most golden honey, and heavy winter snows sometime during the war, when the German POWs went sledging on Dovers Hill in an old tin bath.

'The prisoners went to work on some of the local farms, didn't they?' She poured the tea. 'Would the War Agricultural Committee have allocated them, like they did the land girls?'

'No. It'd have been the camp commandant, I should think,' Mr Samuels said. 'He'd have been the one in charge of organizing the prisoners' workgroups.'

'A rifleman from the camp would have escorted them to their work, kept watch and brought them back to the camp to sleep at night,' Miss Dodsworth volunteered.

'Ah, not always,' Mr Samuels corrected her. 'There was that pair living in an old chicken house up at Diggerman's farm. No guard there.'

'They trusted them not to try to escape?' Natasha asked.

'It all became very relaxed later on.'

'I remember we offered them food but they seemed reluctant to take our rations,' Miss Dodsworth pitched in. 'Either they felt they shouldn't or they'd been told not to, I'm not sure which.'

It hadn't really struck her before that hers was the first generation not to have lived through a major war, was no doubt softer and more selfish as a result, took more for granted.

Natasha watched Miss Dodsworth doing her perpetual knitting while she chatted. Knit one, pearl one. When Ann had taught her she'd patiently caught up all the stitches Natasha dropped, looping them back in before everything unravelled. That's what Natasha was doing now, chasing loose ends, chasing her tail, like a sheep dog rounding everything up, following every scent, in the hope that eventually it would all come together.

Cinderella Pateman who'd been friends with Marion Lassiter ... Marion Lassiter who'd been more than friends with Karl Briegel ... Karl Briegel whose name had been written on Marion Lassiter's family tree by Charles Seagrove ... Charles Seagrove whose father had met another German soldier, Hans Koenig . . . Hans Koening who'd left behind a widow, Magda.

Then there was Richard Seagrove, Charles's son, . . . Rosa, Charles's granddaughter, who wanted to marry John Hellier, the descendant of the murderess Alice . . . somewhere, a little girl called Amelia, who was special to Stella Seagrove, Charles's wife.

No genealogical chart linked them all, but they *were* all linked, and more than just in the obvious ways. She knew it. Another day gone, tomorrow was the weekend. She was halfway through the week that John had given her. Only three days left to work it all out.

She came back to it once more, the one thing that did link many of the strands: Germany. The picture she was forming of Charles Seagrove as a young man, and of what might have taken place at Shadwell during the war years, was growing clearer and at the same time darker. Seagrove visiting a widow of the First World War and her little girl in a Bavarian village. Coming home proclaiming himself a pacifist, employing a German prisoner of war, speaking to him in his native tongue.

The rest of them were all there, somewhere, hiding within that picture, like a hologram in which the images rearranged themselves depending on the angle at which they were observed. Marion. Cinderella. Richard. Stella. Maybe also the mysterious little girl called Amelia, but heaven only knew where she fitted in.

Twenty-Eight

NATASHA HAD SENT an email to the National Archives to pre-order the files she needed, so they were waiting for her when she arrived at Kew the next morning. Piles of 'Old Lace', sheaves of tissue-thin carbon copies of typed letters and memos and progress reports in tattered brown folders tied with tape and fastened with green tabs. How were code names chosen; with an eye to poetry or dark irony? 'Old Lace', the fabric from which beautiful things were made, wedding veils and gowns lovingly preserved in attic trunks.

All the folders bore the official stamp of the Legal Division of the Control Commission for Germany and were dated 1947 or 1948. Old papers were like the gateway from a sci-fi movie, connecting two different worlds. The electrifying sensation of reaching through and touching history, of opening once highly confidential documents probably not looked at for decades – it never wore off.

Much emphasis at the 'Old Lace' trials seemed to have been placed on the debate about the definition of the term 'guilty knowledge'. Guilty not by your own deed but by knowledge and by acceptance of the deeds of others.

She read:

The Court found that the accused had knowledge of the persecution of Jews, having heard that they were compelled to wear the Star of David and that they were expelled from Germany and sent East.

Defence Counsel argued that accused's knowledge of the persecution of Jews was based only on rumours.

The accused pleaded ignorance wherever possible, but finally had to admit knowledge of the following: that political opponents of the Nazi regime were sent to Concentration camps and that the SS provided the guards for these camps.

What was astonishing was the leniency of the sentences: *Affidavits read out in court described the accused as a fanatical Nazi: Court found the accused guilty and sentenced him to three years imprisonment.*

A convicted Nazi who stubbornly denied and refused to believe that crimes were committed by the SS: *One year's imprisonment.*

The trials all followed in the same vein: *Sentenced to seven months imprisonment* or *Fined.*

A press release issued in 1947 explained that 27,000 Germans were being held for immediate trial. The toughest sentence that could be imposed was ten years imprisonment plus forfeiture of property and fines.

Natasha couldn't help but remember her last visit here, when she'd surveyed the nineteenth-century assize records, which contained the names of those who'd been transported for stealing a sheep.

Just as the announcement came over the tannoy that the reading room would be closing in ten minutes, she found a translation of a letter from Franz Heffer, the father of a member of the 12th Panzer Division Hitlerjugend, the same division in which Karl Briegel had served.

My belief is that youth cannot be blamed. The persuasive strength of the school education, the radio and general propaganda were more powerful than the warning words of a father, and made my son a stranger in his parents' house. His misfortune cannot lessen my friendship for the English but for that reason I appeal to their compassion and understanding of the fact that German Youth was led astray and harmed by Nazism and cannot therefore be guilty.

That was probably the closest she was going to get to Karl Briegel, except perhaps his ghost lurking in the face of a son who didn't even know his father's name.

She closed the files and took them back to the returns desk, then walked quickly down the long corridor and outside. She stood by the artificial lake as a low-flying Jumbo, taking off from Heathrow, tore the sky apart.

She had told Richard Seagrove that she loved her job. Right now she hated it. She'd once believed, with all her heart, in the power of history, that only by facing and learning to live with the past could you live properly and fully in the present. She'd believed that understanding your own past was the most vital of all. She'd believed that discovering your real parents, your real roots, guaranteed a happy ending, of sorts, guaranteed some peace at least. Because knowing the truth, whatever it was, was infinitely preferable to not knowing. Now that belief had fallen away.

But she had to carry on as if it hadn't, as if she still believed her job was worthwhile, that history was always a precious gift.

She made herself ring Richard. 'Still no news of Rosa?'

'Nothing. The police told me about your visit from John.'

'Oh shit.' Did they have to? 'I'm so sorry. I should have come to you first, only I didn't want to add to your worries.'

'You did the right thing, putting Sergeant Fletcher on to it. He says John's probably making it up. He's probably just telling me that to make me feel better but love can do strange things to people.'

Yes, she thought. It can be murder. Did Archie Fletcher really think John's warning was a fabrication?

'Rosa's very good at taking care of herself, I'm holding onto that.'

'We need to talk. Could you come over?'

'It'll have to be tomorrow morning, on my way to London.'

'You're going back to your school?'

'I promised I'd be there for the last couple of weeks of term. Sports Day, you know. My big moment.'

She didn't have the heart to rib him about egg and spoon races as she might have done, if the innocent fun of an egg and spoon race didn't almost make her want to cry. 'Tomorrow would be fine.'

Nothing much else she could do on a Sunday, though she was trying not to think about that, about the fact that she really only had Monday left to help John and Rosa.

She'd been working at her computer, allegedly, although she'd not achieved much, except for making a detailed inventory of the view from her living-room window. The sun was shining but there were dark clouds in the sky which made the green of the grass and the pink of the honeysuckle more intense.

She'd spent a good proportion of her life staring out of windows, classroom windows, college windows, office windows. The knowledge that she couldn't just unlatch them, lift them, swing them wide and climb through, sometimes made her legs tingle with the urge to run, her chest go so tight she could hardly breathe. Life was always conspiring to trap you, in one way or another.

She felt worn out, and now and then odd shadows and shapes floated across her vision. She tried to replace them with the red maple leaf.

She turned to the black on white of the computer screen, a half-finished genealogical chart spidering across, a list of dead people. She hit 'save'. Too late to save them now, the dead. When she looked up again, Richard Seagrove had appeared at the window like one of their spirits.

He'd regained his composure and she was struck afresh by how tall he was, how athletic and physically powerful. She was suddenly all too aware that here was a man whose daughter was missing, who'd been arrested for the murder of his father.

Instantly, she wished she'd arranged to meet him somewhere else, away from her own home, a pub maybe or a hotel, where they wouldn't be alone. She'd been concerned about his privacy, when maybe she should have been concerned about her own safety. It was impossible to forget that Charles Seagrove's murderer, whoever it was, was still at large. She told herself not to be ridiculous; Richard Seagrove was not a killer.

In the kitchen, Richard studied the depths of his coffee mug, then looked back at her as if he was about to say something intimate. 'There's a photograph of Cinderella Pateman in the papers today. They say she was only seventeen.' Richard looked at Natasha with his blue eyes and she knew with a startling certainty that he was thinking of the teenaged boys in his football team. 'Apparently after they printed the first news of her death one of her cousins came out of the woodwork. A man called Noah Hearn. He told the paper he remembers that she was pregnant and her father threatened to throw her out but she couldn't bear to get rid of the baby.'

If it was the same Noah Hearn, which it surely must be, he'd been a lot less forthcoming when she'd spoken to him on the phone. She wondered if the paper had paid him for his story. Or maybe it was just that he'd not known Cinderella was dead before, had not wanted to give away her secret.

'According to Hearn, Cinderella said her baby was a living being, a part of her, and she wouldn't let it be killed.' Richard spoke as if he agreed wholeheartedly about that.

If she was right, his real father had guilty knowledge of the death of thousands. He had his father's blood running in his veins, yet he was uncomfortable about the idea of aborting an unborn child. It was enough to make you think blood counted for nothing at all. But the knowledge she possessed made her feel guilty as hell.

'Does Mr Hearn know how Cinderella came to be at Shadwell?'

'Apparently she said she knew of somewhere they, she and her child, could go, where they'd both be safe. Said she knew of someone who'd look after them, someone who didn't disapprove of unmarried mothers.' Richard looked at her again. 'He must have meant my father.'

My father. My father. How could she tell him about his real father?

Go on. Tell him who he is.

Since she'd drunk champagne to celebrate his birthday, Richard Seagrove's whole identity, his entire genetic configuration, had changed. He should look to her like a stranger now. Except that nothing had really changed at all. He was the same person he'd always been.

Instead she repeated what Victor Lassiter had told her about Marion, about her being Cinderella's friend and being in love with a German POW, Karl Briegel, who was working on the Shadwell estate. She talked him through friendships and siblings and lovers, but she left out the final connection, how Marion and Karl Briegel might be related to Richard himself.

'I'm amazed you've found out so much. But we're still no closer to understanding what my father had against John?'

Close, but no cigar, whatever that meant. If she'd taken a wrong turning somehow . . . She had to be more certain before she could mention anything at all to John, or to Rosa, or to Richard.

'We're no nearer to finding out who killed my father either.'

'No. But I haven't given up yet.'

'Thank you,' Richard said. 'I was wondering . . . would you know how to go about tracing Cinderella's baby, if it survived?'

'No,' she said, more harshly than she'd intended. 'Why?'

He thought for a moment, gave the slightest of shrugs. 'So a little good can come of all this.'

She wanted to yell at him: What if Cinderella's baby doesn't want to be found? How can it be good, finding out that the woman who'd carried you in her womb has been lying dead all this time in a bluebell wood?

But still she knew what Richard had meant. And it cut her up.

Because he still believed that, no matter what, discovering the truth about the two people who'd given you life guaranteed a happy ending.

Twenty-Nine

CINDERELLA PATEMAN HAD the same unusual colouring as Natasha. The rare combination of fair hair and dark eyes. In Cinderella's eyes, even in a black-and-white photograph, the allure was unmissable. She and Marion would have made a striking pair.

After Richard had said Cinderella's face had been in the local paper Natasha had driven to the newsagent in Chipping Campden.

Sunny days came with a price in the Cotswolds. There were coach loads of tourists pouring into the little town.

Today, everything felt such a struggle, a struggle to which she was beginning to feel unequal. She was suddenly almost incapacitated by fatigue and tried to ignore the feeling that her skull was crushing her brain.

She had to fight down irritation and impatience as she negotiated the hubbub round the Market Hall, the stalls selling wickerwork and woodcarvings under the stone arches and gables, the ambling, well-dressed pensioners and mothers with three-wheeled prams, the spotless 4×4s. She didn't have time for them, had hooted her horn twice already.

Cinderella's photograph was in all of the local papers, on the front page of one under the predictable headline: 'CLOCK STRIKES MIDNIGHT TOO EARLY FOR CINDERELLA.'

Unlike Marion, whose clothes and hairstyle fixed her forever in the forties, Cinderella's portrait could have been taken yesterday. Long, thick hair, unrestrained and uncut, a dark, tight-fitting top with three-quarter-length sleeves and a plunging V-neck. Her smile was vivacious, almost brazen. You'd never guess that she'd been gone from this world for over half a century.

Through force of habit, Natasha came home and immediately clicked the send/receive icon on the iMac. Konrad Wolff's name jumped into her inbox again. Another workaholic who didn't take Sundays off. She'd not really expected much, if anything, to come of the hasty email she'd sent after seeing Inge Ostermeier's entry in the Snowshill Arms guest book. But she had been wrong.

Steinhoring is linked to all members of the SS in one way. You are aware that it was the venue for the first of Hitler's Lebensborn homes for unmarried mothers?

No, she was not aware of that.

She fed 'Nazi' and 'Steinhoring' into Google and waited. Three links came up. You could rely on the internet to dish the dirt. The first was titled 'Hitler's Third Reich: Little-Known Facts'.

The first of Heinrich Himmler's Lebensborn homes was opened at Steinhoring, in southern Germany, on 12 December 1935 ...

She scrolled and read, agitation making her skim.

Lebensborn ... masquerading as maternity homes for single mothers ... Lebensborn means 'Fount of Life' ... breeding programme ... crazy attempt at genetic manipulation. SS to be prime forefathers of new Aryan nation ... Pass untainted warrior blood to future generations ... equally rigorous selection process of willing young women pronounced pure enough to 'make a child for Hitler' ... Flip side of the policy that resulted in the Holocaust ... racially impure to be exterminated while the racially pure were encouraged to multiply

At the end of the page was a photograph of something she'd seen before. Only she couldn't have, because the statue in the photograph stood in the grounds of the Hochland Home, in Steinhoring. An outsized grey stone sculpture of a mother breast-feeding a baby, her classical features and strong physique characteristic of the Nazi's idealized image of the Aryan race. The faces of baby and mother were different but there was no doubting that the statue that stood in Shadwell was modelled on it. Which begged the question: what else in Shadwell had been modelled on a Lebensborn home?

She reopened Konrad's email, hit reply.

What can you tell me about the Lebensborn programme and any connections there might have been to Britain?

Konrad's name appeared in her inbox again within a quarter of an hour. She clicked on it, tapping the mouse as if it might scald her.

There were Lebensborn homes all over the occupied territories of Europe: Poland, Austria, Belgium, France, Holland, Luxemburg and Denmark. Thousands of children were born in them. The only British territory occupied by the Germans was the Channel Islands, of course, the Germans seeing this first conquest of British Isles as a step towards the occupation of mainland Britain. Hitler and Himmler admired Britain's Anglo-Saxon racial composition so Britain would have been a prime hunting ground, as were the Channel Islands. But, because the population was so small, nothing was done until quite late in the war. A German commander there wrote that the children and mothers were racially irreproachable and that many of the mothers had learned German in the hope of being allowed to move to Germany. Many girls formed friendships with soldiers and the SS race office decreed that the children of German soldiers stationed on the islands should be racially examined. Those classified as valuable were to be sent to Germany, and women expecting German-fathered children should be sent to Lebensborn homes.

Just because there were no official Lebensborn homes in Britain, that is not to say similar activity never went on. There were always those who thought Hitler would win the war and were prepared to assist the cause on the assumption that after the final victory they would be rewarded. There would have been German agents in Britain assessing who was friendly to the prospect of invasion and the fostering of

Lebensborn ideals would undoubtedly have been looked upon very favourably.

It was like standing on shifting sand.

The image of Charles Seagrove morphed again.

Visiting Magda Koenig in Steinhoring. Through her or people he met through her, being introduced to radical and dangerous ideas, which he brought home to England and which made him a traitor. A traitor who engineered a relationship between blonde, blue-eyed Marion Lassiter and Karl Briegel, a Nazi.

Thirty

HER EX-COLLEAGUE Will had suggested to Natasha that they meet at the Wellcome Building on Euston Road, a palatial Art Deco edifice with grand stone columns and revolving brass doors.

What made the Wellcome Building seem truly welcoming, as well as an appropriate place for two genealogists to hole up, was the prominently displayed quote by Henry Wellcome, pharmaceutical king and collector of vast arrays of medical artefacts and books: 'I have found that the study of the roots and foundations of things greatly assists research and facilitates discovery and invention.'

Here's hoping, Natasha whispered under her breath. She was pinning *all* her hopes on making some discoveries here. She had to. It was Monday, 3 July. She had just fourteen hours left to help John Hellier. What was going to happen if she didn't succeed didn't bear thinking about.

John hadn't said exactly what time of day whatever was going to happen would happen, all he'd said was that she had 'until the fourth'. Until, not including.

The double-height reading rooms of the extensive Library for the History and Understanding of Medicine resembled photographs of the interior of the Titanic. Edwardian chandeliers, mahogany shelves, wide marble steps with an elegant brass handrail leading to a gallery, around the base of which were plaques celebrating the names of famous medical pioneers: Nightingale, Jenner, Pavlov, Florey, Darwin. The chairs were studded green leather and the walls decorated with oil paintings of Victorian surgical procedures, bloodletting.

Will, workaholic that he was, was already ensconced at a table at the back, near the entrance to the biography room, dwarfed by a pile of books bedecked with yellow post-it notes.

He leaned over the table and kissed her cheek, exuding a scent of trendy aftershave. 'Thought I'd get a head start.' His smile was as bright and crisp as his sixties-inspired Paisley shirt, which, even in such scholarly surroundings and set off by his Mediterranean complexion and inky hair gelled into a Tin-Tin quiff at the front, made him look like an unusually tidy lead singer in a rock band. 'You look done in.'

'Thanks, Will.' She felt as though she'd barely slept all week. In fact, she *had* barely slept all week, and she'd learned to live with the constant headache, faint dizziness and throbbing pain behind her eyes that had been there since the car crash. She didn't have time to be ill or weak, so she simply ignored the discomfort, hoping it would go away. So far it hadn't.

Will knew his way around the subject of genetics in genealogy far better than Natasha and she was hugely grateful for his offer to help. She wasn't sure she'd have been able to handle this on her own.

She glanced at the volumes piled in front of him. Usually, the prospect of a day engrossed in history filled her with quiet pleasure, but this time the topic in which she had to immerse herself killed any enjoyment, the titles themselves a potted history of the most horrific events and greatest evil of the twentieth century.

Eugenics and Fascism; *Human Genetics and Human Failings: The Eugenics Society in Britain*; *Inheriting Shame: The Psychology and Politics of Genocide*; *Building the Master Race*; *The Nazi Doctors*.

If there was a Big Brother observing who was reading what, there was a good chance there'd be a secret service agent waiting outside her front door by the time she got home. She could have sworn that the researcher sitting further down the table was giving them a wide berth, probably reckoning they were a pair of subversive students plotting a dangerous new world order.

All Natasha was plotting was how to get this over as quickly as possible. She and Will halved the stack of books and carried them upstairs to a polished table in a corner of the gallery.

'I hope you're going to enlighten me,' he said as he sat down, 'To say you were vague on the phone is an understatement. I know *what* I'm supposed to be helping you to find but haven't a clue as to *why*.'

She sighed. Where would she start? She hadn't yet voiced to anyone the dark hypothesis that had been shaping itself in her mind. Maybe she should. She slipped into the chair opposite Will. 'OK. If you were compiling a genealogical chart for hereditary, genetic purposes, you'd major on including medical reports, right?'

He looked at her as if she was nuts. 'Of course you would.'

Generations was one of the few companies of professional genealogists in the country, and Will worked for the department that was attracting a lot of attention recently due to its emphasis on genetics, the major revolution in twentieth-century medical science and in genealogy. Because genetics focused on the way characteristics and medical conditions could be hereditary, it proved family history to be crucially relevant to every living being.

'How long since your department was set up?'

'Ten years.'

'And Generations were pioneers in genealogy allied to genetics?'

'You worked there for three years, you must've read the brochure.'

'I think I know the answer to this, but tell me, why would genealogists have been interested in that material sixty years ago?'

Will patted the pile of books. 'The structure of DNA may have only been discovered fifty years ago but the word gene was invented in 1909 and the basic theory of eugenics, improving humankind by selective breeding and eliminating bad genetic traits, has been around since the nineteenth century. However, the nature versus nuture debate divides fascists from communists as neatly as their politics, so basically anyone interested in that stuff sixty years ago ran the serious risk of being accused of being a Nazi.'

'You're saying that wouldn't necessarily be the case?'

Will shook his head. 'Uh-huh. Not at all. After all, the good old British Empire was founded on the concept that the world is split between the enlightened and lesser breeds.' Wind him up and watch him go. 'It was our own Charles Darwin who suggested that advances in medicine would interfere with natural selection, helping the survival of the unfittest. It was Darwin's cousin, Francis Galton, who actually invented the word eugenics.' He shoved Galton's book at her, *Hereditary Genius*, open at the first page. 'Galton used his own illustrious family to argue that distinguished and talented men had distinguished and talented relatives.'

She read how he recommended 'judicious marriage' and called it the 'duty' of authorities to control progressive breeding.

She then explained to Will how Charles Seagrove had asked her to research the ancestry of his granddaughter's fiancé.

'I can see where you're coming from.'

'Seagrove was a member of the Galton Institute. It was in his obituary.'

'So are lots of very respectable people. You're looking at one. With hindsight you could blame old Francis for inventing an idea that would cause misery and cruelty to millions but he couldn't have know where it would lead. But it wasn't just the Nazis who latched on to the idea. Way before them, scientists all over the world were using callipers and craniometers to measure heads and noses to determine genetic make-up. The First International Congress of Eugenics was held at London University in the early 1900s with Alexander Graham Bell and Winston Churchill in attendance. In the 1920s dozens of US states had laws to sterilize people they decided were criminally insane or genetically inferior. Everything is dangerous if you take it to extremes and all that. What you have to bear in mind is, until Hitler showed the world the horrendous implications of where it could all lead, eugenics was seen as a reasonable solution to moral disorder, seemed to offer a way to strengthen families and nations. H.G Wells, Virginia Woolf, T.S. Eliot and George Bernard Shaw all flirted with the idea.'

Charles Seagrove was a farmer who, so his granddaughter had said, was experimenting with breeding programmes ahead of his time. He was also a genealogist with an interest in genetics so it followed, surely, that he had long ago made the connection between family history and the world of science and medicine. The medical records in Marion Lassiter and John Hellier's family trees were testament to that.

But nothing Will had said could prevent her thinking that Seagrove's interests went far beyond the basic principles of eugenics. If he had been a Nazi sympathizer, a collaborator even, as everything she'd discovered so far seemed to indicate, how much of what they stood for did he condone? How much guilty knowledge did he have? There was no escaping the fact that it was medical experiments and breeding programmes and misplaced notions of racial purity that had lead to anti-Semitism and genocide, concentration camps and millions of deaths.

She opened her laptop and as Will quietly talked her through the passages he'd marked for her attention, she made notes and lifted anything that might in any way shed light on what made Charles Seagrove tick, and confirm what he had against John Hellier. And the further she went in her attempt to get inside his head, the less sure she was that it was somewhere she wanted to venture.

In *Building the Master Race* there was a page of Auschwitz registration photographs, a girl with a headscarf and a boy with a shorn head. Each of their faces shot from three different angles – facing the camera, in profile, looking to one side. On the first frame was a number. At the bottom of the page was a quote from a child who'd been born in a Lebensborn home: 'The Nazis gave us numbers too. I am Lebensborn 1029. I cannot help wondering which Jew or gypsy I was supposed to replace. We were at opposite ends of the same distorted ideology. I the wanted and they the unwanted. My life began as theirs was destroyed. Positive and negative they call it. But there was nothing positive about Lebensborn.'

For now Natasha tried to make her fingers a pure conduit of her ears and eyes, typed what she heard and read, bypassing her brain, forcing herself to resist drawing conclusions until she'd assessed all the evidence.

When they'd been through all the volumes, she'd amassed half a dozen pages of notes. Scrupulously systematic, yet at a frenetic pace, she started the process of scrolling up and down, embolden-ing text, clicking the mouse button, cutting and pasting. Gradually, the mishmash of jottings began to take on a dark and disturbing shape.

'So there you have it,' she whispered eventually, resting her head on her elbows and leaning forward in the chair. 'Seagrove's reasons for wanting John Hellier's family tree.'

She read aloud from the top of the screen.

'Before granting a certificate to marry, the Nazi's insisted bride and groom complete questionnaire of physical features and record of medical and racial background of their ancestors over two hundred years. Hereditary Health Courts were set up to provide training courses in family history to determine if the couple's ancestry and blood were sufficiently pure. The right choice of mate was the Nazi's prerequisite for a worthy and prosperous society.'

So it *was* Alice and her unlawful clan who damned the Helliers in Seagrove's eyes. She read on.

'An original aim of the Eugenics Society, now the Galton Institute, was to eradicate the family stock which produced paupers, the feeble-minded, alcoholics and criminals.'

'Well, murder's about as criminal as it gets,' Will conceded.

'According to Rosa,' Natasha said, 'her grandfather had always been passionate about breeding programmes.'

Will nodded. 'Lebensborn homes were basically glorified stud farms. That's what you think Seagrove was up to with Marion Lassiter? Are you saying that he was using the Lebensborn programme as a blueprint for a social experiment of his own?'

What was it Konrad had said? *There were always those who thought Hitler would win the war and were prepared to assist the cause on the assumption that after the final victory they would be rewarded.*

They looked at each other. It was the first time Natasha had seen real fear in Will's eyes and she knew he would see it reflected in hers. It wasn't the kind of fear that made the hairs raise on the back of your neck or your heart rate increase, but a still, cold horror that lodged deep inside. She'd known all along that she was involved in a murder investigation but this was so much more terrible than anything she could have imagined. The implication of these revelations for Marion, for Cinderella, for their children, were too awful to contemplate. She wanted to slam all the books shut, erase all the files on her laptop.

'You say Charles Seagrove had no genealogical chart for Karl Briegel?' Will said quietly.

'If he did have one, nobody's been able to find it.'

'Well, here's your explanation for that at least.' Will read aloud again.

'"*Recruitment into the SS involved candidates proving their Germanic roots back to 1800*". The Nazis had already done Charles's work for him.'

'Doesn't it make you question what we do for a living?' Natasha said.

'No.' Will was adamant. 'There's a difference in worshipping your ancestors and just being interested in them.'

Her gaze fell upon a page describing the naming ceremony of the children of the SS.

We believe in the race, carrier of the blood.
We bow in reverence before our ancestors.
The brotherhood binds man to the duty of guarding this heritage
We ourselves will become ancestors

Hocus-pocus, but it left a nasty taste in her mouth.

The Nazis had given genetics a bad name, and quietly and less publicly, they'd given genealogy a bad name too. She felt tainted.

We ourselves will become ancestors. Charles Seagrove's voice rang loud and clear in her ears. He'd used those exact words the first time she'd met him. It seemed a lifetime ago.

Had he been murdered because of his allegiance during the war? Had Cinderella died because of it too? It seemed inevitable that they had.

She turned back the pages and looked at the photograph of the Lebensborn home in Steinhoring, the white Gothic watchtower like the turret of a medieval castle, the steeply-pitched roofs and balconies and French windows opening out onto long terraces, the light and airy rooms decorated with Germanic insignias and ornaments.

One insignia she recognized all too well: a pierced V. The caption described it as the runic symbol for life, adopted as the emblem for the Lebensborn programme. It was the motif that Magda Koenig had drawn alongside her initial on the wreath she asked her daughter to lay for Charles Seagrove.

Natasha tried to picture Charles Seagrove and Magda in the rooms of that castle-like building in Steinhoring, and found she could do it all too easily.

Thirty-One

NATASHA JUMPED OFF the train at Moreton and sprinted across to her car. It was almost 5 p.m. She was counting time purely in hours instead of days now. Seven hours until midnight, until 4 July.

Her theory was just a theory which still needed refining but she had to let John have it. If she could find him. He wasn't in his room in Bledisloe Court, nor was he in the student's union. According to reception, however, his tutorial group was up at the Royal Agricultural College's pig farm in the small hamlet of Harnhill, just south-east of Cirencester. She followed a tractor up a rough track that passed through wide, open pastureland, the cross-breeze rippling the grass like waves on water. The heat of the day was over but the shadows hadn't started to lengthen yet.

She could see a small huddle of students up ahead, by the perimeter fence of a field dotted with pigsties, which looked not unlike the Nissan huts that had housed prisoners of war at Studely. John was standing aside from a group, all of whom were listening to a talk by a wax-jacketed man with a clipboard. Several spotted pigs with dirty snouts were snuffling around their feet.

She spared herself and the hire car any more bone-shaking, parked in a not-too-deep ditch, got out and walked the rest of the way, barely feeling the sharp stones through the thin soles of her sandals.

She caught John Hellier's wary eye and snatches of the lecture at the same time. Something about Landrace and Large White gilts and sows being 'served via artificial insemination with semen from

Duroc boars' and 'small numbers of Landrace sows being served with Landrace semen to maintain the pure line'. She couldn't help thinking that Charles Seagrove would have approved.

John peeled away from the group.

'You're not an easy person to find.'

His body was taut with expectation. 'You've worked it out?'

'Yes, I think I've worked it out.' For what it was worth. She looked towards the field of pigs. Not Durocs or Landrace or Large Whites, just pigs to her but at least they gave her an opening. She turned back to John. 'I think Rosa was right all along. It *was* something that I found out that turned her grandfather against you, I'm afraid. I can't prove it, or I haven't been able to yet, but the evidence is pretty strong. It's going to sound a little far-fetched though, and not too easy to stomach . . .'

'Just tell me, please.'

'OK.' She took a deep breath. 'What I think is that Charles Seagrove believed people should be selectively bred, just like livestock.' For now she saw no reason to mention that he'd probably borrowed his idea from the Nazis. 'So when I told him that Alice Hellier, your great-great-great-grandmother—'

'Was a murderess, Seagrove decided he didn't want bad blood tainting his precious family? Well, it's too late.' The group standing in the field had turned to watch in embarrassed silence. 'There's bad blood between us now all right. Bucket loads of it. If Charles Seagrove wasn't dead I'd kill him, I swear I would. My almost father-in-law thought mine and Rosa's baby would turn out to be a delinquent? That's why he wanted to keep us apart?'

Someone else is going to die. Someone innocent.

'Rosa is pregnant?' She'd been putting on weight, was moody, emotional and irrational. It had to be.

John stood still. 'For now she is, yes. She's gone to a clinic to have an abortion. That's why she took her money. That's why she didn't tell anyone where she was going, except her friend Milly who's working on a cattle ranch in Texas.'

'Smart move. The only one of her friends nobody would think to ask.'

'Except me. I kept calling Milly and she gave in eventually, on condition that I wouldn't let on to Rosa that I knew. Which I won't, unless I have something to tell her that will make her change her mind.'

'She's having the abortion tomorrow?'

'Nine a.m.'

'What I've told you isn't enough to make her go against her grandfather's wishes?' She looked at John's expressive eyes, his strong, hard-working hands. 'You know, I don't think Charles Seagrove deserved to have someone caring one jot for his wishes. I don't think he was a very nice man and I also think he wasn't too clever. Rosa won't want to hear that but what you *can* tell her is this: How could it not occur to her grandfather that any child you and Rosa have together might have Alice's wild streak but would be equally likely to have your love of the land and appreciation of nature that Charles so valued, as well as Rosa's beauty and determination. That's how it goes, you see. You inherit the good as well as the bad.'

Thirty-Two

SHE WAITED THREE hours, then dialled the mobile number John had given to her.

'Rosa's seeing a counsellor in the morning,' John said. 'She's agreed to postpone the ... operation for a day, until Wednesday afternoon, to give it some more thought.'

It was now nearly 9 p.m. on Monday. A reprieve of over thirty-six hours. Better than nothing. 'That's good.'

'I suppose so.' He didn't sound so sure. 'The doctors are worried about her. She's very confused and she keeps having these terrible nightmares.'

Natasha remembered Mary's bad dreams about giving birth to dolphins, of all things, probably an effect of all the new-age relaxation tapes she'd listened to. 'All pregnant people are the same. It's the hormones.'

'I know. I've read about it. But Rosa won't believe me.'

'She sees it as another sign that she shouldn't go against her grandfather's wishes?'

'Yes.'

'Look, there may be someone else who can help. I'll let you know as soon as I can.'

'Thanks. And ... I really appreciate what you're doing.'

The call waiting tone had been bipping while she was talking to John. The caller had left a message on the answering service: 'We need to talk. My name is Peter Hearn.'

There was the trace of a rolling Gloucestershire accent, but it was nowhere near as pronounced as that of Noah Hearn. If they were related, meaning Peter was related to Cinderella, she was certainly keen to talk to him, but who was he? The number Hearn had left was daytime only, 0207 prefix. The call was taken by a secretary who transferred her.

'I've been meaning to take a trip up your way for years. I'm interested in seeing the prisoner of war camp at Springhill. We can meet there, tomorrow morning.' A man used to organizing others.

'Can I ask what this is about?'

'I think you already know that.'

Who'd put him on to her? 'Are you related to Noah Hearn?'

'He's my cousin, more like a brother really. His parents brought me up. I'll see you tomorrow, Miss Blake.'

The sooner she saw Hearn the better, and it would be good to see Springhill for herself. Places often helped you to get the feel for someone. Maybe she could get a little closer to Karl Briegel after all. She was due to collect the Alpine tomorrow so she could detour to Springhill on the way home. She wondered at Peter Hearn's interest in it.

She felt her eyelids droop, the urge to sleep almost too strong to ignore. She fetched a bag of crisps from the kitchen but the smell of cheese and onion when she opened it made her retch. In front of her eyes there were pale jagged lines, like fork lightning, which were still there when she closed her eyes again.

The garage mechanic displayed the repairs to her proudly. Washed and valeted, the Alpine looked as good as new with her glossy paint and pristine bonnet and front wing.

'If only human beings could have their dents smoothed out so easily, eh?' the mechanic said.

If only.

It was strange, being back behind the Alpine's wheel. A white-knuckle ride. As she eased onto the high street Natasha found she was gripping the thin mahogany as tightly as she had the handlebars of her bicycle when she'd first learnt to ride without stabilizers. Trees along the roadside seemed threatening, as if they had a life of their own, and might jump out at her at any moment.

If you fall, the only thing to do is get straight back on, before you lost your nerve. The same with horses, bikes, cars, life in general. Never one to take the easiest route, she made herself take the long way to Springhill.

Today it hurt when she moved her head and she felt sick again, couldn't focus on the dashboard dials.

She was at the crossroads, the point where the road from Chipping Campden to Snowshill intersected the Fosse Way. She drove along the Moreton to Evesham road at least three times a week, waited at this particular crossroads every time she went to Campden for a postage stamp or a loaf of bread. She couldn't believe it had been there all the time.

Beyond the screen of trees was a different world, a different age.

When she turned onto a dirt track, there, no more than a couple of metres away from the road, shielded from it by a row of conifers and scrub, were the first, unmistakable remains of the Springhill prisoner of war camp. A long, low, weathered redbrick building, part rendered, the single-skin walls strengthened with narrow buttresses every couple of feet, tall narrow chimneys at either end. The bricks were stained with gangrenous lime-green moss, gaping holes in the tarred felt roofs, the windows broken and one wall crumbled away. Beside it was another building in better condition, part of the wall now a corrugated iron door to give access to the rusted and broken-down farm machinery stored within it.

Littered with potholes and stones, it was no territory for the Alpine but she inched the car forward, feeling each bone-shattering jolt travel right up through her body to rattle against the bones of her skull.

A BMW was parked up ahead, a man in a smart grey suit sitting behind the wheel. He was looking at her and gave a smile of acknowledgement as she turned off the engine. She was aware of how very still and quiet it was.

She climbed out of the car and he did the same.

He'd told her on the phone that he'd worked in the Foreign Office for twenty years and it was immediately obvious that he was fairly high-ranking. He wore his success on the sleeve of his grey Savile Row suit as others might wear their heart.

'Peter Hearn.' His handshake was stronger than she'd expected. At first glance he was as unnervingly bland and impersonal as the kind of furnished apartment she instantly imagined as his home, perk of a top civil service job. But up close you could see he was handsome, though he seemed to have tried to tone down his good looks with his plain suit and conventional haircut. The handshake gave him away and she suspected that his neat, almost insipid appearance concealed his true nature, had been carefully cultivated over time, to help him blend in, smooth his career progression. His was the kind of unshowy power that worked best when it was concealed.

'Do we need permission to be here or are we trespassing?'

'All taken care of,' he said.

He didn't manage to make eye contact with her but informed her breasts that the land belonged to a farm. 'I knocked at the house and they're more than happy to let us wander round. The camp was used as a Polish refugee camp after the POWs left, so they get refugees and POWs coming back to see the place.'

Natasha immediately had Hearn down as the kind of man who almost despised strong women, even though he desired them. The type who lived for his job, who, if he did marry, would choose a safe, mousy wife who'd never step out of line. He was the type who'd believe that women who dressed in anything that could be construed as at all sexy, like her skimpy sundress for instance, were asking for trouble, flaunting themselves, not to be trusted.

He gestured like an ingratiating under-butler ushering her through to dinner. 'Shall we explore?' Strangely incongruous in these particular surroundings, he straightened his pale-blue silk tie as they set off down the dirt track.

Ahead were three more buildings, the rotting wooden doors of one hanging loose and revealing a broken cart and threshing machine, almost concealed by ivy, weeds and brambles.

She tried to sense a little of the atmosphere that clung to the ruined buildings like a miasma. This was not a happy place. But it was not a sad one either. The aura was similar to that which surrounded abandoned airfields. A sense that something important happened, a lingering echo of young lives on the edge, emotions heightened, activity, fear and friendships. Way off she glimpsed a deer darting between the shrubs.

'I expect you know that I rang your cousin, Noah, some days ago? He refused to talk to me.'

'I can only say I wish he'd done the same thing where the local papers were concerned. I suppose I should be grateful that at least he knew when to stop, didn't spill the beans about me.'

A jolt of apprehension. 'What beans are there to spill, Mr Hearn?'

'I wish my family hadn't lied to me about my parents, but I can, of course, understand why they did.' It was uttered in the true style of the career diplomat he was. 'I grew up believing my real mother became pregnant by a soldier – I presumed an English one naturally – and that when she decided to do a runner she got her friend, Marion, to dump me with her cousin, my Aunt Daisy. I knew my real mother met my father up at Seagrove's place and I'd been badgering the old man for a meeting for years but I could never get near him. Then he's murdered and the body of my mother is discovered in his garden, which sheds a different light on everything, now doesn't it?'

Her conversation with Archie Fletcher: *Cinderella's child, if he or she survived, is certainly old enough to have killed Charles Seagrove.*

'Your mother was Cinderella Pateman?'

'Correct.'

She'd assumed he was a cousin, like Noah.

Should she make a run for it? Hearn wasn't overtly muscular but he looked in fairly good shape, and he was tall; he'd be able to outrun her. The Alpine was already out of sight. It wouldn't fare well against the BMW anyway. 'And your father?' She managed, her mind frantic. She cursed herself for being naive enough to meet him here, alone.

He halted, looked at her. 'Come, come now. You mean you haven't worked that out already?' He gave a superior smile. 'My father is Karl Briegel.'

All her theories about eugenics and Lebensborn homes instantly crumbled. Karl Briegel was a member of the SS and Cinderella Pateman was a gypsy.

'I prised Briegel's name out of my Aunt Daisy eventually.'

'Have you tried to find him?' With Hearn's Foreign Office connections he'd have more means at his disposal than most.

He adjusted his tie for what must have been the tenth time. 'I've made a few enquiries but they were unsuccessful, so I left it at that. So many former members of the SS went into hiding, changed their names. It's hard to find people who don't want to be found and if the war tribunals failed to track him down, what hope have I? To tell you the truth, I've no great ache to meet him at all. Until I read in the paper that she was dead, it was only my mother I was ever interested in finding.'

Was it the nine months that a biological mother carried her child inside her that so often made her more important to the lost child than its biological father? Natasha was the same; she thought about her real father a lot less than she did her mother, the woman who'd abandoned her at the hospital twenty-nine years ago.

'Did your aunt say anything about Charles Seagrove's activities during the war?'

'Not my aunt.'

'Someone else?'

Hearn made a ball cage with his hands, fingertips of one hand touching fingertips of the other, oddly reminiscent of Prince Charles. 'I know now that Seagrove was infatuated with Germany. That he believed and hoped the Germans would win the war, so that he could be praised for the work he'd done to propagate the master race. So that Karl Briegel's other son, the boy Seagrove pretended was his own because he had supposedly untainted blood, could fulfil his destiny, be born into greatness.'

It gave Natasha no pleasure at all to hear that her theory was correct.

'So Marion is Rosa's grandmother, Richard's mother?'

'Indeed so.'

She'd been right about that too.

So this was Richard Seagrove's half-brother. She could see that he did resemble Richard in his blue eyes, his athletic build and something about the shape of his nose. Which must be Karl Briegel's nose.

'I know that my real mother saw Seagrove as a clever man who, like the Nazis, used science as a smokescreen for evil.' He'd said that with distaste. He'd worked hard for his professional respectability and nobody and nothing was about to sully it.

This time it was his lapels which came in for some straightening. Natasha recognized it as the nervous tick of a person not entirely comfortable in his new skin but as Peter tugged on his jacket again she felt another tug of unease. Her legs were starting to feel wobbly.

'Do you agree with your mother's view?' Now wasn't the time to analyse why the sound of her own voice always made her feel less anxious.

'Seagrove was either a megalomaniac and manipulator of innocent young women or just a rather sad and misguided nutcase with delusions of grandeur,' Hearn said. The diplomat speaking again, a man with the capacity to see all sides of an argument.

But here, most definitely, was a man with a motive, if not the outward emotion, to murder Charles Seagrove.

Her legs felt as if they were about to buckle beneath her now. 'Who told you all this?'

'Someone who called herself Cinderella's friend.'

'Marion Lassiter?' How had he found her?

'I'm not at liberty to say.'

'How long have you known?'

Could he have sent the note? In other words, did he know his mother was buried on Charles Seagrove's land before Charles Seagrove was shot?

'I'm still coming to terms with it,' Hearn said. 'It's my real father I resent most. He was the one who deceived my mother, made her care for him when he never cared for her. I know that I was born simply because my mother fell in love and let herself get carried away,' Hearn added. He cast his eyes in the direction of her breasts again. 'Seagrove didn't take into account sexual chemistry, youthful lust. Karl Breigel saw my vivacious, voluptuous mother and he didn't have the patience to wait for Seagrove to research her family history before he took his roll in the haystack with her. Her blonde hair and healthy body were good enough for him in the heat of the moment. He didn't wait to consider the fact that not all gypsies are helpful enough to advertise the fact with black hair and olive skin.'

Natasha understood much more now. Hearn's artificially insipid personality, his dislike of overtly sexual women, it was all a reaction against his mother and her alluring, audacious smile, which he believed had been the cause of all her problems, all his problems.

But she was struck by a painful irony. Like Charles Seagrove, Peter Hearn had taken great pains to conceal and rise above his lowly beginnings. He'd achieved success and status, inheriting the interest in politics and world affairs his real father no doubt shared with Seagrove. He probably had the kind of influential job Seagrove himself might have enjoyed, might even have wished for Richard. Charles Seagrove would not have wanted Peter Hearn to be born, yet he would have been proud of the man he'd become.

'Charles Seagrove somehow found out that Cinderella was carrying Karl Briegel's child?'

'I understand she made sure he did.'

'And that's why she died?' She didn't need him to answer that. 'You, or Marion, or whoever it is, have to tell this to the police.'

'I was determined to do exactly that, until I was talked out of it by my wife – ex-wife I should say, we divorced ten years ago, all very amicable. She convinced me there was no point going looking for trouble, best just leave the police to do their job, they'd get there in the end.'

A man so easily swayed wasn't capable of taking another man's life surely? He could have pointed the gun at Charles Seagrove, but before he'd had time to fire he'd have come round to seeing Charles's point of view.

They doubled back and eventually came to what must be the heart of the camp. Bigger buildings, closer together, ranged around what was now a straw-strewn farm yard.

The sun was too bright, hurting her eyes. Normally, she had a strong sense of direction, but she couldn't work out which path she'd need to take to get back to the car. Turning her head to glance round made everything tilt wildly like the deck of a ship on a stormy sea and set a herd of elephants stampeding between her ear lobes. She touched her temple to make sure her head was still where she thought it was.

'You say you never actually met him, Charles Seagrove?'

'Never had that pleasure, no.'

'But you tried?'

'As a matter of fact I wrote to him in the spring to ask him if we could get together. Like I say, I was curious to know what he was like, and to see the place where I was conceived. He never answered my letter, which was rather rude of him, I thought. As I told the police, I did drive up to Shadwell last month. I called in at the house but the cleaner fobbed me off with some story about Mr Seagrove being too busy with some big party. I angled for an invitation but I didn't get one, needless to say.'

She needed to sit down before she fell down. 'As you told the police?'

'Oh yes, they interviewed me, didn't you know? They'd found my letter in Seagrove's study, you see. It gave them my name and address but not much else, except that I was someone who wanted to meet him. They know my name but they don't know who I am. And I didn't see the need to enlighten them.'

'Why not?' Her voice had gone squeaky as a mouse and right now she felt as timid as one. Reduced to the kind of woman Hearn would go for.

'I like people to work things out for themselves. You're very good at that, aren't you? Much better than the police.'

'What it is you want from me, Mr Hearn?'

The sun was slanting down through the trees, like the flickering rays from an old movie projector, making the trees dance and sway, hazy and then sharp again, branches like arms reaching out. She felt herself sway with them, reached her own arm out to steady herself.

On one of the buildings were the remains of a large wooden cross, signifying a makeshift church.

Unable to help herself, she fell against the mossy wall of one of

237

the buildings, the cross looming above her. But there were two of them now, and bright stars were shooting out from both, like a modern miracle.

Thirty-Three

SHE WAS LYING in the back seat of a car going down city streets. She sat up groggily. Peter Hearn was driving the car.

'Where are we going?'

He glanced over his shoulder. 'Cheltenham. I'm taking you to A&E. You just lie down now and rest. You'll be OK.'

The way she was feeling, she didn't much care what happened to her. The panic she had felt at Springhill seemed to have receded.

But Peter Hearn was as good as his word. He took her to hospital.

She was X-rayed, scanned, examined.

'Have you had a bump on your head recently?' a white-coat asked her.

'I had a car accident a week ago.'

'And you didn't get checked out?'

'I didn't have time.'

'Well, I'm glad your friend made you make the time. You have concussion. Nothing that twenty-four hours strict bed rest won't put right though.' The doctor glanced at Hearn, then turned back to her. 'Is there someone who can look after you?'

'Actually, my mother's coming to stay tonight.'

'Excellent. Just what mothers are for.'

Peter Hearn insisted on driving her home. She didn't particularly want him coming into her cottage but she owed him a cup of tea at least. He told her he was staying until Ann arrived, to make sure she was all right, and she lacked the energy to argue.

She lay under a blanket on the sofa, still seeing stars, while Boris did his best to lick them all away.

She waited until Peter Hearn was in the kitchen, making tea, to ring Archie Fletcher.

'Peter Hearn is Cinderella's son,' she whispered when she got through to him. 'I think Charles Seagrove arranged, tricked Marion Lassiter and maybe other girls into getting pregnant by a German prisoner of war.'

Archie drew out a long, 'Okaaaaay.' Then he said, 'I can see how that's a very exciting find, from a historian's point of view, but it doesn't mean—'

'You did interview Peter Hearn?' She was sweating under the blanket.

'We did, and that's how we know he has an alibi for the day of the murder.'

'You're positive about that?' She was relieved and also oddly deflated.

'He was in a meeting with three respected and respectable government officials.'

'Government officials have been known to tell the odd lie,' she said weakly.

Some detective she made.

She may have thought Peter Hearn was a murderer but Ann looked as if she was in the process of considering him a possible son-in-law. Natasha couldn't deny that he had been kind and caring way beyond the call of duty.

First impressions may count but they didn't always add up to much. All Peter Hearn's bland exterior was concealing was his colourful heritage. A heritage he wanted to understand and at the same time reject in favour of normality. She of all people should have understood that.

She should learn from Archie Fletcher, not be so quick to judge. The police had been right to take no notice of her. She had no experience of this kind of thing. She couldn't just go around pointing her finger. She was only qualified to solve mysteries that were at least a few decades old; at least she'd done that. She'd been right about what had gone on at Shadwell. But it might not be enough to help Rosa and John. She swung her legs to the floor.

'Where are you going?' Ann asked just ahead of Peter.

'I can't stay in bed.'

Ann tried to gently push her back. 'Why not?'

'I've got too much to do, and I've got to do it before tomorrow afternoon.'

'Anything I can help with?' Peter stepped towards her solicitously, as if he were about to take down a memo.

'Well, actually . . .' If he went to see Rosa . . . 'Charles Seagrove's granddaughter needs to see exactly the kind of man her grandfather was.'

'Then the person who needs to talk to her is Marion Lassiter.' He sounded very confident about that. 'I had one of my contacts in the Home Office find her address.'

So it *was* Marion who'd told Peter about Cinderella.

He reached inside his jacked and produced a slim leather diary. 'I have her address right here. I'd be more than willing to fetch her but, judging from past experience, I'm not sure she'll come with me.'

Natasha asked Ann to pass her the phone. 'I bet I know just the person.'

She'd expected John to want to know more about what Marion would be able to tell Rosa but it seemed he was willing to clutch at any straw she held out, even if it was a two-hour drive away, in Dorset.

'I'll go first thing in the morning. You sure she'll come though? What do I say to her?'

'You won't even have to say anything about . . . Rosa's situation. Just take a photograph of her and tell Marion that Rosa is Richard's daughter. Tell her Rosa urgently needs her help.'

'Why will that matter to her?'

'I can't tell you right now but it will, trust me.'

So long as maternal instincts extended to grandchildren and could still be activated even if grandmother and grandchild had never met, if mother and child had been apart for six decades.

*

Ann had been up been up hours. While Natasha had been having an unprecedented lie-in, Ann had been busy tidying. Clothes had been put in wardrobes and drawers, books on shelves, cushions plumped.

'Sorry,' she smiled. 'I couldn't resist.'

Natasha had worried about what she and her mother would find to talk about all day, had planned on suggesting a drive to Hidcote, sure Ann would like to see the famous Arts and Crafts gardens with their series of outdoor rooms. Instead, here was Ann plying her with tomato soup and hot chocolate, like she was off sick from school.

'Your dad called while you were asleep,' Ann said. 'He was very worried about you but I told him you were being well looked after.' How had he known there was anything wrong? 'Then Steven must have called Marcus because he called too. I told him the same thing.'

Ann had mentioned Steven without even flinching. Natasha flinched at the mention of Marcus.

She watched her mother drinking her coffee with the delicate sips of a cat, serene and inscrutable as ever. She was beautiful. How could Steven do it to her? What had he confessed, or what had Ann worked out for herself?

Just so long as Ann wasn't going to spring the same question as Abby. No mother should have to ask her daughter if she knew what was going on in her own marriage.

'There's no need to look so worried,' Ann said gently. 'I'm not blind, you know.' She'd closed the curtains while Natasha slept. Now she stood by the window and pulled them open, framing herself in sunlight. She turned to Natasha with her beautific smile, the blue dress she was wearing making her look like the Virgin Mary.

'Don't you think I remember how your dad was when I first knew him, when he asked me to marry him? He went around whistling then too.'

Natasha was totally lost for words, though if Steven was here right now, she'd have a thing or two to say to him.

'He's told you about her then?' She asked, resignedly.

Natasha nodded.

Ann came to sit on the side of the bed. 'Don't worry. I'm not going to ask you to repeat what he said.' She touched Natasha's hand. 'I'm sorry. I don't mean to put you in an awkward position. I'm not expecting you to take sides. But Abby's no use at all. She's on the phone to me every five minutes, wailing about how awful it all is. You're the only one I can talk to.'

Natasha felt as she had the first time she learned how to dance on points. She'd grown two inches taller. 'It's probably just an infatuation.' She did her best to sound convincing. 'He'll get over it.'

'Like all the previous ones, you mean?' Ann looked away. 'I'm not so sure.'

Natasha was incredulous. 'Aren't you furious with him?'

Ann gave a tight laugh. 'Oh, my dear, it's too late for that. If I was going to start cutting up his shirts I should have done it thirty years ago, the first time I smelt another woman's perfume on his collar.'

'Why didn't you? I know I would have.'

Ann smiled. 'I know *you* would. And despite what you may think, I've always loved your spirit. That's the thing you see, if you love someone you have to accept them as they are.' Natasha knew Ann was referring back to their conversation last night, when she'd talked to her about the Seagroves. 'I wouldn't want you to be perfect.'

Natasha felt tears prick her eyes. She pleated the duvet cover between her fingers. 'What are you going to do?'

'Something I've always wanted to do. I'm starting a furniture restoration course. I might even open a little shop.' It seemed a perfect choice, combining her two careers of museum curator and homemaker. 'I'll be all right, you know.' Ann stood, smoothed back her hair with the palm of her hand, walked over to the door. 'There's no point worrying about what you can't change. I can't make him stay. Even if I could, I wouldn't. There's no point being with someone if they don't want to be with you. And in a way, I suppose I've been preparing myself for this for years.'

What Ann had said was wise and admirably stoical. But you

243

shouldn't let life control you. You should grab it by the horns and drive it the way you wanted it to go. Just like she was doing herself, right? By prevaricating over that plane ticket. She wasn't sure if she was more surprised that Marcus had called, or that he'd called because Steven had called *him*. She'd always had the impression Steven didn't really approve, didn't like his friend dating his daughter.

It shouldn't surprise her that people cared about her but it always did.

Richard, Peter and Rosa – Rosalind.

Up and dressed and waiting by the phone for John to call to let her know how he was getting on in Dorset, Natasha idly flicked open the dictionary of first names, which she always kept to hand to add some quirky depth to family trees.

> *Richard: One of the most enduringly successful of the Germanic personal names introduced into Britain by the Normans.*
> *Peter: English and German.*
> *Rosalind: Originally an old Germanic female name.*

All names chosen by Charles Seagrove.

An email came in from Will. The title of it made her smile: '*Some points to raise with Charles Seagrove's ghost.*' She opened the message.

> *The genetic differences between two individuals chosen at random from one race are far greater than the average differences between races. Only around three thousand generations have passed since we all shared one common ancestor.*

Thirty-Four

MARILYN MONROE AS an old lady might have looked not unlike Marion Lassiter. Pale hair, blue eyes, shapely figure, a still-beautiful face. She was sitting alone in the pre-arranged place, a sunlit bench beneath a weeping ash in Batsford arboretum.

After Natasha had primed her, she would explain everything to John who was to take Marion to meet Rosa in a restaurant near the clinic. He was waiting now in the falconry centre outside the park.

Marion was very still, staring into the distance, leaning on a walking stick in a way that resembled a shepherdess with a crook. Little Bo Peep, as her brother had once called her before he'd lost her. The ghost of the girl in the land army sweater was well disguised but she was still there, if you looked very closely. Her successor was wearing spectacles, a navy pleated skirt and matching jacket edged in white braid, stout shoes. Her hair was neatly permed beneath a headscarf. There was a determined air about her, a vigour and sense of purpose that would have equipped her well as a young farm hand. She was a lot like Rosa.

'Miss Lassiter?'

'That's right.' Sunlight glinted off her spectacles, hiding her eyes. Natasha thought she understood why Marion would like to hide them.

'Would you rather walk or sit, Miss Lassiter?'

'Walk, I think.'

She was tall, like Richard, and she walked with a resolute spring in her step, swinging her stick like Fred Astaire. It was as if this was a moment she'd been waiting for and now she was ready.

She was wearing perfume, a musky fragrance that mingled with the pungent baked earth smell which hung in the air. The leaves were a deep bottle-green now, a few of them already on the turn, tipped with orange and gold. In two months the whole place would be ablaze.

'I understand from John that my granddaughter is in some kind of trouble.'

She'd mentioned her relationship to Rosa with complete naturalness, as if they'd been part of each other's lives since Rosa was born. Natasha saw now that Marion and Rosa had the same delicate fair complexion.

'Did you know Richard had a child?'

'Not until John told me this morning. But of course I've always hoped and imagined he might.'

A world of sadness in those few words. Natasha didn't think it would be fair to say any more on the matter just now.

'That's all John told you, that Rosa was in trouble?'

'He thought it would be better if you explained.'

'Rosa has an important decision to make and to do it she needs to be made to see what kind of man Charles Seagrove really was.'

'I have to disillusion her, you mean? Ruin her memories?'

'I know it's asking a lot when you don't know me and I'm sorry I can't tell you what this is all about, but please believe me, I wouldn't be asking you to do this if I didn't think it was the only way.'

It had been Marion's suggestion that they meet here. Snowshill was too near Shadwell, she said, but Natasha couldn't help wondering why she'd chosen this particular place.

It was already nearly eleven a.m., only six hours until Rosa's abortion. There wasn't much time but Natasha was experienced enough to know that this couldn't be rushed. 'Do you know Batsford well?' she asked.

'I had a friend who loved it here. Her father was a tree surgeon and he used to bring her with him. She said it was like coming to the Garden of Eden.' Natasha knew Marion was talking about Cinderella and tried to analyse her voice. Not the nostalgic or fond tone that tinged many people's memories of dead friends, but regretful and guilt-ridden.

'How long is it since you were in the Cotswolds?'

'Fifty-nine years.'

Natasha had the feeling that Marion would have been able to tell her the exact date, if she'd asked.

'I somehow knew I'd be back here soon, when Peter came to see me to tell me Charles Seagrove was dead.'

They carried on up the path – Batsford House standing grandly across the wide lawn to the right, a confection of golden stone gables and tall chimneys – and stopped by a small lake. Ducks and black swans were drifting and diving.

Marion stood at the water's edge, leaning on her stick, her back ramrod straight. 'So, what exactly do you want to know?'

'Charles Seagrove was a Nazi sympathizer?'

Marion expelled a little air through her nose. 'Along with half the wealthy landowners and the unemployed workers. All those who were disillusioned by what they saw as the useless slaughter of the First World War, harboured a sense of a debt that needed to be paid to the dead, were angered by the failure of governments to create a home fit for heroes and a society which adequately compensated for the horror of the trenches.'

'Does that include you?'

Marion twisted her stick against the grass, screwing it into the ground. 'Only after I'd been indoctrinated by Charles Seagrove and set eyes on Karl Briegel.' She paused, remembering, or deciding how much to tell. 'I'm not making excuses at all, but if you could see Karl Briegel it would help you understand. He was like a Norse God, the blondest hair, the bluest eyes, tall and strong and powerful, not in the physical sense, but in the sense of someone who never questioned his superior place in the world, believed utterly that he was above the rest of us. He was mesmerizing. And Charles Seagrove was, I think, the most charismatic man I've ever met.'

'You were in love with Karl?'

'I'm not sure exactly what I was in love with. I can't have loved him that much, can I? Or I wouldn't have been willing to share

247

him. I rather suspect that I was simply carried away with my own self-importance. There I was, a seventeen-year-old village girl who'd never been to London, and Charles Seagrove welcomed me into his drawing room, gave me tea in china cups, talked to me about politics and philosophy as if I were his equal. He gave me books to read, quoted Sarah Grand and Ellice Hopkins, and I thought I was a New Woman, that I, and other middle-class girls like me, could play a crucial part in the regeneration of our imperial race just by doing what our bodies were equipped to do best. Fool that I was, I thought I was saving the world by having a baby with the most beautiful man I'd ever seen.'

'Were you the only girl he invited into the drawing room at Shadwell?'

'There were others. I can't say for certain how many. There was definitely a girl called Jennifer. I got her involved. Charles asked if I had any friends, suitable friends, who would be willing to join us. Jennifer and I had shared a bunk at the land army hostel and we'd hit it off right away. She fell for Karl Briegel even faster. He started teaching her German and she thought she was going to marry him after the war. She was an easy recruit. Poverty had made her mother ill. Her father had been out of work for three years. And then along comes Charles, telling her there are ways to solve bad housing and unemployment and the economic situation. Karl Briegel filled her head with more poppycock about the Aryan peoples being the originators of European civilization. How we British were Germanic, that we were therefore Aryan, successors of a favoured, mystical and cultured people. How Hitler initially sought an alliance with Britain to conquer the Soviet Union and the rest of Europe.' Her voice was growing quieter almost as if she was disappearing back in time. Natasha had to lean in closer to hear. 'Because we won the war you look back and think it was always obvious that we would, but that's not so. For most of the time it seemed likely we could lose, and Charles clung to that until the bitter end. He told us we could be the mother of chosen children, pure-blooded sons born to inherit the earth.'

Strands of hair were peeking out from underneath Marion's scarf, glimmers of blonde that hadn't faded.

'I don't quite get it,' Natasha said, slowly. 'I thought Charles Seagrove . . .'

'What I thought of Charles Seagrove and what I have come to think of him are entirely different.' Marion glanced at Natasha. 'I used to think he was the most fascinating, brilliant man I'd ever met. Now I see him as a kind of vampire who was willing to trade his soul for immortality, for blood.'

'How much was he influenced by Karl Briegel?'

'Oh, you've mistaken me. It was the other way round entirely. Charles's ideas were fully formed long before he met Karl. It was Karl's SS blood that was valuable to Charles, not his mind. Karl wasn't much older than me. He had the fanaticism but not the words to express it, until Charles put them in his mouth, fed them to him. I've always presumed that was why Karl managed to unwittingly fool them at the PoW interrogation camps and manage to escape being sent up to the wilds of Scotland with most of the other hardened Nazis. They obviously didn't look too closely, or they'd have seen his SS tattoo under his arm. For Karl, Charles was a magnifying glass that took his ideals like the rays of the sun and concentrated them onto one attainable target. Charles was the one who quoted J. Hooper Harvey's *Heritage of Britain*. Charles was the one who made Karl believe that being a prisoner didn't mean he had to abandon the cause, that he could enjoy the hospitality of carefully vetted English girls and further his Führer's aim's at the same time. And then of course Charles was there to provide a safe haven for the children he helped to create.' She lifted her face now, raised a neatly filed and buffed finger and tucked the stray strands of hair back into her scarf. 'Charles was the mastermind. He brought us together. And then Karl took care of the rest.' Marion seemed lost in whatever 'the rest' meant to her. 'If he'd sworn that the Germans made the stars in the sky and the apples we were picking from the trees I'd have believed him. It'd be easy to say I wasn't interested in what he had to say. Easy to say I was never really interested in the politics. That's what so many did after the war. They regretted their former opinions and tried to pretend they'd never held them.'

Natasha admired Marion's honesty. She could have easily made out that she'd been duped and taken advantage of by a dashing foreigner and a Machiavellian English gentleman.

Across the lake, lights had come on in the house. Batsford had once been the home of Lord Redesdale, the father of the Mitford sisters. One, Diana, had married Oswald Mosley, the leader of the British Union of Fascists, and another, Unity, had been infatuated with Adolf Hitler. It wasn't hard to imagine Marion being just like them.

'I had thought that the Seagroves just wanted a child.'

'Maybe that *was* the start of it. But not just any child would do. Charles had far wider reaching designs. He wanted to ensure that the worthless slaughter of the First World War was never repeated. He wanted peace at any cost and believed the best thing for Britain was to unite with Germany. By uniting the likes of Jennifer and I with Karl Briegel he saw a small way that he could make that happen. His own homage to the Christmas Truce.'

'Did the Germans know what Seagrove was doing?'

'I think they probably had some idea. Charles had a contact, a woman, in Germany.'

Magda Koenig. She wondered now how much Inge knew of this.

'But Seagrove didn't want all Karl Briegel's sons for himself?'

'He wanted just one baby.'

'Yours.'

'That was my choice.'

'Was your child's birth ever registered?'

She shook her head. 'Seagrove was determined to follow the SS's lead and invent his own registration procedure. He wanted total control of everything. Ran Shadwell like a mini state, and he wanted to be the only one with the documentation that proved the children's parentage.'

Natasha didn't have to mention Richard's name to bring him into the conversation. He was there already, in every word his mother uttered.

'Don't think I didn't have second thoughts though. A dozen times I would have run away but I had nowhere else to go. I was carrying the baby of a German soldier. My family had disowned me for just being seen holding his hand. Some gossip had got out about Charles's allegiance to Germany and the locals despised me. I wasn't as brave as Jennifer, who insisted on raising her baby herself, until he died of whooping cough when he was a few months old. I'm not making excuses, but it's hard for young people these days to understand what it was like. Sixty years ago things hadn't moved on a lot since the previous century. Unmarried girls could be ostracized just for falling pregnant, irrespective of the father. Nowadays your baby would be called a love child. I rather like that. It makes the baby sound special and chosen. Richard was both those things but for all the wrong reasons.' Marion turned to Natasha and removed her glasses, revealing eyes that were a cerulean blue. 'You know him, don't you?' Her question was tentative, his name a sacred word.

'A little.' She felt incapable of summing him up adequately enough, of presenting his mother with the accurate picture she so craved.

'You're the only person I've ever met who's ever even spoken to him.'

'He's a sports teacher. An excellent one, I imagine, inspirational.' Even as she said it she thought that he had inherited his magnetism from his real father. Karl Briegel used his to embroil women in his fantasy of a perfect master race and his son encourages disadvantaged children, makes them believe they can be winners. The same but not the same.

Marion's thoughts must have been running along the same lines. 'Cinderella's family were fruit-pickers. She once told me that apple trees have to be grafted to be replicated. The tree that grows from a pip bears fruit that is entirely different from the apple the pip came from. I've always hoped that sometimes it's the same with people.'

'Maybe it is. But I think Richard is a lot like you.'

Marion seemed too touched to speak. 'I kidded myself that he'd be better off with the Seagroves than with me,' she said after a moment. 'But I did know Stella would be a good mother, that she would cherish my baby. I was always sure of that.'

'You two were friends?'

'I liked Stella very much. She conformed to the Nazi ideal, Charles's idea. Domesticated, maternal, healthy and strong, but there was more to her than that. She was good company and open-minded at a time when a lot of people weren't. She knew how to stand up to Charles too. He couldn't stand alcohol, banished it from the house. But Stella said there was something much better than alcohol. Her grandfather was a woodsman so she knew what she was looking for. You're familiar with Fly Agric, magic mushrooms?' A mischievous twinkle flickered briefly in Marion's eyes. 'We had some fun, I can tell you. Stella used to say there was no way Charles could disapprove. She'd read all his books and she told me how, to the original Germanic tribes, the Fly Agric was Soma, the food of the gods, and the Vikings ate it to attain their fighting frenzy, "berserk".'

So Stella was a trippy hippy before her time, as Charles, with his bare feet and habit of sleeping out under the stars, had been an early tree-hugger. They had probably got on very well in their own way.

'She told me that, before I arrived, when Karl first came to Shadwell, he tried it on with her, tried to seduce her, but she would never have been unfaithful to her husband.'

'Did she know what was going on?'

'No. Not so far as I know. We were forbidden to talk to her about it. She knew Charles was against the war, had friends in Germany, but that was all. I've often wondered, though, if she might have gone along with it all quite willingly because she was so desperate for a baby. She told me she'd tried for three years to get pregnant. "Thirty-six months of hope and disappointment," that's what she said. I remember it. I think that's the real reason she needed a substitute for alcohol, something to help her forget her sadness.'

'But Charles wasn't prepared to stop at two babies, yours and Jennifer's?'

'Who knows? If the war had gone on longer there might have been dozens. Even when it had been long obvious to everyone, even the Germans, that we would win the war, Charles would have none of it and carried on with his plans, but eventually even he had to admit that he would never be able to show off his Master Race programme to the occupying Nazis. He gave up at about the same time as the Lebensborn homes in Germany were forced to close their doors. I do know of others though. Another land girl, Christine, who turned out to have a questionable ancestry, so far as Charles was concerned, and was sent back to the hostel before she knew what she'd got involved in. Emma, who got engaged to an RAF navigator and didn't want anything more to do with Karl Briegel. Fortunately for her, she got out before she became pregnant.'

Natasha was sickened. She'd not considered that Charles would have sought to involve so many girls in his experiments.

'The only family tree he seems to have saved was yours.'

'I was the one who gave him his baby. I should imagine he destroyed the others after the war. They no longer interested him.'

Three cots in the attic at Shadwell. Three cots for three babies. Marion's and Jennifer's. Christine's or Emma's would have been the third. Not Cinderella's.

'Do you know who killed Charles Seagrove?'

'I did wonder if it might be Cinderella's son, Peter.'

'He has an alibi.'

'Well, whoever it was, I can't honestly say I blame them.'

'You think his death is connected to his activities during the war?'

Marion looked at Natasha. 'Don't you?'

'But what about Cinderella Pateman? Did you send me that letter?'

'What letter?' Marion's puzzlement was genuine.

She shook her head, confused

'My mistake. Did Charles kill her?'

Marion replaced her glasses. 'He was responsible for her death. But in a way, no more than I was.' She paused. 'In one of our drawing-room sessions Charles showed a film made in the nineteen twenties. I don't know how he came by it. An old reel of film, in a rusting can it was. He screened it in the darkened room, on an enormous old projector. It was a Hollywood movie, not Nazi propaganda, called *The Black Stork*. It starred with pictures of cows being introduced to selected bulls and giving birth to healthy calves, followed by pictures of thin and scrawny babies. Crass and awful. It tried to make an argument for selectively breeding people. It showed a man who had a hereditary disease caused by his grandfather's affair with a slave. He chooses to marry and have children but the baby is born ill and will die if not operated upon. The doctor refuses to do it. "There are times when saving a life is a greater crime than taking one." he says.' Marion paused again. 'Charles didn't take Cinderella's life but he didn't save it either, when I think he could have done.' A single tear ran down Marion's cheek and she didn't even bother to wipe it away. 'Cinderella was my dearest friend. She was also the most sensual girl I've ever known. There was no doubt that Karl was going to be attracted to her, and she to him. Of course it didn't fit with Charles's plans. Oh, not at all. But Cinderella wasn't one to go quietly. She was always pushy and outspoken and she demanded that Charles look after her, as he was doing for me. I had to tell her what was going on and then she threatened to expose Charles if he didn't do as she wanted. He let her stay to keep her quiet. But her gypsy blood wasn't part of his vision. She died giving birth to her son. She haemorrhaged and should have been taken straight to a hospital. I can't tell you how many times I wish I'd found a way to make him take her. If only I could have thought of something clever to say in time, reminded him that this was all for his father, who had come to disbelieve even the wartime paradoxes of killing to save your country and your regiment. Cinderella might have died anyway, but Charles didn't try to help her, he let her die.'

'It was you who saved her baby?'

'It was all I could do, take him and run from that place as fast as I could, even though it meant I was leaving my own baby behind. Cinderella's father wouldn't have been able to raise a child but I knew Cinderella had a cousin nearby, Daisy, who already had a boy. So I just handed over the little bundle, told Daisy he was Cinderella's and she had to take care of him, and then I left the Cotswolds for good.'

They walked for a moment in silence. 'If Cinderella died of

natural causes, why did Charles Seagrove bury her in the woods? It was an admission of guilt.'

'He would have stopped at nothing to protect his scheme. There were mutterings in the village already. I'd just given birth and Jennifer's pregnancy was showing. He couldn't risk anyone asking too many questions about why he'd had three pregnant girls staying at Shadwell.' Marion turned abruptly and started walking back to the main path. 'Does Rosa really need to know all this?'

'I'm afraid she does, yes.'

'Then I'd rather do it alone, if that's all right with you.'

Thirty-Five

WAS BLOOD ALL Charles Seagrove had been interested in, or was he involved in the rest of the fascist movement? Natasha thought as she drove back to Snowshill. There'd been no mention of any active membership of the British Union of Fascists, no indication he'd ever attended the rallies in the East End or been arrested and imprisoned like other known supporters.

Perhaps, as he'd told Rosa, it wasn't politics that interested him so much as life. Life, or how he could manipulate it. He'd liked the feel of grass on his bare feet but he didn't allow it to grow out of control. She pictured the immaculate drive at Shadwell, nature bending to the imposition of his will.

If not for Cinderella's death it might have been possible to believe that he had just been playing a dangerous game that he saw as his own small part in uniting Germany and Britain. At worst, that he had decided to create for him and his wife a designer baby before the term had ever been coined, a child with the best credentials if his friends, the Germans, invaded Britain and won the war. And at the very worst that he had embraced the German's myth of the Aryan race and all the horrors that encompassed.

He'd set up his small British outpost of the Lebensborn programme and had kept it quiet all these years. He'd shut himself away behind his forest of trees and all that had leaked out were vague rumours about his ability to speak German.

After seeing Rosa, Marion had agreed to go to Chipping Campden police station to tell Archie Fletcher what she knew of Cinderella

Pateman's death. She seemed relieved to be able, finally, to talk about Karl Briegel and her activities during the war.

'How did Rosa react to what you told her?' Natasha asked.

'She didn't really say much, poor girl.'

Marion's main concern was that Richard would have to know. Natasha wasn't sure whether Marion was pleased about that or not. But Richard couldn't be protected from the knowledge of how and why and by whom he'd been brought into the world.

Sometimes, when you started out trying to answer one question all you ended up doing was finding answers to other questions you didn't even know needed asking.

This whole thing had begun with Charles Seagrove's death, which remained unsolved. Why had he died, by whose hand?

She kept worrying at the missing piece of the puzzle. The absence of Charles Seagrove's own genealogical chart. He'd meticulously checked out the genetic credentials of the potential father of his grandchildren, his wife and the biological mother of his son, but he had not done the same for himself, the prospective father of his own children. He could not have known then that Stella would not be able to become pregnant. What if . . .'

She ran to find Mary. Who had told her that Inge Ostermeier had mentioned she planned to see more of the countryside before she went home, and would be spending a few nights at the Swan in Bibury.

Natasha parked by the Windrush that flowed adjacent to the main road in Bibury. Children were paddling on the reedy banks, standing on the bridge watching the trout treading water, swimming open-mouthed against the flow.

It was five o'clock and the receptionist at the Swan said that Inge had gone out for the day. Natasha ordered a coffee and downed it in one. She was pacing, doing her hundredth circuit round the little wrought-iron tables in the forecourt, when Inge crossed the bridge.

She seemed pleased and surprised to see a familiar face. 'Hello again.'

'Hi.' She offered to get Inge a coffee but she declined. 'There's something I have to ask you.' Inge sat down at the table amiably. 'It's a bit delicate and please excuse me for asking this. I wouldn't be doing it if I thought there was any other way.' Inge nodded, encouragingly. 'Do you think there's any chance that Charles Seagrove is . . .'

'My father? There's no need to feel uncomfortable. I knew you were wanting to know that when we met last time. It's the obvious question, isn't it? He came out to Germany to stay with my mother, kept a photograph of her in his office. Don't think it's a question I haven't asked myself. For a while I believed it must be true. I couldn't talk to my mother about it. She is a very private person. But a year ago, when she had a stroke and she thought she might die, she told me lots of things she'd kept to herself, things about the war.'

'About Lebensborn?'

'You are a good detective. About Lebensborn, yes. My family didn't always live in Steinhoring. My mother came from Cologne. After her father, Hans, was killed in Flanders she became passionate about helping the fight to regain Germany's supremacy. So you see, I can't condone the Lebensborn programme but I can understand Magda's reasons for condoning it. You understand me, yes?'

Natasha nodded, not sure that she truly did. She saw Inge in a new light. Not just a parochial, middle-aged family woman, but someone who'd had to come to terms with a difficult past, to learn to accept her mother for what she was.

'She joined the League of German Girls and then the Brown Sisters and was sent to the Hochland Home at Steinhoring, when it opened in 1936, to help nurse the young mothers and babies. It was there that she met Gregor Ebner and Max Sollman, the medical director and chief of the Lebensborn programme. I believe she introduced them both to Charles Seagrove.'

Another link in the chain.

'After the war my mother left Steinhoring, went to live somewhere where nobody knew her,' Inge said. 'She always wanted to go back, I think. She said her happiest times were spent there and I think those times were when Charles Seagrove came to visit. She has never said this but I do think she must have loved him. I think she would have liked to have married him and had his children. But I can tell you with absolute certainty that Charles Seagrove is not my father.'

'How can you be so sure?'

'As I expect you now realize, it was under my mother's influence that he came to approve of the work of the Hochland Home, in the Lebensborn programme. He knew his father was an alcoholic, his grandfather too probably. The Nazis called alcohol poison. They categorized hereditary alcoholism as a necessity for sterilization. Charles told Magda that, because of what she'd taught him, his bloodline must end with him. He had a vasectomy in nineteen forty-one.'

Thirty-Six

THIRTY-SIX MONTHS *of hope and disappointment.* The phrase crashed against Natasha's skull. False hope. Wasted hope. Futile disappointment. Until Stella had given up trying to get pregnant. Not knowing that it could never have happened. Had she ever come to realize her hope had been in vain?

Home again, Natasha called up the folder containing all her research on John Hellier's family tree. The dossier of biographical sketches and supporting certificates had been open on Charles's desk the day he died, at a double-page spread that featured the details of Alice Hellier.

Natasha minimized the file, found the certificates Toby had sent to her to support Charles Seagrove's family history. She'd barely glanced at them. Charles's grandfather had died of liver disease. His father had died of cirrhosis. Same thing. Curse of the alcoholic.

She found the notes she'd taken down at the Wellcome Library. The parent group of the Eugenics Society was the Society for the Study of Inebriety, which looked at inheritance of an alcoholic constitution, the theory that alcohol coupled with sexual excess produced insanity within families.

She drove to Campden police station.

'I need to see Sergeant Fletcher.'

'I'm afraid he's unavailable right now.'

'Is he here or not?'

The PC glanced behind him, checking for back-up, as if he expected Natasha to pull a flick-knife at any moment.

She tried to be patient, folded her arms. 'I'll wait.' She sat on a plastic seat.

'He's finished for the day.'

'Practising his aim,' she heard one of his colleagues chuckle.

Natasha sprang to her feet. 'What does that mean?'

'I believe Sergeant Fletcher has gone clay pigeon shooting. He'll be in again in the morning.'

'Thank you. It would have been helpful if you could just have told me that in the first place. But you could contact him, I assume, if something urgent turned up?'

'Well, yes.'

'Then contact him.' If she didn't know the partition would be made of toughened glass she'd be sorely tempted to throw something through it, reach through and grab the phone and thrust the receiver at the PC's ear.

'Has something urgent turned up, Miss Blake, isn't it?'

'Yes. And yes it has.'

'I'm afraid you'll need to be more specific.'

'It's to do with Charles Seagrove's murder. I have new information.'

'Just one moment, please.' He disappeared for a moment then reappeared on her side of the partition. 'PC Harman will see you.'

'Well, I won't see her.'

She left him standing there stupefied.

Richard's Peugeot was parked on the gravel drive. The front door of the house was slightly open but there was no reply when Natasha knocked.

She walked round to the back. It was the first time she'd returned since she'd come looking for Charles Seagrove and found him. As she approached the gap in the high brick wall she felt sick, almost didn't dare look. A hosepipe snaked across the brick path. There was no sign of blood. It had all been washed away. But she could still see it.

The gardener was kneeling between rows of cabbages and courgettes beside a wheelbarrow piled with weeds, continuing the work that Charles Seagrove had started and never finished.

'Have you seen Mr Seagrove?' The exposed and tangled roots of the weeds were pale through the covering of dark soil. The analogy of roots being ripped up wasn't lost on her.

The gardener eyed her warily, no doubt remembering too that the last time she'd arrived to talk to a Mr Seagrove, death had come to the household. 'He probably went out for a run.'

'Where does he usually go?'

'Through the woods mostly.'

Richard wasn't afraid of ghosts then. Natasha liked to think she wasn't either but she felt her heart quicken once more as she approached the outer edge of the trees.

The forensic team had covered their tracks well, assisted by nature. The cordon was gone now and already the grass was renewing itself, obliterating all evidence of the tyre tracks. Natasha steered clear of the area once known as Poacher's Dell. There would be some sign there that the earth had recently been disturbed, a patch of dark bare soil. By autumn, when the leaves fell from the trees, Cinderella's temporary grave would vanish once more.

She followed the bridleway. There were two sets of hoofprints in the dried ground. It had rained recently, but not heavily enough to penetrate the thick canopy of leaves. The hoofprints could have been there since the winter. Rosa and her grandfather's horses perhaps. How could Charles have ridden in these woods, side by side with his granddaughter, knowing there was the body of another young girl buried beneath the earth only metres from where they rode? Cinderella's body at least was gone now, but it still felt as if she, or something else, was still here.

She started as a dry branch cracked under her feet. She was scaring herself. There was nothing to fear. She'd been in crypts and graveyards at dusk and not felt so jumpy. But crypts and graveyards were the peaceful, sanctified resting places of the dead. Shadwell had only witnessed violent death, unceremonious burial.

There was a rustle in the undergrowth ahead, something moving. Natasha froze. Again the crackling of dried ferns and grass, moving closer.

A King Charles Spaniel came darting out across the path, long ears flapping, tongue lolling. He leapt up at her, thumped dusty paws on her thighs.

'Ruby, come here at once.' Stella Seagrove was walking up the bridle path. The little dog obeyed instantly, skulking back to his mistress. Stella kept her eyes on Natasha. 'You're trespassing. I told you to stay away from my family.' Her voice was as superior as it had been when she'd been issuing commands to the dog.

'I came to apologize.'

That did the trick. Stella was thrown. 'For what?'

From the distance came the dull thud of gunfire. Someone out shooting rabbits, or clay pigeons. Like Archie Fletcher, who should be here instead.

'For causing your husband's death. I did cause it, didn't I?'

'I'm afraid I don't understand?'

'Oh, I think you do, Mrs Seagrove.' She stepped a little closer, to make sure Stella could hear clearly, could see her face. 'Your husband researched your genealogy before he married you and did the same for Richard's wife, but you never knew that, did you? He never had to tell you because Kristen's background checked out, satisfied him, as yours did. But you knew enough about your husband's recent family history. You saw the strength of his reaction to those charts I drew up for John Hellier, how much store he set by them, and you realized that the genes Charles didn't want passing on from Alice Hellier to Rosa's children would be no worse, in his eyes, than the ones he believed existed in his own family. You realized what you'd failed to realize all those years ago: Charles would never have let himself father any children.'

The silence seemed to last an age. Natasha was certain that the light had dimmed in the few moments they'd been standing there.

Then another dull thud of distant gunfire. That was how the shot that killed Charles Seagrove must have sounded.

'You're being utterly ridiculous.' Stella's voice was as strong as ever. In fact, she looked stronger than she'd done since her husband's death, the pain easing from her face, her body straightening, as if what had temporarily crippled her had indeed been physical rather than emotional pain.

Another thud. Natasha had been clay pigeon shooting a few times with James. He'd shown her how to tuck the gun in against her body, hold it firmly.

Thud. Like someone was trying to tell her something. Hammering the point home.

She got it now.

'Your granddaughter said you don't like blood sports. You don't know how to use a shotgun, do you? If you did you'd know how to hold one so that the recoil doesn't dislocate your shoulder.' Like Archie's friend. Stella had flinched from Rosa's touch at the memorial, had been doing everything one-handed – stirring her cheese sauce, cradling her arm across her chest. 'Dislocations take a few weeks to heal, even if you manage to put them back yourself. I bet if we looked now the bruise would still be there.'

The crack of a dry branch.

'*I* know how to use a shotgun and I'm not afraid to fire it.' Rosa Seagrove was standing a couple of feet behind Natasha with a double-barrelled shotgun aimed directly at her. 'It's all lies. What you told Marion Lassiter to tell me. It is, isn't it? Admit it.' She jabbed the air with the gun. 'Why are you doing this to us?' She kept her eyes trained on Natasha but started talking to Stella. 'Tell her, Grandma, tell her to shut up. Tell her none of what she says about Grandpa is true.' There was a fierce and ruthless desperation in Rosa's pale eyes. They'd gone from arctic light to the fire of an erupting volcano. Her finger was poised on the trigger.

'Put the gun down, Rosa, dear.' Stella could have been telling Rosa to be careful with a valuable china vase.

Rosa flicked a look at Stella. 'Just tell her.'

'I can't do that, I'm afraid.'

'What do you mean?'

'It's not that I don't love you and treasure you and your father, Rosa. You must never think that.' Stella's voice was as viscous as treacle. 'Richard has always been my pride and joy, because I wanted him, a baby, more than I ever wanted anything else. He was all I had and I'd waited such a very long time to get him. All the love I'd stored in my heart, I threw at him, and then at you.

264

But Richard was never really my baby, and you are not really my granddaughter.'

Rosa spun round so the gun was aimed at Stella Seagrove. 'How can you say that?'

The dog scurried off into the undergrowth but Stella didn't even flinch, just calmly watched him disappear into the ferns.

'Richard's real mother is a young girl who was living with us during the war. His father is German.'

'That's a lie.'

'I wish it were. But the truth is that my husband, your precious Charles, denied me my dearest wish. He pretended to love me and every month he saw me cry. He robbed me of my child and let me believe there was something wrong with me. How could anyone be so cruel?'

'Grandpa wasn't cruel. Don't you say those things. Don't you dare.'

'I so wanted to experience what it was like to have a child growing inside me, Rosa. It's not true, what they say about not being able to miss something you never had. I mourned the child I believed I couldn't give birth to as if she had lived and died. I honestly believe that Charles denied her life just as surely as if he'd killed her.'

'She?' Rosa whispered. 'How do you know you would have had a girl?'

'I just do. Her name is Amelia.'

Amelia. The little girl in the statue. The name on the bouquet that Stella had brought to the churchyard.

Her name is Amelia. Present tense.

'Richard was my life. For years I tried to forget that I'd never given birth to him, I devoted myself to him. I couldn't have loved him more if he'd truly been mine and I love you both still. I did try to protect him, protect you both, from ever having to hear any of this.' She looked at Natasha. 'I tried so very hard to forget the truth, but when your precious grandfather's ancestor obsession reared its ugly head this last time, I couldn't forget it any more. It brought my little girl back to me. I sense Amelia with me sometimes, more strongly than I've ever sensed the dead.' Stella was whispering now. 'I feel her here, very close, but just out of reach. The strangest thing is that I've always felt how angry she is. It's as if she's trapped somewhere and can't reach me, something has always been stopping her getting through. Now I know what that something is. My husband. The man who should have been her father. That's why I did it, Rosa. For Amelia.'

'You're crazy,' Rosa whispered. 'You killed my grandfather in revenge for a person who never existed?'

'She does exist, somewhere. I've heard her voice just as clearly as I can hear yours now. She wanted me to kill him. I heard her laughing as I did it.'

The barrel of the gun had drooped a fraction, as if Rosa had forgotten what she was holding.

Suddenly, Natasha wanted to be anywhere but the darkening woods. She could almost imagine a small spectral nymph skipping behind the trees, hiding behind the trunks. Not a ghost as such but something paranormal, a supernatural energy source. She could almost hear the fizzling echo of malicious laughter, its direction as impossible to discern as the crying of the baby she'd heard in Shadwell Manor Farm, that Rosa had possibly heard too.

'Your grandfather deserved to die,' Stella said. 'He *was* cruel, Rosa. He was callous and cruel and a traitor, to me and to this country. I should have seen through him. I should have known when he tried to get one of his German friends to seduce me when we were there on our honeymoon. Our honeymoon, Rosa, can you believe that? He tried again with the German prisoner he brought to the farm. If I hadn't been so loyal and honourable I could have had a baby. But I wouldn't be unfaithful to him, left him no choice but to create his chosen child without me. I should have seen him for what he was years ago. I should have realized he let that poor girl die just because of her gypsy ancestry. But I've always been able to shut my eyes to what I didn't want to see. Just like you.'

Rosa jerked up the shotgun. 'What do you know about me? You don't even care where I've been all this time? Aren't you even going to ask?' Rosa was close to tears now. 'You wouldn't care if you'd done it to me, would you? Done what you're accusing Grandpa of doing to you.'

'What are you talking about?'

'Robbed me of *my* baby.' She slammed the words down. 'John's baby. But because of all this I thought I couldn't go ahead with it. I thought it would be terrible for any baby to be born into so much death and murder.'

'Oh, Rosa, no.' Stella's face twisted back into its rigour of pain. She stepped towards Rosa, oblivious of the gun.

Rosa jabbed it at her. 'Stay where you are. Don't come near me.'

Stella halted.

Rosa swung the gun like a wild pendulum back to Natasha again. 'This is all your fault. We were fine until you stuck your nose in.' She stepped closer, her eyes locked on target.

Then, over Rosa's shoulder, Natasha glimpsed Archie Fletcher walking up the path with PC Harman. She knew she mustn't let Rosa know they were there, that they'd need the advantage of surprise. But that advantage was abruptly stolen by Stella's Spaniel. The dog bounded out of the thicket just in front of Archie, yapping frantically.

It made Rosa jump. She turned her head at the same time as her already tense fingers flinched on the trigger.

The sound of a gun shot ricocheted round the wood, splitting a second into fragments. Natasha was aware of distinct and yet simultaneous sensations: The thought that somehow it must be the sound-waves that had propelled her backwards. The searing agony that tore through her right arm. Numbness.

She watched the blood oozing through her shirt and was certain then that she would die, just as Charles Seagrove had died. Everything that had happened had been about blood, because of blood, and now hers was pouring out of her too. Red would be the last colour she ever saw. She put her hand over the wound. The stain hadn't been washed from her skin after all, was spreading now. But no, this blood was not sticky as Charles Seagrove's had been but hot and fresh. It started to seep and trickle around her fingers.

'Put the gun down, please, Miss Seagrove.'

Natasha snapped back to reality as she caught the anxiety crackling through Archie's trained calmness. Great, she thought, half hysterical. He hasn't handled this kind of situation before. No one was going to come running to help. They'd hear the shot and think Rosa was just shooting rabbits.

'This is only going to make things worse for you,' Archie said.

Words he'd been taught to say, a bad choice for this particular situation. For how much worse could things get for Rosa? She'd just discovered that her grandmother and her grandfather were both murderers. That they weren't even her real grandparents. She'd just lost her baby.

Natasha replayed what Rosa had said, her memory short-circuiting, a needle jammed in the groove of a vinyl record. *You wouldn't care if you'd done it to me.* If. So she'd not gone through with the abortion. She was still pregnant.

Archie was still rabbitting on with his crisis situation patter. Rosa's finger was still on the trigger, shaking now. There was nothing like pain and panic for fuelling impatience.

Natasha felt herself snap. 'Cut the crap, Sergeant Fletcher.' Archie flashed a look at her, as if he was about to tell her to shut up, but he seemed too stunned. She had Rosa's attention too, so she'd better use it well.

'You said you didn't want your baby to be born into murder and death.' Rosa's gaze was riveted to Natasha's arm, as if she was spellbound by the blood she'd caused. 'Look what it's done to you, finding out the people you loved could kill each other. Is that what you want for your own baby? Monthly prison visits to a mother who is a murderer?' Rosa seemed fixated on the dribbles of red snaking round Natasha's fingers. Natasha knew she had to get her to respond. 'It'll do more damage to your baby than any genes it might be carrying. You do realize that? Is that what you want, Rosa? Is it?'

Slowly, she shook her head. There were tears glistening in her eyes and they blinded her to Archie's approach. Almost tenderly he began uncurling each of her fingers which had frozen round the gun.

Natasha's teeth were actually chattering the way comic skeletons do, yet her jaws felt clamped tight. She was no longer seeing red but shades of grey. She was going to pass out for the third time in as many weeks. As Archie came to her she grabbed him with her good arm. He held her for a moment and she wasn't too far gone to think that it felt nice.

'All you all right?'

'Never been better.'

He inspected the wound. 'Just a graze, I think.'

'Easy for you to say.'

'We need to get you to a hospital.' He wrapped his jacket round her shoulders, produced a bandage and started to fix it in place. She tried to say she was glad he'd paid attention at his first aid sessions but she couldn't get her tongue to work. He was pulling the tourniquet tight round her arm. She could feel her blood pumping against the restriction, a new pulse.

Stella Seagrove was crouching under a tree, as if she'd dropped something small and was looking for it in the undergrowth. She picked something up, something yellow and white, like a piece of crumpled paper, and surreptitiously slipped it into her pocket. Natasha wondered if she should mention it to Archie but the thought floated away.

PC Hard Woman had produced a pair of cuffs. For a moment Natasha thought they were going to arrest Rosa but the PC turned her attention to Stella.

Stella stood, looked down her nose. 'I don't need those things.' She spoke as if she were rejecting some substandard gift. 'I'm an old woman. What am I going to do, for goodness sake?'

The PC looked to Archie for guidance. Archie let go of Natasha and shrugged. 'Leave 'em off, but keep an eye on her.' He went across to Rosa who hadn't moved a muscle since she'd had the gun prized from her fingers. 'Your father's waiting for you at the house.'

PC Hard Woman was leading Stella down the lane. Rosa followed, trancelike, and Archie and Natasha brought up the rear.

'How did you know?' Natasha asked him.

'The station contacted me and said you'd been in, wanting to talk to me. Despite the odd false alarm, you've been one step ahead of us all the way and I knew better than to ignore the fact. I tried your house first. This was my second bet. The gardener told me where to look for you. Same gardener who tipped me off that he'd just told Rosa where you'd gone too.'

'I meant, how did you know it was Stella?'

'I didn't,' Archie said. 'Until a few minutes ago. I asked Marion Lassiter if she thought Stella could have killed her husband and she said no. For the same reason she herself couldn't ever have killed him, much as she sometimes wanted to over the years. Because it would hurt Richard and Rosa too much. In the end, when she was forced to remember that Richard wasn't really hers, hurting him didn't bother Stella, did it?'

Natasha couldn't help thinking for a moment of her own situation. Blood is thicker than water. Even the blood of someone who's never been born. Stella had chosen the child she never had above Richard.

But Marion had measured Stella against herself, Richard's real mother.

'King Solomon's wisdom,' Natasha mumbled.

'Beg your pardon?'

Two women fighting over the same baby. King Solomon said the only solution was to cut the child in half. One of the women agreed to the idea but the other wouldn't let it happen. She said she'd rather not have the baby at all than let it be hurt. Because she'd put the baby's safety and best interests above her own, King Solomon pronounced her the baby's true mother.

Marion, like the mother in King Solomon's story, had proved her love for her child, sixty years after giving him up.

Thirty-Seven

LYING ON STARCHED sheets on a narrow hospital bed, Natasha missed the final chapter, but she heard it from Archie when he came to visit her at home, a few days later, with a box of chocolates.

He told her that, in the interview room at Chipping Campden police station, Stella Seagrove had admitted to sending the anonymous letter. She said she'd sent it when she'd overheard Charles briefing Natasha on the telephone, when his fixation with John Hellier's gene pool, first made her suspect the truth about why she'd never been able to have a child.

She could have gone directly to the police or media, of course, but she said she wasn't convinced they'd have the expertise or the persistence to root out Cinderella's background, to come up with the whole story. What she didn't want and, in her blind fury, didn't expect to happen, was for Richard and Rosa's true background to be exposed in the process.

Natasha was incredulous. 'How could she have even hoped it wouldn't?'

Archie shook his head. 'Here's the peculiar bit. She insisted that it was Amelia who told her to send the letter to you. And she wonders now if her unborn daughter knew very well what the result would be and wanted revenge on Richard and Rosa, the baby and grandchild who'd taken her rightful place.'

After the garden party, Stella had seen how Charles was prepared to ostracize John on the strength of his genes, his genealogy. She'd found the file open on his desk, where Rosa had left it, and she'd seen how John's supposedly tainted bloodline mirrored the Seagrove family tree. She'd seen the phantom of her lost child more clearly than ever and her revenge had to be swift and final.

After confessing this, Stella Seagrove had asked for a cup of tea.

Too late, PC Harman saw her slip something from her pocket into her mouth and swallow.

'It wasn't only my husband who learnt a few things from the SS,' Stella had said cryptically.

It wasn't clear what she meant until she suffered an attack of vomiting and convulsions less than an hour later. She was rushed to the accident and emergency ward from which Natasha had just been discharged. Stella died there within a few hours. The Post Mortem revealed that she had ingested a mouthful of Amanita Phalloides, the Death Cap mushroom, which grew beneath the birches at the heart of the Shadwell Bluebell Woods.

'The Death Cap has been a poisoners' favourite for centuries,' Archie explained. 'Stella's version of the suicide cyanide capsule that the SS carried in case of capture.'

Natasha remembered seeing Stella searching beneath the trees and putting something into her pocket. If she'd not been so preoccupied with the throbbing of her arm, could she have said something and saved Stella's life? Instead, Stella had saved herself from spending the last days of her life in prison, from subjecting her family to a long and painful trial in which the past would have to be dredged up once more.

A note was found in Stella's pocket, in her own handwriting. Archie handed it over now and looked away while she read it.

My darling Amelia,

Let me tell you about the folklore of Bluebells Woods. They are said to be enchanted by faeries who are summoned to dance by the ringing of the bells. Walking in our woods sometimes, through the sea of purple-blue flowers, I can almost believe I heard the bells ringing, I can almost believe in magic.

I have always known the way into the land of faeries. It is, as you would expect, through a ring of toadstools, or Fly Agric mushrooms to give the scientific name.

I've had the most wonderful experiences. I have danced wild dances and seen such wonderful visions and it is only then that I feel happy and calm and at peace with the world. Everything seems clear and I even stop seeing my body as my enemy, my betrayer. Best of all is being able to talk to you for hours, my beautiful faerie child.

Epilogue

THE FIRST WEEKEND of the school holidays meant the Cotswold Farm Park at Guiting Power was teeming. Toddlers in the sandpit, small boys careering round on toy tractors, little girls holding out cupped hands of pellets over the wire netting to feed the rare breeds of sheep and goats.

Rosa and John were sitting on the grass avenue that wound up between the pens of animals. Rosa's tummy was already beginning to show and Natasha couldn't help noticing how intently she was watching a baby in a pushchair, asleep beneath a lace parasol which shielded her peaceful little face from the sun.

When Natasha had told Rosa that she looked well, radiant even, she'd replied that at least she wasn't being sick any more. 'I feel like a different person.' She'd given a significant smile as she'd said that.

It was at Stella Seagrove's funeral, at a crematorium in Cheltenham, that Richard had asked Natasha to join them at the Cotswold Farm Park, to say thank you. For helping to persuade Rosa to keep her baby, and for bringing Marion to them.

It was actually Marion who'd suggested the venue. She'd told them how she used to make herself visit similar places as a punishment. When the baby was born, she had promised to come to the park – with her son, her granddaughter, and her great-grandchild.

Natasha was glad they'd not invited her back to Shadwell. She was haunted still by Stella Seagrove's words about her absent child. Amelia. A little girl who'd never been born, never been

274

conceived. She didn't ever want to see that statue again. She had never considered before that there could be ghosts from the future as well as the past. It followed though, that a person who'd been denied life would be more troubled than the most restless spirits of the dead who had at least once known what it was like to be alive. She was haunted too by the sounds of the crying baby that she'd heard in the house. Had Stella heard that too? Is that what Rosa had heard?

One mystery still remained. Who or what had wreaked havoc in the Shadwell graveyard, torn the bouquets left at Charles Seagrove's memorial? Had Stella brought the wreath of daisies to placate a small, troubled soul?

Considering her job, it was amazing that Natasha had never seen them before, the ethereal family trees that stemmed from all those who died young or were somehow prevented from having children. Spectral branches blossoming and reaching not into the past but into the infinite future.

John and Rosa joined Natasha and Richard and together they walked up the field towards the Highland cattle.

Richard touched her arm. 'How are you anyway?'

'Still sore but healing nicely. Thanks.'

'I didn't mean just your arm.'

'Neither did I.' She smiled.

She could have died in the car crash, she could have died when Rosa shot her. But she hadn't.

She could have been the root of another ghost tree. Could still be.

That's what you became, in a way, when you'd found the one person you knew you were supposed to be with but screwed it up. She had once imagined the children she and Marcus would one day have.

'I can't type,' she added. 'Which means I can't work.'

'Time for a holiday, I'd say,' John said. 'Do you have any friends in far away places?'

'As a matter of fact . . .'

Steven had called and asked her to join him in Tuscany, to talk.

Archie had light-heartedly invited her to go kayaking with him in Scotland.

Go. Don't Go. Go. Don't Go.

She kicked up some early fallen leaves, watched them flutter through the air and drift slowly back to the ground.

One of them perfectly matched the logo on the ticket that had been sitting on her desk for weeks. A maple.

Maybe, like guardian angels, the ghosts of the unborn were sometimes hovering close, protecting their own interests.

Afterword

THIS IS A work of fiction and Shadwell is an imaginary village. The happenings described as taking place there did so only between the covers of this book.

Not so the events further afield.

It is estimated that 7,500 children were born in Lebensborn homes. As part of the Lebensborn programme many more children were stolen from Poland and are still living in Germany with new names and identities, unaware of their true backgrounds.

The first Lebensborn home in Steinhoring was turned into a care home for children suffering medical and physical handicaps.

Acknowledgements

Many books were invaluable in researching this novel.

In particular: *Master Race: The Lebensborn Experiment in Nazi Germany* by Catherine Clay and Michael Leapman (Hodder and Stoughton, 1995); *Nature via Nurture, Genes, Experience and What Makes us Human* by Matt Ridley (Fourth Estate, 2003); *Fascism in Britain, A History, 1918–1985* (Basil Blackwell Ltd, 1987); *The Nazi Doctors, Medical Killing and the Psychology of Genocide* by Robert Jay Lifton (Basic Books, 1986); *The German Occupation of the Channel Islands* by Charles Cruickshank (Oxford University Press, 1975); *They Fought in the Fields* by Nicola Tyrer (Mandarin Paperbacks 1997); and *Christmas Truce* by Malcolm Brown and Shirley Seaton (Pan Books 2001). The Veterans of the Elite website provided much information about German POWs which I couldn't find anywhere else. Natasha's father taught her about the ancient art of conjuring fire but I learnt from Ray Mear's *Bushcraft* (Hodder and Stoughton, 2002).

Genealogy reference sources included the National Archive leaflets plus *Ancestral Trails* by Mark D. Herber (Sutton Publishing Ltd, 1977), Noah Hey's *The Oxford Guide to Family History* (Oxford University Press, 1993), *Tracing Your Ancestors in the Public Record Office* edited by Amanda Bevan (Public Record Office, 1999) and *Criminal Ancestors: A Guide to Historical Criminal Records in England and Wales* by David T. Hawkings (Sutton Publishing Ltd. 1992).

I appreciate the help of the staff at the National Archives, Judith Ellis of the Campden Historical Society, Guy Stapleton of the

Moreton-in-Marsh Historical Group and the members of Chipping Campden Royal British Legion who shared their wartime memories of the Cotswolds and helped me to piece together details of the Springhill prisoner of war camp.

Thanks also to Sergeant Rebecca Mountain, Emma Kropf, Vanessa Sayce – who bought a house very like May Rainbow's – and to Kirsty Swinburn and her legs!

Many thanks also to Carole Blake, Laura Morris, Rachel Leyshon and particularly to Jane Wood.